THE
BOG

THE BOG

Michael Talbot

WILLIAM MORROW AND COMPANY, INC.
NEW YORK

All of the characters in this book are fictitious,
and any resemblance to persons living or dead
is purely coincidental.

Library of Congress Cataloging-in-Publication Data

Talbot, Michael (Michael Coleman)
The bog.

I. Title.
PR6070.A36B6   1986   823'.914   85-21524
ISBN 0-688-05952-X

Printed in the United States of America

First Edition

1 2 3 4 5 6 7 8 9 10

BOOK DESIGN BY PATTY LOWY

For Blanche Mullen and Marjorie Richards
with love and gratitude

"LET THOSE CURSE IT WHO CURSE THE DAY,
WHO ARE SKILLED TO ROUSE UP LEVIATHAN."

—JOB 3:8

Prologue

Hovern Bog: 53 B.C.

GWYNEDD SAT ON a dogskin beside the charcoal fire while her sister plaited her long golden hair. In the corner her mother wept. Gwynedd did not weep because she saw no reason for it. It was not that she wasn't afraid. She was terrified, as any young woman would have been. But she was also very proud, proud that she had been chosen. There were numerous other potential candidates in the village who might have been picked, but the elders had decided upon her. This made her feel important, even exalted, and for the moment all that she could think of was the very special destiny before her.

On the fire a kettle started to rattle, and Gwynedd's sister Maelgwyn took a rag in her hand and removed it from the flame, allowing the steam to drift up over the golden locks on Gwynedd's forehead. After wetting her thumb with spit, Maelgwyn carefully formed each lock into a curl. Then she stood back to admire her work. After all, Gwynedd had to look her best. Next she stepped forward and straightened Gwynedd's linen tunic.

Throughout all of this Gwynedd kept her hands clasped tightly in her lap. Her stomach growled. To purify herself, for three days she had eaten nothing but the seeds of wild and cultivated plants, and she would have sold her soul for a

9

piece of salt meat. But it was not to be. Even if her family had had some salt meat in the house, she could not have allowed herself to eat it. She had to remain pure. Maelgwyn, sensing her sister's discomfort, offered her a cup of cold spring water, and Gwynedd drank it slowly while Maelgwyn put the last touches on her appearance.

At length Ceredic, their father, appeared at the door. Ceredic was a tall man with bright red hair and a beard. He wore a scarlet cloak and, because their family had some money, wore it fastened at his neck with a brooch instead of a thorn. His eyes glowered with the silent intensity that had become his trademark. At the sight of his arrival Gwynedd's mother broke into a wail. Without a word, Ceredic crossed the room and struck her silent with his arm, sending her tumbling into the corner like one of the dogs. All the while he kept his attention trained on Gwynedd. The time had come.

Gwynedd stood and kissed Maelgwyn on the forehead. Then she strode to her father's side and together they walked out the door. Outside, the entire village had gathered. The sky was cold and gray and the winter wind ripped at their clothing. In the distance lay the moors, rising ledge on ledge in blue, and beyond, the dense wall of blackthorn and briar that marked the beginning of the vast expanse of floating peat and inky water that was Hovern Bog.

Gwynedd gazed silently at the moors as she had done so many times before, the eternal moors. And then she looked at the Roman tent on the hill, its imperial banners flapping violently in the wind. At the moment it looked all but deserted, but she knew that this was not the case. Almost certainly the vice-prefect, Lucius Divitiacus, was watching clandestinely from within. Gwynedd had not expected him to put in an appearance, for he had more than voiced his disapproval of the evening's planned events. This, in itself, was curious, for long before the Roman legions had first begun to subjugate their lands, word of their practices had preceded them. And one of the most often voiced revelations was that, far from condemning local gods and customs, the Romans usually shrewdly embraced them and incorporated them into their own pantheon. In this case, however, and for reasons unknown, Divitiacus had scorned their practices, and his absence during the proceedings was evidence of his disapprobation.

Gwynedd and her father were joined by the elders, and started to walk ahead. Behind them the villagers followed quietly. Down the ravine they walked, down the high, heather-covered slopes and through the long rolling hills of the moors. Only once did Gwynedd look back to see a fiery sunset settling over the huts of the village. She looked ahead and saw that dusk had started to purple the distant hills. They had to move quickly, for soon it would be dark.

They reached the thicket and continued on through. They walked carefully here, for they were now in Hovern Bog proper and the marshy ground had a way of suddenly sinking into oblivion. Several times as a child Gwynedd had actually seen cows swallowed up by the bog, and once even a man. She herself had never even been in this far, and only some of the elders now knew the route they had to take. It took them about ten minutes to reach the hill.

The hill itself was completely dry. Gwynedd looked into her father's eyes. He had never been a compassionate man. In fact, he had seldom even treated his daughters as flesh and blood. Dimly, she had expected that this evening's circum-stances might have elicited some small mote of affection or remorse from him, but when none was forthcoming her thoughts drifted only to the great honor that was before her, and the fear, vague but growing, like a leaden tumor in her stomach. Sunk deep into the hill was a wooden pillar, and Gwynedd approached it. One of the elders walked behind the post and withdrew a hide tether from his robe.

Suddenly there was the sound of something coming through the brush, and a frightened murmur passed through the crowd. Some of the villagers even started to run, but then a figure appeared. Much to Gwynedd's surprise, it was the vice-prefect's wife, cloaked and hooded. The bottom of her robe was muddied, and it was clear from her haste that her coming here had been a last-minute decision. She passed quickly through the throng until at last she stood before the pale young woman. For several seconds everyone remained silent and Gwynedd wondered why the woman had intruded. Had the vice-prefect sent her? Was she there to stop the proceedings?

The silence continued for many tense seconds, then at last the woman reached into her cloak and withdrew a beautiful comb carved of horn. Slowly she reached out and proffered the treasure to Gwynedd. Without thinking, Gwynedd accepted it. She had never before owned such a beautiful object. It was only after she had admired and tucked the comb into her tunic that she looked into the woman's eyes and saw. Although her face was shadowed by the cowl, there was terror in the woman's eyes. Something in the past several weeks had caused her to become a believer, and the comb was an offering, a votive in attempt to make some humble amends for her former disbelief.

Then the woman stepped back, and the elder proceeded to tie Gwynedd's hands firmly to the post. The elder finished, and because it was becoming so dark, the villagers left quickly. Few of them even looked back. Gwynedd's father did, and this surprised her. The vice-prefect's wife also looked back. But soon everyone was out of sight and she was completely alone.

It was only in her solitude that she began to focus on how numbingly cold she had become. She also realized more clearly that she was frightened. Whatever feelings of exaltation had tinged her mood earlier had now all but departed, and she started to squirm within her bonds. Before long, all she could think of was how hideous and dark the fate was that had befallen her, and her only solace was in knowing that it would all be over soon. But as the night closed in around her and she anxiously surveyed the growing shadows, she knew only that death would come. But she did not know in what form, or when.

1

THE CALL FROM Brad Hollister had come at five o'clock on a
Saturday morning, and David Macauley was still very much
asleep. As his grogginess slowly dispersed, the first thing he
noticed was that his wife, Melanie, had neatly rolled herself
up in all of the blankets and left him shivering with nothing
but a sheet. The second thing that entered his consciousness
was the ringing of the telephone, relentless and annoying. He
glanced out the window, saw that the sun had not yet begun
to peep over Oxford's Bridge of Sighs, grunted, and answered
the phone.

"Professor Macauley?" came Hollister's voice from the other
end, a slight crackle of static on the line because it was long-
distance.

"Hollister? Do you know what time it is?"

"I'm sorry it's so early, but I've found a body."

David went silent for a moment, allowing the words to fully
sink in.

"What kind of condition is it in?"

"Perfect. You should see it. The flesh around the neck and
chest has disintegrated a little, but other than that she looks
as if she died yesterday."

"She?"

"Yes, the body's definitely that of a young woman."

"Is it naked or clothed?" David asked in a tone of voice more dispassionate than might have seemed appropriate in posing such a question. Melanie stirred restlessly in the bed beside him as she became cognizant of the conversation. She propped herself up on her elbow, blinking.

"She seems to be naked, although there's some cloth arranged over her. The lower half of her's still buried, though. I just wanted to call and let you know about the discovery. I've been digging all night."

"Where are you, anyway?"

"I'm in a tiny village known as Fenchurch St. Jude. It's about four miles from the Hovern Bog site." Hollister, being an American, expressed the distance in miles instead of kilometers, and David, also an American, had no objections.

"Any indication of how old the body is?"

"Well, since she is naked and what cloth there is is fragmentary and rotted, it's difficult to identify her by her clothing. However, she does have an object buried with her. It's a comb carved out of horn. And guess what, it's Roman."

"My God, do you think she was a Roman?"

"I don't know. Her features look distinctly Celtic and she does have blond hair . . . or did. The comb indicates, however, that she at least had some sort of contact with the Romans. That suggests that the body is at least sixteen centuries old, maybe older. We'll have to run other tests to date it any more precisely than that."

The rest of the conversation concerned details of how and when David would drive down from Oxford to examine the body firsthand, who owned the land the body had been found on, and other mundane particulars. When David finally hung up the receiver he could hardly contain his excitement. Melanie gave indications that she was about to say something, but stopped when the familiar sound of nails tapping against linoleum met their ears. They both looked up to see Ben, their black Labrador retriever, standing expectantly in the doorway of the bedroom. Although it was several hours too early for his normal morning walk, he had heard voices and had decided to test the waters. He wagged an exuberant good morning.

"Is this it, then?" Melanie asked worriedly.

The *it* she referred to was an eventuality they had both known about for some time—brought closer by Brad Hollister's entry into the matter two months before. David Macauley was an archaeologist and a visiting lecturer at Oxford. His special area of interest was in so-called bog bodies, bodies of Iron Age men and women that—because of the remarkable preservative properties of certain chemicals in bog water—had been almost completely protected from decomposition for hundreds and even thousands of years. A number of important bog-body finds had been made in various bogs throughout England and north-western Europe since the 1950s, but it had long been David's cherished hope to discover and extensively study a site of his own. To this end, two months previously he had commissioned Hollister, a Rhodes scholar and a graduate student of his, to travel around England's West Country bogs looking for just such a location. The telephone call this morning had been the first fruit of that effort.

David disengaged himself from the covers and sat on the edge of the bed. He turned and looked at Melanie. She was concerned because she loved the life they had made for themselves at Oxford. She knew it was inevitable that Hollister would make such a discovery, but she had long dreaded the day that the family would actually have to pull up their roots and once again relocate.

"I don't know, honey," he said in answer to her question.

"But Brad's found a body, hasn't he?"

"Yes, but that doesn't mean that the site is important enough to become a major dig. Maybe we won't find anything else there."

Melanie sat up in bed and scrunched her knees up against her chest. Her expression was distant and troubled. "You will," she said.

David looked at her skeptically. "Now how do you know that?"

"I just do."

He shook his head. "You and your woman's intuition," he said as he lovingly stroked the side of her face. He tilted her head up and looked in her eyes. She was still every bit as beautiful as when they had married, almost a decade and a half before. On occasion she had what few gray hairs she possessed artfully lightened at some top-notch salon, but most of her hair was still luxuriantly blond, and her complexion flawless. She had also kept her figure, and possessed a frame that might, were she a few inches taller, be called voluptuous, and her clear blue eyes still flashed with all of their former fire. It was no wonder that David often observed his colleagues and even many of his students flirting with her.

He turned and looked at himself in the mirror, trying to assess if the years had been as kind to him. His brown hair was flecked here and there with gray, but he had been told that it looked distinguished, and he was still certainly as trim as he had been when they had met, his busy schedule saw to that. But was he still as handsome? He did not know. He had never really even thought of himself as handsome until, as a teenager, to his surprise and delight, girls had seemed to find him so. It was true that his features showed no great imperfection. His jaw was square, his cheekbones high, and his nose straight, but beyond that he was incapable of appraising his looks any further. He was not the sort of man who would.

He became aware of a sensation in his hand and he looked down to see Ben's black head pushing up against his fingers as the retriever gently tried to recapture his attention.

"I'm going to take the dog out for a walk," he said as he slipped out of bed.

Outside, Ben wasted no time taking advantage of his premature good fortune and quickly raced to a nearby tree. David gazed at the dog briefly and then surveyed the landscape around him. It was a chilly spring morning. The sun was just beginning to peek over the gray colleges and Gothic traceries of Oxford, and in the crisp cool air he found himself swept anew with excitement. He could scarcely believe it. It had seemed an eternity since he had first set out in his powder-blue Volvo and checked off on a map the sites that his intuition and keen eye had told him were archaeologically promising. Then he had waited for over a year for the funding to send Hollister out on the first wave of exploratory digging, and even then the most he had expected were a few promising artifacts. But the fact that Hollister had actually located a body during his preliminary explorations was more than David could have hoped for in his wildest imaginings. It was the fulfillment of a dream that had been a long time in the making.

In the archaeological world David had a reputation for being both brilliant and a maverick. Part of this was due to his unlikely beginnings. He had been born and raised in Chicago's industrial South Side, and in a working-class family not at all appreciative of academic learning. In spite of this, he had always possessed an inordinate love of history in general, and archaeology in particular. As a result, at the age of sixteen, he had left his squalid and unhappy home life and set out to make his mark upon the intellectual world. After living a year in Illinois, moving from town to town and surviving any way that he could, he discovered one of the most remarkably appointed Indian burial chambers of the Hopewell culture ever found. When news of his discovery, and of his tender age and lack of formal training, became known, it set the archaeological world on its ear.

In time, scholarships poured in. He quickly finished high school by going to night classes, and by dint of good grades, luck, and his reputation as a boy wonder, he was admitted to Harvard. There, he excelled; he published a series of articles on the "new" archaeology, and under the auspices of various well-known archaeologists assisted in making a number of further important discoveries. It was on one of these field trips, at a dig at Haraldskjaer Bog in Denmark, that he saw his first bog body. From that first moment he was entranced. What intrigued him the most was that he had previously only known the people of the past through their bones. But in the bog bodies even the flesh was preserved. When one looked at one of them one was actually looking at the features of a person who had *lived* history.

What was strange about David's life was that although he had assisted in a dozen such excavations since then, and had himself become one of the world's foremost authorities on bog bodies, he had always worked on the finds of others and had never actually manned a research site that he himself had discovered. Part of the reason for this was that he had somehow allowed his earlier adventurous spirit to become sidetracked. When he was outside of the institutional structure, when he was young and had no guidance other than his fervid interest in archaeology, he had no recourse but to go out and scour the countryside on his own. But in becoming a part of the archaeological establishment he also became enmeshed in it. It was easy for him to accept positions working on the digs of other, more established archaeologists. And seduced by the comfortable embrace of academic life, he had allowed just a few more years to go by than he would have liked to. Now, however, he hoped all that was going to change. For the first time in as long as he could remember, it looked as if his dream were about to come true.

He looked at the refaced facades of the colleges just beginning to glow palely golden in the advancing sun. He would miss Oxford. It had been good to them for the two and a half years they had been there. And he would miss it, the distinguished features and vague eyes of the various dons whom he had developed rapport with, even the smooth, dull gleam of the academic poplin. Most of all he would miss old Burton-Russell, the silver-haired antiquities scholar whose thoughts were forever riveted on some aspect of ancient Mesopotamian culture. Like David, Burton-Russell shared an almost passionate enchantment with the past, and the two had spent many long hours discussing the intricacies of some ancient Celtic verb tense, or the psychological implications of some long-forgotten Babylonian ritual. He would miss Burton-Russell's encyclopedic knowledge of history most of all.

Once again he became aware of Ben's head pushing up against his hand, and he patted the dog lovingly on the neck. Ben gave a doggish smile in return.

"Come on, boy," David said as he turned and walked back into the house.

On his way back to the bedroom he decided to look in on the children. He quietly opened the door to thirteen-year-old Katy's room. The first thing he saw were the posters of Michael Jackson and Duran Duran illuminated in the morning light, and then Katy herself, asleep under her frilly French comforter. He smiled when he saw how angelic she looked. Fortunately, she had inherited her mother's looks, and long, strawberry-blond hair framed a face that was still a little girl's, but had a cast about it that was clearly on its way to becoming a woman's. She was the apple of his eye, his firstborn, and although they shared very little of the world and possessed almost totally dissimilar interests, there was a closeness between them, a bond formed out of their great mutual respect and deep but often unstated affection for one another.

He closed the door and quietly padded on. Next he approached the room of his six-year-old son, Tucker, but when he opened the door he saw to his surprise that Tuck's bed was empty. He quickly rushed in to see if Tuck had fallen out of bed, but when he got there he still found no sign of his son. Worriedly, he turned and went out into the hall. He looked in the bathroom and then the kitchen, but still no Tuck. Finally he walked toward the living room and felt a wave of relief when he saw the distinctive glow of the television set shimmering on the wall. He looked in to see Tuck sitting about four inches from the set with the sound turned down low, feverishly playing a video game.

"Tucker, what are you doing?" David demanded sternly.

Tuck turned around, startled. He had dark-chestnut hair and matching eyes and a gaze that might have seemed disturbingly wise had David not known him to be one-hundred-percent boy, an inexhaustible tornado of arms and legs, unyieldingly curious, and capable of producing a wide range of startling and unexpected sounds.

"I couldn't sleep anymore, Dad," he said guiltily.

David was angry about not finding Tuck in his bed, but couldn't stare into his son's freckled and guileless face long without melting. He had to force himself not to smile. "Well, try hard, Tuck. I want you to go back to bed and I don't want to see you out here again until after seven o'clock." He walked over, turned the set off, and lifted his son up in his arms. He allowed himself to smile only when he felt Tuck's arms close around his neck. Tuck was also very special to him, in some ways even more special than Katy, for he was a boy and in David's eyes, as with most fathers and their sons, this made him a little homunculus of himself.

He took Tuck back into his bedroom and once again drew the blanket up over him. "Now get some sleep. I'll see you in a little bit."

"Okay, Dad," Tuck said amiably.

David shut the door to Tuck's room and returned to his own bedroom. He found Melanie looking distant and deep in thought.

"You know what I found our son doing?" David asked, grinning, as he threw off his robe and got back into bed.

Melanie seemed not to hear.

"He was playing a video game with the sound turned down low so that we couldn't hear."

Melanie turned to him. "Brad said that the body was in good condition?"

David looked at her sympathetically, realizing that she was

still troubled. "Come on, Mel, I told you it doesn't mean anything yet."

This did nothing to assuage her.

"Are you trying to make me feel guilty about this?" he asked.

She smiled. "Of course not."

"Because we talked all this out long ago and you said—"

"—and I said that it was all right, that I would go along with your decision."

"So I don't know why you're doing this."

"Doing what?"

"Acting this way."

"Listen, I said that I understood this move was important to your work and that I would go along with it. But, in turn, you've got to understand that I've got feelings in the matter too. I'm not totally happy about the possibility of pulling both Katy and Tuck out of school and moving to the sticks, but that's my problem. You at least have to allow me my feelings."

"Fair enough," he said as he snuggled closer to his wife. At that moment, had he paid attention to it, a tiny voice in the back of his mind was telling him that there was more to his wife's sullen mood than just her unhappiness over the possibility of their moving. But at the time too many other thoughts were crowding for his attention, and he failed to pay it any notice. Instead, he moved closer still and started to kiss his wife on the back of her neck.

Melanie could think of a thousand different reasons why she didn't want to move. To begin with, being the wife of an Oxford academic was about as rustic as she wanted to get. Her father was a wealthy Boston Brahmin, and living on a professor's salary had been a difficult enough situation for her to adapt to. She had been on digs before with David, and the thought of returning to the back woods was almost more than she could bear.

She had also never told David, but once as a small child she had been separated from her parents while on vacation and had been lost in the Vermont woods for a day and a night. The experience had left her with a deep and irrational fear of any tract of land that did not have pavement or stoplights within twenty feet of it.

Still, she knew there was more to her unhappiness than just reluctance to leave Oxford. She had successfully overcome such misgivings before, but this time something was different. Something formless had been troubling her for months now. She did not know what. She was only just beginning to realize that it was there, that she also had a tiny voice trying to communicate something to her. But she loved her husband and she still tingled beneath his touch.

"I think we can do something about your mood," David said. She looked at him and saw that he had the devil in his eye. Suddenly he began to tickle her, and she thrashed wildly in the sheets, breaking into gales of laughter.

"Oh, stop it," she cried. "We'll wake the kids."

"Then we'll just have to be a little more quiet," he returned as he kissed her again and drew her into his arms.

* * *

On the following Monday at nine o'clock in the morning David Macauley set out in his Volvo for Fenchurch St. Jude. According to his instructions he was to meet Brad Hollister at an intersection of two roads known locally as Nobby Fork. The purpose of this, Brad had explained, was to protect David from getting lost, for although David had chosen the mile-long strip of bog where they were to dig, the precise location of the camp was deep in a labyrinth of country lanes in a valley that held both Fenchurch St. Jude and Hovern Bog and was known to geologists as the greater Devon basin. Although it was almost noon when he reached Nobby Fork, the sun had not yet cut through the cloud cover, and a veil of early morning mist still lay over the land. He found Brad standing beneath a tree, framed by a sheath of fog that made him look very much like the ghost of Hamlet's father.

The younger man spotted the car coming and waved. He was tall, standing over six feet, broad-shouldered, and slim but muscular, with a mane of shiny black hair and a neatly trimmed black beard and moustache. He might have looked Mephistophelian had David not known him to be one of the quietest, most gentle individuals he had ever met.

"Professor Macauley," the younger man greeted him as he got into the Volvo.

"How are you, Brad?" David returned. "Boy, sure is spooky with all this fog about."

Hollister shrugged apologetically. "I'm sorry."

"Oh, I'm not criticizing," David interjected quickly, recalling how self-effacing the younger man was. "Actually, I kind of like it. Lends an air of mystery to everything. Just tell me where to go."

Hollister nodded and motioned for David to take the left turn in the fork.

As they drove on, David noticed that a slight tension had developed momentarily between them. This was not because there was any animosity between the two men. On the contrary, when the two of them were heavily into a project they worked as if they shared a single soul. The tension was due instead to the fact that Brad was the archetype of the shy and reclusive intellectual. He was brilliant and fanatically dedicated to his work, but a very quiet and private person, and always a little ill at ease in the company of other people. Consequently, whenever the two of them had been apart for any length of time it always seemed to take awhile before the younger man relaxed and settled back into the routine of their working together.

Eventually the landscape started to look more familiar to David, and he recalled the thoughts that he had had when he first passed through these parts. He looked out his window and remembered that first and foremost he had been struck by the beauty and seclusion of the place. Through the ever-clearing mists, rolling pasture lands curved upward on either side of the road and scrub oaks lined the distant horizon. Farther on, the land got hillier, and he shifted gears as they headed up through a lane worn deep by centuries of wheels and surrounded by high banks dripping with moss and fleshy hart's-tongue ferns. Here the vegetation became unusually lush and verdant and David thought again, as he had thought the first time he drove through here, that it was almost as if he had entered a more primeval England, an England as it might have looked when giant herbivorous reptiles still roamed the landscape. In the distance, bronzing bracken and mottled bramble rose out of the veil of the fog, and through the trees one could see only a dreamlike pall of gray.

Still rising steadily, they passed over a narrow granite bridge surmounting a noisy stream, foaming and roaring amidst a concourse of great boulders. Both road and stream wound up through a countryside dense with hemlock and fir until at last they rounded a curve, the vegetation cleared, and before them lay an outlying spur of the moor.

It was a beautiful and peaceful region, but, David thought, tinged with a strange melancholy. It occurred to him that part of the desolate quality of the region was due to the fact that it seemed so untouched by human hands. It was true that the granite bridge was an artifact of human origin, but it could easily have been there for centuries, perhaps longer. Even the wind seemed momentarily absent, and it struck him anew that the entire place was pervaded by an unearthly calm, an almost palpable timelessness, as if the valley were more than just geologically separate from the outlying countryside, as if there were some actual quality to the air itself that set it apart.

At last, in the far distance, there appeared the misty spike of a church steeple. "Thank God!" David said. "At least where there is a church there is civilization."

Brad looked at him curiously. "That's the church in the village Fenchurch St. Jude. Didn't you see it the first time you came here?"

"No, I approached the bog from a different direction," David replied.

At length the road narrowed, and the Volvo slowed down. Finally there rose beyond the gloomy curve of the moor a dense wall of foliage and the almost endless sweep of peat land and blackthorn that was Hovern Bog. Also visible and set off from the road was Brad's own rusted Volkswagen, on high ground the tent where he had made his camp, and a little farther into the bog several gaping wounds in the peat where he had made his excavations. David pulled the Volvo up onto the high ground near the tent and got out. Then, before he did anything else, he paused and looked around.

On the hills to their left and rising up out of the last remaining fingers of the mist were half a dozen or so piles of stone rubble. To the untrained eye they might have looked as if they had been placed there by farmers clearing their fields, but to David, their distinctive arrangements revealed that they were all that remained of an ancient Neolithic settlement, no doubt the first version of Fenchurch St. Jude, or whatever it had been called up until Roman times. It was these ruins and their proximity to the bog that first told him they should dig here. However, even if the ruins had not been so readily apparent, he would have been drawn to excavating in this region. Like most archaeologists, David had developed his powers of observation to a level of almost superhuman acuity, and he could often see details in the landscape that to other people were quite invisible. In a barren patch of ground he noticed a tiny fragment of bitumen and knew that it was quite possibly the remains of an ancient campfire. And on a nearby hill he observed an angular embankment that, in spite of the fact that it was now covered with vegetation, his discerning eye detected had once been a path and been well trodden by human feet. It was only after he had assessed these features and once again recemented them in his mind that he turned and faced the great Hovern Bog.

Although he had scrutinized it before, now that he knew an important archaeological find had been made there he looked at it with new eyes, his mind greedily reassessing its every detail. The first thing he noticed about it was its size. It was vast, and it broke out of the great plain of the moors like a mysterious continent unto itself. Later he was to learn that it was a full thirty-five square miles in area. It was also a brighter green than the olive and russet slopes of the moors—the vegetation in the bog able to wrench more nutrients out of the black water than the heather could out of the barren plain. To many, the bog might have seemed a frightening and foreboding place, but not to David. He knew the subtleties of the bog too well for them to frighten him, and thus for him it was a place of fascination.

He knew that the many hills scattered throughout the bog were not hills at all, but really islands cut off on all sides by the impassable mire. He knew there was a good chance that somewhere in the bog was a bog lake. This was the nexus of the bog, and over the centuries, even the millennia, the mire had slowly crept outward from it, had wound through the countryside, engulfing some portions of the landscape and making islands of others. Here and there in saucerlike depressions in the land it would have settled into so-called bog caldrons, seemingly bottomless pits filled with a waterlogged and spongy soup of peat and rotting vegetation. In a way, these were the most dangerous parts of the bog, for they could easily swallow an unwitting creature alive. However, there were other dangers as well. During the rainy seasons, like the spring rains they were in the middle of, the endless mire would have expanded and formed numerous other inky pools and rivulets, and these in turn would have become covered with semifloating mats of sphagnum and entangled with water lilies. Thus, sometimes the land itself was not even land, and if one tried to jump from grass clump to grass clump in attempts to avoid the caldrons, one could just as easily be swallowed up by the land itself and drown, hopelessly ensnared in the sinewy tendrils of the lilies.

In fact, the sinister beauty of the entangling lilies was only one of many contradictions that flourished in the bog. As David continued to ponder the vast and marshy expanse, he thought of others. On one hand, the bog was a haunting and eerie place, with the wind perpetually rustling through its many sedges of bulrushes and the forlorn silhouettes of the numerous dead trees whose roots had drowned but not yet rotted that dotted its banks. But on the other hand, it was teeming with life. What hilly ground had survived within the perimeter of the mire stood tall with a scrub of birch, willow, mountain ash, and alder buckthorn. Bog whortleberry flourished on the dry banks around the mire and every square inch of available ground space was covered with marsh cinquefoil and cranberry, and in the driest areas, anemones and dog's mercury.

Similarly, just as the bog was a taker of life, it was also a preserver of life, for in isolating the many islands of green that dotted its expanse it had also protected them, and often they harbored many rare species of plants and butterflies. In fact, it was not unheard of for a brave amateur naturalist to discover a totally unknown species of plant or animal that had been cut off for centuries by one of the impassable arms of the bog. And even what life was not exclusive to the bog was often, nonetheless, at least uncommon, like the carnivorous pitcher plant and even an occasional orchid, trapped but given sanctuary in this Galapagos of the moors.

Everywhere he looked there were such juxtapositions, the beautiful contrasted with the deadly, the mist mingled with the thorns. In short, he realized that like all great things, like the ocean, the night, and even life itself, the bog was a paradox. The greatest bulk of its substance was dead vegetation, and yet it behaved as if it were curiously alive. It expanded and contracted. It reached out with sinewy tentacles and took and entangled and digested. And it even stirred occasionally in its slumber, groaning and emitting the most mournful and unearthly sounds, presumably from the peat settling, but to many who had heard them, including David himself, it seemed more like the ruminations of some great beast, the restless rumblings of the living bog.

From far overhead came the plaintive cry of a bittern, a rare and heronlike bird that also inhabited the protective confines of the bog, and David looked up to see it flying in the direction of the hills to their left. He watched it for a moment, transfixed by its beauty, when suddenly it squawked and tumbled at a ninety-degree angle, almost as if it had collided with an invisible wall. For a second he thought that it was going to crash, but then it regained its balance and flew frantically off in another direction.

"Did you see that?" he shouted as he ran up the steep and rocky hill to get a better vantage. Brad had apparently not seen it, but followed him curiously.

"See what?"

"That bird. It was flying along when suddenly it veered off almost as if it hit something."

Brad looked up into the air, squinting to see the allegedly invisible obstruction. "I don't see anything."

"Not now," David said. "But I swear it looked like it hit something." He surveyed the landscape beneath where the incident had happened. The first thing he noticed was the picturesque outline of Fenchurch St. Jude in the valley below. The now-bright sun gleamed refulgently off the whitewashed walls of the sprawling cluster of cottages, and here and there an automobile or a pickup truck provided the only clue that the village was indeed a part of the twentieth century. David observed that the church he had spied before was set off some distance from the village and was actually nearer to the bog. Here and there in the far distance other moorland cottages dotted the hills, but these too were few and far between, and their infrequency only added to the sense of isolation that hung over the place.

David's gaze moved to the portion of the valley nearer where the bittern had nearly fallen from its flight, and here another sight met his eyes. Some distance from the village and at least partially encircled by the black waters of the bog was a manor house. Like many English manor houses, the huge and rambling edifice was an eclectic hodgepodge of styles from different eras. David recognized part of the facade as late Elizabethan, but the main block of the structure was much older. A huge tower projected from the central core, ancient and crenellated, and heavy, mullioned windows dotted the walls. From the steep roofs set at different angles to one another sprouted innumerable chimneys, and the entire structure was encrusted with ivy and surrounded by great oaks and firs twisted into fantastic shapes by untold years of storms.

So here was the bog lake, David thought to himself. And moreover, there was a house built upon its edge. How strange, he thought, that someone long ago should have chosen such a bleak location on which to build his home. He knew from the high acidity of the peat that the waters of the lake would be still and black and almost completely devoid of life. He knew also that the lake most assuredly had a false bottom, and the only thing that punctuated its dark and impenetrable surface would be again the semifloating mats of sphagnum and decaying vegetation.

But he discerned nothing that explained why the bittern had behaved so strangely when its course had taken it over the perimeter of the grounds.

"What's that place?" he asked.

"It's known as Wythen Hall," Brad replied. "It's the home of the local gentry, the Marquis de L'Isle."

A small breeze rustled by them, and as David started back down he was struck once again by the oddness of someone building so stately a manse on a location so dominated by the bog. In fact, it occurred to him that in a way Fenchurch St. Jude and, indeed, the entire valley were dominated by the bog.

The thought had lingered in his mind for but a moment when his attention returned to the matter at hand. "Now why don't you show me that body?" he said.

"Let me get you some boots to put on first," Brad replied. He ran into his tent, then returned with a large pair of wading rubbers. David put them on and they strolled toward the excavation. As the land sloped downward it became wet and gushed beneath their feet. David looked at Brad worriedly.

"It's okay. I've checked the area out thoroughly. There are no sinks."

David nodded, grateful for the information, but he still walked carefully.

Finally they reached the side of the excavation, and David

looked down. The hole itself was about six feet square and maybe five feet deep. The first several feet of strata on the sides of the pit were composed of a dark-colored peat David recognized as wood-peat, and below this a reddish peat stratum of decomposed sphagnum known to peat cutters as "dog's flesh." A foot and a half into the dog's flesh and resting peacefully on the reddish and muddy bottom of the pit was the body of a young girl.

She lay on her back, her head twisted to one side and her left arm outstretched. Her right arm was bent up against her chest, as if defensively, and her legs were lightly drawn up, the left one over the right. She looked much like any young girl might have who had only recently settled down for a nap, except for the fact that her skin, once white, was now a shiny and resinous black. It was a jarring contrast, the perfect preservation of her features against the almost metallic and petroleum-like color of her skin. It was as if a talented sculptor had carved her out of coal and then polished the surface of his work to a high gloss. David was spellbound. Her every feature had been preserved, every pore in her skin, her nails, the whorls and lines of her fingerprints, and the gentle creasings of the skin at the bend of her wrists.

The reason for her remarkable state of preservation was, of course, the tannin and other soil acids in the peat and the bog water that seeped through it. Not only did they tan the skin and turn it into leather, but they also combined with other proteins in the body and converted them to a form of synthetic plastic. They had been lucky in this instance, however, for if the acidity of the bog water had been too high it would have dissolved the young woman's bones and left them with nothing but her skin. Fortunately, that had not happened.

To some, David Macauley's macabre interest in the bog bodies might have seemed ghoulish, but it was not morbidity that had drawn him to study such things. Again, it was his love of history, his voracious desire to know everything that was knowable about the past, and now, as he looked down at the body, he felt not horror, but a tremendous excitement. He could scarcely believe it. If she was indeed as old as they believed, she had lived and breathed and smelled flowers nearly a thousand years before the Norman invasion. She might possibly have even caught a glimpse of Caesar himself, and it took his breath away to think that here, he, David Macauley, was looking at the hair, the hands and flesh of the person who had actually done those things.

He turned to Brad. "She's magnificent," he said in a hush.

"Isn't she," the younger man said knowingly and in a tone of voice that revealed he shared David's reverence.

David looked at the young man, still shaking his head in disbelief. "You've really outdone yourself, Brad. This is more than I could have ever hoped for. I'm speechless."

Brad blushed uneasily. "You deserve the credit. It was you who found the site."

"But you've done the initial toil. At the very least you'll share credit for the discovery."

Brad grew even more modest and uncomfortable and David looked at him, marveling at his reaction. It was true that picking the site gave him claim to the discovery, but doing the initial excavations and finding the body were no small achievement either. It was not that David thought he was taking advantage of the younger man. Meting out the more arduous tasks to one's assistant was typical procedure in the archaeological field. What amazed him was that Brad could be so humble about it all. He remembered being in the same circumstances himself so many times before and gazing at his superior with gracious but only slightly concealed envy as he longed for the day when he would be the one in charge of the expedition.

His thoughts were soon interrupted. "There's something else you should see," Brad said.

"What's that?"

"Her face," Brad finished simply.

David continued to stare at him for a moment and then looked back down at the body. From his current vantage only the side of her head was visible, and he realized he was going to have to get down into the hole itself. Trying as best he could not to muddy himself, he lowered himself into the pit. He knelt down, craning his neck as he carefully leaned between the muddy wall of the pit and the body and for the first time caught a glimpse of her face.

"My God," he murmured.

When viewed from above, the deceptively tranquil posture of the body had not prepared him for what he now confronted, for frozen in the young girl's visage, as perfectly preserved as her skin and her nails, was a look of unspeakable terror. Her eyes were open, the white of them still preserved as it was in many of the bog bodies that had been discovered, and even the blue of her irises. And they were wide from the sight of some long-forgotten horror. Her mouth too was still agape in the rictus of a terrible death. Whatever had killed her had scared the soul out of her before it had done it.

"Have you determined how she died?" David asked, bewildered and shaken by the sight of the awful countenance.

Brad shook his head. "Not yet. Could be a knife wound or something on some part of her that's still concealed by the peat."

David continued to stare at the reclining figure. "Where's the comb you mentioned?"

"In the tent."

David climbed out of the hole, wiped the mud from his hands, and followed Brad to the campsite. The younger man vanished through the flap of the tent and reappeared several moments later carrying a large hair comb in his hand.

As Brad had said over the phone, the comb was carved out of horn. What he had failed to mention was that it was also inlaid with ivory and gold, an exquisite object to behold. Aside from that, David did not immediately see what identified the comb as Roman. He turned it over in his hands, examining it. He knew of only one other comb that had ever been found buried along with a bog body, and from his memory of that comb he perceived that this one did not precisely follow that Celtic design. However, he still did not know what was Roman about it. He looked closer, trying to find any distinguishing feature. And then he saw. Scratched lightly into the horn and so darkened by the bog water that it was almost invisible was a phrase scrawled in Latin: *Ut tibi postremum donarem munus moriturae, accipe multum manantia fletu.* He translated the inscription loosely: Bringing you this last gift for the dead, accept this offering wet with tears.

"Do you think she was Roman?" Brad asked.

"I don't know. It was uncommon for Roman women to have blond hair, but it was not unheard of. Where's the cloth that you said was found with her?"

Again Brad vanished into the tent and this time reappeared with a large plastic bag containing several sizable remnants of a coarse and greatly discolored cloth. David took them and examined them closely. Even though rotted, he discerned a check design in the fragments that was clearly of Celtic origin. This posed a puzzle.

"Well what do you think?" Hollister asked.

"I think that there are two possibilities. The first is that she is a Roman and was buried in the bog by the Celts. That means that the comb belonged to her originally, but the cloth, which is Celtic, was placed over her by the Celts who interred her in the bog. But that would not explain why she was buried in the bog by the Celts, or how the Romans allowed one of their number to undergo a burial practice they most assuredly viewed as pagan."

"Or the inscription on the comb," Brad added.

David nodded.

"And the other possibility?"

"The other possibility is that she is Celtic, but somehow came into possession of a Roman comb." David paused, once again gazing meditatively at the inscription. "You know, the inscription almost suggests that the comb was meant as some sort of votive or offering. Perhaps she was a sacrificial victim in some long-forgotten Celtic ritual and a Roman woman who happened to witness the event decided to give her a comb as a sort of oblation to the foreign god."

A diffident smile crossed Brad's lips. "That was my conclusion. Obviously when we figure out how she died that will give us some further clue. But I wonder if we'll ever figure out the second puzzle?"

"The second puzzle?"

"If the woman was a sacrificial victim in some sort of Celtic ritual and was given the comb by a Roman woman who witnessed the event and wanted to make some sort of offering, why was the comb wet with the Roman woman's tears? She must have been very unhappy about something. I wonder if we'll ever know the cause of her unhappiness."

David shrugged. It was an interesting notion, but he knew that their chances of answering the question were remote unless, of course, the bog contained still further clues to the mystery. His heart leaped at the hope, and he surveyed the landscape around them, wondering what else, if anything, lay hidden in the inky depths of Hovern Bog.

Brad seemed to read his thoughts. "I have something else

to show you," he said, and David noticed that the younger man had an uncharacteristic sparkle in his eye. He gestured with his head in the direction of one of the other holes and David followed him.

When they reached the second excavation David looked down and saw that it was almost as deep as the first, but narrowed toward the bottom and was, as yet, nowhere near as wide. At first, as he peered into the conical depression in the quagmire, he saw nothing. He shifted his weight, and his boots squished softly in the mud as he leaned closer. Finally his attention came to rest on an unusually sleek patch in the side of the hole. At first his mind only registered that the area possessed an anomalous texture. But as he continued to scrutinize it, the pieces finally fell into place and he realized what the object was. What he was looking at was the side of a human thigh, darkened by the bog water so that it was the same color as the surrounding peat, but a human thigh nonetheless. There was at least one other body buried in the bog.

"Why didn't you tell me?" he exclaimed.

"I only found it this morning. I thought it would make a nice surprise." Brad grinned proudly, but with a modesty not unlike a child who has just surprised a parent with a hand-made valentine.

David continued to just stare dumbly at the human thigh in the pit below. His mind was reeling. The remarkable state of preservation of the first body had itself been enough to persuade him that this was a spot that demanded further study. But the discovery of the second body clinched the matter. He found himself swept with two very different feelings. He was thrilled at the realization that he had at last found a site where he could vent his talents as an archaeologist to their limit. But he was also filled with misgiving, for he knew that he would now have to confront Melanie with the fact that the family would, indeed, be moving.

He turned to Brad. "Have you checked out the housing situation in Fenchurch St. Jude?"

"Not yet," the younger man replied. "I've got to tell you, I've been into the village several times, but the locals are really weird about strangers."

"Well, that's to be expected in a place as insular as this, isn't it?"

"Maybe so, but I mean *really* weird. It's like they look at you like you've got the plague or something."

Great, David thought to himself, that would delight Melanie no end. "Well," he said, "I'm sure their xenophobia is just due to their parochialism."

"Their what?"

"Xenophobia, their fear of strangers. I'm sure it's just because they're not used to seeing unfamiliar faces in these parts. I bet they're fine folks once you get to know them."

Brad shrugged.

Both men were still staring at the second body when David suddenly had an uncanny feeling that there was something behind him.

"Good God!" he exclaimed when he turned and abruptly found himself face to face with a well-dressed stranger. To his equal surprise, a short distance away, on the country lane that wound next to the camp, was an ancient but well-kept Rolls-Royce with a liveried chauffeur sitting behind the wheel. He was stunned, for all three, the well-dressed gentleman, the Rolls-Royce, and the chauffeur had appeared as suddenly and as silently as if they had coalesced out of the mists of the bog. He noticed that Brad was equally taken aback.

"We didn't hear you drive up," he gasped.

The man said absolutely nothing, but just continued to stare at them malevolently. He was tall, fully as tall as both David and Brad, with finely chiseled cheekbones and a mop of silver-gray hair. In contrast, his complexion was unusually dark, almost tanned in appearance, and his brown eyes were deeply set and penetrating. He was expensively dressed in a tweed jacket typical of the landed gentry, and his fingers were studded with rubies and garnets. In his hand he carried a Malacca cane, clouded and mottled with age. David estimated that he was in his fifties, but trim and very well preserved for his years.

"Who are you, and what are you doing here?" the man demanded sternly.

"Who are you?" David countered.

The stranger continued to gaze at them smolderingly. "I am Grenville de L'Isle."

"The Marquis de L'Isle?" David asked.

The older man nodded imperceptibly, still keeping his dark eyes trained on them, hawklike.

David explained who they were and showed him the papers given to them by the government that allowed them to undertake their excavations.

"Would you like to see the bodies?" he asked brightly when he had finished.

The Marquis seemed only slightly interested. David considered offering him a pair of boots, but noticed that the brown, peat-colored water had already squished up over the Marquis's fine Oxford Street shoes. In true stiff-upper-lip fashion, he scarcely seemed to notice. He glanced but briefly down at the body of the young woman in the pit, sniffed appreciatively, and then strolled back up the hill.

"How long do you intend to be here?" the Marquis asked.

"Quite some time. Six months to a year. You don't know of any available living accommodations, do you?"

The Marquis behaved as if he hadn't heard a word of the question. "Do you have a wife, any children?"

"Yes, I'm married and I have two children."

"Do you intend to have any more?"

David found the question slightly presumptuous, but assumed that it had something to do in some oblique way with his inquiry about prospective living accommodations. "We have no plans to have a third."

The Marquis did not flinch, but just continued to stare blankly at him for a moment, and then, just as suddenly as he had appeared, he turned and started to walk away.

David was nonplussed. "Excuse me," he called from behind, "but are you going to answer my question?"

At this the Marquis once again pivoted and regarded him silently, still giving no clue as to what was transpiring in his thoughts, and then, mysteriously, he turned and continued on his way. The liveried chauffeur was waiting in attendance, shut the door behind him, and within moments the Rolls was driving off into the distance.

"You see," Brad said dryly, "I told you they were weird."

*　*　*

David chalked up the Marquis's odd behavior to aristocratic eccentricity, but was still slightly on edge when he drove into the village of Fenchurch St. Jude. He scanned the streets, prepared for just about anything, and became somewhat more at ease when he noted that it seemed to be a typical little English village. The lane that functioned as Fenchurch St. Jude's main artery was lined with terrace cottages. There was a village store, the customary pub, even a petrol station, soberly decorated and neonless, but evidence nonetheless that civilization had indeed encroached upon the sleepy hamlet.

There was not, however, anything even vaguely resembling a real estate office, and David resolved to make inquiries at the pub. He noticed as he walked through the weathered oaken door that the name of the establishment was the Swan with Two Necks. Inside, it was a typical English pub, dark, smoke-filled, but resonant with the feeling that a lot of living had taken place within the confines of its comfortingly dark walls.

Here and there a few grizzled regulars sipped at their ale, and behind the bar stood a frail little woman with matchstick bones and garish bleached-yellow hair. All eyes were riveted on David as he entered. He approached the bar and ordered a Guinness. For a moment the woman just gawked at him, and he found himself staring back at her unnaturally colored hair, as stiff and wiry as a yellow pot scourer. Finally she slid a Guinness his way and then rushed from behind the bar and joined a table of regulars on the other side of the pub. All eyes remained on David as she whispered something rapidly to one of the men sitting at the table. It was clear they were talking about him.

This did not surprise him. The appearance of a stranger in their midst was certainly an occurrence worth talking about. What did impress him was the generally unhealthy look of everyone in the pub. The little blond woman was as thin as a starved bird, and the insubstantial sallow fabric stretched over her bones looked more like chicken skin than human flesh. It occurred to David that her stridently colored hair didn't help matters much. But even the men had a weedy, weak-eyed look to them, a generally unwholesome air that he couldn't quite put his finger on. Their skin was a little too pale and mushroomlike, and their posture stooped and defeated. As he took a sip of his Guinness he noticed that they were still staring at him and whispering among themselves. He turned around on his stool.

"My name is David Macauley," he announced boldly.

This surprised them. The blond woman straightened and looked at him with astonishment. They had apparently not

35

expected him to speak. She glanced down at one of the men and then looked back at him. Still, she did not respond.

"I'm an archaeologist," he continued. "We're doing some work out at the bog."

This truly captivated their attention. After several more moments of silence the woman said, "You and the other gen'ulman?"

"You mean my assistant, Mr. Hollister?"

"The tall man with the black beard?"

David nodded. "That's him."

The ice broken, the woman hesitantly stepped forward and nodded. "Winnifred," she said simply. "People call me Winnie."

"Nice to meet you," David returned.

She looked back at the men behind her, almost as if for support, and then returned her attention to him. "And what did you say you was doing out at the bog?"

"We're looking for the remains of your Celtic ancestors. We've already found two bodies."

This caused quite a stir among them.

"Oh, you needn't worry," David added quickly. "They've been dead for at least several centuries, probably much longer."

This seemed to make no difference to the woman. "But the bog!" she exclaimed. "You shouldn't be doing no digging in the bog."

"Why not?"

"Why, 'cause that's his place."

"Whose?"

"The Marquis," she stammered, bewildered. "The bog belongs to him."

"Not all of it," David returned. "The government owns a section of it."

"I shouldn't think that'd matter," she snapped. "You shouldn't be poking around in things you don't know nothing about. You should leave the bog alone."

"Why?"

She grew totally exasperated. "Because the bog takes. No one as goes up against the bog comes out a winner. You may think you know what you're doing, but the bog will just wait and bide its time and then, when you least expect it, or maybe when you been expecting it for months, the bog will reach out and take something you love, or maybe some part of you. But it *will* take. It's been taking from us for some time now."

"Winnie!" one of the men chided sharply from behind, and David noticed that the entire crowd seemed to have grown uneasy at her admonition. He almost thought he saw several of the men looking around nervously, as if some unseen danger lurked in the walls or the woodwork.

The same man who had chided Winnie reached out and hushed her sternly as he grabbed her by the arm and drew her back. "But I got to tell him—" she began, but he just shook his head for her to be silent.

He looked at David. "You don't pay her no mind," he said tersely.

David took a large swig of his Guinness. It did not seem especially odd to him that the woman had such an unprovidential attitude about the bog. The bog was a treacherous place, and it was only natural that the people who lived near it should have developed a certain healthy respect for its perils.

"How long do you expect to be here?" the man asked.

"Quite some time," David answered. "At least six months, maybe even a year or longer. In fact, that's why I came in here. I was wondering if there were any cottages in the area that are available to be rented?"

This remark had an even more marked affect on most of the patrons in the pub, and they became increasingly agitated. But the man who had addressed David just continued to look at him unaffectedly.

"That's something it would be best to talk to the vicar about," he said.

David chugged down the remainder of his Guinness, pleased with this granule of information. "What's the vicar's name?"

"Venables," the man returned.

"Thank you very much," David said. He paid for his Guinness, nodded to his rapt audience, and turned to leave. Just before he passed through the door he noticed what appeared to be a stack of newspapers on a ledge. The name of the paper was *The Little Telegraph*, and when he looked closer he saw that the masthead said Fenchurch St. Jude. David purchased one from Winnie and left.

As he had observed, the church was set apart from the village and overlooked the bog. It took him about five minutes to get there. He pulled around to the side and parked his car next to what he assumed to be the vicarage. As he walked to the front of the church he noticed that some effort had gone into maintaining it, but it was still greatly in need of repairs. The rhododendron hedges around it were neatly trimmed, but the walls of the church itself were flaking and crying out for paint, and the roof was in obvious need of patching. He went inside.

As he passed through the door he wondered if he would find anyone in the church, it not being Sunday and all, but he did not have to ponder the matter for long, for standing atop a rickety stepladder and plastering a hopeless-looking crack in the ceiling was a man he assumed to be the vicar. The man looked down at the sound of David entering.

"Who are you?" he asked.

"Are you Mr. Venables?"

The vicar nodded.

David introduced himself and explained why he was there.

"Oh, I see," said the vicar, laying down his board and trowel. He glanced up one last time at the crack. "The church is falling apart," he mumbled disconsolately before he started to descend from his precarious perch.

When he reached the floor, he wiped his hands on a rag and then regarded David more carefully. In feature, he was a gaunt man with a resolute face and luminous gray eyes. As he approached, David noticed that he too was staring at David with a sort of incredulous curiosity, but it was a softer scrutiny than the naked ogling he had received from the people in the pub. In fact, it occurred to David that it was more like the gaze of some of the dons he knew at Oxford. He fancied that the vicar was an intelligent and highly sensitive man, a man who contemplated the deeper mysteries of existence. It also did not escape David's attention that there was a strange sadness about the vicar, as if on occasion some of his contemplations caused him deep sorrow.

"You want a place to live?" he repeated.

David nodded.

"How long did you say you intend to stay in Fenchurch St. Jude?"

"Anywhere from six months to a year, but possibly a little longer. It would be nice if the landlord were willing to be a bit flexible."

The vicar mulled all of this over. He looked at David. "It's an unusual request, you know. We don't get many people wanting to move to Fenchurch St. Jude. The last one was over forty years ago. It was before my time." And after he said this he grew suddenly troubled. Something seemed to race through his mind and then he suppressed it, looking back anxiously at David. "I just don't think this is the place for you."

"Why not?" David asked.

"I just don't," the vicar snapped.

"Well why not?" David repeated, becoming annoyed.

"Because there are no empty cottages in Fenchurch St. Jude except for the hunter's cottage and that would, of course, be out of the question."

"Why?"

The vicar's eyes widened. "Because the Marquis owns it. It's on his estate."

"How near to his home is the cottage?"

"Oh, quite far actually. Several kilometers, but—"

"—but why is it out of the question?" David repeated, pretty much at wit's end.

"Because the Marquis is a very difficult man," the vicar said in exasperation. "I couldn't imagine him wanting the place to be rented."

"Does the Marquis have a telephone?"

"But of course."

"Then why don't we call him and ask him?"

This alarmed the vicar more than ever. "I wouldn't dream of it."

"Why not?" David cried.

"Because I wouldn't want to disturb the Marquis," the vicar returned firmly. "As I told you, he's a very difficult man."

"I know," David sighed. "I met him."

The vicar looked at him with astonishment. "What did he say to you?"

"He asked me if I was married or had children."

"Now you see, isn't that a strange thing to say? The man is difficult."

David had had enough. "Listen, if you are not going to call him for me, I'll simply drive up to his place myself."

The vicar shook his head vigorously. "Oh, I wouldn't do that." He sighed. "Very well, as you wish. I'll call him. Follow me."

They proceeded through the chancel of the church and into

the vicarage. David was at least pleased to see that the vicar's living quarters were stacked floor to ceiling with books. He noticed one open on the arm of a chair. The title of the volume according to its spine was *Serving God on High*.

The vicar's mood became even more rattled as he dialed the telephone. Looking at him, David noticed that the vicar seemed more than just reluctant to make the call. He seemed actually fearful. "This is Mr. Venables," he said into the phone. "I'm terribly sorry to disturb you. Is the Marquis in? Because there's a gentleman here. Says he met the Marquis this morning. Yes. Yes. Because he wants . . ." The vicar paused and looked once again at David. ". . . he wants to rent the hunter's cottage."

Whoever the vicar had been talking to apparently went off to ask the Marquis, and the vicar put his hand over the mouthpiece and dropped the phone to his side. "Now we've done it," he said, and again David noticed honest fear in his eyes. He lifted the phone back up to his ear. "What? Yes. What? Six months, maybe a year. Possibly longer. What? Very well. I'm very sorry to have disturbed you. Please tell the Marquis I had no choice. He was going to come by and visit if I did not. What? Yes. Please, tell him I'm very sorry. Good afternoon."

He hung up the telephone and turned to David in disbelief, his eyes wide with David knew not what emotions.

"He says the cottage is yours."

2

DAVID AND MELANIE sat at the dining room table, a candle burning romantically between them. They scarcely noticed that in the living room the lights were bright, the television blaring, Ben was barking, and Tuck and Katy were bouncing around having what appeared to be a mild fight, Tuck's toy helicopter having somehow gotten tangled in Katy's blond hair. David had just told Melanie the news and she was not taking it well.

"Honey, I still don't know what's wrong."

She looked at him with a sort of vague desperation. "I told you, I don't know myself. I don't want to rock the boat, but it's going to rip something out of me to leave here."

"Why?"

"I don't know. What about Tuck and Katy's schooling?"

"I've talked to their teachers and cleared it for them to leave a little bit early for their summer vacation this year. Then next fall, if we like the school in Fenchurch St. Jude, we'll enroll them there. Or if not, we'll tutor them like we did when we were in Nebelgard. After all, we are college professors."

"You're a college professor," she corrected.

"Well, you're almost one. You've certainly had the education."

Melanie continued to stare into her wine. "What about Katy?"

"What about her?"

"I just don't think it's right to be moving her to such a spooky, lonely place."

"But the house is nowhere near the bog. It's the moors. She's reading *Jane Eyre* and she loves it."

"But that's just the point. She's thirteen years old. She's turning into a young woman. She should be out meeting kids her own age and getting to know herself more. She shouldn't be reading *Jane Eyre* out on the moors and in total isolation."

"She won't be in total isolation. I'm sure there'll be kids there that she'll get to know."

She looked at her husband sharply. "None *you* will approve of."

It was true that David had very high standards when it came to his children's friends. In fact, being a perfectionist, he had very high standards when it came to just about everything.

He shifted uneasily in his chair. "I still don't think it's going to be that bad an experience for them." Again he felt a familiar tactile sensation and looked down to see Ben pushing his head up underneath his hand to be petted.

"Ben will love it," he added.

Melanie smiled wistfully. "Ya, he will, won't he."

"*Will?* Did I hear you say *will?* Does that mean . . ."

"Of course it means I'll consent. There was never any doubt of that."

He reached over and took her hand. "You know I love you so much." He looked deep into her eyes. "You have no idea how much this means to me. I'll make it up to you in some way. We'll move where you want to move next."

"Sure," she said doubtfully.

"No, I mean it."

She smiled as he continued to hold her hand, but somehow there seemed to be such a hovering darkness in the pit of her stomach that she found it difficult to imagine there being a next move, or even that they would have a future after Fenchurch St. Jude.

* * *

It was on their way to Fenchurch St. Jude that Melanie Macauley started to put the pieces of her unhappiness together. On the surface it had to do with the fact that Katy was becoming a young woman. But there was more to it than that. She had met David when they were both graduate students at Harvard.

42

He was the pride of the archaeology department and she was working toward her master's degree in art history. They fell in love. They got married. They had not planned to have any children, or at least not at that time.

When Melanie discovered that she was pregnant, however, it came as sort of a godsend. She had completed all of the credits necessary for her degree, and even most of her research. But she was floundering on her thesis. She was trying to prove the influence of certain obscure Parisian philosophers on nineteenth-century French painting, and although she had amassed plenty of rich ore, she found herself at a total loss as to exactly what precious metal to hammer it into.

In addition, she found herself faced with the dilemma that all married academic professionals face sooner or later, the cold harsh reality that good university positions were nigh impossible to come by, and it was too much to expect that both spouses would be offered equally desirable positions in the same geographic location. For all of her feminist leanings, she realized there was a certain horrible wisdom to one spouse taking a backseat to the other's career. David's work was going well and showed every promise of continuing to do so. She was adrift and unhappy in her research. And there was another person to consider, an unborn child beginning to squirm and kick within her womb. Her instincts welled up, and being a mother and a wife seemed like a marvelous oasis, a way out.

Now, however, Katy was beginning to grow up and Tuck was well on his way to independence, and she was beginning to wonder what it had all been for. She loved her children and her husband. She even loved the dog that all too often she was left with having to walk, groom, purchase food for, and endlessly let in and out. Soon enough her children would be grown, and David would still have his career but what would she have? Another dog? The prospect of another week's grocery shopping to do? She did not regret making the decision to have a family, but she was beginning to realize that her life was nearing the end of a conveyer belt of sorts and she did not know what lay beyond. It did not seem fair. She wanted more.

All of a sudden the Volvo tilted upward and the trailer hitched behind it, carrying all of their worldly possessions, clunked loudly. They had pulled into a driveway.

"Well, what do you think?" David asked.

She looked up to see a lovely enclosure of trees, wild cherry, fir, and willow with long golden catkins and slender, pointed green fronds swaying gracefully in the breeze. And in the center of the green cathedral of trees and surrounded by wildly untended hedges and what had once been a beautiful lawn, was one of the most picturesque cottages she had ever seen. It looked like something out of *Snow White*. Its whitewashed walls were flaking and dappled with rain marks, and its quaint, steep, thatched roof was here and there in need of repair, but it still seemed like something more out of a fairy tale than a place where one might actually live.

She bit her lip, withholding her final assessment until she had seen more. "It looks like it could use some work," she snipped.

David was unabashed. "Wait until you see the inside."

They got out of the car, Ben, Tuck, and Katy piling out like spilled marbles.

"Wow!" yelled Katy as she stood and gazed with amazement at the cottage. Both Tuck and Ben, being less receptive to such aesthetic considerations, took advantage of the moment to run off some extraneous energy and bounded off in opposite directions.

David opened the gate in the old stone fence that surrounded the house, which creaked loudly. "Got to take care of that," he commented.

They went into the cottage. Melanie then realized that because of its simple design the cottage had seemed deceptively small from the outside. It was really quite vast. Before them was a cavernous entrance hall, lofty and heavily raftered with huge balks of age-blackened oak. To the left was a large living room with a huge, old-fashioned fireplace dominating most of one wall, and at the end of the entrance hall a beautifully balustraded staircase led upstairs. As she surveyed the place she took in more of its details, the high, thin windows of old stained glass, the oak paneling, the stags' heads on the walls. She also noticed that everything, the heavy and lugubrious furniture and the long-disused torchères, was covered with a thick layer of dust.

"Does it have indoor plumbing?" she asked.

"It's old, but it works," David replied. He flicked a switch and an ancient chandelier clicked on overhead. "It also has electricity."

She looked at him truculently. "It better have."

"Come on. I want to show you the rest of the place."

They proceeded through the remainder of the house, the huge kitchen and full pantry, the gun room and den, and the five large bedrooms upstairs and servant's bedroom downstairs. And everywhere it was the same. The cottage had once been magnificent, a story-book dream. It was conceivable that it could be so again. But it was in a staggering state of neglect. Everywhere Melanie looked there were things to be done, wallpaper to be rehung, carpets to be washed, grass and weeds to be cut, door hinges to be tightened, and runner boards to be renailed. And every place one looked in the old and rambling edifice there was an almost endless amount of dusting and scrubbing to be attended to.

They ended up in the kitchen, gazing out the back door of the house at an overgrown vegetable garden and still more unkempt lawn.

"Well, what do you think?" David asked.

She didn't know what to say. She knew he wanted her to be happy, but she also knew on whose shoulders the brunt of the housework would fall. Instead of taking the bull by the horns she chose to be evasive. "How much did you say the Marquis whatever his name was, was willing to rent the place for?"

"That doesn't matter. A pittance."

"Have you given him the money yet?"

"Not to him directly. I gave it to the vicar, Mr. Venables. He functions as the Marquis's agent."

Melanie felt a sinking feeling. She thought to herself, so there's no backing out then. It wasn't that she didn't like the house. A part of it tugged at her romantic soul. She was about to turn to her husband and force a smile when she noticed that the windows in the kitchen were composed of an almost uncountable number of little leaded glass squares, each one a grimy nightmare of a cleaning job.

Suddenly Tuck and Ben charged into the kitchen, a bit of yellow fluff from the catkins of the willows caught in Tuck's brown hair. "Mom, I'm thirsty."

"Then go get your cup out of the car and I'll give you a drink."

Tuck reappeared moments later with the requested cup. Melanie turned the tap on and was pleased at least to see that the water that came out of the ancient spigot was cold and crystal clear.

She gave the glass of water to her son and then turned once again toward David. "I almost forgot to ask, what about Brad? Is he going to be living here with us?"

David looked at her with surprise. "Oh, I guess I forgot to tell you. He's going to continue to live in his tent. I'm sure he'll be coming here to take showers and stuff, but he said he wanted to keep an eye on the site at night and make sure no one disturbs anything. I tried to convince him he would be more comfortable here, but you know how strange he is. I think he just can't bear the thought of living with other people."

Melanie looked aghast. The thought of Brad spending his evenings alone in a tent out on the moors and with several dead bodies so close by, no less, was horrifying to her beyond words. "*God,*" she said, her flesh crawling as if someone had drawn a dead lizard across her breast. "How can he do it?"

David shrugged. "I don't know. It even gives me a chill, but you know Brad. He's quiet, but he's got moxie."

Tuck looked up at his father curiously, but David addressed Melanie again. "So, you still haven't said anything. How do you like the place?"

Once again she surveyed the air around her, silently chiding herself for being so phony as to pretend that she had yet to make up her mind. Unable to put it off any longer she looked her husband squarely in the eyes.

"I could love it. It has great promise, but honestly I think it will kill me to try to get it into livable condition."

David grinned from ear to ear. "That's why we're going to hire someone to do it."

Melanie looked at her husband with disbelief. "What do you mean?"

"I didn't tell you because I was saving it as a surprise. Because of the promising discoveries we've made already I got another grant. Along with the fact that the rent is so low here it means we can hire a full-time cleaning woman. And then once the house is in shape she can help with the cooking, do the shopping,

46

take care of the kids. It'll give you some freedom, some time for yourself."

Melanie couldn't believe it. One moment she had felt so depressed, so hemmed in. Now she was swept with such a sudden euphoria that tears welled up in her blue eyes. She rushed forward and embraced her husband.

"You dog. You could have told me."

David kissed her and then drew back and looked her in the eyes. "And ruin the surprise?"

She started to bill and coo girlishly as she squeezed him again. Tuck apparently found such exuberant displays of affection baffling and annoying, and he plunked his cup down loudly on the counter and once again tore back out of the kitchen with Ben, as always, right behind.

Suddenly able to view the entire proposition in a new light, for the moment Melanie put her unhappiness about being there aside and stood back and once again examined the kitchen. "Gosh, give these stone walls a good scrubbing and they'd be beautiful," she purred. She walked over and started to tinker with the stove. Several seconds later, as it turned out, they both happened to lapse into silence at exactly the same time and one of those hushes that occasionally envelopes the world seemed to fall over the entire house. For a few moments everything was lost in the stillness, and then, distinctly, there was the sound of scurrying somewhere beneath the floorboards.

Melanie turned white as a sheet. "What was that?"

David sighed patiently. "I'm sure it's nothing. Probably just some small harmless animal of some sort. You know, the house has been empty for a long time. There's bound to be a few critters taking refuge in various nooks and crannies."

This had not been the right thing to say. Melanie turned a sort of gray color. "What do you mean nooks and crannies? You mean there may be things *in* the house?"

"Nah," David said, trying desperately to assuage her fears. "I mean there are probably only things in places that can be reached from the outside."

Melanie grew paler still. "What if it's rats?"

"We'll get rid of them."

"How?"

"I'll buy some poison the first time I go into town."

Yes, indeed, he would, Melanie asserted, but this was still

47

a solution too remote to offer any comfort right now. And before David was allowed to do anything else, even unload the car, he found himself going from room to room banging on all of the floors, walls, and even the ceilings, with a broom.

It was about half an hour later, while David was unloading the trailer, that Ben first started to behave strangely. At first David didn't really notice. In the back of his mind he was aware that Ben seemed to be barking a lot and was no longer bounding around as happily as he had been, but David did not initially register the behavior as unusual. It wasn't until Tuck came up and interrupted his work that he began to pay attention.

"Daddy, something is wrong with Ben."

"What do you mean?" David said, continuing to work.

"He won't stop barking. I think he's afraid of something."

Grunting, David lowered the box he was unloading and looked across the lawn. For the first time he observed that the black Labrador retriever was no longer running, but had come to a complete standstill and was barking mournfully in the direction of the moors. Occasionally he would pause in his baying and sniff the air carefully, and then, as if he caught a whiff of something that he felt was of danger to the family, he would break into his barking once again.

"Ben!" David called. "What is it?"

The dog paused in his barking and looked in David's direction, and when he saw that he had captured David's attention, whined piteously. For a moment it seemed that he was desperately trying to convey something to David but, on confronting failure, turned and took up his curious vigil once again.

"Daddy, why is he doing that?" Tuck asked anxiously.

"It's nothing," David calmed.

"But why won't he stop barking?" Tuck continued.

David knelt down and put his arm around his son comfortingly. "Tuck, it's okay. This place is new for Ben just like it's new for you. He just needs to tell everyone that he's here."

Tuck seemed to accept the explanation, but was still gazing in Ben's direction when Melanie appeared at the front door of the cottage.

"Tucker, come inside, I need you to help me unpack your stuff."

"Okay, Mom," Tuck yelled as he ran into the house. David

smiled, pleased that Melanie's request had taken Tuck's mind off of Ben's unusual behavior, as he once again hoisted the box onto his shoulder.

After dinner that evening, David noticed that Tuck was glued to the television, newly installed in the living room of the cottage. Katy, as usual, had her nose in a book and was curled up in an armchair some distance away. David directed his attention toward Tuck.

"Have you finished that book on dolphins yet?"

Tuck looked up disconsolately. "Nooo," he groaned.

"Have you done *any* reading today?"

Again Tuck replied in the negative.

"Well don't you think you should get a little reading in before you go to bed?"

"Oh, *Dad*, I'm watching television."

"I know, but I thought you and I had an agreement, that every day you would get just a little reading in?"

At that moment David felt Melanie tugging at him gently from behind. He looked at her and she gestured for him to follow her into the entranceway. They made it a point never to discuss the children in front of the children.

She looked at her husband softly. "Don't you think that today's a special day with the moving and all? I mean, he's only six years old. He's been running around like a banshee all day and he's exhausted. Couldn't he have an occasional reprieve from the heavy reading schedule you demand of him?"

"Oh, honey, but he's watching television."

"You watch television."

"Only the news, and an occasional educational show. Did you see what he's watching? *Benny Hill.*"

She sighed. "I know, but every once in a while it's not going to kill him."

"But it's mindless."

"But every once in a while it's good to be mindless, like when you're exhausted, or battle-fatigued from having your entire world shifted beneath you. And sometimes just for the sheer joy of doing something mindless."

He grimaced.

She looked at her husband imploringly. "Don't you remember how it was being a kid?"

This caused him to regard her sharply. Of course he remembered. He remembered his father ripping up his books if he caught him reading. He remembered drunken brawls, the perpetual mist of alcohol around his father's face. That was why he was so driven in his own thirst for knowledge, why he was so demanding of his children, so critical of their friends. David's father had been a factory worker and a horror. He had wanted David to grow up fulfilling only his strict mold of what it meant to be a man. In short, to learn to fistfight, to eschew books, to become a factory worker, and ultimately to end his life as he himself had, accomplishing nothing, learning nothing, and dying, a spent and broken man amidst an ocean of beer cans and empty Jack Daniel's bottles.

That was when Melanie put the final nail in her argument. "You don't want to end up as demanding as your father was, only in the opposite direction, do you?"

He looked at her solemnly. No, indeed, he did not want to end up like that. "Very well," he conceded. "I guess it won't hurt him to watch *Benny Hill* every once in a while."

He walked back into the living room. "Tuck, if you want to just watch television tonight, go ahead. You can read some more of the dolphin book tomorrow."

"Thanks, Dad," Tuck chirped obliviously, his eyes remaining glued to the glowing tube.

David spent the rest of the evening helping Melanie put the house into some semblance of order. When night finally came he found to his surprise that he was actually looking forward to the unconsciousness of sleep. Normally, he was so consumed in his studies, his own reading, and the constant racing of his thoughts, that he usually found it difficult to pull away from it all and go to bed. Tonight, however, he was quite looking forward to being lost in the arms of Morpheus.

He went upstairs, but before going into his bedroom he paused to look in on the children one last time. He knocked on Katy's door first.

"Just a minute! Don't come in!" she screamed immediately from beyond.

David smiled. She had become so excruciatingly modest and vulnerable since she had entered adolescence. There was a time not too many years back when she would have paraded around in front of him with just a pair of shorts on, but suddenly she had become acutely self-conscious about even the most innocent of things. This afternoon, while they were unpacking the trailer, a pair of her simple cotton panties had fallen out of a box in front of him and he thought she was going to die of embarrassment. Nonetheless, he knew that he had to do everything in his power to refrain from showing his amusement at such incidents. He knew that it was all a part of growing up.

"Ready yet?" he called.

"Okay," she returned.

He opened the door. When he entered he found her sitting up in bed with her flannel nightie laced tightly around her neck and looking decidedly unhappy.

"Katy, what is it?" he asked as he sat down on the bed beside her. He felt a sinking feeling, assuming that her disconsolation could only be due to their recent move. For several long moments she said nothing, and he gently took her hand. "Katy, won't you tell me?"

Finally, she looked at him, her eyes revealing that she was still struggling to find the words to express her misery, and then at last she spoke. "Oh, Dad, why did you have to name me Katharine?"

This was not at all what he had been expecting, and he had to think about it for a moment. "What's wrong with the name Katharine?"

"It's just that it's such an old-fashioned name," she said. She fidgeted nervously, and he realized there was still something she wasn't telling him.

"Come on," he prodded, "this is me you're talking to. What's caused you to suddenly become so unhappy about your name?"

Again she looked at him agitatedly, still reluctant to confide the truth, and then finally she came out with it. "I don't like the name Katharine because it's the same name Catherine the Great had and Rupert Riesdale in my fourth-hour history class told me that Catherine the Great died while she was having sex with a horse."

David just sat blinking silently for several moments. Again, this was not what he had expected. His initial reaction was to be appalled at what his thirteen-year-old daughter had just come out with, but he decided the best tack was to take it in stride and deal with it calmly.

"Well, I've heard that story also, but as far as I know it's apocryphal."

"What's *apocryphal*?"

"Greatly in doubt. Most sources I've read say she died when an artery ruptured in her brain, and she was alone in her bed at the time."

Katy seemed only slightly appeased.

"And besides, we didn't name you after Catherine the Great. We named you after Katharine Hepburn. Just before you were born your mom and I saw her in *Pat and Mike* and we liked the movie so much we started thinking about the name. Does that make you feel any better?"

Apparently it did not, for Katy looked at him sulkily. "I was named after an actress?" she asked disparagingly.

"Well, sort of. But there have been lots of amazing women throughout history named Katharine. You were named after them too."

"Like who?"

"Like Catherine of Aragon, Queen Isabella's daughter, or Catherine de Medicis, widely respected for the shrewdness she displayed in her influence on the governing of France." He judiciously neglected to tell her that Catherine of Aragon was the first of Henry VIII's ill-fated wives, or that Catherine de Medicis was also widely touted for the powers of deceit and treachery that she had inherited in her Medici blood.

Katy began to soften.

Trying a new approach, David said, "Well, if you had been there to be consulted, what would you have rather been named?"

"Natasha," Katy replied without blinking.

He scoured his memory for famous Natashas in history, but drew a blank. "Where did you get that name from?" he asked.

Her face grew slightly red. "From the Natasha on that cartoon show with Rocky and Bullwinkle," she said sheepishly. "I just like the sound of the name better."

David's heart sank, but slowed in its descent when he realized that at least she had blushed. He consoled himself with the affectionate realization that she was still in a curious transition between a child and a young woman, the child unabashedly announcing Natasha as her preferred name, but the woman slightly embarrassed at the ludicrousness of the source.

"So call yourself Natasha," he announced.

"Oh, Dad, could I?"

"Sure," he returned, but then added some small print to the concession. "*If* it's okay with your mother."

Katy's face fell, but then broke into a humbled smile when she realized she had been duped.

He kissed her good night and then went into Tuck's room. Saying good night to Tuck was somewhat less complicated. He found Tuck lying straight as a board on top of his sheet and carefully lining all of his toy cars and trucks up and down along the sides of his legs.

"Tuck, do you really want to sleep with those things?"

"Why not?" Tuck asked earnestly.

"Because if you roll over on them during the night they're going to hurt."

Tuck looked up and down at the metal cars, reassessing the matter. "Ohhh," he said, frowning gravely. Carefully and methodically he took them one by one and parked them in rows on the table beside his bed. As he did so David noticed that he too seemed unusually distracted. Even after he had finished and David was pulling the covers up around him, Tuck continued to stare off into space, absentmindedly doing the itsy-bitsy-spider routine with his fingers, a gesture that always meant something was weighing heavily on his mind.

"Tuck, is anything the matter?"

"Dad, do I have moxie?"

David smiled, remembering that Tuck had been present when he had used the word earlier that day. "Not quite yet, Tuck," he said. "But I'm sure you will someday."

"What is moxie?"

"It's courage. But not just any type of courage. It's like being brave enough to face anything. It has to grow in a person."

Satisfied for the moment, all the tension left Tuck's face and he suddenly looked very sleepy.

"Good night, Tuck," David said, kissing him on the forehead.

"Good night, Dad."

"I love you."

"I love you too."

When he finally retired to his own bedroom he found Melanie sitting up in bed and looking very disturbed about something. He sighed. It just wasn't his evening.

"You're not thinking of changing your name, or asking me if you have moxie, are you?" he asked.

53

She looked at him, perplexed. "What?"

"Oh, it's nothing. You just look concerned about something."

"It's Ben," she said. "Listen to him."

David paused and realized he could still hear Ben whining about something downstairs.

"What do you think it is?" Melanie asked.

"Just the newness of the place. The new smells."

"But he seems so troubled about something."

"Honey," David soothed, "we're out in the country now. I don't mean to frighten you, but there are lots of little animals around, *harmless* animals, but lots of little animals nonetheless. Ben's just not used to their sounds and smells yet."

"What kind of little animals?" she asked uneasily.

"Oh, I don't know . . . rabbits, foxes."

"Will the foxes bite Ben?"

"I doubt it. I suspect they're far more frightened of Ben than he is of them. They'll keep their distance. They do, you know. Things like that can smell a dog."

David decided that perhaps the best thing to do was shut Ben outside for the night. At least that way Ben would start to get more of a feel for the place, run around and urinate on trees and stuff, and do all those things that a dog does to feel more comfortable about its territory. He went downstairs and put Ben out, but was chagrined when Ben's whining did not subside but turned into barking. He continued to howl mournfully, woefully, all night long.

* * *

The next morning when David entered the kitchen he was greeted by the smell of bacon frying. Melanie stood at the stove, cracking eggs into a second skillet, Katy sat at the table with a bowl half full of soggy cereal in front of her and reading a book, and Tuck was crouching on his haunches in front of Ben who was reclining in a corner.

"Good morning, everybody," David greeted.

"Morning," Melanie and Katy intoned together. Tuck looked up at his father's approach.

"Daddy, something's wrong with Ben."

Melanie turned around with an expression halfway between mystification and I told you so. "He won't eat," she explained.

David went over and crouched down beside his son and

looked into Ben's eyes. The retriever stared back at him wearily. In front of him was a bowl of his favorite food, untouched.

"Maybe he's just not hungry," David said.

"Oh, come on," Melanie challenged. "You know him. He's normally famished."

"I'll bet he'll eat this," David said, standing and taking one of the pieces of bacon that was draining on a paper towel next to the sink and then crouching down again and wafting it in front of Ben's nose. Ben sniffed it once and then looked up at him sadly, emitting an exhausted and frustrated whine.

Tuck looked at his father worriedly.

"I'm sure it's nothing. He's just depressed over the move. Dogs get depressed over things like that, you know."

Melanie gave him a skeptical glance.

"Okay, okay," David conceded. "If he's not better in a day or two we'll take him to the vet."

"Is he sick, Dad?" Tuck asked.

"I don't think so, but if he is we'll see that he gets better."

Tuck looked back down at the dog and tenderly stroked his head. "You get better," he ordered gently.

"Tuck, come finish your breakfast," Melanie said, pulling his chair out at the table.

"It's soggy now," Katy murmured from behind her book. Seeing that that didn't seem to make any difference to Tuck, she added another barb. "And there's a bug in it."

Tuck looked horrified.

"Katy!" Melanie broke in. "Why do you say things like that?" She turned to Tuck. "There's no bug in it. Come on."

"Well, I think I'll be going," David said.

Melanie looked at him, dismayed. "But you haven't eaten breakfast yet."

"I know, Mel, but it's my first full day at the digs. I'm kind of excited to get there."

"But I cooked the bacon especially for you."

"I thought it was for the kids."

"The kids have cereal. You can see that."

"I'll have some bacon," Katy offered.

"Me too," Tuck chimed in.

For a moment David thought it might be his out, but when he saw the look on Melanie's face he realized that if he knew what was good for him, he'd better have some also. He sat down at the table.

"There are eggs too," Melanie said in a stern monotone.

David watched as she whacked two rubbery yellow eyes down on his plate.

"She makes us eat them too," Katy said dryly from behind her book.

Melanie turned around holding a spatula aloft threateningly. "Remember the movie *The China Syndrome?* Well, Mom's about to have a meltdown, so watch it."

David took a large bite of egg and bacon, grinning widely and chewing with gusto. Mollified, Melanie turned back around.

Trying to change the subject, David noticed that she had been looking through the copy of *The Little Telegraph* that he had left on the counter for her.

"See any ads for housekeepers?" he asked.

"There's a classified section, but no ads for housekeepers looking for work. Looks like I'm going to have to place an ad in myself."

"Are you going to ask for live-in, or just days?"

Melanie looked around her at the house. "Well, this place is big enough for a live-in. What do you think?"

"I'll leave it up to you. I don't really care either way." Melanie smiled and David secretly felt pleased. He knew she liked it when he left such judgments completely up to her.

He quickly wolfed down his breakfast, kissed Melanie good-bye, and turned to leave. Just as he reached the door, Tuck ran up to him.

"Dad, can I come with you?"

"No, Tuck."

"Why?"

"Because Daddy's going to be there all day long, and you'd get bored."

"Can I come for a visit?" Tuck countered.

"Not today. Maybe sometime." He noticed Melanie looking at him reprovingly from behind. They always made it a point not to discuss the bog bodies in front of Tuck because Melanie deemed it a subject unsuitable for a six-year-old's consumption. Personally, David recalled all of the ghastly and lurid things he had been into as a young boy and thought that Tuck would

56

have been able to deal with it. After all, they had allowed him to see the mummies at the British Museum. But to this Melanie always countered that the bog bodies were far more frightening than mummies because they were unshrouded and much more perfectly preserved, and with this David had to agree—although he still thought Tuck would be able to deal with it.

He was just about to leave when Tuck looked up at him again. "Dad?"

"Yes, Tuck?"

"I'll finish the dolphin book today, okay?"

"That would make me very proud of you, Tuck."

Tuck smiled jubilantly and padded off.

Melanie came up beside him, and together they watched as Tuck vanished into the living room. "He worships you, you know."

"I'm pretty fond of him too," David said. He kissed Melanie one last time and then left.

The digs were about two and a half miles from the hunter's cottage, and he had agreed to travel the distance on foot so that Melanie could have the car for errands. As in his trip here to see the body Brad had discovered, there was a nip in the air, and a pall of early morning fog still hung over the moors. He walked briskly, but to his surprise it still took him about half an hour to reach the campsite.

He arrived to find Brad already hard at work, continuing to enlarge the pit containing the body of the young woman.

"Good morning," David greeted him.

"Good morning," Brad returned with an air of excitement. "This is just amazing. I've just about uncovered all of her body, and she's one of the most perfectly preserved specimens I've ever seen."

David too felt a crackle of excitement as he looked down at the body. Her legs, her feet, everything except for the slight decomposition around the neck was in perfect condition.

"Any sign of how she died yet?"

Brad shook his head. "Nothing. I just can't figure it out. There are rope marks here on her wrists, so at least we know that she was tied before she was killed, but that doesn't tell us all that much. And even though part of her neck is covered, I've removed the peat from the side here and there's no sign that she was strangled. There are also no knife wounds, no visible contusions or fractures. As I say, unless her wounds are concealed under her body we have a real puzzle on our hands."

David crouched down beside the pit and stroked his chin. "You know, I've been thinking about this. From the expression on her face and the rope marks on her wrists it seems clear that she didn't die of illness or natural causes. She had to have been murdered in some way. However, if she had been murdered because of adultery or some other social crime, her head would have been shaved. That was the Celtic custom. And if she had been accused of being a witch or possessed or something, she would have been weighted down with rocks or oak palings to prevent her spirit from returning and once again walking the earth. By process of elimination, although we have yet to determine the precise cause of death, the only thing I can come up with is that she was a sacrificial victim of some sort."

Brad grunted from exertion. "That's exactly the same conclusion I arrived at."

David chuckled. "Sorry, Brad. I keep forgetting, you hardly need these lectures. Don't worry, I'll learn."

Brad looked up at him and smiled, and it struck David that the slight tension between them had dissipated.

"I just wish we could figure out the cause of death," Brad said.

"Don't worry," David returned. "As soon as we begin to get the sludge off of her I think we'll find that out."

For the next several hours David took over the digging, and by midafternoon they had expanded the pit enough so that they could fit a large sheet of plywood under the body lengthwise. Only then could they lift the body out plank and all, and thus avoid the risk of breakage. Finally they began the long and arduous task of separating the body and the sheet of plywood from the sticky and tenacious peat beneath it. Then, together, and with their boots sinking deep into the peat at the bottom of the pit, they lifted the body out.

David looked up at the campsite. While he had been busy packing and moving his family, Brad had also been busy setting up a second tent, much larger than the one he slept in, and filling it with all of the equipment, barrels of solvents, tables, and the portable generator they would need to operate their field laboratory. They climbed out of the pit and carried the body up the hill to the tent.

After they had placed it on the examining table, David's first task was to determine whether the tanning process that had been begun by the bog water had extended uniformly throughout all of the young girl's internal organs. To accomplish this it would be necessary to make a deep incision in both the young girl's abdomen and her hip, but as he looked down at her he found himself filling with qualm over the procedure. For all of his drive and yearning for knowledge, he always felt mixed when it came to cutting into one of the bog bodies. They were so perfectly preserved, and were such silent and awesome emissaries from the past that part of him viewed it as an extraordinary sacrilege to slice into them as if they were no more than just another specimen for dissection. He looked at Brad and saw that the younger man was filled with the same apparent misgivings.

"Well, here goes," he said, taking a scalpel and neatly cutting into the young woman's eerily obsidian flesh. To his relief, he noted when he peered into the resulting wound that the flesh was a uniform brown throughout. That meant that they would not have to continue tanning the body, soaking it in a wooden trough filled with distilled water and oak bark for untold weeks. They would, however, have to further preserve it using other processes. As Brad prepared the first chemical bath, David took a small sample of the young woman's flesh and placed it in a plastic bag. This they would send to Oxford to be carbon-dated.

Once Brad had the equipment ready, they lifted the girl, plywood slab and all, and gingerly placed her in a large polyurethane tub. As they did this David once again caught a glimpse of her face, and found himself wishing that the cleaning procedures could be done more quickly, but he knew that it would still be several hours before they even had the peat off of her.

Then he placed the end of a long rubber hose next to her side and turned the spigot on a nearby drum. Slowly the tub began to fill with a mixture of Formalin and acetic acid. Once the body was completely submerged it would have to sit for several hours. Then they could slowly start to siphon off the Formalin and acetic-acid solution and gradually replace it with alcohol. After that they would replace part of the alcohol with toluene, and only then could they initiate the numerous other processes that lay before them. They would lave the body in Turkish red oil and then lanolin to protect it and keep it pliant. Next they would treat different portions with mixtures of various hot waxes, and finally they would inject the more decomposed areas of the anatomy with collodion. David knew that only after all of these steps were complete could they feel secure that they had made the girl as immortal in the open air as she had been during the many centuries she was buried in the bog.

As soon as they finished with the first phase of the procedures, the pungent smell of the Formalin and the acid forced them to leave the tent. Outside, David once again surveyed the excavations. Both of the bodies they had discovered thus far lay on the rim of an ancient bog caldron. Presumably, when they had been interred the peat in the caldron had been much soupier and the bodies had just been tossed onto its surface and then slowly sank. Nonetheless, samples taken at various levels of the peat and then carbon-dated should give them reasonably accurate corroborative evidence to compare against the age of the body once they had it carbon-dated. He was about to turn to Brad to instruct him to proceed with the taking of peat samples when the younger man smiled knowingly.

"I know," he said, holding up several sample bags.

David smiled. "While we're waiting for the first soaking to be finished, I'm going to take a walk around."

Brad nodded. "See you in a bit."

David turned and strolled in the direction of the hill to the west of them. His purpose in the walk was to get more of a feel for the land these people had inhabited. Part of the "new" archaeology that David was helping establish was the philosophy that to truly understand an ancient people, to see the world through their eyes, one had to do more than just catalog their artifacts and their bones. One had to also try to put oneself in their shoes, as it were. This included not only understanding what they experienced when they physically moved about the land they inhabited, but also knowing the plant life, the climate, even the animal species that had come and gone since they had lived. This was why David was so knowledgeable when it came to the flora and fauna and even the geological conditions that went into the making of the bog. But even if he had not deemed it useful to his profession to know and understand such a wide-ranging array of information about the world around him, he would have learned it anyway, for when it came to knowledge his appetite had no limit.

When he reached the top of the hill he looked up and noticed that a kestrel had caught an air current and was hovering motionlessly high above the moors. The sight made him recall with curiosity the incident involving the bittern a few days previous. As he continued to watch the kestrel he wondered if it too would collide with the apparently invisible barrier, but then it caught another vagary of the breeze and slowly soared off in a different direction. For a moment David wondered again what had caused the bittern's strange behavior, but as he gazed into the tranquil gray sky he dismissed the incident as just a freak occurrence.

Then he noticed the kestrel again hovering motionlessly at an even higher altitude, and suddenly jealous of its superior vantage, he decided to move to the top of the next hill. From this new location he could now see a part of the valley that he hadn't seen before. He scanned it with interest, and some distance away spotted a ramshackle little moorland cottage with a crumbling stone roof and surrounded by a clutter of junk, dilapidated plows and wagons, a chopping block, and several sloppily stacked mounds of wood. Sheep dotted the hillocks around the cottage, and the entire place, although clearly inhabited, had a look of waste and ruin about it. As he continued to gaze at the rustic but peaceful sight, he noticed something else. Not too far from the tumbledown cottage, and strolling dangerously close to one of the seductively verdant arms of the bog, was a little girl.

She looked to be around six or seven years old, roughly the same age as Tuck. Her hair was a drab brown, and even in the distance he could see strands of it straying across her face in the wind. Her white calico frock also had a look of the hand-me-down and the timeworn about it, and seemed more Victorian than something a contemporary child would wear.

She walked toward the bog with determination, and strode so close to its treacherous edge that David almost called out to her. But then she stopped and just gazed into the abatis of blackthorn and dead trees. She stood there for many long moments, lost in some apparent contemplation, her dress fluttering sadly in the wind. And then she turned and walked back toward the house.

* * *

As soon as Tuck and Katy were finished with breakfast Melanie herded them quickly into the car. Seeing the amount of cleaning that needed to be done in the house, she wanted to put an ad for a housekeeper in *The Little Telegraph* as quickly as possible. Fenchurch St. Jude was about six miles from the hunter's cottage, and as they drove along she noticed there were only a handful of other houses. Nonetheless, she observed that a number of them had people out and about them, and whenever they drove by, their new neighbors would stop what they were doing and stand and stare at them silently as they passed. The appearance of newcomers in the community was clearly something to stand up and take notice of. What disturbed her was the indescribable solemnity of the people. It was not that she expected anyone to wave. But always everyone seemed so grim in their deportment. Nowhere did she see people running or children playing or anyone even striding with anything approaching gusto about life.

Katy noticed it too. "What a bunch of stiffs," she said.

"Don't judge others until you get to know them," Melanie chastised, but then, on passing yet another moribund farmer, she said, "Ah, heck, go ahead and judge them."

In the backseat Tuck was totally unaware of the entire situation, and from the rocket noises he was making seemed to be somewhere between Jupiter and Mars.

When they reached Fenchurch St. Jude their reception did not improve. Here and there people dotted the street, and they too all stopped and gaped at them as they drove by. Melanie pulled the Volvo up in front of the village store. As she shuttled the children out of the car, she became aware that in the windows of a few of the shops and in some of the homes, faces pressed unselfconsciously up against the glass and observed their every movement.

They went into the store.

Inside, the small establishment was packed floor to ceiling with a carefully but prudently broad selection of just about anything one would ever need for basic survival. In a room off the side of the shop was what appeared to be an office, containing a printing press and a clutter of papers. In here worked a woman with short, plainly cut black hair speckled with gray, and severe features. She was neatly but somberly dressed, and she glared coldly at Melanie as she entered. Melanie gave Katy the shopping list and nodded for her to start collecting the things they needed. Then she approached the woman.

"My name is—"

"I know," the woman cut her off. "Your name is Mrs. Macauley. You're the professor's wife. News like your moving in doesn't take long to travel in a village as small as this. My name is Thoday . . . Miss Thoday." She looked down at her hand and grunted when she saw that it was covered with ink. It occurred to Melanie that for a moment maybe the woman had considered shaking her hand, and this seemed like a good sign.

"What can I do for you?"

Melanie tried to make the best of the situation and smiled. "Well, as you probably know, we've just moved into the hunter's cottage and it's a wreck."

"No doubt, great ol' barn of a place."

"And I was wondering if I could place an ad in your newspaper for a housekeeper?"

"Don't know of anyone who's up for some extra housekeeping."

"Aren't there any young girls who would appreciate the employment?"

"A few."

"What about them?"

"Don't know that their parents would let them do it."

"Why not?"

If Melanie had nurtured any hopes of the woman being friendly they were now dashed, for the woman broke into a contemptuous glower. "I know you just moved in, but there's something you should know. In the village of Leeming, about fourteen miles from here, a couple of nights ago a woman was murdered, shot twice, and in the back, no less. I hope I don't have to tell you that such things are unheard of in this part of the country. This is a small community and we just don't have that kind of crime here. It's got people quite shaken. So if your reception is less than warm here, it's because people are quite leery of strange faces right now."

"Do they have any idea who killed her?"

"No idea. They don't even know why. She wasn't even robbed. She was just walking home from work one night when somebody shot her, neat as you please, two bullets right through the base of her spine."

Melanie looked across the store and was pleased to see that both Tuck and Katy were out of earshot. She turned back to Miss Thoday. "And you think people will be reluctant to allow their daughters to work for us because of this crime?"

"I do."

"Well why should they blame us for it?"

"It's not that they blame you, it's that they don't want their daughters walking home at night."

"Oh," Melanie returned. "Well I suppose we could drive them to and from work."

"Doesn't matter."

Melanie sighed exasperatedly. "Well could I place the ad in your paper anyway?"

Miss Thoday considered the matter for half a moment. "I suppose. It's your money. Just as long as you are aware that you are not likely to get much of a response."

Melanie nodded as she reached into her purse for the copy. "We'll see," she said optimistically.

As Miss Thoday surveyed the copy the silence was suddenly broken by a loud and grating sound, and both women looked out the window to see a young man on a motorbike tearing through the village. He parked the bike before the pub and got off. As he was loosening his helmet, a small wiry woman with artificially blond hair came out to meet him.

"That's Luther Blundell," Miss Thoday informed. "And that's his mother, Winnifred Blundell. She's one of my best friends."

As Melanie continued to look out the window she noted that Winnifred Blundell wasted no time in alerting young Luther to their presence in the village, jabbing a bony finger repeatedly in the direction of their car, her mouth flapping at an astonishing rate. From the pursed expression on her face it did not appear that she was organizing a welcoming committee for them.

Melanie turned to Miss Thoday one last time. "When will

the ad appear in the paper?" she asked, still keeping half an eye on the scene taking place in front of the pub.

"I'll put it in the edition I'm working on now. It'll be out by late afternoon today."

"Very good," Melanie said, as she paid for her purchases, gathered her children, and left the store. Outside, both the blond woman and the young man on the bike paused in their dialogue and gazed coldly at them as they got into the car and pulled off.

Driving back home, Melanie found that she could not take her mind off their strange reception. The gloomy cloud of apprehension that she had felt about moving to Fenchurch St. Jude started to build once again in the pit of her stomach. Her moody reverie broke only when she realized that Tuck had sat up in the backseat and was leaning forward, his small elfin face poised right beside her own.

"Mom?"

"Yes, Tuck?"

"Are you sure there was no bug in my cereal this morning?"

"Yes, Tuck. Katy was just teasing you."

" 'Cause I can feel something moving in my stomach."

"It's nothing, Tuck," she assured him as she cast a condemning glance at Katy, who was smirking like a Cheshire cat at the success of her ploy.

* * *

David arrived back at the site to find Brad busy excavating the pit containing the second body. "Did you know there's a cottage just over the hills back there?" he asked when he reached the spot where Brad was working.

"Ya, I've seen it," Brad said, glancing up and wiping his brow. "It belongs to someone the locals call Old Flory. The first time I went into the pub in town and mentioned to that wretched blond woman, the one who calls herself Winnie, where I had set up my camp, she remarked that it was near Old Flory's place. Apparently he sells firewood to the people around here."

"Did you know that he had a little girl?"

"Can't say that I did," Brad returned, grimacing. "That's too bad."

"Why do you say that?"

65

"You'll see when you see Old Flory," he responded cryptically.

When the time came for them to drain the first bath of liquid, they both went back into the tent. The first thing David did was examine the coloration changes in the young girl's flesh. Then, when he saw that they were to his satisfaction, he started to siphon off the Formalin and acetic-acid solution. As it flowed off they passed it through a filter, mixed it with alcohol, and then routed the liquid back into the drum perched beside the body.

David looked down at the glistening but still sediment-encrusted cadaver. In the next step they would allow the liquid to wash over her with enough force to rinse away the last of the peat that still obscured the finer details of her anatomy, and David was excited, for he hoped that at last they would decipher what had brought her life to a close. He looked over at Brad. He could tell that the younger man was also filled with anticipation, and this caused David to once again look down at the rubber tubing that he held in his hand. At times like these, during the final moment of reckoning when they were about to reveal some important aspect of the past for the first time, archaeologists often became very competitive and self-seeking, and David was not unsusceptible to these feelings himself. There was nothing more he wanted than to be the one to wash away the final patina of mud from the body of the young girl. But, in spite of Brad's withdrawn nature and occasionally grating humility, David knew he was very lucky to have him as an assistant. He was not contentious. He was totally devoted and hardworking, and he was bright, but quiet about his brilliance. David fought down his own selfish feelings and decided it was only right that he allow Brad the honor of washing away the last bit of dirt.

"Would you like to take over from here?" he said, offering him the hose.

Brad looked at him unbelievingly. "You mean it?"

David nodded and smiled.

Overwhelmed, Brad took the rubber tubing and positioned it over the woman's abdomen as David went behind the table and once again released the spigot. The clear liquid quickly snaked through the translucent tubing and gushed out the other end.

As it streamed out Brad moved the hose back and forth in slow and rhythmic sweeps, and both men watched closely as the last remaining peat broke away from the woman's flesh and collected at the bottom of the polyurethane tub.

At first they saw nothing, just larger and larger portions of the eerily preserved and sloe-black skin, but finally, when Brad moved the stream of the solution up around the woman's neck, the first unusual features began to appear.

"This is strange," Brad said, leaning closer.

David's own interest grew keener, and he moved a second portable light into position so that they could get a better look.

What drew their attention was not the extent of the deterioration, but the form that it had taken. When he had first looked at the body, David had assumed that the area had simply rotted away before the tanning processes of the bog could fully take grip. Now, however, he was able to see that the damage was far more regular than would have occurred by rotting alone. Scooped out of the woman's flesh was a profusion of strange, half-moon-shaped gouges. Most notably, the gouges clustered around what had been the woman's jugular, and indeed, large chunks of her flesh were missing here. Over the woman's upper breast and sternum the craterlike holes were fewer and less deep, as if whatever had caused them had languished here, choosing instead to concentrate primarily on the neck.

As they continued to wash away what debris remained in the wounds, they saw something else. Some of the gouges on her upper breast had rasped away the flesh entirely and cut deep into the bone. Here, as David looked closer, he was able to make out a little circle of furrows lining the edge of each wound, and like the gouges, these striations were also very regular in shape and arrangement. They appeared to be teeth marks.

"What do you think could have made those?" Brad asked.

"I don't know," David said, frowning and shaking his head. "I've never seen teeth marks like that before." As he continued to stare at the wounds he was also bothered by the size and shape of the bites. Whatever had made the incisions had obviously had very sharp teeth to be able to slice so neatly into the bone, but the wounds themselves were too small to belong to any large predatory animal that he could think of. He was also troubled by the shape of the gouges. If she had been bitten by an animal like a wolf or any similar carnivore with opposable jaws, it would have ripped at her flesh and left puncture wounds, but not the strange, sickle-shaped hollows that they now saw before them. However, the wounds were also too large and regular in shape to have been made by any small gnawing animals that he knew of. They were anomalous bites, as if whatever had attacked her had had a small but powerful mouth and had rasped away at her flesh instead of biting away chunks of it.

In light of this recent discovery both men looked once again at the rope marks on her wrists.

"Are you thinking what I'm thinking?" Brad asked, disconcerted.

David looked at the younger man, but said nothing. Both knew that they were thinking the same thing. The conclusion was inescapable that the woman's hands had been bound together shortly before her death, probably around an upright stake, and that something had been allowed to feed upon her. If that had been the case, and if she had been alive during this occurrence, it would certainly go a long way to explaining the look of unspeakable horror wrought on her face.

David's mind was reeling. If they had in fact found evidence of the Celts sacrificing a young woman to an animal of some sort, it was a stupendous archaeological discovery. This excited him greatly, but he was also filled with disquiet. Not only was he horrified at the idea that the people who had lived in these hills might have sacrificed a young girl in such a manner, but even more he was baffled at what species of animal could have possibly created such unusual wounds.

* * *

These questions still weighed heavily on his mind when he and Brad arrived back at the cottage that evening for dinner. What had turned into puzzled brooding for David momentarily dispersed when Tuck came bursting out the front door to greet them.

"Dad!" he squealed as he catapulted his little body through the air and into David's waiting arms. Although the feat had taken David somewhat by surprise, it was an often enough repeated ritual for David's arms and body to just reach out and catch whenever there was the slightest indication that Tuck was about to blast off. However, an equally ingrained part of the ritual was that Ben was usually barking exuberantly close behind, and it did not escape David's attention that the retriever was nowhere to be seen. Nonetheless, he refrained from mentioning it, because he did not want to make Tuck unduly aware that there might be a problem.

"How are you, Tuckaroo?" he greeted his son as he hoisted Tuck's diminutive body into a more secure position in his arms.

"Fine. Mom's making hamburgers."

"She is? Great!" he said as he nodded for Brad to follow him into the house.

In the kitchen they found Melanie standing at one of the counters patting ground beef into patties. Katy sat at the table reading, and David noticed that Ben was still in his position in the corner, but had at least stopped his incessant whimpering.

"Hello, Brad," Melanie said.

"Hello," Katy burbled at the same time as she quickly took off her glasses and concealed them in her lap.

David smiled. "Have a seat, Brad," he invited, gesturing at the table. He put Tuck down and then sat down himself.

"Dinner will be ready in about twenty minutes," Melanie said as she placed the first hamburger patty into the waiting skillet and it started to sizzle.

"In that case, you better wash your hands, Tuckaroo," David said.

Tuck became deeply concerned. "Dad, I can't reach the sink."

"Maybe Katy will help you." He looked at his daughter proddingly.

"Oh, jeez," she groused, closing her book, as she reluctantly took Tuck into tow and accompanied him upstairs.

"So how did it go today?" Melanie asked.

David related the day's events to her, and when he got to their somewhat unnerving discovery late that afternoon, he paused. On one hand, with all of the talk they had been having about little animals and Ben's odd behavior, he knew that it would alarm Melanie. But on the other hand, it had never been part of his nature to be anything but totally honest with his wife, and he saw no reason to go back on that policy now. He took a deep breath and related the entire incident. When he had finished he looked up at her and saw that she had taken it about as well as he had expected she would.

69

"Do you think whatever killed that poor girl is still wandering about now?" she asked.

"Of course not."

"What makes you so sure?"

"When's the last time you read about some sort of wild animal mauling a person to death in England?"

Melanie accepted the information and seemed to relax slightly.

"And besides," David went on, "one thing you've got to remember is that this event occurred nearly two thousand years ago. The native fauna has changed a lot since then."

"How so?" she questioned.

"For one thing, there were wolves."

"But we don't think she was killed by a wolf," Brad added quickly, and David cast him a sharp glance.

"Why not?" Melanie asked.

Brad looked at David awkwardly, realizing that he had made an error.

David sighed and, comprehending that the cat was out of the bag, related to Melanie the unusual and rasping nature of the wounds.

"Oh, my God," Melanie murmured, appalled. "Why on earth would an animal behave in such a peculiar manner?"

An uneasy silence filled the room. She looked at the two men, once again wielding her spatula in a subtle but threatening way. "I'm an adult. I can be told," she urged.

Still, both men remained silent, until finally Brad shifted uncomfortably in his seat. "Well, I've been thinking about this, and I know it sounds a little farfetched, but it's almost as if the animal, whatever it was, wanted the girl to die slowly, had enjoyed her anguish and had lingered and caressed her with its bites in a way that seems less animallike and more . . . well, almost more passionate."

Thank you, Brad, David thought to himself as he rolled his eyes up toward the ceiling. To his extreme relief, however, the children came running back into the room, and he knew that this would keep Melanie from asking any more ghoulish questions. He knew that his best approach now was to try to change the subject and get her mind off of this.

"Have any luck finding a housekeeper today?" he asked.

Melanie placed another hamburger in the skillet as she related

her own experiences that day. When she reached the part about
the murder of the woman in Leeming she tried to be as low-
keyed as possible, spelling pertinent words here and there so
as to avoid frightening Tuck. It was an unsuccessful ploy.

"Did a bad man shoot the lady?" Tuck asked almost immediately after she had finished.

Melanie looked at her husband.

"Yes, a very bad man," David assured him.

"Is the bad man around here?" Tuck continued with thoughtful alarm.

"No, he's very far away from here," David answered as he
smiled at his son and patted him comfortingly on the back of
the head.

For several seconds everyone remained silent, busy in their
respective thoughts, and then finally Melanie spoke again.
"How many hamburgers do you want, Brad?"

Brad looked up sheepishly. "I'm afraid I don't eat hamburger.
I'm a vegetarian."

"Well then what are you going to eat?" Katy asked worriedly.

"What are you having with it?"

"Green beans and mashed potatoes," Melanie replied.

"I'll eat that."

"But that won't be enough," Melanie said.

"Sure it will. Did you know that the Roman army conquered
the world on a vegetarian diet? Caesar's troops actually complained when grain stores ran out and they were forced to
eat meat."

She looked skeptically at her husband for confirmation. "He's
right," David agreed, pleased that the conversation was at last
taking a more innocuous turn. "Roman troops lived primarily
on vegetables, bread, and porridge. They disdained eating flesh."

The conversation proceeded on about several other aspects
of Roman history until at last Melanie said, "That comb you
found was Roman, wasn't it."

David nodded.

"What did you say the inscription said?"

"Bringing you this last gift for the dead, accept this offering
wet with tears," David replied.

"And what did you interpret that to mean?"

"Since the evidence suggests that the girl is Celtic and the
comb is Roman and a considerably more costly object than

we would expect a girl of this region and time period to possess, we believe her sacrifice might have been witnessed by a Roman woman, and that she presented the girl with the comb as a sort of offering."

"What would a Roman woman have been doing here?" Melanie asked.

"There were Romans all over the country during that time period. The woman was probably the wife of an official who was sent here on some political mission."

"And she gave the girl the comb as some sort of votive?"

"Exactly," David returned.

Melanie looked puzzled. "But why was the comb wet with the Roman woman's tears?"

"That's the fifty-dollar question," Brad broke in.

"But it could be any number of reasons," David added. "We know that Caesar first conquered Britain in about 55 B.C. This comb is an expensive enough object that the woman it belonged to had to be the wife of a Roman official reasonably high up in Caesar's political hierarchy. If she had accompanied her husband to England it means that they must have arrived here at least several years after the skirmish, when things had settled down enough that it would have been safe for a wife to accompany her officiary husband to a conquered land. They were here, most likely, to set about the more mundane task of the political and social reorganization of the Celtic people. A woman separated from her native soil and forced to travel with her husband to a totally foreign environment might have any number of reasons to be unhappy."

Melanie was caught off guard by this and stood blinking at her husband for several moments, but soon saw that he did not realize that an analogy might be drawn between what he had just said and their own situation. She started to take the hamburgers out of the skillet and lay them on a plate with paper towels to drain. As the chat continued on behind her, it once again returned to the subject of sacrifice, and she looked at each of her children anxiously, wondering if the talk was having any adverse affect on them. To her great relief it did not seem to be. Now that no attempt was being made to conceal the conversation from Tuck, he was paying not the slightest bit of attention, and instead, was moving his fork around the table like a tractor-trailer with several sugar cubes on the back of it as cargo. And Katy, Melanie quickly observed, had something entirely different on her mind. Her daughter seemed to be paying an unusual amount of attention to Brad. She was gazing at him attentively and virtually hanging on his every word. And whenever he said anything even remotely resembling a joke, she laughed heartily. It suddenly hit Melanie that her daughter was developing a crush on her husband's graduate student, and for some reason this surprised her.

Perhaps it was simply that she was not yet used to her daughter becoming a sexual being. As she considered the matter she realized her surprise was equally due to the fact that she had never really viewed Brad as a sexual being either. True, he had once mentioned a brief liaison with a woman named Jean, but it had been a comment made in passing, with no other details added, and she had long ago accustomed herself to the fact that Brad was far less interested in relationships with women, or for that matter anyone, than he was in his work.

Now as she looked at him, however, she realized that he really was very attractive. Beneath his plain but tightly fitting clothing he was lean and muscular, and a whorl of dark hair showed through his loosely buttoned shirt. He was also, she realized in her sudden reassessment, very handsome, and his hair and beard were a shiny and lustrous black. Equally striking were his eyes, which, in spite of their furtive modesty, had a sort of smoldering sensuality about them. She realized that if she didn't know him so well, and had come upon him suddenly in an appropriate setting, she might easily view him as a satyr or some god of the forest, a Bacchus or a Pan.

"Honey, should that be doing that?" she heard David's voice in the background.

"What?"

"That pot on the stove," he said, pointing, and she noticed that the potatoes were furiously boiling over the sides of their pan.

She looked at him, annoyed that he had called it to her attention instead of simply getting up and turning it off himself.

After they ate they had coffee in the living room. Finally the evening grew late, and it was time for Brad to leave.

"Are you sure you won't stay?" Melanie offered politely, once

73

again aghast at the idea of anyone spending a night all alone in a tent out on the moors. "We have clean sheets and plenty of room."

"Oh, stay!" Katy piped in brightly.

Brad considered the matter for a moment. "It's a tempting invitation, but I just don't like the idea of leaving the camp unattended for that long. We've made an important discovery and I wouldn't want anyone to go in and mess it up."

Melanie looked at her husband, wondering if he too was at all discomfited by the notion of Brad returning to the camp at so late an hour, especially considering the dismaying revelations of the day. But David scarcely even seemed to register Brad's leaving and was in the process of taking Tuck upstairs to bed.

Brad said good-bye and left.

Melanie noticed also that since they had come into the living room, Ben had at long last moved out of his corner in the kitchen and followed them in. He still had not eaten anything, and ever since nightfall he had once again grown increasingly agitated. Now, with Brad's departure, he padded cautiously over to the door and was sniffing deeply at the air coming in through the crack above the threshold. Suddenly he once again let out a low and plaintive howl.

"I'm going to let him out," David said when he came back downstairs.

Melanie looked at her husband incredulously. "After what you discovered today?"

"What do you mean?"

"I mean, what if something gets him?"

"Mel, I thought we went through this. There's nothing out there that's going to hurt him."

"Then why is he behaving this way?"

"I told you, there are so many new smells about that it's just going to take him awhile to get his bearings."

David approached the door.

"—but," Melanie argued, but her husband looked at her so sternly that she quieted.

He reached for Ben's collar, but the retriever instantly backed away. "Come on," David coaxed. "Don't be a big chicken." He grabbed Ben around the middle and propelled him outside. "Now go get 'em," he said as he shut the door.

Melanie felt a sinking feeling. She was sure this was not the thing to do, but she knew her husband well enough to know that this was not a point on which she should challenge him. Outside, Ben just continued to yowl.

While they were undressing for bed upstairs, they could still hear Ben's barking, and for the first time David himself grew a little worried. He went to the window in his underwear and peered out. The evening sky was still overcast and the night was an impenetrable black. He could see nothing. For lack of knowing what else to do he went back to bed.

It was about half an hour later that Ben's barking became unusually vigorous, and David once again jumped out of bed and ran to the window. He threw it open. Even he could tell now that something was seriously wrong. Ben's barking was no longer just the slow saraband of warning, but had accelerated in tempo and taken on a desperate and frenzied tone. "Ben! What is it?" David called, but the dog just kept up his feverish cries. From the sound of his barking it appeared that he was only a short distance out in the yard. Occasionally the barking moved, as Ben apparently raced from one side of the yard to the other in his impassioned attempt to ward off the unseen danger, but for several minutes he maintained the same distance from the house.

Finally, even Ben's already feverish barking crescendoed into a rapid series of staccato yelps, as if whatever the menace was that he was trying to keep at bay had drawn even closer, and from the sound of his barking David could tell that he had once again broken into a run. And then suddenly his barking was cut short in an abrupt and strangely truncated yelp.

"Ben!" David called again. For several moments he listened carefully, but he heard nothing. No barking. Not even the rattle of the retriever's collar as he padded across the lawn. "Ben!" he repeated, but still the only response he got was silence.

Behind him Melanie had turned the light on and was sitting up in bed, her faced creased with worry. "David, what is it? What's happened to him?"

For the moment David hushed her with a finger placed to his lips as he continued to listen. He did not know what had happened. He had only heard Ben make a sound like that once before, when they had still lived in the States. Melanie had allowed her clothesline to hang too close to the ground and one evening, not seeing it, Ben had run into it headlong and had had the wind knocked out of him in midbark.

This reminded him of that incident, for as he continued to listen he could still hear absolutely nothing, no sign of growling or a struggle that might indicate that Ben's silence was due to a confrontation with another animal. Finally he slipped on a robe.

"David, what are you doing?"

"I'm going out to check on him."

"You've got to be kidding."

"Honey, don't worry. I'm sure it's nothing."

She looked at her husband beseechingly. "Please, David, don't go. I have a terrible feeling about all of this."

"Melanie, it will be all right," he repeated as he grabbed a flashlight from the dresser drawer. She too got out of bed and slipped on a robe, but before she could stop him he had gone downstairs.

Outside, he still heard nothing, and as he stood there listening carefully it occurred to him that even the night itself had gone oddly silent. Normally, after darkness had fallen, around the cottage could be heard the cadence of crickets and other night insects, and even the call of an occasional night bird, but as he stood there now it seemed that everything had been enveloped in an unearthly hush. Only the rustle of the wind through the willows gave any indication that he had not entered a tomb. He called Ben again and again, his bare feet clammy in the dewy evening grass, but there was still not a sound, not even a whimper. He shone the beam of the flashlight across the lawn and through the trees, hoping at least to see Ben's eyes glowing comfortingly in the clear white light, but the retriever was nowhere to be seen.

Melanie appeared at the door behind him and called out. "Please, David, come back in."

"Go inside," he told her. "I'll be right back." And then, as an afterthought, he yelled back to her. "And lock the door until I get back."

He heard Melanie let out a little cry of distress as she did as she was bid, and he walked farther into the darkness. He passed through the creaky rusted gate in the stone fence and went out into the lane that ran by the house. He pointed the flashlight down the road in one direction, and then the other, but still saw nothing. He walked a little farther in the direction of the moor, and then suddenly he thought he heard something. He stopped.

"Ben?" he repeated. But still there was only silence. He waited a few moments, and then he heard the sound of a twig snap somewhere in the thicket behind him. He turned and directed the beam into the tangle of wisteria and blackthorn. He still saw nothing, but he suddenly got the distinct and eerie feeling that something was gazing back at him. He continued to move the beam of light around, still seeing nothing, and as he did so it began to flicker and then went out.

He heard another sound, as if whatever was concealed in the underbrush had taken the disappearance of the light as a signal to advance, and had taken another step forward. He shook the flashlight and it flickered weakly once or twice, but it did not come back on. He got a terrible feeling that whatever it was that was watching him from the thicket would be even more encouraged by this, and he heard another twig snap.

And then he got a most peculiar feeling. It started in the back of his jaw, a low, dull throbbing. Something rustled in the brush again, apparently taking another step forward, and the throbbing spread throughout his entire jaw and into his teeth and gums. It was as if someone had embedded little rods of steel in the center of the bones in his mouth, and was moving a powerful electromagnet all around him. Little spasms of pain shot up through his molars and into his skull as the unseen force tingled and tugged at him from all directions.

Suddenly his unseen assailant crashed full force through the brush, and David screamed, turning and tripping headfirst over a fallen log. He quickly clambered to his feet as whatever it was continued to close in on him. Without his flashlight it was too dark for him to see anything. His only thought became to make it to the house before it got him.

He broke into a run, but to his horror he realized that the fall had disoriented him and he was blundering deeper into the thicket. A blackthorn branch gouged him painfully in his face as he turned around madly, trying to get his bearings, and the pain in his jaw intensified. Whatever it was was just a few feet behind him now. Gasping like a marathon runner, he lunged forward, but again he became entangled in the underbrush and fell. He screamed again. Before him branches and twigs snapped as if something was ripping them apart to get at him. Any second now he would feel its teeth and claws.

Suddenly all was silent and a light clicked on. He looked up to see Melanie standing a few yards away, holding a flashlight. She was pale and frightened. "David, what is it? What's the matter?"

He looked around him in the thicket and, to his astonishment, saw that he was quite alone. The brush around him seemed broken, but there was no sign of any intruder, not even a small animal scurrying away. Whatever it was, if there had been anything at all, had evaporated like a mist into the darkness.

3

Hovern Bog: 53 B.C.

THE ROMAN VICE-PREFECT, Lucius Divitiacus, gazed out silently over the moors. His expression was impassive, but inwardly he was in torment. He had never faced a problem like this before. Now that the brunt of the fighting was over, and Celtic rage had been broken on Roman discipline, it should have been child's play to effect political reorganization in this isolated and unimportant tribe of the Britanni. The Romans had long ago established themselves as old masters of the game. They knew just how much of a culture to allow to remain intact, and just how much to change. With the consummate skill of a professional gambler and a keen eye for human weakness, they would seduce a foreign race, gradually acquaint them with the pleasures of public baths and develop in them a taste for colonnades, until they were drunk for want of experience and no longer realized that their growing hunger for Roman splendor was only contributing to their greater subjugation.

But these tricks had not worked here. The people of this valley tribe were peculiarly apathetic to Roman ways. It was not that they were hostile or combative. On the contrary, they had not even put up a struggle when the first phalanx of Roman troops had entered the valley. They had simply stood and scowled, but there had been something in their glower that

79

had troubled him, even then. It was as if deep in those submissive eyes there was a smugness, even a sort of pity. It had puzzled him for a long time. Now he agonized because he was beginning to understand.

Behind him in the tent he heard something stir, and he turned to see that his wife, Valeria, had come up behind him. She put her arms around him and rested her face against his back.

"Why don't we just leave, Lucius?" she asked.

He laughed, a short, bitter laugh. How could she ask such a question? He had been educated for war since childhood, and had spent most of his life in field or camp. The major element of his existence was discipline, and that meant cowardice was an unforgivable sin. He himself was empowered to behead any soldier or officer who strayed in any way from orders, however favorable the result. If he pulled up and left the valley before completing his assignment, the very least he could hope for was death by flogging.

"You know that I cannot do that," he said.

"But you saw the body of the girl before they tossed her into the bog. You saw what happened to her. How can we consider staying?"

Lucius turned and faced his wife. "I also saw that you attended their abominable ceremony."

Her gaze fell to her husband's feet.

"And I've noticed that your most expensive comb is missing. The one that I bought for you in Campania."

She grew even more penitent.

"May the gods preserve us, Valeria, why did you do it? You know that Caesar himself has ordered us to eschew their rites. I could have your hand cut off for such a deed. I just hope none of the soldiers saw you." He paused a moment in thought. "Do you know what has become of the comb?"

"They buried it with her . . . in the bog."

Lucius was somewhat relieved. "We may at least be grateful for that. But my question still remains. Why did you do it?"

She looked away, feeling too wretched to suffer the sharp scrutiny any longer, and he noticed something in her expression that alarmed him.

"Valeria, is there something else that you're not telling me?"

She looked at him entreatingly, her eyes filled with pain. "No, it's nothing."

"What's nothing?"

"I'm just upset. I'm frightened by what's happened, and I'm terribly sorry that I've offended you. Can you ever forgive me, my husband?"

He looked at her harshly for but a moment longer and then his expression softened. "Of course I can forgive you this time. But you must never let it happen again."

She nodded submissively as she collapsed into his arms. She was pleased that he forgave her, but inside she was still in turmoil. She wanted desperately to tell him, but how could she? She knew that her husband was obdurate in his adherence to rules and a Roman to his soul. If he had threatened to cut off her hand for her infraction when it came to the comb, what would he say or do if she told him her most terrible *secret*? And yet she was bursting to tell him. A part of her knew that she had to tell him, regardless of the consequences, for if she did not reveal to him what she knew, had witnessed, and now suspected, she had an awful feeling that they would never leave this valley alive.

4

DAVID SPENT THE better part of the morning looking for any sign of Ben. In the clear light of day the almost existential fear that had gripped him the night before had dissipated, and although he was still deeply troubled by everything that had happened, it was easier for him to accept that there had to be some rational explanation.

When he found no trace of the retriever, he procured a long stick and carefully poked away at virtually every square foot of land within several hundred feet of the house. Although he had done this before they had moved in, he thought that perhaps there was an undiscovered sink or an abandoned well somewhere in the yard that he had missed. At least, if Ben had been running and had fallen into some sort of pit, that would explain the suddenness with which his barking had been cut short. It would not explain the strange experience he had had in the thicket, or the pain in his jaw, but if he were to find a simple explanation for Ben's disappearance he knew he could more comfortably chalk those events up to overactive imagination.

When he still found nothing, he reluctantly went back into the house. When he entered he found Melanie waiting for him in the living room.

"Did you find him?" she asked.

"Not a trace."

She dropped down into one of the living room chairs. "My God, what do you think has happened to him?"

Although David's own alarm was growing, he knew that if he expressed his honest feelings it would send Melanie into a blind panic. He tried to look unconcerned. "I think he probably just caught wind of something and ran off chasing it. You know, when I was a kid we had a cat that would stray off and it wouldn't come back for days."

"But you heard the way his barking ended. It was as if a giant hand just reached down and plucked him right off the face of the earth."

"Maybe it was just a trick the wind played on our ears. Or maybe it was his last yelp before he went off chasing something. Dogs can make funny sounds sometimes. Remember how Ben used to make that funny wa-wa sound and we used to think it was Katy crying?"

"Oh, David, if that were the case, wouldn't we have heard him barking in the distance as he continued to chase the animal? I mean, dogs bark when they chase things. They don't just stop barking abruptly and then chase them in silence."

"Maybe he kept barking and the sound was just swallowed up by the trees."

Melanie grew cross. "Don't be ridiculous."

David found his own patience growing short. Basically he agreed with her, but because he had opted for the adversarial position he found himself growing annoyed at her persistence in shooting down everything that he said. "Okay, then what do you suggest? There was no blood. No body. What could have possibly happened to him if he didn't just run off?"

"I don't know," she returned. "That's what scares me."

He gulped down one last swallow of his coffee and then turned to leave.

"Where are you going?" she asked unbelievingly.

"I'm going to the digs. After all, that's why I'm here, isn't it?"

Melanie lost her temper. "You mean you're going to go traipsing off to be with your dead bodies and just leave me and the kids here alone?"

He looked at her incredulously. "What am I supposed to do, sit out in front and stand guard with a gun?" He looked at his wife angrily and then stormed toward the front door. Melanie jumped up from her chair and followed him.

"I can't believe it!" she exclaimed. "I just can't believe that after last night you can take this thing so lightly."

David's own temper had now reached boiling point. "So what am I supposed to do?" he demanded again. "What would make you happy?"

"I think we should leave."

"What do you mean?"

"I think we should pack up and move."

"Oh, that really takes the cake! I make the archaeological discovery of the decade, and just because our dog disappears you tell me that we should gather up all our things and move away." He threw his hands up in the air in exasperation.

Melanie seemed to see the ridiculousness of this suggestion, but the incidents of the previous evening still had her deeply shaken. "Well I don't know what else to suggest!" she cried.

"Well neither do I!" he shouted back, and at almost precisely the same instant the air was split by several loud banging sounds. They looked at each other in confusion. Something had pounded on the door.

David approached it and opened it cautiously. Outside, standing on the steps, was a tall, grim fright of a woman with severe features and salt-and-pepper hair tied back in a matronly bun.

"I heard you shouting," she said dryly. "I knew I had to knock loud to get your attention."

David blushed, growing slightly embarrassed. Both he and Melanie stared at the woman curiously.

She looked back at them with equal uncertainty. "You did advertise for a housekeeper, did you not?" she said. "If I've come at an inopportune moment, I'd be glad to come back some other time."

This time it was Melanie's turn to be embarrassed. "Oh, no, please come in. You see, our dog vanished inexplicably last night, and it's just got us a little rattled."

"As I can see."

"Please come in," Melanie repeated. "What did you say your name was?"

"Mrs. Comfrey," she said.

"Have a seat, won't you, and please forgive us."

Mrs. Comfrey did as she was invited. Both David and Melanie looked at each other sheepishly, not knowing what to say to the other next. Mrs. Comfrey intervened. "Please pardon me my presumption, but if your dog has vanished, I shouldn't fret too much about it."

"Why?" David asked.

"Because the brambles around these parts are filled with enough rabbits to lead a dog astray for days."

"You see," David said, casting Melanie an I-told-you-so glance. He looked back at Mrs. Comfrey and assessed the features of his new and unexpected ally. To his regret, Mrs. Comfrey was a dour-looking creature with a rather too-small head, and sharp, pale features. Her dowdy, navy-blue cotton dress covered a large and bony body, and on her long, shapeless legs she wore heavy brown nylons. He noticed also that her lilac perfume was just a little too oppressive and marveled once again at the bizarre creatures Fenchurch St. Jude seemed to turn out.

Melanie offered Mrs. Comfrey a cup of tea and when Mrs. Comfrey accepted Melanie vanished momentarily into the kitchen to fetch it. David followed her. After the kitchen door shut behind them he walked up to his wife's side and gave her a hug. "Honey, I'm sorry for losing my temper."

Melanie turned around. "Oh, David, I'm sorry too. I know I can't expect you to abandon your work just because Ben's disappeared, but I have a terrible feeling that something awful has happened to him."

David stared affectionately into his wife's eyes and decided to express his true feelings. "Well, I think something might have happened to him also, but I don't know what. Let's give it a few days and see. Maybe he'll turn up."

As they continued to embrace, David wondered if he should mention his slightly less than favorable opinion of Mrs. Comfrey, but decided against it. So far Melanie had not expressed any similar criticisms, and he decided it was best to leave well enough alone. He did, however, resolve to stay awhile and see how things went.

They returned to the living room and Melanie proceeded with the interview. David was pleased to see that in spite of her off-putting appearance, at every twist and turn Mrs. Comfrey handled the questions like an old pro, and near the end of their conversation Melanie seemed quite taken with her.

Suddenly Melanie blurted out, "You're so nice, you can't be from—" She stopped abruptly, realizing that her remark could be taken as quite offensive.

Mrs. Comfrey smiled knowingly. "—from Fenchurch St. Jude? No, I'm not, and I must say that I'm pleased that you're not also." Then she looked from side to side and lowered her voice as if to make sure no one was listening in and said: "Just between you and me, the people of Fenchurch St. Jude have quite a reputation in these parts for being . . . well, for being a bit queer. I'm from Leeming."

"Oh, the place where the woman was shot," Melanie interjected.

Mrs. Comfrey's features darkened. "What a nasty bit of business that was. Twice in the back. Still haven't caught the fellow, you know." She shook her head in concern.

After a few other sundry exchanges Melanie looked across at David and he perceived the meaning of her glance. She wanted to hire Mrs. Comfrey and she was looking for his approval. He nodded favorably.

Melanie turned back to the older woman. "Mrs. Comfrey, if you like, the position is yours."

"Very good," Mrs. Comfrey said amiably.

"There's just one other thing."

Mrs. Comfrey regarded her quizzically.

"Would you like the position to be live-in, or would you be returning home every evening to . . . your husband or something?"

"I'm widowed," Mrs. Comfrey said matter-of-factly. "And I don't fancy making the long haul back to Leeming every night, especially with the shooting and all. I'd prefer it if the position were live-in."

"Then live-in it is," Melanie said, clinching the deal.

David was surprised at the outcome, for given Melanie's mood earlier in the morning he would have thought it impossible to please her in any matter. But he was delighted that in this one small item, their life seemed to be working out. He decided to test the waters further.

"Would it be all right if I left for the digs now?" he asked cautiously.

Melanie looked at him quickly and for a brief moment her

eyes still seemed to be filled with anxiety. But then she smiled. "Will you excuse me for a moment," she said to Mrs. Comfrey as she stood and accompanied her husband to the door.

She looked at David apologetically. "Darling, I just wanted to say one more time that I'm sorry about this morning. I know things are going to go better now that I have some help around here." She kissed her husband good-bye and he departed.

Outside, it was another gray day, bright, but with a solid layer of clouds still completely obscuring the sun, and on his walk to the excavations David found himself once again troubled about the episode the night before. He looked at the thicket uneasily as he passed by, and wondered anew what could possibly explain the mysterious pain he had experienced.

When he reached the camp he found Brad, as usual, already deeply immersed in work. David looked down into the pit and saw that the younger man had almost completely excavated the second body. David whistled appreciatively and felt a chill of excitement when he saw the state of preservation of the second fallen form. This time, resting on the murky red mat of dog's flesh was the body of a man, an old man, again as eerily intact as if he had died only a few days earlier. On his head he wore a pointed skin cap typical of men during the Iron Age, and around his waist there was a smooth hide belt. Other than that he was naked. Whatever excitement David felt, however, was quickly alloyed with fear when he looked at the old man's visage. Although peat-encrusted, around his neck and chest were the same distinctive marks of deterioration as they had first observed in the young girl, and his face was contorted with the same terrible rictus of death. He too had been a sacrificial victim to the ancient and unknown animal.

"My God, what are we on to here?" David murmured.

Brad looked up. "It's really incredible, isn't it?"

"It's more than incredible," David returned. "It clinches the importance of the find."

"What do you mean?" Brad asked. "I thought we knew the find was important as soon as we discovered the bite marks on the young girl."

"True. But if we had only that information to publish, it would have been challenged in the academic literature as a fluke, a one-time occurrence. But with the discovery of this second body we have far more persuasive evidence that it was a regularly practiced ritual. The people who lived in these hills had quite a relationship with the creature responsible for this. I honestly can't think of any historical precedent for such a thing. I mean, the Aztecs used to feed portions of their sacrificed victims to animals in the royal menagerie, but that was only after they had been killed by human hands. In this instance, however, it seems that the Iron Age tribe to which these two people belonged had developed a regular and consistent relationship with an animal that roamed wild, probably lived in the bog. I really can't think of another instance of that happening in history."

"Any idea what the animal was?" Brad asked.

David frowned. "Well, the problem is that it had to be both large enough and aggressive enough to be able to attack and bite a person around the neck while they were standing and tied to a stake, and there just weren't many fauna in this region at that time capable of such behavior. It's conceivable that it might have been a wolf, but wolves, we know, tend to nip and bite their victims all over, and both of these individuals seem to have wounds only around their necks and sternums." David stroked his chin thoughtfully. "There is another possibility, however."

Brad looked at him quizzically.

"It may have been a badger."

"A badger? Come on," Brad challenged.

"Now hear me out. As you may know, badgers belong to a family of carnivores known as *Mustelidae*, and although they're typically smaller and thus aren't usually considered in the same league as, say, a panther or a tiger, they're often fierce flesh eaters. The Arctic wolverine, for example, lives on large herbivores like reindeer and even small elk. In India and parts of Africa the honey badger or ratel can also develop incredibly bloodthirsty habits, especially in its old age. There are reports on record of them killing pigs, sheep, and even cattle, and although there are no documented cases of it, it is generally acknowledged that an aging and ill-tempered ratel could quite easily kill a man."

Brad fidgeted uneasily.

David continued. "Similarly, the North American badger or wolverine is also acknowledged as a vicious killer and will eat dead animals as well as prey it kills."

"So, what kind of badger lived here?"

"The European badger."

"And is it known as a killer?"

David's expression changed. "Not really. They're normally considered peaceful animals unless molested, but there are always freak occurrences. It could have been an uncommonly large and mean animal. And . . ." He paused.

"And?"

"Well, it could have been domesticated in some strange way. Perhaps it had been trained to feed on people tied to stakes, and once it had tasted human flesh, acquired quite a liking for it."

"Domesticated? Come on," Brad protested again.

"Stranger things have been known to happen," David retorted. "Did you know that in 1899 the geologist Rudolf Hauthal led an expedition to Ultima Esperanza in Chile and in a cave in the mountains discovered a pen containing the bones and droppings of the now-extinct giant sloth? Keep in mind that the bones of that animal reveal that it averaged fifteen feet in height. In the cave, Hauthal also found the remains of an ancient kitchen, mussel shells, and charred pieces of guanaco and deer bones. It seems that the cave's inhabitants kept the terrifying beasts as a ready food source."

Brad just stared at David for several seconds and then shook his head. "You never cease to amaze me. How do you know all of these things?"

David blushed and tried to shift the focus of the question to a more impersonal level. "But that's exactly my point. To be an archaeologist you have to have a tremendously broad base of knowledge. You never know when you're going to run into special circumstances, such as this, where you're going to have to know a lot more about a situation or environment than just the age of the geological strata you're digging in."

Brad nodded dutifully, as one duly chastised. "Getting back to this badger theory. From what you know about badgers, do these bite marks look like something they would make?"

This took all of the wind out of David's sails. In truth, when he had suggested the badger theory it was less because he believed it and more because he was growing increasingly desperate to construct some sort of theoretical framework with which they might begin to understand the puzzles they were continuing to unearth. "I'm afraid not," he said reluctantly. "Here the badger idea has two counts against it. First, badgers have incredibly sharp claws and somewhere on the bodies we would expect to find someplace where they had scratched or hooked into their victims, but we do not. Secondly, they usually kill by a blow to the top of their victim's skull and then disemboweling. Obviously, we do not find instances of that here."

Both men looked again at the newly uncovered body before them.

Brad paused and leaned meditatively against his shovel handle. "Well, when it gets right down to it, neither of these bodies has any claw marks or scratches anywhere on it. Can you think of any animal that could stand and gnaw away at their necks, but not leave any marks where it gripped them?"

"Only one that had been declawed," David said uneasily.

"Or one that had hands less like an animal's and more like a human being's," Brad countered with equal trepidation.

"Brad, those bite marks are not human."

"But that's just it. They're not anything we can think of. None of this seems to fit in."

For several moments both of them just stood silently as they nervously studied the frozen terror of the ancient form before them, neither of them able to penetrate any further into the strange regions their thinking was leading them.

Finally Brad spoke. "Now is maybe not the time to bring it up, but I have some slightly unpleasant news for you."

"What's that?" David asked.

"Well, obviously we've got a pretty rich site here. We've dug in six spots and already come up with two bodies, and there's every reason to believe that we may dig up more."

"Yes?" David said, nodding, still not understanding what was unpleasant about the news.

Brad continued. "Well, you'll note that the exploratory pits I've already sunk pretty much cover most of this half of the old bog caldron we're standing in. That means that the most promising area for us to continue looking is in the other half of the caldron. The problem is that the Marquis owns the other half. You're going to have to get his permission if we're to dig any further."

* * *

David ruminated for the rest of the afternoon over how he would go about this, and that evening Brad once again accompanied him back to the cottage for dinner. When they arrived home this time they discovered Tuck sitting disconsolately on the steps.

"What is it, Tuckaroo?" David asked.

Tuck looked up sadly. "Daddy, Ben's gone."

David's heart sank. He had forgotten that he was going to have to come up with something to tell Tuck tonight. He lifted Tuck's sad and listless form up into his arms. "I know," he said softly.

Tuck's dark brown eyes searched his face for further comfort. "Do you know where he is?"

David felt a pang. He wanted desperately to tell Tuck that he did, but his drive for honesty insisted that he not lie. Still, he deliberated over the best way to dilute the truth.

"I don't know where he is, but I think he's only run off to chase animals through the woods. Dogs do that sometimes."

Tuck brightened. "Then he'll be back?"

"I hope so," David said gently. "We just have to be patient and see."

He carried Tuck into the house and was greeted by Melanie, who, he was both surprised and happy to see, was smiling broadly. He put Tuck down and affectionately ruffled his hair as he looked at his wife curiously.

She continued to just beam from ear to ear, and when he finally looked around, he saw why. Every inch of visible floor, wall, and ceiling space had been scrubbed and was three shades lighter. He could hardly believe his eyes. Even the huge balks of age-blackened oak in the ceiling shone with new life.

"My goodness!" Brad exclaimed. "Did Mrs. Comfrey do all of this?"

Melanie nodded happily.

"Where is she now?" David added. "I for one would like to commend her."

"She's out back beating all of the rugs," Melanie informed. "Oh, but of course she didn't start doing that until she had put dinner in the oven. Pot roast for us and Welsh rarebit for you," she said, looking at Brad. "And cooked carrots and salad and trifle for all of us."

It was more than David could fathom. "How does she do it?" he asked as they came in and took off their muddied boots and sat them on papers that Mrs. Comfrey had apparently placed there for that purpose.

"She just never stops," Melanie explained. "I've had several nice chats with her today. It seems that she no longer has any family and she's always been used to taking care of a lot of people. She's really very nice. You know, I think she would do all of this for free if we'd let her."

"Which we won't," David added, feeling a surge of righteous honor.

Since Melanie was no longer burdened with the cooking and serving, they ate in the dining room of the cottage, and as she served the dinner, Mrs. Comfrey continued to demonstrate her unusual prowess. The very moment a course was finished, she would sweep in and silently clear the dishes and with equal unobtrusive proficiency quickly serve the next. And true to form, everything was delicious, the roast superbly succulent, the vegetables cooked perfectly, and the custard in the trifle so indescribably light that even Katy, who did not like custard, ate it.

The only flaw in Mrs. Comfrey's impressive first showing remained the potency of her perfume. She was efficient, silent, polite. But every once in a while when she was present David would almost find himself gagging on the pall of lilac that followed her around. When he mentioned it, however, although Brad nodded vaguely in agreement, Melanie quickly rushed to Mrs. Comfrey's defense, noting chidingly that at least she had managed to place healthy doses of rat poison throughout the house, including attic and cellar.

During the dinner David also noticed that Tuck was taking Ben's absence rather poorly, barely touching his food. Even the trifle he only poked at, and this truly set David to worrying.

David became so focused on Tuck's mopish behavior that he did not notice that Katy's already flourishing crush on Brad was flowering even further. Melanie, however, noticed its every advance. She noticed when Katy moved everything that was placed on the table an inch or two closer to Brad, the butter dish, the salt and pepper. She noticed each time that Katy's adolescent hand brushed close to Brad's when they were both reaching for something, and she observed especially the long, moonish gazes that Katy proffered the older man, accompanied by almost ludicrously coquettish flutterings of the eyelashes.

Oddly, Melanie found herself greatly annoyed by all of this, and once or twice she made subtle overtures to Katy to tone her flirtations down, petitions that Katy more often than not responded to with sharp glances. She noticed also that Brad was becoming increasingly aware of Katy's budding fancy and responded to it with the same unease with which he seemed to respond to most things.

At length, they finished dinner, had their coffee in the living room, and in due time the children were sent off to bed.

Mrs. Comfrey appeared at the door.

"Mrs. Comfrey," David said. "I must commend you, the dinner, the dessert, everything was magnificent."

"Glad you enjoyed it," Mrs. Comfrey said with stern dignity. "Shall I put another kettle on?"

David got an impish glint in his eye as he looked first at Melanie and then at Brad. "I think not. I think we're going to go for a drive."

Both Melanie and Brad looked at him curiously.

"Very good, sir," Mrs. Comfrey said. "Then, if there'll be nothing else, I'll take my leave."

"Yes, of course," David said. "And Mrs. Comfrey?"

The older woman paused.

"I just wanted to say thank you. We think you're doing a tremendous job."

"Glad to oblige, sir," Mrs. Comfrey ended and withdrew.

"A drive?" Melanie questioned.

David smiled. "Well, with Mrs. Comfrey's coming and her great success, I think we have reason to celebrate. I thought we'd all go into the village and have a drink at the Swan with Two Necks."

Neither Melanie nor Brad seemed very taken with the idea.

"Oh, come on," he prodded. "We could all use a drink."

"But what about the kids?" Melanie asked.

"Mrs. Comfrey is here," David said. "That's why we got her, isn't it? So that we could do things like this."

Both Melanie and Brad finally gave in.

"I'm going to look in on Tuck just one more time and then we'll go," David said as Brad began to chip the mud off of his boots so that he could once again put them on.

David rushed upstairs, taking two steps in each stride. He said good-night to Katy, but before he reached Tuck's room he heard Tuck cry out. "Dad, dad!"

David rushed to the door and flung it open. In the darkness he could see nothing that might have alarmed Tuck. He snapped the light on and looked around the room. "What is it, Tuck?"

"Over there!" Tuck said, pointing at a chair with a jacket flung over it. His eyes were wide with fear.

David crossed the room and lifted the jacket up quizzically. "What?"

"*Oh*," Tuck sighed. "I thought it was a monster."

David went over and sat down on his son's bed. "Tuck, there aren't any such things as monsters."

"Katy says there are."

"When did she tell you that?"

"When we first moved here. She told me that a bogey man lives in the bog and that's why they call him a bogey man. At first I didn't believe her, but now I think the bogey man has Ben."

Nothing could have disturbed David more. He stroked the side of his son's face lovingly. "Honey, there are no bogey men. Ben's just run off. Nothing bad has happened to him."

"Well I miss him," Tuck muttered as tears welled up in his eyes and he began to cry.

David pulled him into his arms. "I know you do, honey, and Daddy's going to do everything in his power to try to get him back."

"You are?"

"Of course, did you think Daddy would do anything else?"

"I guess not," Tuck sniffled.

For several minutes David just continued to rock Tuck in his arms, making sure that all of his tears had subsided. As he gazed off into space he also found himself thinking that they should not go out tonight, but he knew going out for a drink would do them all a world of good. Finally he looked down at his son once again.

"Daddy's got to go now, Tuck. Are you going to be all right?"

Tuck still looked disconsolate, but his tears had abated and a discernible drowsiness had crept into his eyes. "I think so," he said.

David kissed him lightly on the forehead and then tucked him beneath the covers. "Is there anything else you need?"

"Could I sleep with the light on tonight?" Tuck asked.

David smiled at his son. Under normal circumstances he demanded a lot from his children and would have tried to talk Tuck out of needing to sleep with the light on, but tonight he gave in.

"How about this light?" he asked, clicking on the little lamp sitting on Tuck's desk.

"Ya," Tuck murmured, almost asleep.

David kissed him one last time and then turned to leave. Just before he departed he looked back at the tiny mound beneath the covers and the mop of chestnut hair. He knew that emotionally he could deal with the weirdness of the people of Fenchurch St. Jude, with Ben's disappearance, with Melanie's mood changes, and with most of the other sundry problems arising in their new life. But one thing that he could not tolerate was the unhappiness of his children. As he went back downstairs he thought again of how sad Tuck had looked, and for the first time since they arrived he began to wonder if their moving to Fenchurch St. Jude had been a mistake.

Outside, the sun had not quite set, and the sky was the deep ultramarine blue of late twilight. They piled into the Volvo and drove off. The nights were growing more humid, and both David and Melanie rolled down their windows for air.

"I still don't think this is such a good idea," Melanie said, her blond hair blowing delicately across her face.

"Why not?" David asked.

"Going into town to have a drink at the Swan with Two Necks? I mean, even the name gives you the creeps."

"Come on, Mel," David countered. "Loosen up a little."

"Pub names are always a little ominous sounding," Brad added from the backseat. "Like the King's Head or the Lost Dog."

David cringed silently at the mention of the latter and noticed that a dark cloud fell over Melanie's expression.

"I wonder what did happen to Ben?" she said distantly.

"Well, you don't live that far from the bog," Brad continued. "He could have always blundered into a sink and been sucked under."

"Brad, please!" David said, raising his voice.

"Sorry," Brad said, but it was too late. Out of the corner of his eye David noticed that Melanie grew gloomier. Brad's grim observation also struck a nerve in him and he remembered again Winnifred Blundell's warning that the bog always took something from everyone.

They all went silent for several minutes.

Suddenly Melanie leaned forward in her seat. "Look!" she exclaimed. They were now passing the hills near the site of the excavations and down in the valley, illumed in the ghostly blue twilight, was a flash of white. David could not be sure, but it looked like the little girl he had seen the day before. She seemed to be running frantically, and around her were several other dark forms in apparent pursuit. Suddenly the other forms, which appeared to be other children, caught up with her and threw the little figure to the ground. Then they jerked her up roughly and started to drag her in the direction of the bog.

"David, do something!" Melanie gasped, and David stopped the car and jumped out. He ran quickly down the hill.

"Hey, what are you doing there!" he shouted. As he approached he could see that the little girl's attackers were, indeed, children, four young boys ranging in age from about nine to thirteen, and they all looked up in surprise. As he drew nearer and observed them more closely, he discerned that they were definitely from Fenchurch St. Jude. Their foreheads were overly flat, and there was something just a little too weedy about their skeletal structure, something oddly misproportioned. He remembered seeing pictures of a family in the Appalachians in which the children had been the product of incest, and it struck him that there was a similar look to these children. He found an incredible dislike welling up inside him for them.

"What were you doing?" he demanded.

They all looked at him silently. The little girl straightened her ancient-looking frock and gave indications that she was going to run off, but then stopped and looked up at him shyly. By no stretch of the imagination could she be considered anything but plain, but there was something strangely appealing about her. Her hair was tangled and badly in need of brushing, but her round eyes were wide and beckoning, and her expression so innocent and so ineffably sad that he had to use all of

97

his will to suppress his urge to strike out and pull her attackers to the ground.

David could overlook many things, but one thing he could not tolerate was the mistreatment of children. He had never thought about it, but perhaps it had something to do with his own childhood and all of the inequities he had suffered. Even under normal circumstances he would have run to the little girl's aid, but tonight, because of Tuck's tearful session earlier, he was especially sensitive, and he glowered at the older boys. Then he knelt and looked the little girl in the eye. "What were they doing to you?" he asked.

She was obviously extraordinarily withdrawn, and once again she almost turned and ran, but then she paused and seemed to detect something that she could trust in his eyes. "They was goin' ta throw me in the bog," she said timidly.

"Aw, it was just a lark, mister," the oldest boy broke in. "We wasn't really goin' ta throw 'er in the bog. We was just havin' a bit 'o fun."

David looked at them angrily. "But she's just a child, just a little girl. How could you pick on someone so much smaller than yourselves?"

The logic of the question seemed beyond them, but they at least appeared cognizant of the fact that he was rebuking them. "I told you it was just a lark," the oldest boy repeated.

"Well, I don't ever want to see anything like this happening again," David continued. "It's getting dark now. You should all be home." He gestured with his hand for them to leave. The little girl looked at him one last time, meekly but appreciatively, and then ran off in the direction of the ramshackle cottage, and the boys reluctantly dispersed. As they backed off they continued to stare at him, puzzled and annoyed.

"Aw, it's only Amanda," another one of them interjected one last time before they turned and were swallowed up by the darkness and the distance.

David returned to the car.

"What was going on?" Melanie asked.

He explained to them what had happened.

"Shades of *The Woman in White*," Brad commented.

David glanced slightly in his direction, but kept his eye on the road. "Come again?"

"*The Woman in White*. The nineteenth-century gothic novel

98

about the woman in the tattered white dress who wanders the lonely moor."

"I don't think it was the moor," Melanie pointed out. "Just some desolate part of the English countryside."

"Well, whatever. In any case, she was a sad, haunted creature, a portrait of innocence victimized by the evil forces swirling around her."

"Evil forces! Really, Brad," David reproved.

"I don't know, there seems to be evil in this valley."

David mentally rolled his eyes to the ceiling as Melanie looked back in astonishment at the younger man. "What makes you say that?"

"Don't forget, these are the people who staked out that young girl and allowed some animal to feed upon her while she was still alive."

"Not *the* people," David hastened to add.

"No, not *the* people, but the descendants of those people. And certainly some of their blood still courses through these people's veins. And besides, even if they did not share their blood, an evil like that lives on in some way. Takes some other form."

"What sort of form?" Melanie asked.

"Who knows? Over the centuries it would permute, change many times, and become something entirely different. Perhaps the strangeness of these people, or even the cruelty of those boys out there, is nothing more than the last remaining resonance of that evil."

"Or perhaps it has taken another form entirely," Melanie said darkly.

David grunted. "Brad, will you please tell her that you are speaking in sociological terms and not supernatural ones."

Brad looked at Melanie, surprised. "Oh, purely sociological ones. I'm talking about the habits and customs of these people, you know, units of cultural transmission."

"But couldn't the evil committed here, if it was powerful enough, manifest itself as something physical, an animal or something?"

"I don't know about that," Brad said quickly.

David sighed. He had intended this outing as a recreation, something to get their minds off of Ben's disappearance, and he did not at all like the direction the conversation was taking.

99

He tried desperately to think of some way to reroute it. "Who did you say wrote that novel?" he asked.

"What novel?" Melanie replied.

"The Woman in White."

"Wilkie Collins," Brad responded, and David was grateful when he saw that this piqued Melanie's interest.

"Are you interested in nineteenth-century literature?" she asked.

"Very much so," Brad returned, and the conversation went on from there.

David smiled at the fact that his ploy had worked so well. He himself was not interested in nineteenth-century literature, perhaps because it had so little bearing on his archaeological endeavors, but he was pleased that Melanie and Brad were having a rousing discussion about it. He knew that not only would it improve Melanie's mood greatly to enjoy some intellectual stimulation, but it also would allow him the luxury to lapse into his own thoughts.

As for Melanie, the conversation did lift her spirits. It took her mind off the troubling events of the past several days, but it also called her attention to something else. As she continued talking animatedly about nineteenth-century literature with Brad, the first notion that crossed her mind was that she had not enjoyed herself so much in months. However, as they continued with their conversation, she slowly experienced a sort of epiphany. There was something distantly familiar about the exchange she was having with Brad. It took her some time to realize that it made her recall the way that she and David used to talk before they were married. With this realization came a second thought, even more jarring. One of the reasons she had fallen in love with David was those discussions. Before they were married, when they were merely fellow graduate students, their friendship was vibrant and he treated her as an intellectual equal. As the years passed, however, their ability to converse in this manner had slowly atrophied. David treated her less and less as an intellectual comrade, and more as a wife. And she too had allowed herself to become a silly creature more concerned with whether there were mice in the house than with the challenge of interesting ideas. In a flash of painful and yet liberating light, she realized that this had a great deal to do with the unhappiness that had been brewing in her for

months. A part of her was dying and she had not even realized it.

Suddenly the car came to a halt, and she saw that they had
pulled up outside the Swan with Two Necks. They all got out.

As they approached the pub, David noticed that Melanie
had grown temporarily silent, but he assumed she was thinking
about some issue that she had just raked over with Brad. They
entered the pub.

It was unusually crowded inside, the bar lined with people.
In a corner several men played darts and behind the counter
Winnifred Blundell scurried back and forth, her garish blond
hair glowing like a neon sign through the haze of smoke. The
buzz of conversation ceased instantly when they entered, and
all eyes turned in their direction. David motioned to an empty
table near the back.

As they approached it, Melanie, in her heightened state, also
noticed something else that had never really penetrated her
consciousness. David sat down before she did. Normally such
behavior wouldn't have concerned her, but again, as she thought
back, she remembered the time when he would never have
dreamed of sitting down before her, or at the very least would
have asked her which chair she would prefer. She lingered
but a moment in the thought, and was about to sit down when
Brad suddenly held one of the chairs out for her. She blushed,
startled.

"Thank you," she said. As she went to sit down, out of habit
she reached out to take a hold of the chair herself, and her
hand accidentally closed over one of Brad's fingers. She half
expected him to pull his hand away, but he did not. For a
second or two, their fingers continued to touch, and she thought
that she should do something about it, but she too found herself
strangely immobile. She looked up into Brad's eyes, and for a
few seconds longer they just gazed at each other until finally,
uneasily, Brad moved his hand, and she took her seat.

For a moment Melanie was filled with disbelief. It had never
occurred to her that she was even remotely sexually attracted
to Brad. Furthermore, she had never even fantasized about being unfaithful to David. She loved David. They had their problems, but she was nowhere near being ready to throw in
the towel.

She did not remain lost in thought for long.

After they sat down, the conversation in the pub resumed slightly, but they remained the object of intense scrutiny. At length, Winnifred Blundell approached their table.

"Get you anything?" she barked.

They each ordered a beer, and when she returned with them she slammed them down vigorously on the table.

"What is wrong with these people?" Brad asked under his breath after she had left.

David tried to think of something to say that would make light of Winnifred Blundell's surly behavior, but given that most of the patrons were still staring at them as if they were naked and had expletives tattooed on their foreheads, it seemed a lost cause. He took a sip of his beer, and from the pain he felt when it washed down his throat, he realized that the inside of his mouth had become as dry as the Sahara.

They sat there for several minutes, desperately trying to act as if nothing were amiss, but it was to no avail. They continued to remain the object of almost searing attention. Only a fraction of the patrons even continued to talk with one another, and one of these, an incredibly filthy old man sitting at a table in the corner, suddenly cackled loudly at some secret joke.

It did not seem possible, but as David looked at him he realized that he was even more misshapen and unwholesome than most of the other natives of Fenchurch St. Jude. His clothing was grimy and hung like dirty sacks over his stooped and bony body, and he possessed virtually no chin at all. When he tilted his head back he revealed an almost toothless jack-o'-lantern mouth, brown with venomous spittle, and his eyes were vacant and crazed. A thick but blotchy stubble covered what passed for his face, and in the cracks and creases of his leathery neck, hairlines of dirt had collected. It was clear that he was roaring drunk, but it was also equally obvious that he fit into the general look of the place. He was simply the extreme.

Brad leaned over to David. "That's Old Flory," he said, "the father of the little girl you just saved from those kids."

David suddenly felt even more compassion for the sad little waif.

He looked back at the crowd and saw that even more of the patrons were watching them. The men who had been playing darts had stopped. Even Old Flory began to glower in their direction. And most discomfited of all was Winnifred

Blundell. She continued to slam pints of ale down in front of regular denizens of the Swan with Two Necks, all the while her gaze remaining fixed on David and his troop. On occasion he could hear her clucking loudly and he caught fragments of what seemed to be a disgruntled diatribe about their presence. At length, her antics became so overblown that several other of the patrons actually made efforts to calm her down. But it was no use.

A miasma of tension spread through the pub, like ozone after a lightning strike, and it became apparent that a confrontation of some sort was imminent. The same man who had spoken with David when he had first visited the pub reached out and tried to pull Winnifred Blundell back, but she stormed forward and looked the three of them in the face.

"You shouldn't be here, you know!" she shrilled.

"Why not?" David asked angrily.

This irritated her even further, but through her ire another emotion rippled briefly, an emotion disturbingly like pity or great concern. "You haven't been here very long. It isn't too late. If you went home and packed up your things and left right away, it might be all right. But you must not stay another night. Because if you do—"

"Winnifred!" shouted the man behind her, and the entire pub fidgeted nervously. David couldn't be sure, but the little blond woman's words seemed to stir some terrible fear in the other people in the pub.

"Because if we do, what?" David asked.

The emaciated little blond woman started to completely lose her composure as if she were torn between telling him and her growing fear of something else, of some powerful but unseen enemy. Suddenly her eyes fixed on something behind them, something over their heads, and her gaze widened with terror. In an instant she went white and screamed, a gurgling, mindless scream, and like a crack of thunder, a blind panic ensued in the pub as grown men gasped like whimpering animals and fell over one another in a mad attempt to get out.

Not knowing what to think, David, Melanie, and Brad also leaped up from their chairs and stumbled frantically toward the door. Melanie fell and David nearly pulled her arm out of its socket as he yanked her up, and they scrambled on toward the exit. It was only when they were nearly out and every one else had fled into the night, that he turned, perversely, wondering whether he would be faced with a roaring ball of fire or a maniac wielding an ax. And then he saw.

Brad too turned and became transfixed by the sight, and then Melanie. For several stupefied seconds they just stood there, mesmerized, and the only movement that was anywhere near them was the shadow that passed over their faces and then flickered lambently over the overturned chairs and tables. For the unspeakable sight that had sent Winnifred Blundell into a blind panic, the terrible menace that had caused grown men to whimper and run, was a small white moth that lazily circled the single bare bulb in the ceiling in the back of the pub.

5

AFTER THEY GOT over their initial shock at the behavior of the people in the pub, their reaction became one of confused amusement, so much so that they laughed convulsively all the way home. It was only after they had dropped Brad off and returned to the cottage that, for David, the event once again took on an unutterably ominous quality. He could tell that Melanie was also mystified and troubled, but as usual he continued to downplay the matter to keep her from becoming completely unhinged. Nonetheless, as he drifted off to sleep that night he found himself haunted by questions. Why should the inhabitants of Fenchurch St. Jude have reacted so bizarrely to the presence of such an innocuous creature? What had Winnifred Blundell meant by her warning? And why had the man in the pub silenced her so brusquely when she had attempted to speak?

The next morning when he got up he found Melanie and the kids sitting at the kitchen table with Mrs. Comfrey doing dishes at the sink behind them. Tuck still looked down in the dumps as he twirled his fork in what looked like a plate of completely untouched scrambled eggs. Melanie looked up at David with concern.

"What's the matter, Tuckaroo?" David asked.

"*Ben,*" Tuck said simply.

David sat down beside him and Tuck looked up. "You said he'd come back. But he hasn't."

"It's only been a short time. He may still come back."

Tuck's eyes went back down to his cold scrambled eggs. "What if he doesn't?"

David looked sadly at Melanie. "If he doesn't, we'll figure out something else to do. Maybe we'll get another dog."

"But I want Ben," Tuck said.

"Well hopefully we'll get Ben back," David reassured. "Daddy's looking for him. I'm looking for him every day. But I can't keep looking for him if you're going to be sad and not eat because that'll make me sad too, and then I won't eat and then where will that leave us?"

This seemed to make sense to Tuck.

"So won't you please eat something?"

Tuck looked his eggs over and then looked entreatingly up at his father. "These are cold," he pouted shyly.

"Well, maybe just this once Mrs. Comfrey will warm them up for you. But in the future you've got to learn to eat them when they're warm so that you don't make extra work for Mrs. Comfrey. Now ask her nicely."

Tuck glanced over at the woman at the sink and she looked back at him with what seemed to be her expression of compassion. "Just this once," she said in her usual clipped manner. "But little boys must learn to be men about things. That's the way of the world."

It annoyed David slightly that Mrs. Comfrey had injected a bit of her own philosophy into the matter, but he decided to overlook her remark.

Mrs. Comfrey rewarmed Tuck's eggs and served David his breakfast, and then several minutes later Tuck said, "Maybe I should go to work with you today, Dad."

"Why's that, Tuck?" David asked guilelessly.

Tuck took another mouthful of egg. "Because it would be good for me to get out of the house," he returned.

David looked at Melanie, smiling, but the expression on his wife's face made it clear that she did not think it would help Tuck's state of mind any to see them pulling dead bodies out of the bog.

"Not today, Tuck. Maybe sometime."

"But that's what you said last time."

"And it's what I'm saying this time also. Maybe someday, when you're a little older, Daddy will take you to see his work, but you've just got to be patient."

"Okay," Tuck said begrudgingly, but at least continued to eat his eggs.

It was just as David was about to pull away from the table that the sound of a motorbike met their ears, and both he and Melanie stood and saw Luther Blundell pull into their driveway.

"Now, what can he want?" David asked.

As David left the kitchen he noticed that Melanie followed close behind. Tuck also went to pull away from the table, but David admonished Mrs. Comfrey to keep both him and Katy in the house. He went out into the yard.

As he watched Luther get off the motorbike he noted that the gangly teenager had inherited, in a masculine version, all of his mother's looks. His long, simian arms were pale and the size of sticks, and his face the spitting image of his barmaid mother, save that it was dappled with adolescent acne. Even his hair was a strident and artificial yellow, although it was short and choppily cut in what, David bemusedly thought, might be called Fenchurch St. Jude punk. His amusement faded, however, when he saw the look on Luther's face. The teenager was clearly upset over something.

"What can I do for you?" David asked as Luther ran up to where he was standing. His face was pale and frightened and he seemed on the verge of punching David out.

"My mother!" he blurted out.

"What about her?"

"She's missing. Have you seen her?"

"Not since last night."

Luther's panic increased. "Oh no. Oh my God."

"When was the last time you saw her?" David asked.

"She didn't come home last night."

David did not know what to say. "Might she have stayed with a friend?"

"Not without calling."

"Perhaps this time she forgot."

Luther turned to him angrily. "No, she didn't. She's gone. Without so much as a good-bye." He seemed torn between fury and tears.

"Have you been to the authorities?"

"Of course. I've talked to Constable Crease. But he knows . . ." Luther trailed off into silence.

"Knows what?" David asked.

The teenager just looked at him in frustration. "If it was your mother, I'm sure you would care."

"I'm sure I would," David agreed. He noticed that tears were beginning to well up in Luther's eyes as he turned to leave. He strode down the driveway and once again straddled the bike.

"But, Luther!" David called after him, and the boy looked up one last time in his direction. "Constable Crease knows what?" David asked again.

Still, Luther Blundell regarded him with irritation, as if he considered the question somehow superfluous. "That it's happening. That it's starting again."

"What's starting again?" David called, but Luther only revved up the motorbike and left.

David stood there for many long moments puzzling over what he could have meant when he noticed Melanie had come up beside him.

"Winnifred Blundell is missing?" she asked.

"So he says."

"Oh, David, what do you think could have happened to her?"

"I don't know, honey. But you saw what happened last night. She ran out of the pub in a blind panic when she saw that moth. Maybe when she got outside she saw another and just kept on running."

Melanie was not amused. "Come on, David, this is serious. You don't think she's been shot, do you?"

"Why do you say that?"

"Like the woman in Leeming. Maybe that's what Luther meant when he said 'starting again.' Maybe there's a serial murderer in Fenchurch St. Jude, one that's never been caught and has been inactive for a number of years, but who's starting once again to kill people."

"Don't you think you're jumping to hasty conclusions? I mean, we don't even know that Winnifred Blundell is dead, let alone if she's been shot. Let's wait until we know a little more before we try to piece this thing together."

"Okay," she said begrudgingly.

He hugged her, but as he looked again in the direction of the moors, he wondered if she was on to something.

* * *

The next day David and Brad received from Oxford the results of the carbon-dating tests and discovered, as they had expected, that the bodies were indeed from the first century B.C. Although the question of their antiquity had never really been in great doubt, confirmation reinforced the zeal with which the two men went at their work. They also sent off photographs of the bite marks to a zoologist at Oxford and continued to explore various intellectual culs-de-sac, conjecturing what the creature might be as they awaited the results.

Although David's work continued to go well, his home life deteriorated further. They still had found no trace of Ben, and this caused Tuck to sink deeper into depression. Try as he might, David seemed only temporarily able to raise his son's spirits, and this fact increasingly eroded his own. In addition, no trace of Winnifred Blundell was found, and although Melanie continued to revel in Mrs. Comfrey's prodigious and extraordinary success at running the household and cleaning every stray and remote corner of the cottage, David could tell that the moth incident continued to weigh heavily on his wife.

Three days after Winnifred Blundell's disappearance he went into town and asked Mary Thoday what Luther might have meant by his "starting again" comment, but Miss Thoday was as vituperative as ever and asserted that she did not know. As for Luther, he spent his days in the Swan with Two Necks drowning his sorrow, and avoided David like the plague whenever he came near. Indeed, after Winnifred Blundell's disappearance, everyone in Fenchurch St. Jude avoided them as if they were contaminated, and it was rare to get so much as a furtive glance from even those who had previously been the most prying.

It was for these reasons as well as the memory of his previous encounter that David brooded for another day before he finally placed a telephone call to the Marquis de L'Isle to ask permission to continue their excavations on his land. The phone was answered by the butler and David was put on hold for nearly five minutes. Finally he heard the click of another extension being picked up and a second click as the first extension was placed back on its receiver.

"Hello?" came a voice that he presumed to be the Marquis's.

"Hello," David returned nervously. "This is Professor Macauley, the archaeologist you've rented your cottage to. I'm sorry to disturb you at home like this, but I'm afraid we've run into a snag at the site of our excavations."

For several seconds there was a deafening silence on the other end, and then finally the Marquis spoke again. "Yes?"

David swallowed. "Well, I was wondering . . ." He paused. "I mean, as I showed you when we met, we've made some amazing discoveries at the bog, and our evidence indicates that there are still more to be made. The problem is that one of the richest sites encroaches upon your land, and I was wondering if you might possibly give us permission to dig up some of the portions of the bog that you hold ownership to?"

Again there was another awful silence at the other end of the phone and David braced himself for a pyrotechnic outburst from the temperamental Marquis.

After another moment the Marquis said calmly: "We may be able to arrive at some terms."

"Terms?" David asked.

"The time has come for us to get to know one another," the Marquis said emotionlessly. "If you, your assistant, and your wife would be kind enough to honor me with your presence here at Wythen Hall for dinner tomorrow night, I will grant you the permission you seek."

This time it was David's turn to be silent as he recovered from the shock of the Marquis's invitation. "That's very kind of you. We would be flattered to be your guests for dinner tomorrow night."

"Very good," the Marquis ended. "Then I'll see you at seven thirty. Will that be convenient?"

"Yes, we'll see you then."

"Very good. Tomorrow at seven thirty. Good-bye then."

"Good-bye."

David hung up the phone, surprised, to say the least.

As the evening approached, his surprise turned to unease as he started to wonder about the Marquis's mysterious show of hospitality. At their first meeting he had been disconcerted enough by the Marquis's granting them permission to rent the hunter's cottage. Now, the Marquis's invitation to dinner only increased his bewilderment and he could not shake the feeling that somewhere there was something vaguely fishy about it all.

Nonetheless, to his delight, Melanie was thrilled by the invitation and even Brad seemed uncharacteristically excited at the idea of rubbing elbows with a nobleman.

About half an hour before they were due to leave and while Melanie was putting the last finishing touches on her appearance, David decided to look in on Tuck. As he approached the door to Tuck's bedroom he caught a glimpse of his son inside, sitting on the edge of his bed. What drew David's attention, however, was the look on his son's face. It was rapt, as he apparently listened to something with spellbound interest, but also oddly tortured, as if whatever he was listening to were disturbing him to his deepest fiber.

David could also hear the sound of Mrs. Comfrey's voice coming from the room, and as he came closer he could make out her words.

". . . and a terrible looking old wizard with a face dark and knotted as the faces you may sometimes think you see among the tree boughs, said to the wicked fairy-men, 'What we must do is persuade a human maiden to marry one of us. That way, the child will be half man and half fairy, and we may once again regain the power in the world that we are losing so fast.' "

David stepped into the doorway and both Tuck and Mrs. Comfrey looked up at him wonderingly.

"Mrs. Comfrey, may I see you out here in the hall for a moment?"

Mrs. Comfrey set down the book she was reading and walked out into the hall. "Yes, sir?"

David stepped back and lowered his voice so that Tuck couldn't hear them. "Mrs. Comfrey, I wonder if you'd mind playing a game with Tuck or doing something else that isn't so frightening."

"My goodness," she clucked. "It was only *Stories from King Arthur.*"

"I know, and I don't mean to condemn what you were doing. It's just that Tuck's been overly sensitive since Ben's disappearance, and I'm not sure stories about wicked fairy-men and faces in trees is the right thing for him to be hearing right now."

Mrs. Comfrey stared at him blankly, a glint of strange

disapproval in her eye. "I've raised many children in my lifetime and I haven't failed yet," she said, clearly piqued that he was challenging her judgment.

David too grew irritated. "I don't mean to cast doubt on your ability to take care of Tuck, but he's my son and I just wish you wouldn't read such things to him right now."

Mrs. Comfrey gazed coldly at him for a moment, and as David stood looking back at her it occurred to him for the first time that he really didn't like her very much. As he continued to examine her features, her lilac perfume enveloping him in a suffocating pall, he also realized why. She was efficient and remarkable in the way that she performed, but there was an odd emptiness in her eyes, as if there really wasn't much more going on inside her head other than her almost mechanical dedication to her work.

At length, she conceded. "As you wish, sir." But he could tell that she was still annoyed.

He went downstairs. In the living room he found Brad sitting and sipping a martini that Katy, as was her new habit, had prepared and served. Katy sat across from him, pummeling him with questions about the digs.

"You've never been this interested before in archaeology," David said, smiling.

"Sure I have," Katy argued, trying to save face. She turned and was about to ask Brad another question when behind them Melanie swept down the stairs. She was wearing a white, high-collared Victorian blouse and a long Norma Kamali skirt.

"You look great," David said.

"Thank you," Melanie said, pleased. She looked over at Brad to see if he greeted her efforts with equal approval, and then, when she realized what she was doing, nervously glanced away.

"I'll go pull the car out in front," David offered as he straightened his tie in the mirror and went outside.

Melanie walked into the middle of the living room. "You know, Brad, I've been thinking about what you said last week about the impetus Horace Walpole's *The Castle of Otranto* gave to the gothic revival."

Katy rolled her eyes to the ceiling and sighed audibly.

Melanie glanced at her daughter but continued. "The only question that remains is whether Walpole went about his task consciously or unconsciously."

Brad shifted his weight nervously. "That's a good question. I would imagine unconsciously, but what do you think?"

"My first guess would be unconsciously also, but Walpole was an avid collector of gothic memorabilia. He could have known what he was doing. There are several pieces of information to back this up."

"I've been thinking of changing my name," Katy announced abruptly.

"Katy, you interrupted me," Melanie pointed out, somewhat peeved because she was in the middle of making what she considered a very clever point.

Katy ignored her. "To Natasha," she said, looking only at Brad.

Brad grew uneasy, knowing something was going on but not knowing quite what.

"*Katy,*" Melanie repeated.

"What, *Mommmm*?" Katy sneered.

"You interrupted me."

"Well you were only talking about some dumb old novel."

"It doesn't matter, you don't just interrupt someone when they're speaking."

"But if I didn't interrupt you I wouldn't get a word in edge-wise. Sometimes you don't even come up for air."

Melanie was mortified. "How dare you speak to me like that!" She was about to add something else when they noticed that David had come back inside.

"What's going on?" he asked.

Melanie turned to him, her face red with anger. "Katy just interrupted me."

"Well, it can't be that bad." He looked at his daughter. "Katy, tell your mother you're sorry."

"I'm sorry," Katy said petulantly.

"She wants to change her name," Melanie continued, still nettled by what had just transpired.

David smiled, trying to spread oil on troubled waters. "I told her she couldn't."

"You told me I couldn't unless Mom said it was okay," Katy corrected, and David blushed, realizing he had committed that most horrendous of parental crimes, the old pass-the-buck ploy.

"And, of course, Mom won't let me," Katy ended unhappily.

"We'll discuss it later," Melanie said sharply as they stood and prepared to leave. David went back outside and Brad followed close behind. Melanie and Katy were left momentarily alone and Melanie turned resentfully toward her daughter.

"That was very rude the way you just treated me in front of Brad."

Katy remained belligerent. "I don't think so."

"Katy!" Melanie cried. For several seconds they just glared at each other, Katy's normally innocent eyes filled with an unusually mature hostility.

Finally Melanie pulled a shawl around her shoulders and started to leave.

"You've got a crush on Brad, don't you," Katy challenged suddenly as Melanie passed just an arm's length away from her. Melanie turned and looked at her daughter with utter astonishment, and again was shaken to see that the venom in Katy's look was disturbingly adult. And then, before she knew what she was doing, she reached out and slapped Katy very hard across the face.

"How dare you say such a thing to me!" she cried, and suddenly Katy was once again a child, blinking and looking very hurt and very stunned. She burst into tears and ran upstairs.

It took Melanie several seconds to compose herself. Of course she didn't have a crush on Brad, she thought indignantly to herself. Why the very idea was absurd. Her hand stung and she was abruptly filled with remorse over the force with which she had just struck her daughter. She looked worriedly upstairs, but realized that she would have to deal with it later. Her thoughts still in tumult over Katy's suggestion that she felt more than friendship for Brad, she turned and left.

As they drove to Wythen Hall, David noticed that his wife was unusually quiet, and he worried that she was getting into one of her moods again. He hoped that her spirits would improve when she was confronted with a new social situation, but he was much too preoccupied with his own thoughts to ponder over her reticence for long. Brad had also reverted to his normally silent self, and they made the remainder of the drive with hardly a word said among the three of them.

At length, they passed through the huge and rusted wrought-iron gates that marked the perimeter of the Marquis's estate, and against the jagged backdrop of the hills, Wythen Hall came into sight. As he had first observed from the hill overlooking the bog, the facade of the old manor house was late Elizabethan, but the crenellated tower and several of its wings dated at least from the Middle Ages. As he might have expected, the dark and imposing granite walls of the structure were weather-beaten and deeply eroded by wind and time, and the casements of the windows were almost completely concealed by a vast sea of leather-green ivy. What he had not expected, however, was the well-manicured appearance of the lawn. Beneath the canopy of the great oaks and firs that filled the grounds it was as smooth and velvet green as the green baize of a gaming table, and through this fairy-tale glen of emerald and jade, the black waters of the bog lake beyond seemed restful and even strangely beautiful.

They pulled up to the front of the ancient edifice and parked the car. As they approached the door, David noted that it was so roughly hewn and weathered that it had to date from at least the fifteenth century. Each of the two massive sections composing it was divided into four quadrangles, and they peaked in a high Gothic arch over their heads. He hoisted up the immense black iron knocker in the right-hand panel of the door and let it fall back loudly. A deep and resonant thud echoed throughout the unknown spaces beyond.

After several minutes they heard the sound of shuffling foot-steps, and the door creaked open. There stood a gaunt and baggily liveried butler of typical Fenchurch St. Jude stock.

"Good evening, sirs, mi' lady," he greeted, glancing briefly at them before he respectfully returned his gaze to the floor. "Please come in. The Marquis is expecting you."

He stepped back and allowed them to enter. Inside was a vast entrance hall, sparsely furnished and dimly lit. High above them a square, balustraded gallery ran around the top of the huge and shadowy enclosure, and opening off this were other faintly visible doorways and corridors. The place was filled with the smells of an ancient dwelling, a faint background of mustiness overlaid with subtle resonances of cool stone, fine woods, and the smell of polish and torch smoke.

David also noticed something else. At first he thought it was a wind, a faint susurration moving across the floor stones, but as he looked to the side of the corridor it occurred to him that it was less a sound and more a sensation. He looked first at Melanie and then at Brad, but neither of them seemed cogni-zant of the movement. Still, as he glanced around, he half expected to see a dust devil flailing cobwebs in its wake, save that his every tool of perception told him that the air in the cavernous entrance hall was deathly still.

Finally they reached a door at the end of the hall, and the butler pushed it open for them and motioned for them to go in. They entered and David gasped silently at the sight beyond.

Before them was an immense drawing room, refulgently aglow with the light of uncountable lamps, flaring torches on the walls, numerous sconces, and a great and kingly fireplace crackling and roaring at one end. The walls of the room were opulently paneled in deep walnut and superbly appointed with rich old tapestries and large wall hangings of lush red damask. The furniture and carpets were also all befitting the home of a Marquis, and various candelabra here and there added still more light to the already intense atmosphere of the place. Most startling of all, however, was the Marquis's sizable collection of ancient Sumerian and Babylonian art, and his curious array of exotic animals, both caged and stuffed.

Here and there on the walls were the heads of okapi, impala, and other exotic antelope with long, stiletto horns curving upward. In various cages around the room were bright-colored finches and other tropical birds that David did not recognize, with flowing and iridescent tails hanging lazily out of their wicker prisons, and in a large golden pagoda of a cage at one end of the room, a strange and melancholy monkey with haunting and blood-red eyes.

The art was equally exotic. David recognized bas-reliefs of bird-headed deities from Ashurnasirpal, stone statues of Mesopotamian demons; Chaldean votives of goats and lion-bodied gods; horn-shaped cups of Scythian gold; bronze dragons, and statues of a host of other Babylonian creatures of the night. Most impressive of all was a huge stone stele hanging over the fireplace, an ancient calendar, as far as David could determine, inscribed with the Babylonian version of the signs of the zodiac and a great deal of accompanying text written in cuneiform.

Sitting in a chair near one of the Babylonian idols was the Marquis, and standing at the fireplace was one of the most distractingly beautiful women David had ever seen. The Marquis stood.

"Professor Macauley, I believe," he said, extending his hand. "Please, call me David."

"And you must call me Grenville," the Marquis returned graciously. Indeed, the Marquis now behaved with such cordiality that David looked him over once again to make sure that he was the same distinguished and handsomely silver-gray gentleman who had conducted himself so rudely when they had first met at the excavations.

David introduced Brad and Melanie, and then it was the Marquis's turn. He reached out his hand toward the beautiful woman and she slowly stepped forward.

"This," said the Marquis, "is Julia Honaria."

"How do you do," the woman said, speaking for the first time, and her eyes caught David's. She was, he thought, one of the most breathtaking creatures he had ever encountered. Her hair was a luxuriant raven black and cascaded down her bare white shoulders in a way that was at once faultlessly coiffed and yet suggestively erotic. Her features were perfectly formed, like some exquisite porcelain doll's, and her smoldering dark eyes were wide and flashed with suggestive fire. Her lips too were full and poisonously scarlet, and her complexion as pale and flawless as a piece of Italian marble. Contrasted against the perfection of her features, her attire seemed almost unimportant, save that it too was spectacular. She wore a black gown that looked as if it must have cost at least a thousand dollars and across her large full breast was a splay of rubies and diamonds that, although dazzling, still only ran a close second to her beauty.

It was only after he had taken in all the details of the woman before him that he noticed the portrait over the fireplace behind her. It was a large and moldering family oil, and from the style looked to be late eighteenth century. In it was depicted a man, a tall man, aristocratically dressed, with a hunting dog beside him. The scenery framing him was relatively nondescript and could have been any wooded glade in the valley, or for that matter, in any other part of England. But what caught his eye, what froze his attention for several long moments, was the fact that the man's face was totally concealed by a little muslin curtain suspended on gold cord and draped across the front of the painting.

David looked bewilderedly at the Marquis and could tell that the older man had noticed his reaction to the veiled portrait, but he offered no explanation.

"Please, won't you sit down," he invited, gesturing toward the various sofas and chairs encircling the fireplace. "Would you like something to drink?"

As if on silent cue the butler once again appeared and took their requests.

Then Grenville turned and directed his attention toward David. "May I begin by apologizing for my unseemly behavior toward you at our first meeting."

"Quite all right," David said, accepting his apology.

"You see, this land has been owned by the de L'Isle name for quite some time now, and it has become, in a sense, a part of my flesh. When I first became aware of the intrusion of your digging, I couldn't have been more shocked and pained than if you had taken a scalpel and sliced into my arm. I was livid. Now, of course, I have calmed down and realized that you were in the right and I was in the wrong. I do hope we can overlook my former rudeness and arrive at some sort of *rapprochement.*"

"I think we already have," David said politely. "I mean, with you renting us the hunter's cottage for such a reasonable amount."

"My pleasure," Grenville said, smiling. He lifted his drink. "May I propose a toast to your lovely wife."

"Oh, why thank you," Melanie said, blushing slightly and clearly touched by Grenville's gallantry. They all toasted.

"This is quite a collection of statuary you have here," David complimented. "I had no idea you had such an interest in antiquities."

"Thank you," Grenville replied. "I've gathered it all myself over the years."

"Have you studied ancient Near Eastern art?"

"Oh, my goodness no, at least not in the academic sense. I'm really just a dilettante. Do you have any expertise on the subject?"

"Only cursorily," David returned. "I took a few graduate courses on the subject and have attended a seminar here and there, but it's really not my area of expertise."

"What about you, Mr. Hollister?"

"I know a little," Brad stammered, surprised that he had been brought into the conversation.

Grenville stood and retrieved one of the horn-shaped cups of Scythian gold. "What do you think of this?" He handed the cup to Brad. The younger man turned it over in his hands, scrutinizing it carefully. "I think it's extraordinary. It must be worth a fortune."

"Really," Grenville purred with a faint lack of interest. "I must remember that if ever I need the money."

He strolled over to the mantelpiece. "This is really my prize possession," he said, motioning toward the huge cuneiform calendar. "You know, the Babylonians were really very fine astronomers. They had the lunar month worked out to an incredibly precise decimal point. Astrology was everything to them. They didn't do anything without consulting the stars. Everything was cycles. They wouldn't crown a king or even bury their dead unless it was favorable to the stars."

"Really," Julia interrupted for the first time. "Don't you think you're getting a bit tedious on the subject?" She cast Grenville a sharp glance and then immediately resumed her aura of lascivious charm, her eyes flashing at David and then at Brad.

"Sorry," Grenville said emotionlessly. He once again took his seat.

Julia turned toward Melanie. "So what do you do?" she asked.

"I'm just a housewife," Melanie replied somewhat shamefacedly. "But I'm going to return to college just as soon as the opportunity affords. I have all of the credits necessary for a degree in art history. I've just got to finish my dissertation."

This came as news to David, and he looked at his wife with surprise.

"I hadn't mentioned it yet to you because I've only just made the decision myself," she said, seeing the incredulity in his glance.

He didn't know why, but the notion of Melanie returning to graduate school disturbed him slightly. The thought quickly flitted out of his mind when he realized that Julia was gazing at him rather penetratingly, and as he looked back it occurred to him that when Grenville had introduced her he had offered no clue as to what their relationship was. Was she his mistress? A relative? A friend?

The butler appeared at the doorway and nodded to Grenville.

The Marquis turned again toward his guests. "It appears that dinner is ready. Shall we go in?"

They all stood and followed Grenville and Julia through yet another hallway and into a dining room that was every bit as sumptuous as the drawing room. Large Sheraton-style sideboards stood on either side of the exquisite chamber, and another massive and crackling fireplace filled one entire wall. Lighting was provided by the literally hundreds of candles that filled the room, some in several large chandeliers that hung over the table, and others in the countless dozens of candlesticks and candelabra that cluttered the furniture, mantelpiece, and various ledges in the room. Equally striking were the chairs around the dining room table, which were high-backed and of elaborately carved and polished bog oak, and the liveried footmen that stood behind each one of them, waiting dutifully to seat the guests.

But what again drew David's attention were the portraits on the walls, half a dozen or so of them done in various styles and from various centuries, all men, and again, each with the countenance of its subject completely concealed by a small curtain of muslin.

He noticed that Melanie and Brad were also riveted by the sight as they took their seats around the table.

Grenville sat down and sighed. "I suppose I should explain this little family mystery."

David looked at the Marquis with interest.

"You see, my venerable ancestor, one Gervase of Shrewsbury, and the first Marquis de L'Isle, had a deformity of the face that he sought, at all costs, to conceal from everyone. Even his portrait he had veiled, and from that point on decreed that all portraits of the de L'Isle lineage should be veiled in a similar manner. In deference to my ancestor it has become our family custom."

David nodded as he mulled the explanation over.

Grenville picked up a little bell and jingled it. "And now, that over, I have a very special treat for you."

They all looked at him expectantly.

"As you may be aware, the Celts who lived in this valley around the time that the bodies you have discovered were buried in the bog did not have the pleasure of drinking distilled liquor as we have just done in the drawing room. However, analysis of sediments in bronze vessels from that time show that they were not completely without alcoholic drink. They occasionally imbibed a type of wine made from the bog myrtle. The only recorded reference to that notorious beverage was made by the Roman historian Tacitus in his work *Germania*."

"Right!" Brad interrupted. "Bog-myrtle wine."

Grenville smiled tolerantly. "Precisely, and as it so happens I have in my possession the recipe for that ancient beverage, handed down for centuries through the de L'Isle family. In fact, in my cellar I have quite a stock of the heavenly liquid, homemade of course, but I would now like to share a bit of that rare elixir with you, my honored guests." He snapped his fingers, and the footman who had appeared at the sound of the bell stepped forward with a decanter of a deep-purplish liquid and started to fill their glasses. When he reached David's, Julia leaned across the table and said loudly, "Be careful. Bog-myrtle wine is purported to be a powerful aphrodisiac."

David laughed and noticed that Melanie was beginning to grow uneasy over Julia's flirtatious attentions. He looked back at their host and to his surprise saw that Grenville was also cognizant of Melanie's reaction. Furthermore, he was aware that David had noticed that he had noticed. David was beginning to realize that Grenville was an unusually observant man.

"To your marriage," the Marquis said urbanely, his brown eyes glinting knowingly at David as he raised his glass aloft in another toast.

They all drank and David washed the first cold swallow over his tongue, tasting carefully. A pungent burst of flavor exploded throughout his senses, and at first it was so overwhelming that he almost winced. But then the piquant, strangely musty flavor unfolded into a pleasant cacophony of tastes, and he found himself craving a second swallow. He noticed that both Melanie and Brad seemed to be experiencing the same reaction, first uncertainty, and then a craving for more. Grenville and Julia watched carefully.

"Well?" Grenville asked.

"Quite delicious. In fact, amazing," David commended and Melanie and Brad soon joined in the accolades.

"I'm pleased you like it," said Grenville. "There will be an unending supply of it during dinner." He snapped his fingers again and the liveried footmen began to serve the meal.

"And as Lord Markham, that great seventeenth-century arbiter of social decorum, once observed, the first course in any proper English banquet must be primarily for show," Grenville added, and on that cue one of the footmen brought forth an immense silver serving tray on which there was a cooked pheasant with a small bejeweled crown of gold on its intact head and its tail feathers streaming out behind it.

David noticed that Brad, being a vegetarian, looked slightly less than enchanted, and once again Grenville instantly detected that something was afoot. "What is it, Mr. Hollister?" he said, glancing briefly at David.

Brad shifted uneasily. "I'm afraid I don't eat pheasant. I'm a vegetarian."

David thought that Grenville and Julia were going to choke. They both gaped disbelievingly at the younger man for several seconds, Julia seeming especially disturbed. Finally Grenville composed himself. "Well, no matter," he said amiably. "But I'm afraid you're not going to enjoy the meal very much."

"Oh, don't worry," Brad added quickly. "I'll make do. I'm used to this sort of thing."

As the meal proceeded David understood more fully Grenville's warning that Brad was in for a less than perfect evening, for as the courses came one by one, it quickly became apparent that the menu was tipped heavily in favor of meats. There was a thick Yorkshire pudding, quail, venison steaks, and a large and succulent brisket of beef. On the stranger side, there was a salmi of owl, tiny roast songbirds, and a dish that Grenville asserted was prepared from the tongues of flamingoes. There was also an assortment of other odd dainties, quinces in syrup, cinnamon water, gingerbread, and little cakes called jumbles, paste of Genoa, Banbury tarts, marzipan, and fruits preserved in sugar that Grenville referred to as suckets. In all, it was more like a feast that one might have imagined encountering in Epicurean Rome rather than in an old English manor house.

Those dishes that David was courageous enough to sample he discovered were indescribably delicious. Others, like the flamingo tongues, he found too disconcerting to brave. And all was washed down with the ever more dizzyingly wonderful bog-myrtle wine.

With each glass of wine Melanie seemed to loosen up more,

and she started to engage in an increasingly animated discussion with Brad, Grenville, and Julia. David noticed that she even sampled the salmi of owl, which so far was the stunner of the evening. And several other things piqued his curiosity. First, he noticed that although Grenville was quaffing down glass after glass of bog-myrtle wine, as were they all, it seemed to have little or no effect on him, and he continued to watch their every move with the unsettling acumen of a falcon watching its prey. Grenville also continued to notice David noticing him, and indeed, a strange sort of silent dialogue had developed between the two of them, Grenville sometimes behaving as if he were entertained by David's own formidable powers of observation, but other times slipping and appearing to display a mote of annoyance over them.

The second thing that struck David as out of the ordinary was Julia's appetite. To say that she was ravenous was putting it mildly. She ate more than any of them, partaking of each and every dish and having seconds and thirds when she did. Once she even emitted a short sort of animallike snarl when Grenville appropriated a slice of brisket that she apparently wanted. On another occasion, when Brad asked Grenville why he owned so many exotic pets and Grenville replied that it was because Julia liked them, David looked up to see Julia smiling, with the wing of a roast songbird protruding from her mouth, and he actually felt an odd chill.

It was toward the end of the meal, between a serving of oxtail soup and seviche of flounder, that David suddenly and inexplicably felt the same strange neuralgia of the jaw that he had first experienced in the thicket. True to form, Grenville also immediately detected his discomfort, but instead of making his normal inquiry about what was wrong he looked quickly at Julia. For a moment she did not notice and was engaged in a boisterous swig of bog-myrtle wine. But then she became aware that she was being stared at. She looked at Grenville and seemed to perceive some message in his eyes. Then she looked at David, and as quickly as the pain had begun, it ended.

For several seconds he sat staring at them, wondering if the exchange that he had thought he had seen had actually transpired, when suddenly he heard another strange rustling sound scraping along the floor behind him. He turned quickly, assuming that it had to be one of the footmen, but saw that they were all standing motionless and at attention. He looked around the room, still searching for some sign of the mysterious draft, but saw nothing. Not even the candle flames flickered.

"Is something the matter?" Grenville asked.

"I thought I heard something."

"What did it sound like?"

"A rustling, like a leaf being blown across the floor."

Grenville smiled. "This old house has been here for many years. When a structure gets as old as it is, it takes on a life of its own. It becomes filled with many strange sounds."

"There are a lot of strange things in this valley," David commented nervously.

"What do you mean?"

"I mean, for example, an experience we had the other night at the pub, the Swan with Two Necks." Melanie and Brad both looked up with interest as David explained the reaction of the villagers to the appearance of the moth. "How do you explain that?" he asked when he had finished.

"I don't," Grenville returned simply.

"You don't have any idea why they behaved so strangely?"

"None at all. Why don't you ask them?"

"I did. They won't tell me."

This seemed to please Grenville. He shifted languidly in his chair. "You must understand, I really don't have much contact with the villagers. We live a rather solitary life out here, Julia and I. However, I can tell you, if you have not already figured it out for yourself, that the people of Fenchurch St. Jude have always had a disarming way about them. They keep to themselves. They behave peculiarly at times. No one knows why. Perhaps they see more in the moth than you see."

"What could they possibly see that we don't?" David said skeptically.

Grenville took a slow sip of his wine. "Who knows? But what was it Hamlet said? 'There are more things in heaven and earth than are dreamt of in your philosophy.' "

"Bah!" David said, reacting emotionally. "It's a nice turn of phrase, but I've never really bought that line."

Grenville looked at him, his eyes flashing, almost as if he took the remark as a challenge. "Oh, really," he said, munching on a piece of candied fruit.

At the same moment David noticed that the flame of one of the candles in a candelabrum sitting on the mantelpiece began to sputter and elongate, sending a ribbon of black smoke upward toward the ceiling. As it did so, a rivulet formed on its side sending a stream of hot wax downward onto the mantel.

"You know, there's a Norse version of that saying," Brad interrupted.

"The quote from *Hamlet*?" Melanie asked.

Brad nodded. "I don't recall the name of the epic poem it comes from, but I do remember that it's tenth century. Translated loosely it goes something like, 'There are more things beneath the tree of life than any stupid ape would suppose.'"

"The name of the epic poem is the *Grimnismal* and it dates from A.D. 950," Grenville informed them.

David looked at the Marquis, impressed that he should be in possession of such an obscure fact. Because of the unpleasantness of their first meeting and his generally unfavorable opinion of the inhabitants of Fenchurch St. Jude, it had not really occurred to him that the Marquis might be of more than ordinary intelligence and character. But as he looked into the older man's eyes he realized that something unusual did indeed dance in their depths. More than that, now as he reassessed the striking figure before him, he realized that there was even a special air about Grenville, a sense of power and presence.

"So Shakespeare took the line from the *Grimnismal*?" Melanie asked.

"There's no way that we can know that for sure," Brad returned. "But we do know Shakespeare was a great borrower. Many of his plots he lifted from older and lesser-known classics."

The conversation continued until finally Julia shifted restlessly. "Shall we retire to the drawing room for our void?" she asked.

Melanie and Brad looked at her questioningly.

"A 'void' is a medieval expression for a dessert or an after-dinner cordial," David explained. "It refers to whatever victual one uses to cleanse the palate after a large meal and in another room while the servants are busy clearing or 'voiding' the table of its dishes."

Grenville looked at him admiringly. "Quite correct," he

commended. And then he cast a somewhat reproving glance at Julia. "Sometimes Julia has a tendency to use terms that are a little out of date."

"In any case, I don't think I could consume another drop of anything," David said. He went to pull away from the table and suddenly noticed that he wasn't feeling very well. He felt painfully bloated, and realized that everything had taken on a gauzy appearance. His temples throbbed.

"Ooo," Melanie added, "I don't feel very well." She raised her hand to her head as if to suggest that she too were feeling a sudden pounding in her forehead.

David chalked up both of their reactions to their unrestrained gluttony.

"Oh, I'm so sorry," Grenville said, concerned. "Is there anything I can get you?"

"I think I just need a bit of fresh air," David returned.

"Oh, then let's you and I go for a walk by the lake," Julia said to him, hopping up excitedly.

David noticed that Melanie was not at all thrilled at the prospect of him going for a moonlight stroll with Julia, but his head was spinning, and he feared that if he did not get some air he might be ill. Given that Julia had offered to accompany him, he saw no tactful way of getting out of it.

"I don't feel very well at all," Melanie repeated firmly, and she looked at David as she assumed the pinched expression that she always employed when she wanted to go home immediately.

David looked at her peevishly. First, he resented the fact that she did not trust him. But of equal importance, he did not think that it would be polite of them to stuff their faces and then immediately leave. Given that their coming to dinner had been Grenville's requirement in return for giving them permission to dig on his land, David did not want to risk offending their host in any way.

The Marquis intervened. "You and Julia get some air. I'll take care of your wife. I'll get one of the servants to bring her some clear tea. We'll sit by the fire in the drawing room and have a nice chat. She'll be all right."

David stood, and Julia immediately crossed around the table and latched on to his arm. "This way," she directed. As they departed he noticed that Melanie was looking at him with daggers in her eyes and he realized that there would be hell to pay later for his insubordination.

As they approached the door, David glanced once again at the mantelpiece, and to his astonishment saw that the candle that had been dripping wax was gone. Indeed, the entire candelabrum was gone. The room was still filled with countless other candles, and he might scarcely have noticed its absence, were it not that he had been lost in reverie staring at it earlier. Even the stalagmite of wax where the candle had guttered was now completely absent and the mantelpiece was absolutely clean.

David looked quickly at Grenville, and the older man smiled faintly, but continued with some piece of courteous patter he was carrying on with Melanie. David was stupefied. He looked again at the empty mantelpiece. Had the candelabrum been carried out by one of the footmen, surely he would have seen it, or at least he would have noticed when someone cleaned up the accumulation of dripped wax. But he had seen nothing. His head spun, and he wondered if he could possibly have imagined the entire occurrence.

"Come along," Julia prodded, pulling him out the door.

Outside, the night was cool but comfortable, and an evening fog had begun to roll in from the lake. The sky had also begun to clear a little and occasionally, through a rift in the clouds, a bright and nearly full moon was visible. As they strolled across the grounds David was impressed again by the strange beauty of the place. The well-manicured lawn was like a dewy emerald carpet beneath their feet, and the languid wisps of fog that inched slowly through the trees gave the landscape a dreamlike cast. They reached the ancient balustraded terrace at the end of the lawn, and David observed that even the stagnant waters of the bog lake possessed a darkling beauty. Here and there lilies glowed ghostly white in its calm and obsidian surface, and occasionally, when it broke momentarily through the clouds, he could see the cratered reflection of the moon.

He looked at Julia. In the bluish glow of the moonlight she appeared even more beautiful than before, and he found himself fighting his attraction for her. Had he not been married, he fancied that he would have thrown himself at her feet. Seldom in his life had he encountered anyone he found more tantalizing and desirable. Her pale white flesh was almost luminous in the moonlight and her perfect visage even more radiant. In a momentary indulgence he imagined himself making love to her, running his fingers through her dark hair, and kissing her full and exquisite lips.

She seemed to reciprocate his feelings and suddenly pressed up against him until he could feel her large, full breasts through the black silk of her gown. He pulled away.

"Is something the matter?" she asked.

"I'm married," he said simply.

"Does that matter?"

"To me," he returned. He was extraordinarily drawn to her, even hungered for her, and he sensed that she felt an equal intensity of desire for him. But David had always prided himself on being a man of principle, and he loved both his wife and his children dearly and would do nothing to jeopardize his marriage.

"I'm sorry," he said, and the very moment he mouthed the words, the haze of the bog-myrtle wine suddenly welled up in him with a vengeance, and he almost found his lips forming an adulterous invitation in spite of himself. For several moments the strange visceral storm swept through him, as if every fiber of his body were suddenly pliant and no longer had any will of its own. The very night itself seemed to take on a more gossamer cast, and he wondered for a moment if he had been drugged.

Julia looked at him as if she knew what he was experiencing, and she waited patiently as if to see which opponent, he or the bog-myrtle wine, would come out the victor.

Several times he found his brain sending out the command to pull her into his arms, but he fought the impulse. Finally, the influence of the wine seemed to pass.

Julia looked at him oddly and stepped back. "You are a man of unusual will and conviction. Too bad," she sniffed. "I could be quite entertained by a man like you."

She turned and strolled ahead of him and then leaned against the balustrade, gazing out dreamily over the lake. At length, she looked at him again. "Have you ever been unfaithful to your wife?"

He looked at her with surprise. "No," he said falteringly, and then suddenly looked down at his feet.

"Are you telling me the truth?"

Again he hesitated. "Well, I've never really been unfaithful, but . . ."

"But?"

He looked at her, slightly affronted by the brazenness of her questions, but then the entire story came pouring out of him, almost as if he had needed to tell someone for years. "Once, when I was quite a bit younger, I was in Amsterdam strolling on the grounds of the Rijksmuseum when a girl asked me to take her picture." He leaned against the balustrade and gazed out over the water. "I don't know if you've ever had this experience where once or twice in your life you see someone who's exactly right. The face, the hair, everything, is just how you would design it if you could design your own perfect lover." He grew wistful. "Well, this girl was it. The face, the figure . . . and she had the greenest eyes, like chips out of a jade idol, those eyes." He shook his head.

"So what happened?"

"I took her picture."

Julia looked at him, dumbfounded. "That's it? That's the transgression that it was just so difficult for you to tell me?"

He shook his head. "There's more. After I took her picture I saw that it was the last one on that roll of film, and while she was getting her things, I stole it. I stole the roll of film." He withdrew his wallet and out of a secret compartment took out a snapshot, trimmed so that it would fit into the credit-card-size enclosure, and handed it to Julia. "I had the film developed, and I've carried around that picture ever since."

Julia examined the picture carefully.

He looked at her while she continued to scrutinize the snapshot. "You know, I've never told anyone about this before," he said.

She shrugged as if she did not consider the honor that extraordinary, and handed the photograph back to him. Again she directed her gaze out over the lake, and he noticed a strange smile cross her face. After several moments he spoke.

"Julia?"

She looked at him. "Yes?"

"Tonight I saw something very strange happen. When we were leaving the dining room a candelabrum sitting on the mantelpiece just vanished. I can't be sure, but I think Grenville may have made it disappear, as some sort of trick or something."

"It was no trick," she murmured.

"You mean it did happen?"

"I did not see it happen, but it's the sort of thing Grenville would do."

"How did he do it?"

She turned to him, her eyes strangely afire. "Grenville is a man of unusual power, great power. Such a feat would be child's play for him."

"You mean he's an illusionist?"

She laughed tauntingly. "Of great ability, I should say. But not an illusionist in your sense of the word."

"I don't understand."

"Then it's time you learn more about Grenville. It's time you witness a little more of his power." She walked up behind him and stood just out of his sight. He saw her hand extend beyond him as she pointed in the direction of the house. "Just watch over there," she said, allowing her hand to fall.

He squinted at the distance, at the fog moving lazily through the trees, and at first he saw nothing. He continued to look in the direction he had been instructed, but it wasn't until a minute or two later that it seemed to him the fog had started to glow. At first the light was so faint that he attributed it to the moon. But then, when the moon passed behind a cloud and the light remained, he realized that there was more to what he was seeing than just moonlight. Suddenly the ghostly luminescence grew brighter, and out from behind the trees walked a sight that caused him to freeze with disbelief.

In certain respects it seemed to be a centaur, in that it had the torso of a man and the lower body of a horse. In height it stood about eight feet tall, and even in the moonlight he could see the sinews of its massive and well-developed muscula-ture. As it strolled farther into the clearing he saw that the human portion of it was male and possessed handsome and finely chiseled features. Still, a number of its features were distinctly uncentaurlike, and suggested to him that perhaps the true nature of the beast was something quite different. First, and most anomalous, were its fore and middle fingers, which projected some six inches longer than the other fingers on its hands, and these it allowed to droop in a relaxed way like the pincers on some great insect. Equally striking was the look of its flesh. Although all portions of its anatomy were massive and powerful looking, somehow its muscles seemed to have rotted and were only hanging against its body. Here and there its ghostly bluish-gray flesh was flecked and pitted, and withal it had the look of something carious and nearly decomposed.

It took a step forward, and as it did so he was astonished to discover that the pain in his jaw suddenly throbbed into wakefulness. It stood in the clearing for several moments, preening itself, the fog glowing around it in faint swirls and eddies as it became infused with its preternatural light. And then it stopped and turned its gaze in his direction.

The moment it did so he felt another sharp spasm of pain in his jaw. The creature smiled, as if it seemed to understand the influence it was having upon him, and took another step forward. For a moment David remained frozen, staring into the centaur's hypnotic and strangely beguiling eyes, and then he looked behind him to gleen some hint of what to do next from Julia. To his surprise and growing disconcertion, he discovered that she was nowhere to be seen. He was alone with the thing.

He turned around and started to run. When he reached the end of the balustraded terrace he looked madly about, wondering if he should try to make his way back to the house, but he realized he was trapped. Even if he did break and try to make a run for it, surely the creature could outrun him. He looked back with horror at the advancing centaur. It continued to smile at him malevolently, the fog parting before it as it walked, and with its every step the pain in his teeth and gums intensified.

Finally, when it reached the balustraded terrace, instead of coming up onto it, to David's astonishment the creature walked right by and ambled down to the edge of the bog lake itself. It looked at him bewitchingly one last time and then strolled leisurely into the inky black water. The normally placid lake rippled gently as the centaur vanished beneath its surface. Shaken, David ran to the end of the terrace and looked down, and to his continued amazement saw that he could still see it walking along the bottom. He watched, mesmerized, as the eerie luminescence moved deeper into the lake, and finally the glow faded, and all that could be seen in the dark water was the undulating reflection of the moon on its surface.

In the distance he heard a rumble of thunder and he noticed there was a smell of rain in the air. Still, he could not take his eyes off the lake. He continued to lean against the balustrade and gaze outward, until about twenty minutes later, he thought he saw something come out of the waters on the opposite shore. It seemed to glow dimly in the moonlight, but if his eyes were not deceiving him it no longer possessed the shape of a centaur, but seemed more amorphous, even larval, like a giant and faintly glowing worm.

Now, seeing it at a distance, his courage returned to him, and instead of being frightened, he became intensely curious about the thing. His burning passion to understand every unknown facet of the world returned to him, and he could not help but think that there had to be a simple and rational explanation for what he had experienced. He knew that he would not rest until he had discovered the truth of the thing.

The thunder rumbled again, and casting caution to the wind, he started off around the lake to follow it.

* * *

"It sounds like rain," Grenville said.

Melanie looked up at him, frowning. "It certainly rains a lot here."

"Get used to it, my dear," Grenville returned companionably. "This is England."

On any other occasion she might have smiled at the remark, but as it was she was losing patience with just about everything. Her head continued to pound as the strange and oppressive influence of the bog-myrtle wine continued to course through her, and she looked at her watch. David had been gone for almost an hour and she had had enough. She looked at Brad and saw that he almost seemed to be dozing, except his eyes were open.

"I'm going out to see what's keeping David," she announced.

At first Grenville looked as if he might make a move to stop her, but then apparently decided against it. She stood and discovered she was still much drunker than she had realized. Walking was not going to be easy. Summoning all of her abilities, she negotiated the drawing room, walked through the vast and dark entrance hall and out onto the grounds of the estate. To her surprise, neither David nor Julia was anywhere to be seen. She called out their names and still heard nothing. She walked down to the balustraded terrace that overlooked the lake. Again, she called their names, but her ears were only met with silence and the mounting rumble of the thunder.

Well that's torn it, she thought to herself with irritation. She could not believe it. She never would have thought David would do such a thing, but clearly he had gone off somewhere to be alone with Julia. She stormed back to the house, fighting to keep tears from flooding her eyes.

She strode back into the drawing room and looked down at Brad. Under the influence of the bog-myrtle wine she found him even more attractive than usual, and her gaze lingered as it traced over his face, down the open buttons of his shirt. She caught herself when she realized that Grenville was watching her carefully.

She grew embarrassed for a moment, but then composed herself. "Brad, will you please drive me home?"

Brad looked up at her, dazed. "What about Professor Macauley?"

"He can go to hell!" she cursed, not caring any longer about propriety.

Grenville took the remark in stride. "There, there," he soothed. "I'm sure they're just off walking somewhere. They simply lost track of the time."

"Well, he can just walk home when he gets a mind to," she retorted. "Come on, Brad. We're taking the car."

Brad stood up, still blinking worriedly. "Doesn't Professor Macauley have the keys?"

"I have a set," Melanie shot back. She turned to Grenville. "Thank you very much for a lovely evening," she said with all of the pleasantness she could muster.

"Yes, thank you," Brad echoed.

"My pleasure," Grenville ended as he nodded to the butler to see them to the door.

On the drive home it started to rain, lightly at first, but then in torrents. That'll teach him, she thought to herself angrily. When they reached the cottage and Brad pulled the car to a stop, she looked over and saw that the younger man was feeling very uneasy about the entire situation.

"Would you like to stay the night?" she asked innocently, thinking mainly of the weather, but after she had said the words she felt an overwhelming urge to jump on top of him and begin mauling him. This took her completely off guard, for although she was beginning to recognize that she was drawn to him in a way, her sexuality had never been channeled in such an overt and aggressive manner. She mentally rebuked herself and remembered her violent reaction toward Katy when Katy had suggested such a thing, but even as the thought passed through her mind, a second voice in her head kept shrilling, *It would serve David right, it would serve David right.*

To her continued surprise she wanted suddenly to see Brad with his clothing off, to run her fingers through the hair on his chest, and again she fought to constrain her own libido. She recalled once more Julia's warning that bog-myrtle wine was a powerful aphrodisiac, and she wondered if there could possibly be any truth to the matter.

She looked at Brad and thought that even he seemed to be fighting an inner onslaught of desire. He looked at her lips and then into her eyes.

"Thank you, but I really should be getting back to the camp."

She looked at him for a moment longer. "Very well," she said conjuring all of her will. "Then I'm sure I'll see you tomorrow night when you come over for dinner."

"Yes," Brad returned stiffly. Then, in his silly and utterly self-effacing way, he started to get out of the car as if he had every intention of walking back to the excavations.

"What are you doing?" she asked.

"Going back to the camp."

"Well, take the car."

"But—" he stammered.

She started to get angry. "Don't be an idiot!" she said, getting out of the Volvo herself. The rain instantly started to drench her hair. "Take the car and we'll get it tomorrow." And with that she slammed the door and Brad reluctantly drove off. She went into the house.

Mrs. Comfrey had left the living room lights on for them. Upstairs, Melanie found that she had also thoughtfully built a fire in the fireplace in their bedroom, no doubt on account of the poor weather, but as she looked around the room she saw that there was no sign that David had come home yet. As she proceeded to take off her wet clothing, a black and agonizing depression started to swell up in the pit of her stomach. How could he do this? she thought to herself. How could

their marriage mean so little to him that he could meet that
. . . that harlot, and cast everything that they had worked so
hard to build to the wind?

The rain continued to pelt down and the lightning cracked,
and every time the house creaked or groaned with each renewed
assault of the storm, she grew deathly still and listened, hoping
it would be David. She began to regret leaving him stranded
in the rain, but still she felt that it had been the right move.
Nonetheless, with Mrs. Comfrey and the children fast asleep,
and David gone and God only knew where, she began to grow
afraid.

It was while she sat arranging her stockings in front of the
fire that she heard the distinctive squeak of the gate at the
front of the house. She sat up, her ears pricked. Was it David?
She hoped it was, but suddenly she tingled with the fear that
it might not be. She remembered Ben's disappearance, and then
Winnifred Blundell's, and a shudder passed through her. She
had had a bad feeling from the start about coming to this place.
And now, feeling alone and dispirited, she was gripped with
the terrible realization that it could be almost anyone or anything that now approached the house. As she sat listening carefully, she was swept with another horrifying thought. She did
not remember locking the front door.

Suddenly something crunched on the gravel outside.

It now occurred to her that if it was David he would have
reached the house by this time. But whoever it was was hesitat-
ing, lingering for some unknown reason on the walk. Her only
thought became to get downstairs and to latch the front door
before it reached the house.

She pulled her nightgown around her and ran out into the
hall. As she raced down the stairs she heard another crunch
of gravel and she realized that it was now done deliberating
and was heading straight for the door. As she ran frantically
through the now seemingly endless living room, the seconds
seemed to tick by slowly, almost as if in a dream. The thunder
cracked, and her hand reached out as she sprinted the last few
feet that divided her from the latch. She reached it and silently
engaged the lock just a fraction of a second before whatever
was on the other side slowly tested the knob.

She paused, not knowing what to do next, when she heard
another crunch of gravel and realized that it had started around

the side of the house. It was making its way to the back door, which was probably not locked either. Whoever the unseen intruder was, its footsteps were heavy, and she could trace its steps clearly as it plodded toward its goal. She raced toward the back door, but as she approached one of the side windows it hit her that the curtains were not drawn, and the prowler would see her if she continued. She flattened herself up against the wall beside the window and was horror-stricken when she heard the footsteps also pause. She realized that just inches away something was peering into the house.

The lightning flashed and she held her breath, not daring to move. Finally the thing started again, this time with renewed determination in its stride, and she broke into a run in a mad attempt to reach the back door before it did. Thunder shook the house again as she crashed into a kitchen chair and lunged desperately for the door. Again the passage of time was dream-like. With aching slowness, her hand stretched out frantically through the darkness, every fiber of her body praying that she would reach the latch in time. But she did not. She watched in horror as the knob turned and the door flew open.

Melanie let out a scream. But, standing rain-soaked in the darkness beyond was only Brad. The lightning flashed behind him and she could see that he was thoroughly drenched by the downpour. Also, even in the dim light, she could see that he had a peculiarly brazen gleam in his eye.

"I decided to come back," he said.

For a moment Melanie was so out of breath from her panic that she could not speak, and her heart was beating so rapidly that it felt as if at any moment it would come bursting right through her rib cage.

"Oh, Brad, I'm so glad it's only you," she gasped when she had finally composed herself.

"I'm sorry," he said. "Did I frighten you?"

She nodded. "I'll say." And then, still holding her heart, she pursed her brow. "Why did you come back? Did you forget something?"

He shook his head and smiled strangely, and another thought occurred to Melanie.

She looked beyond him into the darkness. "I didn't hear the car drive up."

"I hid it. I didn't want Professor Macauley to see it."

She looked at him, bewildered, wondering why he should care, when suddenly he stepped forward and ran the back of his hand down along the side of her neck and then placed it firmly on the bare skin above her breast. With his other hand he started to unbutton his rain-soaked shirt.

Her first impulse was to pull away, to respond indignantly to his presumption, but she found her will quickly receding. He pulled her to him and kissed her passionately, the warm, sweet taste of his tongue flooding her senses as it probed deep into her mouth. Then he lifted her into his arms and carried her upstairs.

She could not believe that she was going along with it, but she felt oddly powerless to do anything but acquiesce to the incredible desire coursing through her.

In the bedroom he placed her gently on the bed while he finished taking off his clothing. She watched as he undressed in front of the fireplace, admiring his trim and muscular body flickering golden in the lambent light of the flames. My God, she thought, what was she doing? What if David came home? But then, as he approached her and slowly slipped her night-gown off, her desire exploded and she became lost in sensation.

It was new and exciting making love to someone else. She enjoyed sex with David. She knew every portion of his body with comfortable intimacy, but Brad's body was novel and foreign and she explored it hungrily. He was vigorous in his love-making, but attentive to her silent cues, and soon they were locked together. The pleasure she felt was intense. She ran her fingers through the thick mat of hair on his chest, his mouth continuing to engulf her own as the bed started to rock with the rhythm of their lovemaking.

In time he started pumping faster, groaning loudly with plea-sure, and some distant part of her worried about waking the children. He continued to groan, and as his ardor increased she noticed that the sounds he was making became more animal-like, and this surprised her. His movement hastened and her own pleasure intensified, but still he continued to moan ever more loudly until at last when she looked up at him, still golden in the light of the fire, he seemed like some wild thing baying over her with his head tilted back in an almost mindless ecstasy.

He pumped madly, letting out a primal and guttural howl as he climaxed, and as soon as he had finished she thought she heard something. Downstairs the front door slammed. My God, she thought, David is home. She looked up in a panic at the man hovering over her. But at the same, almost orchestrated moment that he had climaxed and the door had slammed, the naked form that one moment had been so palpable and so intensely real, vanished, instantly and without a trace. She looked madly toward the fire and noticed that even his wet and discarded clothing was gone, and, inexplicably, she was totally alone in the room, her legs parted widely and her body still covered with the sweat and fluids of their lovemaking.

6

VALERIA STARED LISTLESSLY into the flames leaping up from the small tripod of beaten brass, and the smell of scented wood filled the tent. She tossed a handful of verbena and other herbs into the fire and carefully watched the smoke that issued forth. The smoke turned black, and again the augury was unfavorable. It was a very bad omen.

She knew that she should tell her husband, but how could she? How could she explain to him that she had had indiscreet relations with one of his subordinate officers, let alone that the man had vanished afterward as if by artifice or sorcery? She had heard of such spirits that prey on the weaknesses of women, and she was grateful that the thing had at least not harmed her, for they were known not only for their carnal appetites, but for their ferocity. And at least this much about the thing was evident to her husband, given the other events that they had witnessed in the valley.

She had hoped her offering of the comb might appease the thing, but it was now obvious that it was not to be so easily placated. She had no other choice but to do what she had done almost constantly since they had arrived in the valley, and that was to pray.

She added some more scented wood to the fire and lowered

her head. "Oh, chaste Diana, if there is any way that you can find it in your heart to forgive me for my sins, and deliver us from this evil—"

Her husband entered the tent behind her. "What are you doing?"

"What does it look like I'm doing?" she said, turning to him, her eyes red from crying.

"Praying, but I thought I heard you ask for forgiveness for your sins."

"We have all sinned, Divitiacus. Is that so strange a request?" she said evasively, and then hated herself for not having the courage to tell him the truth.

"I suppose not," he said, accepting the explanation. From his expression she could tell that he had his own troubles to think about.

"What is it?" she asked.

"Two more men have vanished," he said. "I will, of course, have two more of the villagers put to the sword, but I have no hope that it will do any good." He paced anxiously through the tent, wringing his hands together in exasperation. "I just don't understand, first the horses and now my men, almost a dozen in all so far."

"And don't forget the girl," she added.

"And the girl," he conceded begrudgingly, and then laughed a short, scornful laugh. "I don't know what good they think it does them sacrificing their people to the thing. It still just devours them and waits hungrily for more."

"But at least they have some control over who dies next." He looked at her harshly.

"And it's only one at a time. Look at you, you're beginning to lose two and three men a night now."

"So what do you suggest that I do?" he demanded angrily.

"Perhaps we should start giving it men. Or perhaps we should have slaves brought in for it."

"We're Romans!" he cried.

"But Divitiacus," she argued, "at least then *you* could decide who dies next." She looked around with a tormented expression. "It's too hellish going on the way we've been doing, not know-ing who it's going to take next; each evening not knowing which face will vanish during the night. It could be one of us next. Or both."

"But Caesar—"

"I know," she interrupted. "Caesar has decreed that we reject the local religions." She looked out over the moors. "Well, Caesar does not know what is going on in this valley."

"Nor would he ever believe me if I told him," Divitiacus added bitterly. "But I have another plan."

Valeria looked at her husband hopefully.

"Their local tribal chieftain, the one who lives in the fortification on the edge of the lake—I think we should go to him." Divitiacus's eyes darted hither and thither as he mulled the thought over. "You know, when we first came into this valley I thought that the man was a coward and not worth the fight it would take to draw him out of his battlement. I mean, he just remained in his fasthold and didn't even come out to challenge us. He doesn't even have an army." Divitiacus's expression became optimistic. "But I'm beginning to think that he holds the key to this thing. At least, he doesn't seem to fear the creature. And it never seems to harm him. I think we should pay him a visit."

"The two of us?"

"Yes, the two of us. Not as members of the invading army, but as fellow patricians, as diplomatic emissaries wishing simply to raise a glass or two with him and perhaps negotiate some sort of understanding. I'm beginning to think that he knows more than we may have suspected. I'm beginning to think that he may be the key to this entire thing."

Divitiacus instructed his wife to put on her best gown. Valeria did as she was bid, and together with her husband, and with a garrison of Roman soldiers following only a diplomatic distance behind, they made their way to the battlement on the lake.

As they approached the escarpment leading to the formidable hulk of granite and stone, she found herself hoping that her husband was right. But she was also worried, and feared that he might not be, for she could not forget the augury and the handful of leaves that she had thrown upon the flame. And the blackness of the smoke.

7

THE EVENTS OF that evening left David in a state unlike anything
that he had ever experienced before. When he had reached
the other side of the lake he had found nothing. When he had
returned to Wythen Hall he was informed by one of the servants
that the Marquis and Julia had retired. Even when he arrived
back at the cottage he found Melanie in a curious state, although
mercifully she was not nearly as angry as he had expected her
to be. His first urge had been to tell her everything that had
happened to him, but given that he himself did not know what
he had seen, he refrained. To explain his disappearance he told
her only that he and Julia had gotten separated and that he
had followed a strange animal through the woods in the hopes
that it might be Ben, or at least provide him with some clue
about Ben's disappearance. But even this she greeted without
question or argument, and he was left to ponder the night's
occurrences alone.

He thought about it restlessly through a good portion of
the night, but by morning he had still come no closer to explaining what he had seen. It was not that he was troubled by enig-
mas. Throughout his life he had always thrived on puzzles.
But what bothered him so much about this was that he had
no context in which to tackle it. The only thing that seemed
to make sense was that it had been a hallucination of some
sort, but assuming that this was the case still brought with it

several problems. If it was a hallucination, how had Julia been able to so precisely anticipate its onset? In addition, if it was a product of his own psychology, why had there been no other clues about what was happening to him? No blurring of the vision previous to his sighting the centaur? No flashes of light or other perceptual distortions? The more he thought about it the more convinced he became that he could not explain what he had seen as an aberration of his own mental functioning; but the alternative, that the centaur was somehow real and existed "out there," was equally untenable to him. He was left only with an unsolvable problem, and the sentence that kept returning to him endlessly in his thoughts was Julia's strange allusion to Grenville's power.

When he got up that morning he went for a long walk outside, like a man possessed. It was only when he came back in and found Melanie agitatedly sipping her coffee in the dining room in the dark and with all of the shades unopened that he realized something was bothering her also.

"Honey? What is it?" he asked, sitting down beside her.

"Nothing," she returned unconvincingly, still gazing off into space.

This irked him, for he hated it when she made him drag it out of her. "Come on, Mel, don't play this game. Can't you just tell me?"

She hesitated for another moment and then looked at him frowning. "Do you think there was any chance we were drugged last night?"

This took him by surprise. "What do you mean?"

Again she hesitated. "I don't know. I just felt that that bog-myrtle wine hit me rather hard last night. I just wondered if you thought there was something in it other than alcohol, something that might cause . . . well, hallucinations, maybe?"

Not knowing what she meant, he assumed that she had to be referring to the experience he had had. "So you know what happened to me last night?" he said.

The look of agitation on her face intensified. "What do you mean?"

This time it was his turn to become flushed as he fidgeted and told her the entire experience. When he had finished the look on her face had escalated from concern to fear.

"David, what do you think it was?" she asked urgently.

He became confused. "I don't know, but I thought you knew about this already."

"Of course not. How would I?"

"Then why did you ask if I thought the bog-myrtle wine was drugged and might cause hallucinations?"

"Do you think it was?"

"No . . . well, I don't know. I'm not sure." He told her the reasons that he could not accept that his vision had been the result of a psychoactive experience.

"But, David, that means that the centaur was real."

"No it doesn't."

"Then what was it?"

"I don't know!" he snapped, and then grew penitent. "I'm sorry. But I can't help but think that it was a trick of some sort. I mean, obviously Julia knew about it. She even said that Grenville was an illusionist. I think he perpetrated the event as some sort of practical joke, or mind fuck. I don't know."

Melanie clearly remained unconvinced that it had been a trick and stared off into the distance, even more mysteriously tortured than before. Finally, after several minutes and with her eyes still fixed off in space, she said darkly, "David, I don't think it was a trick."

Too exasperated to respond, David just allowed the comment to go by.

Melanie spoke again. "Did you see the Volvo outside?"

"No. I've been meaning to ask you what happened to it."

"Are you sure? When you went for your walk did you see it anywhere, hidden or pulled off the road?"

"No. Why do you ask?"

"Because I thought Brad might have driven it back. He drove me home last night and since it was raining I let him borrow the car." She paused in thought. "But you know how considerate Brad is. I just thought he might have driven it back already."

David accepted the information without question, but Melanie's thoughts raced. It was the final vindication, she thought. Already she suspected that whatever it was that had been in her room had not been Brad. Brad was a human being, a creature made of flesh and blood, and flesh and blood didn't simply evaporate, fade away into nothing like a vapor or a morning mist. But even if she had been mistaken, had unknowingly fainted from the shock of David arriving home, if it had been

Brad, he would not have been able to drive the car away without alerting David. The Volvo should still be hidden somewhere near the house. But it wasn't.

And yet she was also convinced that she could not simply have imagined the entire experience.

Her thoughts in tumult, another question came into her head, incongruous and inexplicable. "Grenville seems awfully dark-complected for an Englishman. Do you have any idea why that might be?"

David shrugged. "Well, the Romans do mention that when they came to conquer England the Celts were unusually dark-complected. Perhaps his family line just maintains a more pure strain of ancient Celtic blood."

She accepted the answer and both of them continued to brood for a moment. Suddenly David stirred.

"Now I have a question. If you didn't know about the centaur why did you ask if I thought we had been drugged?"

She looked down into her lap. "Well, I felt pretty strange last night myself."

"How so?"

She hesitated for a moment longer and then looked into her husband's eyes, and when she saw him staring back at her, so compassionate, so trusting, she knew that she would rather walk over burning coals than have to tell him what she had done. But she realized also that, given what he had told her, she had experienced something, something that frightened her more and more. She looked back down into her lap. "Well, to begin, do you remember Julia saying that bog-myrtle wine is an aphrodisiac?" She paused. "Well, last night when I got home I . . . well, I felt very peculiar, and I'm not trying to blame it on the wine, but I—"

And suddenly he thought he understood. "Honey, I know what you're going to say."

"You do?" she said, her eyes widening.

"Yes, I do. I know that you weren't thrilled about the way Julia was coming on to me, and I have to admit the wine made me feel pretty peculiar too." He shifted nervously. "I wasn't going to say anything, but Julia made a pass at me, and although it pains me to admit it, I damn near came close to accepting it."

"David, I—"

"Honey, please let me finish. I came close to accepting it, but then I thought of you and the kids. I thought of how a relationship like ours is built on trust, and then I turned her down, and you know why?"

"Why?" she asked weakly.

"Because I knew you would never do anything like that to me." He paused. "Honey, I'm sorry."

After several seconds he realized she was still just looking at him, her eyes glazed and behaving as if all of the life had been drawn out of her. "Honey, do you forgive me?" he asked.

"Forgive you?" she repeated distantly. "Yes . . . I forgive you."

"Now, what was it you wanted to say?"

She continued to ruminate over some unknown and mysterious thought. "Nothing," she returned. "It's nothing."

* * *

David noticed that his wife continued to brood for the rest of the morning, but it was just before he was about to leave for the digs that he found her looking even more troubled as she stood in the living room and sniffed the air carefully.

"What is it?" he asked.

"Do you smell something?"

He sniffed, and at first detected nothing. But then he took another deep whiff and became aware of a faint and unpleasant odor. The scent was familiar, but as he stood focusing his senses on it, it remained hazy and ill-defined. He took another, even deeper inhalation and at last recognized what he was smelling. He had smelled that stench before in his life. It was the smell of putrefying flesh.

"What do you think it is?" Melanie asked, seemingly on the verge of panic.

"You had Mrs. Comfrey put rat poison around the house, right?"

She nodded.

"Well it's probably just the poison working. Somewhere in the walls or beneath the floorboards a rat who has eaten some of it has crawled in and died. The smell will go away in a few days."

To his amazement Melanie seemed almost relieved.

Although he didn't mention it, David thought of another possible and even more unpleasant explanation for the smell.

147

It occurred to him that it might be Ben. And so after Melanie had gone back into the dining room, he got a flashlight and went beneath the crawlspace of the house. To his relief, however, he found no trace of the retriever's moldering body, or for that matter, the remains of any small animal that might explain the mysterious odor.

The next several days were less than idyllic. Although he continued to work at the digs, he remained driven to distraction by his inability to understand the events that he had witnessed at Wythen Hall. When Brad asked him what was wrong he declined comment, but more than ever he was haunted by every detail of the evening, and turned every word, smell, and perception over and over again in his mind in attempts to wring some sense out of it. As a result, he existed in a state of agitation equaled only by Melanie's. Since that evening, she too seemed like a changed person, and she padded listlessly around the house, sulking and brooding almost as if she were in a state of grief or moral breakdown. When Brad came over for dinner she no longer even engaged in animated discussions with him, but behaved instead as if he reminded her of something she wanted to forget. At first David had blamed the change in her on his confession of near infidelity, but as her moods continued, he started to wonder if there was more to it than just that.

He noticed also that Katy was unusually pensive and became especially unsettled when Melanie was around, but he did not know why. And Tuck, although his appetite improved, remained disconsolate over Ben's disappearance, no longer ran and laughed or even played his video games, a gloomy and spiritless shadow of his former self, in the charge of the equally cheerless Mrs. Comfrey.

What bothered David most about it all was that he was so involved with his own internal struggle that he felt powerless. He knew that he should reach out and try to help his family, try to initiate some communication that would release them from the torpor that had enveloped them, but he seemed trapped behind his eyes and hands. And throughout it all, as the emotional ties that had once bound his family seemed to disintegrate, there remained in the house the subtle but omnipresent odor, the faint miasma of decay.

It was on the morning of the fourth day after their dinner

at the Marquis's that Brad appeared unexpectedly at the front door of the cottage. It was still so early that Melanie and the kids had not even arisen, and David answered his unrestrained knocking still wiping the sleep out of his eyes.

He looked wonderingly at the young man shifting his weight excitedly on the front step.

"Get dressed!" Brad ordered.

"Why, what is it?"

"You're not going to believe it. Get dressed!"

Still curious about what it was all about, David quickly dressed and they piled into the Volvo. On the way to the digs Brad still refused to divulge the reason for his strange fervor. They reached the campsite, got out, and it was only as Brad ran ahead that David realized it had something to do with the excavation they were doing in the portion of the bog that belonged to Grenville. They reached the edge of the pit and David looked down.

This time in the red strata of the dog's flesh there was not one, but two of the eerily obsidian bog bodies, curled slightly in fetal position and facing one another, one male and the other female. What had excited Brad so was obviously their dress. Unlike the other bog bodies they had found, the couple in the pit wore tunics and blouses, discolored but preserved by the bog water and of a far more sophisticated weave than the clothing of the Iron Age inhabitants of the valley. In addition, the hairstyle of the woman, her bracelets and the bracelets on the man, the woman's soft leather shoes, and the *fasciae* or leg bands of the man, all were not Celtic but unique to quite a different culture. The bodies before them were Roman.

David knelt down slowly in stupefied reverence. Nothing like it had ever been found before. Perhaps no other ancient civilization had inspired as much interest, been the subject of more archaeological endeavors, of more books, films, museum exhibits, essays, and intellectual ponderings than the Roman. And yet no one, no living person, had ever done what they were doing now. They were actually looking at two denizens of that glistening and bygone empire, two ancient Romans *in the flesh*.

He looked back at Brad and realized why the younger man had been so excited. It was the sort of discovery archaeologists dream of. The bodies before them were perhaps the only two of their kind in the world, and when news of the find got out it was sure to inspire a flurry of media attention.

"It's amazing," David murmured, and then realized that such superlatives palled in light of the momentousness of the discovery. He slipped down gingerly into the excavation. As he examined the bodies he tingled all over. This was the moment that drove all archaeologists on, that brief starburst of exhilaration, perhaps akin to the feeling a painter experiences when he puts the master stroke on a great work of art, or a photographer who, after years of work, captures that one ineffable moment on a roll of film. He savored the electricity that now coursed through his body as if it were the finest wine, for he knew that in years to come he would thirst for its memory.

And then he looked at the way that the bodies had met their end. Because these bodies were in a drier section of the peat, and he now knew what he was looking for, he was able to discern more readily what had caused their demise. Like the first two bog bodies they had unearthed, the body of the man displayed the same telltale bite marks around his neck and chest. Strikingly different, however, was the fact that his head had been savagely twisted a full three hundred sixty degrees in its socket and was almost totally severed from the body. In addition, compared to the other bodies, his expression could almost be considered tranquil. His eyes were open and the look on his face one of surprised horror, but it was not the look of unutterable dread that had been wrought in the faces of the previous two corpses. It was almost as if whatever had twisted his head nearly off had hit him with such force that he had scarcely had time to react. Given that this might be the case, David wondered if perhaps the bite marks had come after the fact, that first the man had been killed and then the beast had been allowed to feed.

He turned his attention to the woman beside the man. Determining the cause of her death was at first more difficult. Her neck and chest showed no traces of having been bitten, and although her expression was desperately sad, her eyes were closed and her head intact. It was only after David knelt down and leaned over her that he saw. In her small clasped hands was the handle of a knife, which she had apparently plunged into her own abdomen.

David straightened. Although dying by one's own hand seemed a far better mode of demise than being mauled by an animal or having one's head twisted off, for some reason, seeing how the woman met her end had a strangely disquieting affect on him.

"Do you think it was *her* comb?" Brad asked behind him.

"What?" he said, still distracted and gazing off into the distance.

"The Roman comb we found buried with the girl. Do you think it belonged to her?"

David looked again at the woman and at the depth of the sadness frozen in her ancient face. "There's no way of knowing, is there?" he said. "At least not yet." He climbed back out of the hole.

Brad continued to look down at the bodies. "No, I guess not. But she certainly looks sad enough to have wept the tears of our lady of the comb." He noticed that David was strolling off in the direction of the hills. "Hey, where are you going?"

"To think," David called out without looking back. "I have to think."

As he walked he realized that what had bothered him about the woman's suicide was the parallel he was drawing between her and Melanie. From the man's dress it was evident that he was high up in the Roman power structure, and the woman was no doubt his wife. If the man had come here to officiate, as David surmised that he had, his wife would have accompanied him very much as Melanie had accompanied David. In fact, if the man had brought his wife, like David, he would have done so only if he believed she were in absolutely no danger, that she would be completely safe in a strange and foreign land. What, then, could have happened that had caught the man so off guard? And why hadn't the same fate befallen his wife, instead of allowing her to linger and take her own life? David knew that it was silly to think that the events of over a dozen centuries previous might have something to do with anything happening today, but somehow he could not get the growing sense of gloom and despair that was encompassing his own family out of his mind.

He walked up to the top of the first hill and then the next, and it was only when he had reached the promontory of the tallest hill that he stopped and looked out over the valley. There was every likelihood that if the man were a Roman envoy he would have set up his camp here. Not only was there plenty of room for the soldiers, but also the prominence of the bluff afforded a clear view of anything that approached. As he looked out over the vista he wondered again what could have so savagely overcome a Roman soldier and military strategist who no doubt would have taken every precaution to protect himself.

Suddenly, as David mulled over the thought, in the thicket at the foot of the hill he heard a sound. He looked down at the wall of brush, but saw nothing. As he continued to look at the thicket he heard another sound. Something was definitely moving behind the bushes. He started down the hill, and the very moment he initiated his advance whatever it was that had been watching him took off. He too broke into a run, but it wasn't until he had nearly reached the thicket that he saw what it was. Running at breakneck pace and heading deeper into the bog, was the little girl Amanda.

Fearful that she was headed toward certain disaster, he continued after her.

"Hey!" he yelled. "I won't hurt you. Stop!"

It was of no use. She continued blindly on. When he first entered the thicket, his feet pounded against solid ground, but a little ways in, the ground became wetter. Not thinking of his own safety, he continued.

Amanda moved like a wild thing, like a rabbit or a deer that had been frightened out of hiding, and as he crashed through a tangle of alder buckthorn he saw that she was already some distance ahead. He penetrated deeper into the undergrowth and was once again transfixed by the primeval beauty of the bog. Along a fallen cedar to his left, luxuriant masses of rusty woodsia grew and tubers of bladderwort nestled among the spreading roots of the larger trees. Ahead, in a shaft of sunlight, the delicate little crosiers of a royal fern uncurled, and beneath a rock a boreal bog orchid with a raceme of small but exquisite white blossoms perfumed the damp air.

He leaped over one of the stagnant black rivulets of the bog, and as he came pounding down on the other side he was relieved to find that the ground did not vanish deceptively from beneath his feet. He pressed on.

Finally, realizing that he was pushing his own luck far beyond its limit, he paused, and his boots sank several inches into the spongy ground before stopping.

"Amanda!" he called out. "Please!"

Perhaps it was the desperation of his entreaty, or perhaps the fact that he had called her by her first name, but he saw the flicker of white far ahead come to a stop.

"Amanda, I'm not going to hurt you. I just want to tell you that you're in danger in here. The bog is not a safe place to play in."

The patch of white moved again, and he realized she was coming toward him. Within moments the dirty but angelic face appeared among the briar. He looked down and noticed that he himself was cut by the brambles and flecked here and there with blood, and there were pieces of plant debris caught in his hair. But although her hair was disheveled, it was free from such chaff, and her skin, he noticed, had also fared far better than his.

In her hand he observed for the first time that she carried what looked like the jawbone of an animal. She looked up at him shyly, but a definite curiosity shone in her cheerless brown eyes.

For several moments neither of them spoke and they just stared at each other like two creatures of the forest slowly negotiating their territory. Finally he broke the silence.

"You don't need to worry. I'm not going to hurt you."

She looked at him suspiciously.

David smiled. "Come on, I know you can talk. I heard you, remember?"

For the first time a flicker of recognition passed through her face and she nodded timidly, seeming to recall the incident several nights previous.

Realizing that she was shy, he continued. "The only reason that I chased you just now is I was worried about you running into the bog as you did. You know, it's very dangerous in here."

She stared at him perplexedly, as if she were startled that anyone should care about her safety, but still she remained silent.

He decided to try a new approach. He decided to ignore her. Picking up a stick, he sat down next to one of the stagnant bog ponds and started to dab lightly at its surface. As he continued to pay her no mind he once again became absorbed in still other features of his surroundings. He noticed that shiny scavenger beetles covered the muck of the shallower portions of the pool, and a mob of back swimmers jostled across its watery surface. Still deeper in the dark mirror he saw the real lords of the pool, rough-skinned newts in various stages of development with pink, frilly gills and pebbled orange bellies scraping slowly across the bottom.

The bog was also rich with smells, the deep muggy scent of wet earth and vegetation, and sounds, the high stridulations of the cicadas and the distant buzzing of the flies. Suddenly one of the buzzing sounds grew louder, as a dragonfly swept past his face and narrowly missed the floating web of a filmy dome spider. It was a short-lived victory, for it immediately landed on the gelatinous cap of a bright-orange toadstool David recognized as the deadly fly agaric. The bog, in many ways, was a treacherous place.

As he continued to gaze at the arboreous landscape it became easy for him to imagine that the Batrachian age of great fern forests and endless swamps had never ended. In the pool before him a bubble of marsh gas erupted from the ooze and rushed upward in a swirl of silt, only to break the surface and vanish, with nothing to mark its passing but a tiny pop.

Out of the corner of his eye he noticed that Amanda had finally sidled up beside him.

"You know, I really won't hurt you," he said, turning to face her.

"Then why were you chasin' me?" she inquired unexpectedly.

"I told you I was afraid for you. The bog is a very dangerous place."

She thought this over carefully and then looked down at the stick he was wafting in his hands. "Why are you pokin' at the water?"

"Just for something to do."

"Wo' ya like to see wha' I found?" she asked.

"Sure," he said, happy that he was gaining her trust.

But before he could say anything else she had again bounded off deeper into the bog.

"Hey!" he shouted as he once more had to break into a run to keep up with her.

Several times, as they pressed farther into the green labyrinth, she would point at a bed of lilies or an innocuous-looking clearing and announce simply, "Sink."

Finally they reached a large and muddy clearing encircled by an almost impenetrable wall of blackthorn and mountain ash, and Amanda stopped. As they stood there for a moment David slowly became aware that another smell now mingled with the background scent of the place. It was an unpleasant smell, a fetor of putrefaction not unlike the stench that had begun to filter through the cottage. Equally foreboding, he noticed that the cacophonous buzzing of the flies had grown even louder. Amanda pointed at a large clump of brambles.

David stepped forward, his boots squishing ominously in the black muck, until he saw what she was pointing at. There was a body beneath the brambles. He crouched down to get a better look, and recognized the garish yellow hair immediately.

It was Winnifred Blundell. Her pencillike legs protruded gracelessly out from under one side of the bush and her face was turned sideways and was half buried in the black ooze, but the wounds around her neck and chest were clearly visible. He leaned closer to gain a better vantage, and a small cloud of flies rose up as he approached. Her skin was gray and swollen, and he noticed that one of the carrion beetles that now harvested her rotting flesh had become entangled in her yellow hair. She had been dead for quite some time, but what attracted his attention the most was the manner of her death. Although many of the wounds were now obscured by maggots, their odd crescent shape was distinctive and unmistakable.

He straightened when he could take the smell no longer and batted at the flies that now besieged him. His mind was spinning, and for several minutes he just stood, staring at the body and contemplating the implications of the discovery. He did not like the conclusion that he was forced to reach, but the evidence was irrefutable. Something unfathomably rapacious prowled Hovern Bog. In the distant past the inhabitants of the valley had been so fearful of it that they had sacrificed living victims to it in attempts to appease it. It was capable of killing humans and even seemed to do so with relish. But what disturbed him the most was that it was still there. Whatever it was, it, or its descendants, still prowled the bog.

In the background he became aware that Amanda was

rhythmically whacking the jawbone she was carrying against a tree. He turned, intending to lead her away from the horrific sight, when the bone finally captured his attention.

"What is that?" he asked.

"Jussa bone."

"May I see it?"

She looked at him with the same puzzlement with which she seemed to greet all of his remarks and diffidently offered him the ghoulish object. He took it and examined it carefully. As he had previously surmised, it appeared to be the jawbone of a smallish animal, old and bleached white by the sun. What drew his interest, however, were the numerous gouges on its surface, rasplike grooves identical to the teeth marks in the sternum of the bog bodies.

"Where did you get this?" he asked.

"Over there," Amanda replied, and started off to show him. Growing increasingly cognizant of the fact that she knew the bog like the back of her hand, he allowed her to guide him. A short distance from where Winnifred's body lay were numerous other muddy hillocks surrounded by dense vegetation and bounded by the inky rivulets of the bog. The hillocks, he noticed, had a trampled look, and over the entire place there hung a faint but malodorous odor. As he looked at the hills more closely, he realized they were literally covered with bones. Some of the bones were white and appeared to be relatively recent deposits, but as his eyes took in more of the details, he discerned that beneath these there were smaller fragments of bone, discolored and half rotted from exposure to the elements. As he looked closer still, he saw that the very mud itself was largely composed of even smaller bone fragments, blackened and nearly pulverized by wind and time, but evidence of a vast and inconceivable carnage nonetheless.

He also noticed something else. Projecting from various locations on the hillocks were short wooden stakes with pieces of rotting ropes trailing from them. Here and there he also saw snippets of hide and mud-trampled fleece. And suddenly he realized why Old Flory kept sheep.

The place was a feeding ground, and from the look of things its unknown inhabitant had fed there quite a lot. Furthermore, it was apparent that the villagers were well aware that something of voracious appetite lived in their bog. Thankfully, they had apparently de-escalated their sacrifices from human beings to sheep, but he now reasoned that the attitude they conveyed to strangers about the bog had something to do with their fearful and lengthy involvement with the thing.

He turned to Amanda. "Do you know what's responsible for all of this?"

"Why, Ol' Bendy," she replied.

"Who?" he asked again.

"You know, Ol' Bendy," she repeated, not understanding why the term held no meaning for him.

"Do you know what Ol' Bendy looks like?"

She shook her head slowly as her eyes widened with alarm. "Oh, no. If I'd see'd him, he would 'a eaten me."

Growing fearful himself, David asked, "Where's Ol' Bendy now?"

Amanda shrugged her tiny shoulders. "I dunno. He don't come out durin' the day."

Thank God for that, David thought to himself as he looked around nervously. "Come on," he said to the little girl. "We're leaving."

"I'll lead," Amanda offered and once again hastened off.

When they reached the edge of the bog she ran brightly down the hill ahead of him, and by the time David had himself left the thicket he noticed that she had run right into Old Flory.

"Where 'ave you been?" he demanded angrily and jerked her up by her frail little arm. She let out a cry and he cracked her soundly across the face. "Shattup! 'Asn't I told you never to go—" He stopped abruptly when he noticed David approaching. He looked at David coldly. "What were you doin' wi' 'er innair?"

"I saw her run in. I was frightened for her."

Old Flory looked down again at the pale and frightened girl. "Now see! 'Asn't I told you?" He yanked her up again as if she were no more than a little rag doll and pushed her in the direction of the ramshackle cottage. "Now, you get 'ome."

He looked back at David and scowled, searching David's eyes as if to glean some hint of what he might have seen. But before he could say anything else, David spoke. "You'd better get the constable. Winnifred Blundell's body is in there."

"Where?" Old Flory demanded, fear in his eyes.

"*Innair,*" David mocked, tilting his head in the direction of the bog. "Near where you stake out sheep for Ol' Bendy."

Old Flory's eyes widened with surprise, but before he could add any further comment David had strode off. As he walked back toward the camp he turned and saw Old Flory hobbling angrily after Amanda. He reached her and again jerked her up sharply by the arm.

He started yelling at the girl again and David felt a terrible aching in his heart when he realized that he had perhaps made an error in telling Old Flory that he knew about the stakes. He watched angrily, bitterly, as Old Flory continued to drag his helpless daughter all the way back to the house.

* * *

Considering in total the events of the past several days had a strange effect on David. He told Brad about finding Winnifred's body, about the bite marks, and even about the feeding ground, and although the younger man reacted with dismay, his excitement over discovering the two Roman bodies kept him from discerning the gravity with which David viewed the situation. On another occasion, David might have been more conscious of the danger he believed the younger man to be in, would have spent more time stressing the implications of the discovery to him, and even urged him not to pass any more nights in so vulnerable and unprotected a dwelling as a tent. But as it was, the discoveries of the afternoon had left David in an almost trancelike state.

Even Melanie he only told about the discovery of Winnifred's body in the vaguest terms and left out all mention of the bite marks, the feeding ground, or even the bite marks on the two Roman bodies they had unearthed. She naturally pressed him for more information, but this he stalwartly withheld, and he spent the better part of the evening in seclusion. He had only one thought on his mind. His vision of the centaur had been too mercurial and insubstantial for him to pin down and understand. But the creature that roamed the bog was physical and subsisted on living flesh. And this fact brought his driving curiosity forth full force. Regardless of the dangers, he had to discover what it was. He resolved to go into the bog that night to look for it.

He waited until Melanie had gone upstairs to bed and then

he went into the gun room of the cottage. He surveyed the once-dusty cases, now shining brightly from Mrs. Comfrey's skilled hand, and opened one of them.

He detested guns, mainly because his father had counseled him so firmly to like and use them. Because of that he had never even fired one. But as he removed one of the ancient rifles from the gun cabinet, he realized that they were really quite simple in mechanism. It was as he was searching through the various drawers in the cabinets for bullets that Melanie came into the room.

"What are you doing?" she asked, seeing the gun in his hand.

He found a box of bullets and placed them on the table. He also found what appeared to be an array of paraphernalia for cleaning the guns, and decided it would be prudent to do so before attempting to use the aged instrument. He sat down at the table. "Cleaning this gun, why?"

"For God's sake, David, you hate guns."

He kept his eyes trained on the piece of gun batting before him, trying desperately to think of some sort of excuse. "I'm just going for a walk," he blurted out feebly.

"And taking a gun?"

"Well, given what happened to Winnifred Blundell, it seemed like a good idea."

"Oh, come on, David," she said. "I'm not a child." And then she looked at him, her eyes growing suddenly wider. "There's more to it than that, isn't there? Something happened today that you're not telling me?"

David sighed and realized that it was useless to keep up the ruse any longer. Taking a deep breath, he told her everything. When he finished, Melanie collapsed into a chair opposite him.

For several minutes she said nothing and just stared absently off into space as she processed the information. And then she turned to him, pale with fear. "David, what in God's name do you think it is?"

"I'm sure it's just some animal of some sort."

"No, it's not just some animal," she muttered darkly.

"Oh, Melanie," David chastised as he stood and proceeded to load the gun.

She reached over and clenched his arm. "But what about the centaur!"

The comment hit a nerve in him and he pulled sharply away.

"What about the centaur?" he snapped, more rhetorically than wanting an answer.

"Don't you think it has something to do with this thing?"

"Don't be ridiculous. How could it?"

"I don't know. I just think it does."

He went over to one of the drawers and took out a flashlight. He flicked it on and off several times, making sure it worked, and then started for the door. But before he reached it Melanie caught up with him and grabbed him beseechingly by the arms.

"David, please don't go. It's not just an animal. I know it's not. It's something beyond us. It's something unearthly and evil and far more dangerous than I think we've begun to suspect."

He looked down into her eyes and was galvanized by the depth of the terror he saw in them. He too felt a growing and irrational fear about whatever it was that was out there; and a small part of him had even begun to suspect that what she was saying was true—that was part of the reason he was so driven to seek some resolution to the matter. But no matter what he thought awaited him, his obsession to know had been aroused. He had to understand what he was up against, whatever the cost; for the alternative, to drift, awash in a murky sea of questions and ignorance, was a fate far more intolerable.

He frowned, his face full of pain. "I'm sorry, Mel." And then he left.

Outside, the night was clear and the moon was bright over the lawn. The air was muggy with the grassy smell of the advancing summer, and the crickets, the katydids, and the occasional and mournful call of a whippoorwill added a deceptively lulling cadence to things. He walked out into the lane. As he passed the thicket where he had first experienced the strange pain in his jaw, he glanced at it nervously and again wondered why he had experienced the same enigmatic pain both in Grenville's house and when he later saw the centaur.

As he neared the moors he remembered Amanda's assertion that Ol' Bendy only came out at night, and he found himself looking over his shoulder and glancing uneasily at the extended shadow of every grassy sedge. At the bend in the road where he normally turned left, he turned right instead. He did not want to circle around the part of the bog where their camp was and risk frightening Brad. And besides, he had another destination in mind.

He walked on for another twenty minutes, and when the great wall of the bog finally rose up on one side of the road he found himself steering as far to the opposite side of the lane as possible. To his left he spotted Old Flory's cottage, with its windows gleaming jack-o'-lantern yellow in the distance, and next to the cottage the ghostly outline of the sheep in their dilapidated pen.

As he paused before an outbreak of thorn apple he saw a truant swallow fold its long narrow wings and drop into the darkness. He looked back in the direction of the lane. He knew that he had to keep his wits about him now and push his memory to its limit. He cocked his gun and entered the bog.

The first several dozen feet he negotiated without difficulty, carefully recalling every twist and turn that he had seen Amanda take earlier that day. But then he ran into trouble. Because of the density of the vegetation, far less moonlight trickled down in the bog than out on the moors, and it was difficult to see various landmarks, let alone place them on the mental map of the maze that he had formed in his mind. He also did not want to use the flashlight, for he knew that its beacon could be seen far off through the bog and he did not want to prematurely alert the creature to his coming. After a moment of deep concentration he deciphered where he was and pressed on.

Not surprisingly, at night the bog revealed yet another side of its ever-changing nature. The buzzing of the flies was now replaced by crickets, the distant croaking of frogs, and every once in a while, the plaintive hoot of a screech owl. Instead of the fly agaric he made out the phosphorescent gleam of armillaria fungi winking on and off like greenish yellow embers along the ridges of dead twigs and bits of bark among the oak litter. Clouds of midges and tiny moths batted around him and occasionally, as he passed, the damp air was loaded with other exhalations, the rustlings and slitherings of other nocturnal denizens of the bog as they moved heedfully out of his way.

Once, when he was about to step on what he thought was solid ground, at the very last moment he noticed a solitary lily growing impropitiously a few feet away. Mindfully, he pushed the area with a stick, and was horrified to see it vanish into oblivion as it was quickly covered over by black water. On another occasion he walked full into one of the webs of the filmy dome spiders and found himself momentarily gripped by a silly and almost primal fear of the thing. Still he pressed on.

As he neared his destination he slowed so as not to broadcast his arrival, and finally he detected the faint but acrid stench of the feeding grounds. He assumed that the villagers had taken away Winnifred Blundell's body, and that the smell was coming from the other profuse remains in the area. At last he saw the muddy clearing in the moonlight, and he froze in silence when he became aware of another sound in the night.

It was the bleating of a lamb. He crouched down behind a short clump of blackthorn and peered through the thicket. In the clearing ahead and illuminated by a shaft of moonlight, he saw the poor creature staked out like its predecessors on one of the muddy hillocks. However, there was no sign of its unknown adversary. Given that the thing now seemed accustomed to feeding on sheep, he reasoned that the bleating would attract it before long. He settled in to wait.

He had been there for well over an hour, and to his dismay had found the incessant bleating of the lamb on the verge of lulling him to sleep, when at last he heard something coming. He slowed his breathing and suddenly wondered fearfully how keen the creature's hearing was, or whether it would smell him, but he then dismissed the fear. He knew that the question would be answered before long.

Whatever it was, at least it did not slither, for he could clearly make out the sound of slow and ponderous footsteps. However, he could not tell whether it walked on two feet or four. In the distance a sapling snapped as the creature made its way toward the clearing. Then, to his amazement, he suddenly felt the familiar amorphous pain buzzing into wakefulness in his teeth and jaws. He squinted in the dim light, keeping his eyes trained in the direction of the approaching footsteps. The lamb also detected the intruder's presence, and its bleating became even more desperate and frantic as it pulled madly at its tether.

David could hear the squishing of the creature's footsteps as it entered the clearing, but he still could not see it. Suddenly the lamb ran out of his vision as it apparently tried one last time to evade its attacker, but it was of no use. He heard it give a piteous squeal as the thing apparently cornered it. The lamb continued to squeal agonizingly as the night was rent by a snap of bone and then the slow and measured sound of mastication. Still, the lamb bleated heartrendingly as David could hear its flesh ripping and the almost lazy munching continuing.

Able to stand it no longer, he crept forward, and there, in the moonlit stillness, he finally saw what he assumed to be Ol' Bendy.

At first glance the creature was humanoid, but some seven or eight feet in height. It was also naked, and like the centaur, possessed an awesomely powerful musculature, but with the same sagging look of moribundity and decay. Unlike the centaur, it did not glow or give off any luminescence of its own, but was instead a cadaverous and stony gray, and possessed the mottled and bumpy look of a toad, or an ancient and battle-scarred lizard. From its massive and sagging sexual organs, strangely human in design, it was clear that it was male.

Its most anomalous feature, however, was its head, which was immense and oddly misshapened, as if a square pillowcase had been filled with concrete and allowed to harden. In the middle of the flat and almost featureless expanse of its face were two large and sulfur-yellow eyes with shiny vertical pupils that were occasionally eclipsed by reptilian and semitransparent nictitating membranes. Its ears were massive and pointed like a bat's. For a nose it possessed only two vertical slits in which grew small fleshy protuberances that fluttered in and out as it breathed, and its incongruously tiny mouth was human and almost disconcertingly feminine.

As it ate the still-writhing lamb, for the first time David discerned how it made those peculiar lacerations. Completely lining its tiny round mouth was a perfect circle of small, razor-sharp teeth. These teeth, it seemed, were capable of independent movement and rasped in and out as it munched, almost like the mouth of a sea urchin, or a snail as it rasps away algae from the side of a fish tank. In time the lamb that it suckled went limp, and when this happened the creature held the small dead thing high above its head and literally wrung it out, hungrily drinking the remaining blood that drizzled from its body, almost as one might hold a wine skin above one's head and squeeze it to drink its contents. When it did this, David noticed that its hands were humanoid but, like the centaur, its fore and middle fingers were peculiarly extended.

Finally it tossed the carcass aside and belched heartily. And then, squatting slightly, it evacuated its bowels. As David watched the disgusting and fantastic spectacle, he realized that part of the stench of the place was due to the fact that the creature had apparently repeated this function often on the muddy hillocks. Indeed, with growing repulsion, he looked down and saw that the very ground he knelt on showed traces of well-trampled excrement. He also noticed something else. Illuminated faintly in the moonlight he saw gobs of hair mixed with the excrement, only it wasn't white, like fleece, it was shorter and darker. With growing horror he thought that he recognized the hair, but in the feeble light he could not be sure. Swept with uncontrollable loathing and curiosity, he shielded the flashlight with his body and held it just a fraction of an inch above the ground. And then he clicked it on. In the small circle of light he saw what he had so feared. He had seen the hair before. It was Ben's.

At the same instant that he had clicked the flashlight on the creature apparently had heard the sound and turned around. Fearing discovery if he clicked the light off again, David lowered the lens of the flashlight into the mud to ensure that none of its light escaped. And then he returned his attention to the creature. Whatever the thing was, the click of the flashlight had clearly alarmed it. It pricked its massive and pointed ears and listened carefully. David held his breath and tried to maintain himself in as motionless a state as possible. As he kept his terrified pose he saw the thing lift its huge and ferocious head and then, almost like a deer or other wild animal trying to catch the scent of an intruder, it sniffed the air carefully, the fleshy protuberances in its breathing slits fluttering in and out. And then, to his astonishment, it smiled as it seemed to pick up his scent. It turned in his direction and started to advance.

For a moment he was frozen in terror, unable to believe that the thing was real. The centaur at least had been more phantasmagoric, and seemed more tenuous and ephemeral. But as the creature before him advanced, he could see the dull solidity of its flesh, hear the labor of its breathing, and see the striations of its pupils change as it struggled to discern more details in the darkness.

Its feet squelched loudly in the mud as it continued to plod forward. Soon it would be upon him.

He stood up quickly and, bracing the butt of the rifle against his shoulder, he pulled the trigger. The hammer clicked, but it did not fire.

The creature gurgled in a way that might almost have been construed as amusement.

In a panic, David quickly cocked the gun again and pulled the trigger one more time. Still it clicked uselessly. Not knowing what else to do, he quickly lifted the flashlight up and turned the beam into the creature's saucer-size eyes. Its pupils narrowed instantly as it squealed and raised one of its massive arms to shield itself from the light. But before David could do anything else, with its free arm it reached out and knocked the flashlight from him with a force that made his hand ache as if it had been struck by a two-by-four. By now the thing was so close to him that he could smell the cold decay of its breath, and he realized that whatever the thing was, in spite of its decomposed appearance, its strength was preternatural. His jaw and his teeth throbbed as if they were going to explode.

Still holding the rifle, he turned and ran.

The thing broke into hot pursuit behind him and he could hear it crashing loudly through the underbrush as it tried desperately to catch up with him. In some distant part of his mind a voice cautioned him about the dangers of the bog, and he attempted as best he could to retrace his path out, but in his own blind panic he devoted most of his attention to simply running as hard and as fast as his legs would support.

Because he had been on the opposite side of the blackthorn bush he had gotten a lead of perhaps fifteen to twenty feet on the creature, and because of the creature's greater size and hence reduced maneuverability through the dense vegetation, he was able to maintain a certain measure of that lead, but he knew it was a losing battle. Suddenly one of his feet struck the matted and tangled edge of a sink, and with no other option he hurled himself forward, leaping over the open area and hoping that he would come down on solid ground on the other side. To his great relief he did, and he glanced briefly behind him only to see that the thing was taking advantage of his momentary pause to quickly close what slight distance still separated them. He ran on, his heart pounding, when he suddenly heard a great crash behind him. He turned, and to his momentary relief saw that the creature had itself blundered into the sink. He stopped and watched as it flailed around and snarled ferociously, but only succeeded in further entrenching itself in the mire. It snorted once or twice, desperately trying to clear its breathing slits, and then vanished beneath the dark surface.

At first he felt a great wave of relief pass over him, but he immediately cautioned himself not to be so quick in claiming victory. Instead, he fumbled with the gun, opening it up and rattling the rifle cartridge in its barrel to make sure that it was properly in place. In the sink something stirred.

He closed the rifle, cocked it, and pointed it over his head. He pulled the trigger, and to his delight a shot rang out and a flurry of small creatures rustled in the night. He quickly discarded the empty cartridge and loaded the rifle again. It was none too soon. In the sink a terrible foment started to bubble forth, and suddenly the creature came crashing up through the surface like a great whale leaping out of the ocean, as it snorted and sent large clots of peat and strings of mucus streaming out of its breathing slits.

As it continued to shake its massive head, loosening what peat that remained, David cocked the gun again and aimed it squarely at the creature. It struggled to look at him, its nictitating membranes slowly clearing the last bit of the black ooze from its eyes. Then it realized what he was up to and emitted a hideous snarl. It lunged forward. David prayed the gun would work, and pulled the trigger.

The thing let out one last menacing and furious scream as a second retort echoed through the night and a large chunk of the creature's torso was blown to bits. Ghastly gray and white viscera dangled from the wound as the creature's head lolled to one side and it stumbled backward. But before David could savor any sense that he had won out over the thing he realized that something strange was happening. At first it sounded like the buzzing of an angry horde of bees, but as he squinted into the darkness he realized that the pieces of flesh and severed bone that the rifle shot had scattered over the ground were now waking into a strange new state of life.

Like the armillaria fungi he had seen earlier, they glowed a dim but phosphorescent white as they rattled and moved across the ground and the remaining hulk of the thing seemingly effervesced into a cloud of glowing, blue-white mist. Then, with the same strange buzzing, as of a thousand furious hornets spurred into action, the entire mass coalesced and went whipping through the forest like an angry ghost. A terrible wind enveloped him as the glowing mist continued to move at lightning speed, occasionally enwrapping trees and nearly snapping them with the force of its passing, until, like a heavy stream of sand, it all hit the earth in one spot and congealed into a larval mass. As he continued to watch breathlessly, the mass pulsated and a splay of veins suddenly snaked through its surface. Vestigial organs coalesced in its luminous depths, and then the features of the thing that had chased him started to sculpt themselves once again in the waxlike mass.

The conclusion was inescapable that somehow the creature was repairing and reconstituting itself. And at the rate it was going he realized that it would not be long before it completed the task.

He turned and once again broke into a run. He moved as quickly as good sense told him was possible, and he had scarcely reached the edge of the bog when he heard an enraged howl echo behind and around him. He realized that the thing was once again whole.

Another furious blast of wind moved past him as if it were some advance guard of the force now pursuing him, and he ran out into the moonlit lane. As he looked around he realized that he had exited the bog from quite a different point than he had entered and in the distance, across the purpled moors, he saw the silhouette of the church. A light glowed dimly in one of its windows and he ran toward it. He did not have time to reflect deeply upon his actions, but he hoped, prayed, that this house of God might provide him some sanctuary from the thing that now stalked him.

As he tore across the moors he heard the creature howl once again and he realized the sound was frighteningly close. It would not be long before it reached the road.

He ran up to the church and pounded frantically on the door.

It seemed like an eternity before he heard footsteps inside, and finally the door opened. The vicar looked first surprised and then apprehensive when he saw the gun in David's hand.

"What is it?" he asked worriedly.

"Please!" David shouted, pushing past him and entering the church. The vicar shut the door behind him.

"Lock it!" David commanded and the vicar's eyes grew wider still at the desperate tone of his injunction. "It's after me!" he explained.

"Dear God!" the vicar cried. He looked at the door as if to double-check the fact that he had bolted it, and then scanned the windows. David also looked at the windows and saw that these at least were too narrow to allow the thing through.

The vicar opened a small peephole in one of the doors and peered out. "Dear God!" he repeated. "It's coming." He slammed the peephole and looked madly about.

David cocked the rifle.

"That will do no good," the vicar warned.

It had been a reflexive action on David's part. He was well aware that the rifle was ineffective against the thing. "What will do us any good?" he demanded.

"Nothing that I know of," the vicar returned in a terrified voice.

"What is it?" David asked finally.

The vicar collapsed before the altar. The creature howled again, this time even closer.

"*What is it?*" David repeated, grabbing the older man by the shoulders and turning him around.

The vicar looked up at him, his eyes filled with torment. "It's a demon, Mr. Macauley. Something my profession pretends to know about, but doesn't know at all. And something your profession is aware of even less. It is older than the bog itself, and it is pure evil. And beyond that there is not much else that I know."

David looked back in the direction of the howling and seconds later the thing hit the door with the force of a charging bull. The old wood warped and buckled inward.

"But this is a church!" David argued, his heart beating so violently that he thought his chest would explode. "It can't come in here!"

The vicar shook his head despairingly. "It can and will. There is no force we have ever discovered that is effective against it. Even the power of the Lord seems futile."

David had never been a religious man, but it seemed to him that if demons existed they were somehow in the province of the metaphysical. The thing hit the door again, and still having no success, started to circle the church. As it moved David noticed that the pain in his jaw also moved, providing a lodestone of its location. He noticed that the vicar was also stroking his jaw.

"The pain," he said. "What's causing it?"

"It is," the vicar returned. "One always feels the pain of its presence. I don't know why."

The demon bashed against one of the narrow windows and shards of glass went flying through the church. Unable to contain himself any longer, the vicar started to cry, and through his blubber he began to slowly sing a hymn.

The demon shattered another window, still snarling hideously, as a fetid and unearthly wind tore through the church.

"Oh, Holy Father, source of mercy," the vicar sang feebly. "Watching o'er us from above."

The demon roared again, and from the pain in their jaws it appeared that it was making a second run toward the door. It struck the wood and this time a splinter appeared.

David thought of his wife and his children and realized that he was about to die.

"Forgive us all our earthly sins."

The demon crashed against the door again and a piece of it broke free, allowing the terrible wind to enter.

David thought of all the things he had wanted to do before he died as he stepped backward and huddled next to the vicar.

"And fill us with the Savior's love."

The demon crashed against the door one last time and the bolt snapped. The door went crashing aside and such a torrent of wind and debris swept through that David thought he was going to be knocked off his feet. He struggled to remain standing as he squinted into the onslaught. A strange cold filled him as he made out the outline of the thing, the massive and rotting muscles, the predatorily sentient eyes.

"Hallelujah, hallelujah," the vicar croaked valiantly. "Every tongue sing hallelujah." And the moment he uttered the words, the wind stopped and the pupils of the demon narrowed as if it were actually frightened by the proclamation.

The vicar stopped singing abruptly, speechless at the sudden calm, and the wind started once again to rustle around them.

"The hymn!" David ordered. "Don't stop."

"But I don't understand. It's not supposed to have any effect."

The thing started forward once again.

"Just sing!" David shrilled.

"Oh, Holy Father, Lord of Glory," the vicar continued, but the words no longer seemed to have any power over the beast.

David's mind raced as he quickly arrived at a different conclusion. "The word, then!" he shouted, and the vicar looked at him, bewildered.

"Hallelujah!" he screamed, and once again the demon shrank back. "Hallelujah," he repeated and the demon continued to recoil, looking at him with what seemed to be fear.

The vicar soon joined in and both men started to shout in unison. "Hallelujah! Hallelujah! Hallelujah!"

The terror that had only moments before been theirs now gripped the impossible creature before them and it turned, went out of the church, and started down the hill. Rejuvenated by their newfound power, they ran after it. "Hallelujah! Hallelujah! Hallelujah!" they cried as the thing turned tail and lumbered all the way back to the bog.

8

After the creature left, the vicar once again became unyield-ingly reticent about it. David quickly sensed that it was more than just casual reluctance or some sort of misplaced feeling of shame or guilt that kept him from talking about the thing. It was a bond of fear that kept him from discussing it, the same bond of fear that he now realized gripped all of the inhabit-ants of the valley. He did not know if it was superstition, or a terrible pact they had made, or something even more sinister, but it was clear that they were sent into a blind panic if they even so much as mentioned Ol' Bendy to an outsider. The only fragment of information he was able to extract was that none of them believed anything religious would have power over the creature, that this feeling had apparently been handed down to them since time immemorial, and that no one was more astonished than the vicar that the world *hallelujah* had seemed anathema to the demon. In the end, David was forced to leave the church and make his way home knowing little more from the vicar than he did from what he himself had witnessed.

A part of his pragmatic nature still tried to understand the thing as a new type of life form, something zoological, but in the end he knew that this was an untenable position. He had never been a religious man, and he had no idea what the word *demon* even meant, but he realized that he could no longer allow himself to flounder in incredulity and confusion. He still had no real idea what he was up against, but it was obvious from his encounter with the creature that he had to be prepared for anything, that he was entering a world that was perhaps far beyond his understanding, and that he had no way of predicting its ultimate dangers or ramifications. All he knew was that something inside him had surrendered itself, had stepped over into the acceptance of that world, and although it stirred within him a deep foreboding, frightened him more than anything in his life had ever frightened him before, it also left him dazzled. For him it represented the edge of the universe, the very boundary of human understanding, and nothing, not even the discovery of the two Roman bodies, now intrigued him more. He knew that now more than ever he had to penetrate the secret of the matter, unravel every last thread of the mystery that hung over the valley, or for the rest of his life he would be haunted by it.

When he arrived home he found Melanie waiting up for him, and although he knew it would be difficult to persuade her of the reality of what he had seen, he felt he had no recourse but to tell her. After he had finished he was surprised to see that she accepted it all without question. She looked up at him tormentedly.

"David, what are we going to do?"

"We're going to pack up and get the kids out of here," he said.

She greeted his remark with tremendous relief. "Oh, thank God. Where are we going to go?"

"Back to Oxford. I'll call friends tomorrow and try to make arrangements for you to stay with them."

She drew back quickly. "What do you mean *us* stay with them?"

He drew in his breath, knowing that she was not going to like what he had to say next. "Melanie, I'm not going to leave yet. I've got my work to finish, and besides . . ." His voice trailed off.

"Besides what?"

He sighed and looked in his wife's eyes searchingly. "Melanie, I know you're not going to like this, but I just can't leave without knowing what makes this thing tick. Whatever's going on here is quite extraordinary. Why, the scientific implications alone are enormous. I couldn't call myself a scientist if I just picked up and left without getting to the bottom of the thing."

"Bottom of the thing?" she repeated scornfully. "I'll tell you what's at the bottom of the thing. It's evil, pure unadulterated evil!"

"Melanie, don't be absurd."

"I'm not being absurd. I've sensed it ever since we came to this place. Don't you realize that there are some things that are not meant to be studied, some things that are better left alone?"

He hated that attitude. He hated bans on certain areas of knowledge. It reminded him too painfully of his father, who thought that most things were not worth a person's interest or study. His own temper rose. "Melanie, you really don't understand me very well if you think there's any possibility of me pulling up and leaving this valley now."

This seemed to fluster Melanie more than anything and she turned to him, her face growing red. "And you don't understand me very well to be so against my going back to college to finish my dissertation!"

He looked at her in confusion. "What?"

"You heard me," she said wearily.

"When have I ever said that I didn't want you finishing your dissertation?"

"You don't have to say it. It's true, isn't it?"

"I guess so," he admitted.

"Well, why? Why are you so against it?"

He continued to brood about the matter. He did not really know. "I guess I just don't want anything rocking the boat. Things seem to be going along fine as they are and I'm afraid . . . well, I'm afraid of ruining it."

"Well things aren't going fine for me," she blurted out.

He looked at her with surprise.

"Oh, I love you, David. And I love what we've built together, but I need more. I've only just realized it, but I'm afraid if I don't start using my mind more, start doing some of the things that I want to do, I'm going to wither and die."

This pained him to hear. He had had no idea that Melanie felt this way, and the last thing he wanted was to be party to her unhappiness. After mulling everything over for a moment he said, "Then I think we should make a deal. I think you must understand that I have to stay here. You must understand what I have to do for myself, and in return I will understand what you must do for yourself."

Melanie seemed to soften.

David's own expression grew somber. "Melanie?"

"Yes, David?"

"You're not going to leave me, are you?"

"Oh, no, David," she said rushing into his arms. "I love you too much to ever do that."

It was only later, as they readied themselves for bed, that she felt a terrible darkness when she realized that somehow in the deal she had agreed to her husband's staying in the valley.

* * *

The first thing the next morning, Melanie started to pack, and as soon as Mrs. Comfrey saw what she was doing she became very agitated. David told her that she had no need to worry about losing her position, for he intended to keep her on. But apparently she had become very attached to the children and did not find this concession much consolation. He did not tell her about the thing in the bog. He saw no reason to unduly alarm her, even in the remote chance that she would have believed him. Neither did he tell the children.

It was as he walked through the house to retrieve one of Melanie's suitcases that he again noticed the unmistakable smell of something foul. He wandered through all of the rooms on the first floor and still found nothing. A few minutes later Melanie came in to help him with a box, and after they had paused to tape it shut they heard a knock on the door. At first Melanie looked alarmed, but David reminded her of Amanda's observation that Ol' Bendy only came out at night. He opened the door and to his surprise saw Grenville's chauffeur standing beyond. Grenville's Rolls-Royce also sat in the driveway, but David saw that there was no one in it. The chauffeur had come alone.

"Yes?" David asked, disconcerted.

"Excuse me, sir," the chauffeur said politely, "but the Marquis wondered if he could have a brief word with you."

"Well, as you can see we're a bit busy right now," David returned. "Could it be later this afternoon, or possibly tomorrow?"

"I'm afraid it's a matter of the utmost urgency, sir."

This piqued David slightly. He did not like command

appearances. "I don't know," he said, irritated, and was about to add his further thoughts on the matter when the chauffeur cut him off.

"It is in regards to your encounter last night with the creature you might have heard the villagers refer to as Ol' Bendy."

Melanie looked at David sharply, but his curiosity had been aroused. "I'll get my jacket," he said. But before he could walk away, the chauffeur added another bit of news.

"He would like Mrs. Macauley to come also. He would like to have a small conversation with both of you."

David looked at Melanie and saw that his wife was apprehensive about the entire matter. She also looked down worriedly at her casual dress.

The chauffeur anticipated them once again. "The Marquis understands that at such short notice proper formalities cannot be attended to. He apologizes for the profound inconvenience of this request and promises that you will find the meeting most enlightening."

David and Melanie looked at each other perplexedly as Melanie removed the bandanna she was wearing and shook her hair loose. Together they went out the front door as the chauffeur strode ahead of them and opened the door of the Rolls.

When they arrived at Wythen Hall they were immediately ushered into the massive drawing room *qua* menagerie. They found Grenville sitting in a gigantic thronclike chair of elaborately carved bog oak beside the now-dead fireplace. He wore a deep-purple velvet smoking jacket and gold brocade slippers. The various tropical birds twittered nervously as they entered, and the monkey with the blood-red eyes watched them silently from his golden pagoda.

Grenville stood graciously to greet them. "Come in, come in. I'm so glad you have obliged me yet again in one of my requests. Won't you please have a seat. Would you like a drink?"

Both of them stiffened, recalling the last time they had had a drink in Grenville's house. "No thank you," David said, and Melanie also shook her head in the negative.

"But, of course not," Grenville said, his eyes flashing but not revealing whether he understood why they had declined or not. "It's too early in the day for you." He motioned for them to sit on one of the sofas near him.

"What is this all about?" David asked, sitting down.

Grenville smiled. "It's simply that I've heard you've had an encounter with the creature the villagers quaintly call Ol' Bendy, and I thought that you might have a few questions about it."

David assumed that the vicar must have called and informed Grenville of the incident, and he marveled at the communications network the older man had in the valley. "Yes, I do have a few questions about it," he replied. "The first one is what do you know about the creature?"

"Quite a bit, I daresay," Grenville returned.

David's eyebrows raised. "All right, I'll bite. For starters, what is it?"

"It's a demon," Grenville returned as he absentmindedly picked a bit of lint off of the sleeve of his smoking jacket.

Under normal circumstances David would not have dignified such a remark with further question, but after his experiences of the night before he was prepared for anything.

"And how do you define *demon*?" he asked cautiously.

"A creature of the night, an inhabitant of the underworld," Grenville returned.

"You mean hell?"

Grenville pursed his brow. "I so dislike that term. It carries with it so many misleading mythic connotations. Let us just say that demons inhabit another region of reality, a vibration that is normally not available to the human senses."

David became increasingly uneasy. "How do you know all of this?"

Grenville frowned. "Know what? You mean, know that the creature is a demon?" He paused as a look halfway between a smile and something darker crept into his face. "Because it's my demon."

David grew confused.

Grenville stood. "Perhaps things would be easier if I showed you. Won't you follow me?"

David and Melanie exchanged anxious glances, but stood and followed.

They passed through a large set of Amboina wood doors and into an adjacent parlor. Inside, the room was almost totally dark, but from what dim light there was coming from the open doorway, David could see that it had been converted into a makeshift bedroom. Huge and funereal velvet curtains had been

176

drawn across the windows and kept out all encroaching sunlight, and in the middle of the room, placed haphazardly amidst the pushed-aside furniture, was a large four-poster bed completely draped in gauze.

As they entered, David noticed something else about the room. In addition to being dark, it was hot and stifling, and had the humid and sour smell of a sickroom.

Grenville lifted a candelabrum from a table in the drawing room and strolled forward into the darkness. Hesitantly, David and Melanie followed. As they approached the bed, David became aware of movement within the gauzy enclosure. And as they drew closer still, he could hear the raspy exhalations of troubled breathing. Melanie clenched his arm as Grenville thrust the candelabrum aloft and motioned for them to step up to the very perimeter of the bed. Then, glancing at them briefly, he drew back the bed-curtains.

Melanie gasped and David clasped his own hand over hers when they saw what lay beyond. Lying half naked in the bed was Julia. Her eyes were closed and she was drenched in sweat. But the most striking aspect of her feature, what captured their attention immediately, was the gaping wound in her chest and shoulder. A massive chunk of her torso was missing and clearly visible was half an eviscerated lung and a dangling section of esophagus. Still, remarkably, she was alive. What remained of her breast rose and fell, and the shredded fragments of her windpipe fluttered as she breathed, but David failed to comprehend how anything biological could survive the wounds that she had apparently sustained. Equally astonishing as the fact that she was alive was the color of her internal organs. Unlike human viscera, they were a nacreous and cadaverous gray, and the veins that entwined them a darker and more leaden color still. Most incredible of all was her black heart, which protruded prominently from the bloody splay of her abdomen, and it too pumped and quivered like some creature from the deep stranded on land by a storm.

At first David did not connect Julia's wound with the creature he had seen in the bog, but as he continued to stare at her, it slowly dawned on him that the bloody cavity was exactly the same as the gunshot wound he had delivered to Ol' Bendy the night before. He looked at Grenville incredulously.

Grenville returned his stare. "She's going to be quite

angry with you once she's up and around again."

David blinked. "You mean Julia is the creature?"

"One and the same."

"But how?"

Grenville smiled. "Certainly in your encounter last night you gleaned some hint of the fact that Ol' Bendy possesses somewhat remarkable powers of transformation."

David still could not believe his eyes. He looked down once more at the reclining form in the bed, at the remaining breast and the distinctly feminine figure. "But the creature I shot was male!"

"Strictly speaking, Julia is a male spirit, but you must understand, she can assume virtually any form that she wants. In addition, her appetites are rather wide ranging, so it becomes somewhat meaningless to speak of her as possessing gender."

At this last remark David noticed that Melanie went completely white, but he assumed that she was merely reacting to the extraordinariness of what they were witnessing. Still searching madly for some flaw in what he was being told, he said: "But the creature reconstituted itself after I shot it. When it chased me to the church the wound had already healed."

"It was a temporary measure on Julia's part. She was furious with you, and just as humans display more than normal abilities in times of trauma, Julia was able to affect some semblance of her normal self. But it will take her a couple of days to recover completely."

At the very moment Grenville finished saying this, a tremor passed through Julia as she was apparently wracked by an unseen pain, and arching her back like a woman in labor, she let out a wail. As she did this a cloud of acrid and sour air flooded forth from the bed, and at the same time the enigmatic pain that he had first experienced in the thicket shot through David's jaw. He looked at Grenville questioningly.

True to form, Grenville perceived what was puzzling him instantly. "You must forgive her. Most of the time she can suppress the painful effect she has upon people."

"Why does she have that effect?" David asked, still stroking his jaw tenderly.

"Julia is no normal physical entity. You see, under normal circumstances she does not belong on this plane of existence. But because she's here, quite literally she has a foot in two worlds, and when you feel the pain in your jaw you are feeling the tug of her realm. You are feeling the dissonance of the two worlds coming together, a sort of static."

David was about to ask another question when suddenly Julia's head lolled to one side and it looked as if she were about to regain consciousness. Her eyes opened and rolled about in her head as her lids fluttered. And then her eyes stopped rolling as her gaze fastened on David and recognition came.

"You!" she hissed, rising up like a serpent about to strike, and shot a long and pitchy tongue at him accompanied by a ferocious snarl. Drawing on some unearthly reservoir of power she lunged at him, but Grenville stepped quickly between them. She looked at him, infuriated.

"*Ip bur ib du ni!*" she cried.

"*Ish ma na ni ia ip!*" Grenville shot back as he glowered at her. For a moment she hesitated, still challenging his authority, but then she fell back into the bed and lapsed once more into her feverish delirium.

Grenville turned to David once again. "She really is very peeved with you."

Noticing not at all the immensity of Grenville's understatement, David focused his attention instead on the unknown language that Grenville had just used to address Julia. It sounded to him vaguely Phoenician, although he knew enough of that ancient tongue to know that it was not.

"What language was that?" he asked.

"Its name would mean nothing to you," Grenville returned. "You would not know it."

"It's not Celtic," David countered.

"No, it's not," Grenville replied and seemed unwilling to comment any further on the matter.

Another tremor wracked Julia and Grenville allowed the bed-curtains to flutter shut.

"I think it is time we return to the drawing room," he said, holding the candelabrum aloft and motioning for them to follow him. He closed the parlor doors as they once again took their seats on the sofa.

"So why are you telling us all of this?" David asked as Grenville sat back down in his chair of bog oak.

"Well, you see, Julia has been in the trust of the de L'Isle family for quite some time, many centuries, in fact." Grenville paused as if to allow the ramifications of what he was saying to fully sink in.

"So she *is* responsible for the deaths of the bodies we've unearthed in the bog," David filled in as he glanced at the portrait of one of Grenville's ancestors over the fireplace and noted once more the mysterious veil that was draped across its face.

Grenville nodded. "Indeed, but more important is the fact that it has long been the duty of the de L'Isle family to watch over Julia, to protect her, and in this regard it is most imperative that her existence remain a complete secret. You see, we have learned to control her and understand her ways, but if news of her existence went beyond this valley, and curiosity seekers started to rain down upon us, heaven only knows what the consequences would be."

"So what do you want out of us?" David asked.

"I would like to make you an offer. I would like to propose that you and your family stay in the hunter's cottage and you continue with your work, but with the promise that you will say nothing of the events of these past several days to anyone, not even your assistant. And in return I will promise you that I will keep Julia away from you and not allow her to harm you or your family in any way."

David's hackles began to raise. "But Julia is a murderer!"

"You mean the bodies in the bog? But that was centuries ago. As you have seen for yourself, we now keep Julia restricted to sheep. Surely you cannot call that murder."

"What about Winnifred Blundell?"

"That was an accident."

"But I thought you said you could control Julia?"

A hint of rancor flashed in Grenville's eyes, but he remained calm. "True, but that was the first such accident in over a hundred years and it was due to an oversight on my part. It will not happen again."

David remained unappeased. "And what if we don't agree to your demands? What if, as a scientist, I cannot simply forget what I have seen and heard in the past several days, and I decide that I have no recourse but to tell the world about Julia's existence?"

Melanie clenched his knee as she sensed that this had somehow been a dangerous remark to make.

Grenville made a church with his rubied fingers. "Then I would be forced to allow Julia to do with you what she will," he said placidly.

This caused David to completely lose his temper. "How dare you threaten me in this manner!" he said, standing. "Who do you think you are to presume that just because you are the local gentry you have absolute powers of censorship over anything that happens in this valley?"

Following David's outburst Grenville just continued to stare at him, offering no hint of what he was thinking.

David continued to pace angrily. "And where did this creature come from, anyway? And how is it that you are able to control it whereas others cannot?"

He looked again at the veiled portrait hanging over the fireplace and on impulse he charged over and snatched the drapery away from the canvas. As he did so, Melanie gasped, and he himself stood back and stared mutely at the countenance himself. For the face, the visage done in a style from over a century before, was not of Grenville's facially deformed ancestor as he had said, but was none other than Grenville himself.

Grenville stared at David icily. "I do wish you hadn't done that."

He continued to gaze at them silently for several moments and then he stood. "But now that you have, you certainly deserve to see the others." He strode briskly in the direction of the dining room. He turned and cast them another sharp glance. "Come along. Come and see, if you are so curious."

With growing trepidation, they followed. Once in the dining room, Grenville moved from portrait to portrait, removing the little curtain from each, and each was in turn revealed to be another yet more ancient likeness of himself. As the paintings increased in apparent antiquity, his clothing style changed, and the manner of the brushstroke altered according to the fashion and sophistication of the times, but in each, the face, hair, and eyes were undeniably his. Even the ruby ring had been recorded, and the Malacca cane that David had seen him carrying at their first meeting.

David rushed forward to examine the crackle in the varnish.

"They are not fakes," Grenville informed him. "They are all of me."

"I don't understand," David said.

"It's really quite simple," Grenville returned. "You see, there is no de L'Isle family line. I am the only one. I'm as old as Julia is. It was I who first conjured her up."

David's understanding of the world was once again assaulted, but this time the mental siege that followed was short-lived. With Grenville's last revelation he laid down what remaining vestiges of skepticism he possessed and stood ready to face whatever lay ahead.

"What are you?" he asked.

Grenville's eyes narrowed as he at last seemed relieved in being able to reveal his true colors. "In colloquial terms you might say that I'm a sorcerer."

"How old are you?"

"My precise age is not important, but I am very old, certainly as old as the bodies you are digging out of the bog."

With this final surrender to the strangeness of Grenville's world David also discovered new courage, and he looked his adversary fixedly in the eye. "I know what has preserved them all of these years. What has enabled you to weather the centuries?"

"Why, Julia, of course," Grenville said, folding his hands and walking around the side of the table. "Surely you must be cognizant of the relationship between a magician and his demon? Since time immemorial it has been understood that there is great power in the world of darkness. It has long been the role of the thaumaturgist to break through into this world and bring one of its inhabitants under submission. It is true that one must have some innate talent to accomplish this, but the brunt of a sorcerer's power comes from his enslavement of the demon and his channeling of the ocean of unfathomable energy available to that darkling creature."

"So it was you who made the candelabrum vanish the other evening?"

Grenville smiled. "A simple trick, really."

"What other powers has Julia enabled you to wield?"

"Oh, a vast number of them. Even more power than most who have preceded me in my profession. You see, under normal circumstances the magician is only able to allow the demon to manifest on this plane of existence for a short period of time. But long ago I discovered a way to make Julia manifest permanently, to give her actual physical form. That is what has enabled the two of us to survive so long. It is the perfect symbiotic relationship. I provide her with physical form and allow her to sate her needs, and she functions as the energy source, the conduit through which all of my powers flow."

"And what do you want with us?" David asked.

"Ahh, here we come to the meat of the matter. To begin, I want you and your family to remain in the hunter's cottage and I want you to continue with your work."

"That won't be possible," David retorted quickly. "My family is leaving this very afternoon."

Grenville looked at him quiescently. "You don't understand. I'm not giving you any choice in the matter. The truth is, I've never had any intentions of ever letting you leave this valley. It is regrettable that you forced my hand in this matter because I wanted to apprise you of this fact more slowly, but I'm afraid that this is the case nonetheless. You see, as you are no doubt aware, I have quite a number of human servants to take care of this house, the grounds, and in general maintain the standard of living to which I am accustomed. When they grow old and die, I need replacements. Normally, I get them from among the villagers, but as you may have noticed the people in this valley are becoming quite pithless. The trouble is that, as the years have passed and times have changed, the valley has become an almost totally closed community, and inbreeding and incest have become quite a problem. To put it bluntly, I need new blood. That is why I gave you the hunter's cottage. I want you to stay, and ultimately I want your children to intermingle and marry into the community."

"Forget it!" David cried.

"But you have no choice."

"What if we just refuse and pack up and leave?"

"I have ways of stopping you. Just because Julia has been temporarily downed does not mean that the flow of my power has ceased. I have eyes everywhere and there is nothing in this valley that I do not know about." He looked at them smugly. "Do you remember the moth in the Swan with Two Necks? Do you wonder why the villagers were so afraid of it? Well, I'll tell you. You see, the moth too was one of the ways I have of keeping an eye on things around here. The moth was Julia.

I had her assume that form so that I could send her there to spy on you. That was how I knew that Winnifred Blundell so foolishly tried to warn you to leave."

"So you did murder her?" Melanie interrupted.

"I had Julia kill her," Grenville replied. He turned to David. "As you have seen in your exhumations of the bodies in the bog, it is a task she does with unusual relish." He smiled. "And please be advised that Julia is only one of the tools of surveillance I have at my disposal. There are others. And so, if you tried to leave you would never know what set of eyes watching you might really belong to me, a tiny moth between the folds of the clothing in your luggage, a gnat following a discreet distance behind, or even a flea sequestered amongst the hairs of your scalp, any one of them might actually be one of my little emissaries."

The notion that Julia could shrink down and become the size of an insect once again challenged David's reason, but given what he had witnessed so far he did not doubt that it was true. He shook his head. "But I have my work, my reputation. If I do not return to Oxford people are going to start wondering why. They'll come looking for me."

"I'm sure something can be worked out," Grenville returned. "You must understand, we are not totally cut off from the outside world. Some intercourse is allowed. For example, when we need a new vicar I always arrange a way for one of the villagers to attend seminary." He paused. "In fact, I see no reason why you could not come and go as you please as long as your wife and children remain here to remind you that you must ultimately return."

"What about Brad?" Melanie asked.

"Good point," Grenville said. "I'll tell you frankly that I would prefer that he didn't stay. Two outsiders at a time I can handle with ease. Three makes me uncomfortable and might bolster your courage and inspire you to dissent and rabble-rouse. However, I warn you, if you say one word to him about either Julia or myself, at the very least he will become a prisoner in this valley as well. At most, I might even decide to let Julia have her way with him. She's most intrigued by the fact that he's a vegetarian."

Melanie looked horrified.

"The same goes for your housekeeper," Grenville went on.

"And anyone else you may be in touch with in the outside world." He looked at them harshly. "Please don't underestimate the range and scope of my power. Others have made that mistake in the past, and all who have are among the bodies you are now unearthing from the bog."

David and Melanie just sat staring at the ancient magician.

"One final word," Grenville murmured. "I am aware that I have just given you a great deal about which to think. On the brighter side let me add that life need not be so grim for you here. To begin, when I say we need new blood in the valley that does not mean I am going to force anything. So please do not feel any undue pressure on that count. Just relax and I'm sure as the years pass nature will inevitably take its course." Grenville paused and looked distractedly at his fingernails. "If I am not mistaken, the floodwaters of womanhood are already beginning to flow through your daughter. Who knows, she may fall in love with one of the village boys on her own accord."

The thought of one of the scrofulous boys he had seen in the village laying a hand on his daughter filled David with revulsion.

"Never!" he shouted, lunging at Grenville. He was halfway to him and filled with enough venom to strangle him barehanded, when the old sorcerer suddenly raised one of his hands and passed it swiftly through the air in front of him. Then something invisible hit David with the force of a bag of concrete and sent him flying across the room into a row of chairs.

Grenville stormed forward and glared down at him as Melanie rushed to his side.

"Do not try my patience, Professor Macauley. I am in control of forces far beyond your ken and I have enough power in the tip of my little finger alone to rend you asunder." His eyes flashed with fury as he spoke, but then something curiously respectful came into his gaze. "But do not think it has escaped my attention that you are a man of unusual spirit and intelligence. Who knows, perhaps in time, as I become persuaded of your loyalty, there may even be things that I would be willing to teach you."

And with that he ended.

Although his insides were twisting with rage and defiance, David found that this last remark by Grenville plucked something deep within him. He knew that nothing would ever get him to sell out his family, or induce him to accept Grenville's tyranny, but his insatiable curiosity, the part of him that always strove to know more and more, could not help but be allured by the possibility of learning even a fraction of the fantastic knowledge that Grenville apparently possessed.

He was still lost in this thought when he looked up and saw that Melanie was gazing at him terror-stricken. Grenville stood back, and as Melanie helped David to his feet the silence in the room was abruptly punctuated by a sound in the distance. Curious, Grenville walked back out into the drawing room, and after David had brushed himself off he and Melanie followed.

By the time they reached the drawing room Grenville was already standing at one of the windows and looking out, and cautiously both David and Melanie walked up behind him to see what was going on.

In the distance David saw Luther Blundell tearing up the drive on his motorbike. From the speed he was going and the wild expression on his face, it was clear that he was very upset about something. David could only imagine that the discovery of his mother's body had been more than he could bear.

For several seconds they all just watched as Luther continued to race toward them.

"I knew that boy would be trouble someday," Grenville muttered. "But no matter." He looked at David and Melanie with priggish self-satisfaction, and then turned and unlatched the double windows and calmly flung them open.

By this time Luther was a scant few hundred yards from the house, and Grenville watched for just a moment longer. Then, as Luther was about to rip up onto the lawn, Grenville flung his hands out as if he were shaking something off of them, and a mist rolled out of his fingertips as they snapped in the air beyond. As David and Melanie watched, the inchoate mist coalesced a few feet beyond into a blue-white ball of coruscate energy that crackled and went roaring off with lightning speed. The fireball hit both Luther and the motorbike with hammerlike force, but instead of knocking them backward it froze them motionless, the energy ball expanding and enshrouding both the boy and the motorbike in a glistening cocoon of intense white light. Luther screamed, but his scream was quickly truncated, as first his skin and then the red ligaments underneath vaporized. For a few seconds his skeleton sat motionless on the now-melting bike, the brilliant fire glowing dazzlingly from his eye sockets as it incinerated his brain and other internal organs. Finally, it consumed his bones and the metal of the bike and then vanished, sending an oily black mushroom cloud pillaring ominously into the air, the only sign that anything had been there in the first place.

Grenville shut the window and turned back to his guests. His gaze fixed on David. "Please think about all that I have said, and three days from now I'd like you to visit me once again. That will give you a chance to more fully absorb all that you have seen and heard today, and we will at that point continue our conversation. Until then, I bid you adieu. I will see that the chauffeur gets you home."

Grenville turned to once again face the window, and as if on unseen signal, the butler appeared. He led them out of the drawing room and back through the entrance hall. As they passed through the cavernous enclosure, unnaturally dark because it too had all of its curtains drawn, David once again became aware of the susurration, the mysterious rustling that he had heard on their first visit to the old manor house. Neither Melanie nor the butler seemed to register it, but he was sure that he heard something moving in the shadows against the wall. His eyes scanned the darkness, but again he saw no trace of what was making the sound.

It was when they were almost to the front door that the sound grew louder and David realized that it was coming right for him and at incredible speed. He turned suddenly, expecting to see some wraith or ghostly apparition closing in on him, but still he saw nothing. As he squinted into the half light, however, he felt something invisible touch his skin. For a moment it danced like a midge across his face and arms, and then, like a rotted drapery passing swiftly over him, it was gone. He turned, his eyes wide with alarm, but the expressions on both Melanie and the butler's face remained impassive; they sensed nothing. The butler held the door open and stared at him vacantly. David turned and looked into the empty darkness one more time, wondering what other unseen energies inhabited the old house, and then, not knowing what else to do, he departed.

9

FOR SEVERAL HOURS after they got home they scarcely spoke a word to each other, and it was only after they had recovered from their shock that they discussed all of their options. At first David was sorely tempted to simply pack up his family and get them out of the valley as quickly as possible, but in the end he realized that this entailed a risk he was not willing to take. Although he would never have believed it a few weeks previous, he now accepted that they were engulfed by forces far beyond his fathoming, and given that he had no real measure of their sweep or magnitude, combined with his memory of what had happened to Luther Blundell, he reluctantly concluded that he should take all of Grenville's threats seriously until he had reason to believe otherwise.

In the end, Melanie also came around to this point of view although she did so with considerable resistance. David had not expected her to deal with the matter well, but he also had not anticipated the reaction she displayed. He had thought that she would be wild and hysterical, but instead she behaved as if all of the life had been drained out of her. Her gaze was blank and defeated and she lapsed into long stares as if she knew or understood something about what was happening that he did not, something that spoke even more forebodingly about what fate lay ahead for them.

As for Mrs. Comfrey, she displayed obvious worry over Melanie's despondent state of mind, but she seemed not at all cognizant that it had any darker underpinnings. The children also sensed something was amiss and moped around the house cautiously as if they suspected at any moment they might be blamed for the mysterious cloud of gloom that had now overtaken their parents. David tried to assuage them by telling them, and Mrs. Comfrey, that it was a new discovery at the bog that had brought about their change in plans.

David spent the rest of the morning unpacking the car, and when he had finished he turned his attentions to the problem that now towered so menacingly before them. This effort manifested itself in two endeavors. First, he went through all of his books to find what he could about sorcery and demonology, which he discovered, to his dismay, was precious little, for all of the academic texts he owned assumed without question that such subjects were mere superstition. They therefore dealt with them only as cultural eccentricities, offering no real insights into their workings.

The second thing he did was try to track down some clue about the identity of the cryptic tongue that Grenville had used in his exchange with Julia. But again he met with failure. Various of the syllables of their dialogue could be found in half a dozen languages, but none in sequence or with any meaning that shed light on what language they had been speaking.

Finally, frustrated and thwarted, he did what he felt was the only option left to him. He went upstairs and spent an hour looking through dresser drawers and old jewelry boxes until he found three small crosses, and these he made his wife and two children wear. He had never been devotedly religious, but given the effect the word *hallelujah* had had upon Julia, it seemed an inevitable precaution. For himself he fashioned a cross out of two bits of old wood bound together by a rubber band, and this he wore on a cord of rawhide concealed beneath his shirt.

And then, late that afternoon, he went to the campsite to attempt the unsavory task of persuading Brad to pack up and leave. It took him an hour to do this and it was no easy feat, but finally he told the younger man that Melanie was having what appeared to be a nervous breakdown and he trumped up the wild excuse that she was threatening suicide if either of them continued to have anything to do with the bog bodies.

To fuel his argument he told Brad that she had concluded from the moth experience and the bite marks on both the bog bodies and Winnifred Blundell that there was a curse upon the place. Remarkably, Brad bought it, but agreed to leave only on David's assurance that it was a temporary hiatus.

As for himself, David found that not surprisingly he had lost all passion for his work. Instead of staying and continuing with the chemical treatment of the two Roman bodies as he should have, he went back home. That night, after forcing down one of Mrs. Comfrey's typically hearty dinners, he retired to the living room to think. Melanie went upstairs, complaining of a headache, and the children remained in the kitchen with Mrs. Comfrey.

A short time later, David headed for the kitchen to get himself a glass of water. As he approached the kitchen door, however, he heard something sizzling on the stove, and this surprised him, for he knew that both Mrs. Comfrey and the children had already eaten. Curious, he paused outside the doorway to listen.

"Why are you doing that?" he heard Tuck ask.

"It's a scrap cake," Mrs. Comfrey's voice returned. "After every meal you should fry up some of the table scraps with a little batter to make a scrap cake for the goblins."

"How do you give it to the goblins?" Tuck continued.

"You put it out on the back porch, and during the night the goblins come and get it, and that way the goblins don't get mad."

David leaned forward so that he could see the scene transpiring in the kitchen. Katy was sitting at the table, almost completely oblivious to what Mrs. Comfrey was saying, but Tuck sat on a high stool by the stove, his face filled with fear, as he hung on to Mrs. Comfrey's every word.

"What do the goblins do if they get mad?" he asked worriedly.

David stepped quickly into the kitchen. "Mrs. Comfrey, I thought I told you not to tell the children frightening stories."

She blinked dumbly, taken aback. "But this isn't to frighten the children. This is to protect them."

"Well they wouldn't worry about needing protection from goblins if you hadn't brought them up in the first place."

"Well, I never! I only—"

Irritated that she was still challenging his authority, David lost his temper. "Mrs. Comfrey, this is my house and if I catch you talking about frightening things again I'll dismiss you!"

Mrs. Comfrey turned red as she continued to be both angered and humiliated by his reprobation. Stunned by the fierceness of his father's outburst, Tuck began to cry. "Daddy, don't fire Mrs. Comfrey. She just doesn't want the goblins to get me."

Still crying, Tuck jumped off his stool and ran out of the room. Mrs. Comfrey's chest swelled as she put on an expression of righteous vindication.

David glared at her. He knew that he had perhaps been too harsh because of his own frustration over the situation they were in, but for some reason he could not bring himself to temper his fury. He continued to glower at her for several moments as she defiantly scowled back. And then he turned and went after Tuck.

David found him in the living room, curled up in one of the large horsehair chairs and crying. He sat down beside him and lifted him into his arms.

"Tuck, Daddy's sorry for yelling at Mrs. Comfrey. I'm not really going to fire her, I just think that it's bad for her to tell you stories about goblins."

"But what if the goblins do get me?" Tuck asked, concerned.

David smiled. "But that's just it, Tuck. You see, there are no such things as goblins. That's a lie people like Mrs. Comfrey tell children to scare them into being good. I get angry at Mrs. Comfrey when she does that because I don't believe in lying to children. I think adults should tell them the truth."

Tuck wiped the tears from his eyes as he pondered this. "Daddy?"

"Yes, Tuck?"

"Are we still going to move?"

"Not for the time being. Maybe in a little while."

Tuck fiddled with a button on his shirt. "I'm glad we didn't leave," he returned. "You know why?"

"Why?"

"Because that would have meant that we were leaving Ben behind." After this remark Tuck continued to fumble distractedly with his shirt button, gazing meditatively off into space. David drew in his breath, grateful at least that Tuck had not phrased the remark in the form of a question, and hugged his son tighter. Nonetheless, a moment later David noticed that

Tuck's expression had taken on a darker cast, and as he continued to stare off into the distance some inner voice seemed to
be speaking to him, prodding him with things he found painful.

"Daddy?"

"Yes, Tuck?"

"Is Ben ever coming back?"

David closed his eyes as he embraced his son tighter still.
It was the question he had been dreading. As long as he himself
had been ignorant of Ben's fate it had been easy to be evasive,
to postpone confronting the matter. But now that he knew
the truth he was left in a quandary. The last thing in the world
he wanted to do was tell Tuck the truth, for he feared it would
send Tuck even further into his ever-increasing depressions.
But after what he had said about Mrs. Comfrey he felt he had
no right to lie. He took a deep breath.

"No, Tuck. Ben isn't coming back."

Tuck remained absolutely motionless, absorbing the information with no visible sign of distress.

"Why not?" he asked.

David took another deep breath. "Do you know how every
fall the flowers die and the leaves fall off the trees? Do you
know why they do that?"

Tuck shook his head in the negative. " 'Cause winter's coming?" he offered tentatively.

"Partly because the winter's coming," David returned. "But
partly because they have to make room for the new flowers
and leaves. You see, that's the way nature works. Everything
has a beginning and an end. If it didn't the world would become
stagnant, like a bucket of water that you just let sit and sit.
Can you imagine what the world would be like if everything
lasted forever? Just think about it. Every bee that ever lived,
every tree and every person would still be here, and what a
crowded place it would be. The only problem is that it's painful
when things we love go away. We miss them and that's okay.
But what's not okay is to think that it's bad that things have
to go away, because it's not bad. It's a very important thing.
It's what allows new flowers to grow, and new leaves to replace
the old, and the world to renew itself."

"And Ben went away?"

"Yes, Ben went away."

"Where did he go?"

"To heaven," David replied.

Tuck's lower lip started to quiver. "But why did he have to go to heaven?"

"Because it was his time to go."

A large tear rolled down Tuck's cheek and hit David's arm, and he gave his son another reassuring hug. "Hey, now, I don't want you to be upset about this. I told you the truth about Ben because I don't want you to be afraid when things have to go to heaven. Too many people in this world spend too much time being afraid of that, and it's just silly. When something goes to heaven it's a scary thing, and it's a painful thing. But you've got to be brave about it. Things don't go to heaven very often, but when they do, you've got to face it like a man."

Tuck wiped the tear from his eye. "I've got to have moxie, huh, Dad?"

David smiled. He had forgotten about that. "Yes, Tuck. You've got to have moxie."

* * *

David spent the rest of the night going over every word that Grenville had said, searching for some chink in his story, and continued with the pursuit all the next day. On the morning of the second day he went walking on the moors, and his continued absorption in the matters at hand was broken by only one occurrence of note. As he neared the low grouping of hills that marked the border of Old Flory's land, he once again came upon a group of children taunting the little girl Amanda. As he once again dispersed her assailants he noticed that most of the children now boasted shiny new crosses around their necks, he assumed as a result of the vicar's newly enkindled faith following the hallelujah incident. Amanda was the only one who did not possess such a prophylactic and, indeed, this seemed to be the basis for the other children's jeering. To remedy this, after her attackers vanished, he took the crude wooden cross from around his neck and offered it to her. She accepted it as reverently as if it had been made out of the purest gold, and it nearly brought him to tears to see the furtive and incredulous gratitude that shone in her eyes as she ran off with it. When he went home he fashioned himself another.

By the third day his lie about Melanie had started to develop into a self-fulfilling prophecy, for she had become so eaten up by nerves and fear that she was no longer able to keep down solid food. Mrs. Comfrey nursed her attentively, but with little success, for she continued to spend increasing amounts of time in bed.

By nightfall her state of mind had deteriorated to such an extent that David resolved he had no choice but to take Grenville up on his offer of continuing their conversation. The prospect of meeting with Grenville, especially after nightfall when presumably Julia would once again be up and around, frightened him, but he felt he had no recourse. Given all that he had witnessed he knew that every encounter with Grenville meant one was taking one's life into one's hands, but he hoped perhaps to learn more about the old magician's world, to gather some small piece of information that might lead to their escape.

Just moments before he was to exit the front door, he looked up and saw Melanie, ashen and spent in her white nightgown, coming down the stairs.

"Where are you going?" she asked.

"To Grenville's."

Her eyes widened with alarm. "Why?"

"Just to talk. He invited me back, if you recall. I was hoping I might learn more about him, maybe discover some of his limits and his blind spots."

"But why would you want to have anything to do with him?" she continued, as if she still did not understand.

"I told you, to try to help us out of this thing," David repeated.

She sank down heavily onto the steps. "Oh, no. I knew it."

"Knew what?" he said, growing more confused.

She looked at him fearfully. "He's pulling you in. I knew when he told you that there were things he might be willing to teach you that sooner or later he would have you. You're going there because you hate it when there are things you don't know. You're going there because you're hoping that he'll teach you more about his world."

David grew angry. "Do you really think I would sacrifice you and the kids for what I could learn from him? I won't deny that I would give my eyeteeth to understand the forces he wields, to know a fraction of the things that he seems to know, but for God's sake, Melanie, the man is a cold-blooded killer. I would love to tap his knowledge, but I have only one motive in going there tonight, and that's to get you and the kids out of here."

She stared at him tremblingly for several more moments and then started to cry. "I'm sorry, I guess this thing is really getting to me."

He went over and put his arm around his wife. He tilted her chin up with his finger and looked into her eyes. "I know it is, and you can't let it, Melanie. We're up against enough without you cracking. You've got to be strong. Try and eat something, will you?"

She nodded and he noticed that Tuck and Katy had come out of their rooms to see what was going on. He called up to them. "Kids, your mom isn't feeling very well. Do you think you could take care of her and keep her company while I go out for a while?"

They nodded and started down the stairs.

"Be careful, will you?" Melanie said as he kissed her goodbye. Tuck and Katy reached her side and he turned to leave. He was almost down the stairs when Katy called out.

"Dad, what's going on?"

He turned and looked at her, and her gaze was bold and challenging.

"I mean, it's obvious something is going on," she continued. "First we pack up the car and then we don't leave. And then Mom gets sick and you make us wear these things." She lifted up the little cross that she was wearing around her neck. "I mean, you can keep things from Tuck because he's just a kid, but I wish you wouldn't treat me like I'm just a ninny."

Tuck suddenly looked concerned.

David continued to gaze at his daughter, and his first reaction was one of ire. But then he realized that she did have a right to know more than he had told her. He maintained his stern expression. "I can't talk about it right now, Katy. We'll talk about it later."

"But, Dad—"

"—later, Katy."

She remained defiant for but a moment longer and then gave in. "Okay."

He turned and left.

Outside, he got into the Volvo and drove off. The drive

through the moonlit moors was uneventful, but as he neared the ivy-encrusted old manse he realized that he had broken out into a cold sweat. He had no reason to doubt Grenville's assurance that no harm would come to him or his family as long as they abided by his rules, but given the number of bodies they had pulled out of the bog he realized that anything was possible. He recalled Grenville's warning that Julia was going to be "very angry" with him once she recovered, and he wondered again if she would be up and about, or how she would behave toward him if they met.

He swallowed to get rid of the tightness in his throat as he parked the car and got out. Approaching the house, he looked up and noticed that the lights in the tower were burning brightly. He felt the cross concealed beneath his shirt. He hoped that it would be his secret weapon if things became difficult. He lifted the knocker and let it bang heavily against the door. Again after a wait of several long moments, the door opened and he was greeted by the shuffling butler.

"Come in, sir. You've been expected."

He was shown into the dark and gargantuan entrance hall, but instead of being led into the drawing room, to his discomfit he was instructed to remain where he was. As soon as the butler left he searched the shadows for signs of the mysterious presence that he always sensed in the room. For several minutes he was pleasantly disappointed, but after a longer while he slowly got the feeling that he was not alone. Unlike his last encounter, the presence did not manifest itself as a focused scraping, but this time seemed more subtle and encompassing, as if the entire house were slowly sighing. Here and there a drapery appeared to move, or a banister seemed to emit a faint sound, not as distinct as a creak or a tap, but a ghost of a sound, as if it had been only lightly touched by an invisible but insistent hand. It occurred to him that it was not his physical senses that were picking these things up, but something else, some other system of awareness he had never before understood he possessed; and once this realization dawned on him, the shadows in the room became even more alive, swayed and whispered as if it were only a thin veil that divided him from whatever it was that inhabited the darkness.

The movements became so relentless that he was about to turn and flee when suddenly the balustrade creaked overhead

197

and he looked up to see Grenville leaning against the banister and peering down at him. He was wearing a full-length dressing robe of black and gold brocade fringed with Russian sable, and his deep-set eyes were pools of darkness, framed by the shock of white hair.

"Good evening, Professor Macauley," he greeted. "I had almost given up hope that you were coming. Forgive me for making you wait so long. I was busy with something."

David nodded. "That's all right," he said politely.

"Why don't you come up here," Grenville continued. "We'll have our little meeting in the tower."

David nodded and started hesitantly up the stairs. When he reached the ancient magician's side, Grenville turned and motioned for him to follow. They strode down the hallway and through a large door. David was beginning to notice that many of the doorways in the old house were of huge proportions, and he wondered if this was to facilitate Julia's occasionally massive bulk. Beyond the doorway the Elizabethan splendor of the house ended abruptly and the walls and floor were of older and more crudely hewn stone. From the circular staircase before them it was clear that they were now in the tower.

Unlike the drawing room, the tower was lit only by an occasional blazing torch, and as they ascended David had to be careful not to lose his footing on the dark and greatly worn steps. Finally they reached the top and entered what appeared to be Grenville's study. The first thing that David noticed about the vast and circular room was the huge medieval fireplace that burned at one end of the chamber. The nights were now warm and muggy and it struck him as odd that Grenville should still stoke so large a fire. As he looked around he took in the other features of the room. Toward one end of the shadowy and spacious chamber was what appeared to be Grenville's work area, several large tables cluttered with a plethora of apothecary jars, crucibles, bell jars, and flickering retorts. Aside from the disarranged look of this area, the rest of the room was impeccably well kept and possessed the sort of baronial splendor that he had become accustomed to in Grenville's house. Here and there on the floor were several large Persian carpets, and artfully arranged over the expanse of these were various reading tables, wing chairs, and a number of resplendant ottomans. Besides the amber glow of the fireplace, additional light was provided by an array of Victorian floor and table lamps as well as two massive torchères flanking the fireplace, each aflicker with a small galaxy of candles. All told, it might have been a sitting room in a fashionable English gentleman's club.

But the most prominent feature of the room was its many books. Towering two stories over their heads and covering most of the available wall space was one of the largest private libraries that David had ever seen. Most of the volumes were of worn and satiny leather, but there were quite a number of more recent vintage as well. As he continued to look at the monolithic wall of books he noticed that it was divided in half by a narrow balcony and traversed here and there by movable ladders set in tracks so none of its numerous volumes were beyond its owner's reach. For some reason it surprised him that Grenville was such an apparent lover of books. He realized he had been so fixed on the fact that Grenville was so callous, so ruthless, and capable of such evil, he hadn't considered that there might be deeper and more human facets to Grenville's character as well.

"Shall we sit down?" Grenville said, gesturing toward a grouping of furniture before the fireplace.

David nodded, and as he approached the enclosure of chairs he noticed for the first time that someone was sitting on the high-backed sofa facing away from them. To his surprise it was a woman, and from the chestnut color of her hair it did not appear to be Julia. As he passed around the sofa he noticed that there was a table with a tray of dainties before her, *petits fours* and glazed ladyfingers, and she was nibbling on one delicately. He looked at her face, curious as to who the new presence was, and then gasped. To his amazement it was the girl with green eyes, the girl in front of the Rijksmuseum, whose photograph he had secretly stolen so many years before. At first he could not believe it. Had she been a part of this all along? And then he realized. He had shown Julia the photograph when they took their evening stroll. She had, for purposes unknown, taken on the form of the woman.

"Hello, David," she greeted him, smiling. Even her voice was no longer Julia's, but was lighter, more delicate, and with a melodic and more mellifluous lilt. She stood to greet him and extended her long, slender hand. She had captured the look and essence of the woman completely, but as he looked down at her outstretched hand he felt a chill.

"Don't be afraid," Grenville soothed as he sat down in one of the wing chairs before the fire. "Julia's no longer angry with you for shooting her. She won't hurt you."

He looked again at the woman, and as he did so her perfume reached out to him, sweet and insistent. Diffidently, he accepted her hand. He was surprised to find that it was soft and warm, but he did not hold on for long. He remembered too clearly its true form. Julia, or whoever she was calling herself now, sat back down. Grenville motioned for David to take the chair opposite him.

"Would you like a brandy?" he asked as David sat down.

"That would be nice," David replied, still keeping his eyes on the woman across from him.

"What about you, Julia?"

"Oh, please," she returned, taking a tiny bite out of one of the *petits fours*.

Grenville pulled a tasseled cord beside him, and a moment later one of the liveried footmen appeared and fulfilled their requests.

"Why did you ask me here tonight?" David inquired.

"I told you, just to talk," Grenville returned. "In our last meeting I gave you quite a bit to think about. If you recall, I also said that life need not be so dismal for you here. I thought if we got together and had another conversation you might come to realize that just as I make a formidable enemy, I can also make a very powerful ally. The choice is up to you."

"I don't see that I have any choice," David retorted.

"Of course you do. You can fight me, and go the route that so many of your predecessors have gone. Or you can abide by my wishes and enjoy all the benefits of such an allegiance."

"And what are the benefits?"

"Oh, many. Knowledge, for one."

"What do you mean?"

Grenville languidly traced his finger around the rim of his snifter. "As I said before, it has not escaped my attention that you are a man of unusual spirit and intelligence. In fact, correct me if I am wrong, but I would say that you are more than casually interested in learning about things. I would say that you are driven, that you live and breathe to understand the secrets of the universe. Mostly this desire has manifested itself in your ardent interest in history, but there is a passion in you in general, a deep craving to unravel and decipher all things unknown."

"But what makes you think I would forsake my family to satiate this craving?"

"Forsake? Come now, I do think you are phrasing the situation a little too strongly. All I ask is that your family remain in this valley and that you allow your children to grow up and marry into the community. Certainly there are far harsher fates that could befall you. But even allowing for the moment that fulfilling this request could be construed as an abandoning of your family, has it ever occurred to you that this may not be the sin that you make of it? Couldn't it be argued that the seeking of knowledge is a higher endeavor, a more noble pursuit than mere familial loyalty? Where would we be if the great thinkers of history had valued paternity over their studies? Would the world be better off if Leonardo da Vinci had left us a brood of little da Vincis instead of the corpus of his work?"

Grenville paused, twirling his brandy around in its snifter as he shrugged noncommittally.

David bristled. He realized that there was a certain persuasiveness in what Grenville was saying, but he discerned also that the old magician had a clever way with words and was inveigling him, trying to lure him over to his way of thinking.

"I still say you are wrong. I still say there is nothing you could teach me that would get me to go along willingly with your demands."

"Are you so sure?"

The smugness of Grenville's expression when he asked this took David off guard. "What do you mean?"

"I mean, why don't we lay this matter aside for the moment and just proceed as if we were engaging in a friendly conversation. Why don't you just ask me any questions that are puzzling you, and we will see how powerful your curiosity is."

David sensed a trick of some form in the making, but the prospect of finding out more about Grenville seemed to him worth the risk of proceeding. "All right," he agreed. "To begin, why has Julia taken this form tonight?"

Grenville smiled. "Can't you guess? You see, in spite of her anger with you the other evening Julia's really quite taken with you. She took this form for your sake. She thought it might help her entice you."

"Entice me to do what? Be eaten?"

Julia affected a look of offense.

"Oh, no, not to be eaten," Grenville added quickly. "That indignity is reserved only for those who incur my wrath. Julia has a far more libidinous desire in mind. You see, the truth is she finds you quite attractive."

David looked abruptly at the girl with green eyes and she smiled beguilingly as she took another bite of *petit four*.

"But Julia's a male spirit," he argued.

"Quite correct," Grenville agreed. "But as I told you, her appetites are, well, so voracious Julia enjoys indulging in all manner of the senses."

David shifted uneasily in his chair.

"Do not dismiss her advances out of hand," Grenville cautioned. "If you could put aside the image of Julia's true form in your mind you would find that she is completely everything that she appears to be before you now. In fact, she could become anything that you desired in a woman, any woman. She could fulfill any fantasy that you could conceive of, indulge your every whim or desire. Once, long ago, when we lived in Rome, she posed for a number of years as a courtesan and she had quite a reputation for her skills in the erotic arts."

David looked once again at the girl with green eyes, and to his astonishment, although he was filled with revulsion, on some level the prospect plucked a chord of fascination within him. For the briefest of moments he imagined what it would be like to make love to the long-held object of his fantasies, to run his hands across her naked body and be locked in passionate embrace, but then the memory of the creature that he had seen in the bog flooded back to him and he reddened. He realized that no matter how alluring such a prospect might seem he could never get the image of Julia's true form out of his mind, could never lose sight of the fact that the beautiful lips that now so delicately nibbled at dainties he had only days before seen slowly devour a live sheep.

He shook his head violently. "No, I could never."

As he said this, out of the corner of his eye he suddenly saw a glint of gold and he looked up to see a large metallic object moving sluggishly across the mantelpiece. It was a gold and jeweled maharaja sitting in a gold palanquin and carried aloft by four large and exquisitely crafted gold elephants. What intrigued him the most was that the thing appeared to be an automaton. The maharaja slowly tilted his head back in silent laughter and the legs of the elephants lifted in graceful unison as the entire contraption moved slowly across the mantel. In the side of the thing was the face of a clock.

"It makes one complete crossing of the mantelpiece every hour," Grenville offered, observing David's interest in the object.

"Then what happens?"

"Then it turns around and starts back."

Julia shifted restlessly and David turned and saw that she seemed almost angered at his rebuff. He judiciously decided to change the subject. He turned to Grenville.

"You said that you and Julia lived in Rome. When was that?"

"Before we came here."

"Exactly how old are you?"

"I told you before, that does not matter, but since we are having a friendly conversation I will tell you. I number my years now in millennia. I was born in the year of the second Macedonian war."

David felt as if the ground had been taken away from beneath him and he were falling through space.

"But that makes you over two thousand years old."

"You do have a shrewd eye for detail," Grenville said sarcastically. "But certainly that was clear to you once I told you Julia was responsible for the deaths of the bodies you uncovered in the bog."

David blushed. He had known it, it was just that somehow it was only now more fully sinking in. He looked at Grenville, thunderstruck. He had been enthralled by the link the bog bodies had provided with the past, captivated by the notion that they were the earthly remains of a culture and a people long since dead. But if Grenville was as ancient as he said he was, he predated even Caesar. He might have known Hannibal, or been present at the writing of the Old Testament's Book of Daniel.

"Where were you born?" David asked, and for the first time, before answering Grenville faltered.

". . . here, of course. Or more precisely, in Avebury. But

I was always of precocious intelligence and stricken by wander-lust. And so I traveled the world and learned the secrets of magic."

David paused in thought, wondering why Grenville had hesitated before he replied, and then pressed on.

"And how did you learn the ways of magic?"

"That is a question that I will not answer at this time."

Again David paused and thought of another question. "Then how did you end up here, and how is it that you came to call yourself the Marquis de L'Isle?"

Grenville took another sip of his brandy. "We came here because of the bog. You see, it suits Julia's heart to be in a marshy place, it comes the closest to what you might call her natural habitat. As for how I came to call myself the Marquis de L'Isle, the truth is I really am the Marquis de L'Isle. I was granted that rank in 1067 by William the Conqueror shortly after the Norman invasion. You see, it was William the Conqueror's command to give all landowners noble title if they did not oppose him during his invasion. I oppose no one. I simply wait in my fortress for them to come to me. At that time the lake was much larger and not nearly as choked with peat as it is today, and this house was virtually on an island. It was thus by both geography and default that I became the Marquis de L'Isle."

David thought about Grenville's comment that the bog came closest to what Julia might call her natural habitat. He looked again at the strangely feminine creature on the sofa and at the fire that blazed so warmly just a foot away. He noticed that she had finished her brandy and the entire tray of small edibles, and he recalled Grenville's reference to her voracity. He noticed also that she had inched as close as she could get to the fire and this surprised him, for even he, who was relatively far away from the blaze, felt uncomfortably warm.

"If the bog is her natural habitat and it is such a cold and clammy place, why does Julia also seem so fond of the fire?" he asked.

Strangely, Grenville again faltered before he answered. "Haven't you ever known a turtle or a snake whose natural home is someplace damp and cold to also enjoy warming itself in the sun?"

David accepted the answer, amused that Julia did not seem at all offended at being likened to a snake, but he was also intrigued at Grenville's hesitancy before answering. He could not be sure, but thought that Grenville was hiding something, that there was something else about the situation he deemed it dangerous for David to know.

David thought of another question. "In the bog, just before our fateful meeting the other day, we dug up the bodies of two ancient Romans, apparently a husband and wife. The man's neck had been broken and he had been mauled by Julia, but the woman had committed suicide."

"So?"

"So, why wasn't she killed by Julia at the same time that the man was? Why, out of all of the bodies we've unearthed from the bog, is she the only exception, the only one who has died by her own hand?"

Julia sat up taking a sudden interest. "I had forgotten about them."

"Because she took her own life before we could do anything," Grenville intervened quickly. He took on a curiously wistful look. "The man was the Roman vice-prefect sent here to subjugate the valley. His name was Divitiacus, I believe . . . Lucius Divitiacus." Grenville smiled. "For weeks he ignored me because he thought I was a coward hiding in my castle, and for weeks I allowed Julia to feed freely upon his men. Finally he came to me, terrified, and desperate to know what was going on. But he was too proud to submit." Grenville paused. "I confess I was responsible for his neck breaking, but the woman, his wife . . . when she saw what had happened she pulled out a little knife and plunged it into her own abdomen. I suppose she thought she was sparing herself from the same fate as her husband."

"But if you killed the man does that mean that Julia mauled him only after he was dead?"

Grenville nodded.

"Then why wasn't the woman mauled as well?"

Grenville looked at David sharply. "Because there wasn't time to let Julia have her way with the woman's body. You see, it was learned that another Roman garrison was on its way, a second one called in by Divitiacus for assistance. I wanted to dispose of the bodies as quickly as possible. A disappearance the garrison could chalk up as a mystery, but had they found the bodies it would have brought the whole of Roman forces in this section of England down upon us." Grenville twirled his brandy around in its snifter once again. "Now certainly my powers are such that I could have handled such an onslaught, but I saw no reason to open a hornet's nest when it wasn't necessary."

Again the explanation made complete sense, but for some reason David could not shake the feeling that there was more to the situation than Grenville was letting on. Ever since they had uncovered the bodies of the Roman couple he had gotten the unnerving feeling that in them lay some key, some analog to the terrible predicament in which he and his family now found themselves. He went over Grenville's account of the situation in his mind, searching for some toehold.

"After all these centuries you still remember the vice-prefect's name? Certainly that seems strange. Is there some reason the incident is lodged in your memory?"

Grenville's expression darkened. "You really are very obstinate, aren't you?" He looked down into his drink. "I suppose I cannot fault you. Your questions are understandable, but there is a simple explanation. Look around you," he directed. "Look at all the books you see here."

David did as he was bid, taking in the massive library that surrounded them. For the first time his eye noted the names of some of the volumes. He discerned not only titles by Plato and Aristotle, by Boethius and Avicenna, but works by Malthus and Darwin, by Kierkegaard, Heidegger, and even Freud. Even more intriguing than these, however, were the books with unrecognizable authors and more cryptic titles such as *The Heptameron* of Trimethius of Ancona, *The Black Book of the Hamadryads*, the *Grimorium Serpentis*, and the *Key of Al Dzabar*. As he continued to scrutinize the shelves he saw that there was no end to the expanse of subjects covered, and there were even ancient volumes, bound and clasped, inscribed with calligraphies so mysterious that even he did not recognize their tongue or historical origins.

"Name a title," Grenville murmured. "And then name a page."

David looked at him. "Why?"

"Just pick a title and name a page."

David scanned the shelves and spotted a work by an obscure medieval philosopher. "The *Monologion* of Anselm of Canterbury," he said. "Page seventy-two."

"Very well," Grenville nodded as he tilted his head back and closed his eyes. " '. . . certain attributes are comparative, that is, admit of degree,' " he quoted. " 'Goodness is such an attribute, for one thing may be as good as, better than, or less good than another.' " He stopped, smiling. "Now go look," he directed.

David stood and retrieved the book. He opened it to page seventy-two and saw that the page began with the exact sentence that Grenville had recited.

" '. . . when an attribute admits of degree, there is some element common throughout its variation . . .' " Grenville continued, but David had seen enough. He closed the book and replaced it in the shelf.

"Pick another," Grenville invited.

David looked at him incredulously and shook his head. "I don't need to," he said, returning to his chair.

"You see, it is not so strange that I remember the vice-prefect's name. I remember everything, every book that I've ever read, every face that I've ever seen, every footprint in the dust of these old halls, and every falling star. It was this anomalous mental capacity in part that enabled me to become as powerful as I am."

"But I don't understand. How can you know so much, have so much respect for knowledge, and still be so depraved?" David said.

At this remark Julia suddenly looked at him harshly. "Depraved? What do you mean, depraved?"

"Careful," Grenville warned, looking in his direction. "Remember, you are not yet adept in the etiquette of demons."

"Well?" Julia said.

David swallowed nervously, realizing that he seemed to have put himself on the spot. "I suppose I mean morally corrupt. Lost souls."

It did not take him long to realize that he had said precisely the wrong thing. Julia instantly went rigid as she leaned forward and opened her mouth, but instead of a feminine voice, or even anything vaguely human, out came a deafening snarl, an unearthly roar filled with a cacophony of gravelly clicks and drumlike rattles.

And before David knew what was happening, Julia leaped up from the sofa, knocking the empty tray of delicacies out of her way as she charged forth, and with preternatural strength gripped him by the shoulders and pulled him up just inches from her face. Almost instantly the insistent perfume of the girl with green eyes faded and became mingled with the familiar fetor as there was a frothing sound, and as if a ghastly liquid were being squeezed through a cheesecloth, her flesh flowed and bubbled and she metamorphosed back into the demon. What had been her red lips now became the thin red lips of the thing, and what had been the fabric of her clothing quickly reorganized, and like the skin of a chameleon, became the scaly flesh of the creature. David trembled as he gazed into the now hideous face, and the demon's breathing slits flared angrily as a wave of cold and malodorous breath flooded down across his nostrils and his lips.

"Julia!" Grenville cried. "I'm sure Professor Macauley meant no offense."

The thing's rage remained unabated. "But why is it always we who are the lost souls? We are the superior. We are more powerful. Why is it never they?"

"Perhaps we might find the answer to that if you would put him down."

Julia still hesitated as she glared down at David. "Bah!" she said as she spat a little pool of bubbly black spittle down in front of the fireplace and then tossed David like a rag doll back into his chair.

"I'm leaving," she ended as she lumbered angrily toward an open window on the opposite side of the room, and without looking back leaped into the darkness beyond. For several seconds David waited for the sound of her hitting the ground far below, but when none came he could only assume that she had transformed in midair into something that could fly.

He looked back at Grenville.

"Shall I answer your question now?" the old sorcerer offered.

David blinked in confusion, still trying to reassemble his thoughts.

"You had asked me how I could have so much respect for

knowledge and still, in a word, be so evil." As he said this Grenville kept his eyes trained on David with a gaze that seemed more filled with pity than with anger. "Don't you see, that is just the point. We are all obsessed. Each of us is driven toward our own goals, our own ends. Some do not realize they are obsessed because their goals are so mundane—to eat, to sleep, to procreate. Only those of us whose goals are extraordinary are recognized as the driven ones, the drug addicts and the great artists, the saints and the fanatics. You and I are in this latter category. We are driven toward knowledge. The only difference between us is that you have allowed the distractions of the world to hold you back. But me, long ago I decided that I would let nothing stand in my way, no moral constriction. I have sated my thirst without regard to the encumbrances of the world, and that is why I have been able to come so far, to amass the vast reservoir of knowledge that I have. So you see, if you are truly dedicated, if you hold no goal higher than unraveling the secrets of the universe, you must let evil into your heart. It is the only way."

David felt his flesh go cold as he gazed into the darkness that seethed in the old magician's eyes. He saw perhaps a glimmer of Grenville's reasoning, but every fiber of his body rebelled at what he had just heard.

"I couldn't," he returned. "Even if you promised to teach me all that you know, the price that you have just set forth is too high."

"Do not be so certain," Grenville countered quickly as his gaze became even more penetrating.

"Why should I not be certain about what I know lies in my own heart?"

"Because you do not yet know the full extent of my powers. You know what I have given up, but you do not know all of the doorways that have been opened for me in return." Grenville set down his brandy snifter. "For example, one of your desires is to learn about the past, and to gratify your curiosity you spend your time groveling in the mud. Well, let me show you one further manipulation of reality that magic has allowed me, let me show you one more benefit of my power."

Grenville leaned back in his chair as he did a spider's dance with his fingers and gestured for David to look into the fire before them. David did as requested, but he did not immediately see anything different about the flames. He did, however, feel a most peculiar tactile sensation. It was the sort of feeling he normally experienced in an elevator as it smoothly but quickly accelerated. It was as if from visual cues he was not aware that he was moving, but his stomach, his whole insides seemed to be falling away from him with eerie speed. Next he felt what seemed to be pressure changes building around his head and in his inner ear, and as he continued to gaze at the flames that danced before him, he realized they were beginning to fade away, not die out, but fade, as if they were no more than a picture from a movie projector whose bulb was slowly dimming.

As he looked around he realized that the same phantomlike quality was beginning to overtake the bindings of the books, and the furnishings in the room, and then the walls themselves, until all that was left of the room that just moments before had been so real was the floor and the chairs they were sitting in and everything else was darkness.

For a few moments they just sat there as if they were on the pinnacle of some desert plateau, and then finally the floor itself faded out of existence and they were adrift in a murky void. For several moments David could discern nothing but utter darkness and the feel of his chair beneath him. And then he once again became aware of movement as a gray and shadowy light began to glow around them.

As he watched, the light slowly grew brighter until suddenly something white shot by his face with lightning speed, and then shot by again. It took him several seconds to realize that the ghostly projectiles were clouds. He became aware of Grenville in his chair beside him and frozen in the same configuration as if they were still sitting side by side in the study. But as the light grew brighter still he saw to his amazement that they appeared to be several miles above the earth. No sooner had this realization dawned on him than he perceived they were no longer motionless, but were plummeting downward at a terrifying speed and with their chairs tilted so far forward that he had no idea what was keeping them from falling out. He gripped the arms of his chair tightly as the wind and cold ripped by him and they plunged deeper, until at last they broke through the cloud cover. As the white veil parted he could make out an endless sweep of olive and gray-green countryside far below.

Then, as if their chairs had been fastened onto the wings of an invisible plane, they leveled off and soared along several thousand feet above the ground. It struck him that the landscape looked English, but there were still no landmarks or any other signs of civilization that might have offered him a clue as to where they were.

"What is this place?" he shouted.

"Wait and see," Grenville called back.

David squinted in the direction of the horizon and could make out several large gray objects. Soon he could tell that there were also people moving about the tall and bulky shapes, and as they drew closer still he at last realized what they were doing. The shapes were stones and the people were moving them arduously along on massive sledges. From the arrangement of the monoliths already in place he suddenly realized that he was witnessing the building of Avebury, the largest of the British stone circles, and situated about eighteen miles north of Stonehenge.

He recalled that Grenville had said this was his birthplace, and he looked at the old sorcerer incredulously. "Is this really what I think it is?"

"You tell me. You're the archaeologist."

"But that means that we're thousands of years in the past!"

Grenville only nodded and cackled, his laughter muted by the wind.

David returned his gaze to the impossible scene before him. They were still high enough that an occasional rift of clouds passed between them and the ground, and he struggled to make out more features below. As they neared the army of pale and ghostly workers, he discerned some of the details of how the massive sledges were constructed. He noticed that the Neolithic wooden structure known to archaeologists as the "Sanctuary" was not crumbling or in a state of decay, but was built of freshly hewn wood, had a column of smoke rising from it, and appeared to be used as a charnel house. Most of all he noticed the pale, half-naked bodies of the workers, and the slow ponderous ballet of their toil as they moved like creatures out of a dream across the gray and olive plane.

At length, the spectral army passed beneath them, and as they soared away he realized that in a glance he had solved mysteries of artifact and technique that had puzzled archaeologists for centuries. He was swept with excitement as he watched the bedraggled entourage fade into the distance and he turned to Grenville longingly.

"Can't we go back?"

"Back, indeed," Grenville returned, shouting above the wind. "But not back there . . . back further in time!"

Grenville momentarily lowered his head as he apparently gave some silent, cerebral command, and as if they were on a roller coaster they ascended swiftly once again into the clouds.

David shielded his eyes as a thunder of air engulfed them and there was a flapping sound as of a flag waving violently in the wind. A thousand days and nights seemed to wink instantly by them, and the driving wind became so furious that David had to shield his face entirely. Only once was he able to look up and catch a glimpse of what seemed to be a swirling tunnel of clouds, and then the roar grew deafening and they descended once again into the darkness.

As before, when the roar finally faded he saw that they were flying along through the clouds, and this time when the cloud cover parted he saw that they were high above a desert. Wherever they were, it also appeared to be dusk, for he could make out Venus twinkling on the horizon. They had also entered at a greater altitude than they had over Avebury, and as they plummeted downward David feared that he was going to faint.

At length, as they leveled off, he made out what appeared to be man-made structures on the desert far below, geometric traceries that nearly blended in with the color of the sand. It was only as they descended farther that he realized one of the objects was a ziggurat. He was looking down at one of the first monuments of civilization, one of the city-states of ancient Sumeria.

As they flew in closer they passed over a bluff, and a larger brace of earthwork settlements came into view, surrounded by a filigree of irrigated fields. Most noticeable of all, however, was the immense cloud of dust that rolled across the horizon, raised by an army that appeared to be in the midst of an attack upon the city.

Suddenly, to David's astonishment, they descended so close to the ground that for a moment he thought they were going to crash. But instead, they leveled off once again and glided straight toward one of the desert plateaus. As they drew closer it appeared that there was a small battalion of Sumerian soldiers waiting to greet them. David and Grenville flew right up to the assemblage, and then, like a great bird descending, their chairs floated gently down and alighted on the sandy promontory just a scant twenty feet from the group.

"What are we doing here?" David asked breathlessly, but Grenville only gestured for him to be silent. Incredulous, he turned and looked once again at the soldiers. In the manner of the time, they wore long, flounced skirts, and on their upper bodies they had only fringed shawls draped over one side of their bronzed and muscular shoulders. For the moment they appeared neither friendly nor antagonistic, but just gazed at them sternly as they held their swords and spears motionless at their sides. Behind them stood what appeared to be the tent of their commander, and as David watched, the flap parted and out stepped their leader. He was taller than many of his soldiers, although he still stood only about five feet seven, and his black hair was parted in the middle and braided into a thick pigtail. His long black beard was trimmed into a square geometric block and his features were fierce and determined.

He stepped forward, accompanied by several priestly advisers.

"Stand," Grenville instructed quietly.

They both stood to greet the approaching group.

"Who is it?" David asked under his breath just moments before they arrived.

"It is Lugalzaggesi," Grenville whispered in return.

David looked once again at the army still laying siege to the city in the distance. "Then this must be the taking of Lagash," he replied, recalling the ancient military leader's role in Sumerian history.

"Very good," Grenville commended. "Now, do be quiet if you value your life."

David still could not believe it. He looked down at the sand beneath his feet, at the glint of Lugalzaggesi's sword, and at the solidity of his flesh, searching for some flaw that betrayed it all as a dream. But the rattle of their sandals, the dry desert air, it was all uncompromisingly real.

The cadre reached them.

David looked into the eyes of the warrior king, the conquering Alexander of his day, and was suddenly galvanized by the smoldering darkness he found there. It was not only that they were cruel eyes. What was far more frightening was that they were vacant, soulless eyes, more like an animal's than a man's. It occurred to him that they were the eyes of a creature not yet far removed from the beast, the way the eyes of his race had looked at the very dawn of its humanity.

He trembled, wondering what was going to happen next, when to his surprise, Lugalzaggesi fell to his knees and bowed his head, and all of the soldiers and the priests did the same.

"Inanna igbal kalkatum," Grenville greeted them, and Lugalzaggesi rose to his feet. *"Elam ashak asharu,"* the old magician continued.

Lugalzaggesi's eyes filled with tears. *"Elam shigash shi malakir,"* he returned reverently, and slowly all of the soldiers and the priests returned to their feet. *"Ennatum ashak?"* he added, and David noted that even in these savage times the raised inflection at the end of a sentence seemed to denote a question.

Grenville looked in the direction of the city under siege, his gaze as merciless as always, and then once again turned in the direction of the warrior king.

"Ennatum ashak," he confirmed in reply.

A wave of approval seemed to pass through the attendant soldiers as still more tears flooded Lugalzaggesi's eyes and he strode imperiously to the edge of the plateau. He raised his sword and held it motionless aloft for several moments, then brought it crashing down. Another resounding cry rang out from the army in the valley as battalion after battalion of Lugalzaggesi's troops now flooded through the gates of the city.

"What is it?" David whispered. "What has just happened?"

"He thinks we are gods," Grenville explained, "and he wanted my go-ahead before he laid final sack to the city."

"And you gave it?" David asked contemptuously.

"It does not matter," Grenville replied. "If we had not happened along, he would have found his omen in something tonight."

David's horror remained unmitigated. In the distance he could make out the muted screams of women and children as they were put to the sword. "Why did you bring me here?" he asked.

"To show you something I think you'll like," Grenville returned.

"Certainly not this?"

"The battle? No. . . . Something you'll find far more to your interest. Something that Lugalzaggesi doesn't really consider all that important. Let me show you."

Grenville turned to Lugalzaggesi once again and murmured something else in the tongue that David had recognized as Sumerian, and the warrior king nodded obediently.

"Follow me," Grenville instructed David as he padded off through the sand.

Lugalzaggesi had already conquered much of the perimeter of the city, and at the end of the plateau they came upon a group of buildings David recognized as part of the temple complex. Outside of one of the buildings, Lugalzaggesi, who had followed close behind, pointed toward a door.

Taking a torch from its wall sconce, Grenville motioned for David to accompany him inside. They passed through a tunnel into an anteroom, and then through another tunnel and into a vast chamber. Grenville held the torch aloft and David gasped. Lugalzaggesi's men were obviously using the chamber as a storage room, and there were huge clay jars filled with oil, water, beer, and grain. But what captured David's attention were the clay tablets the room contained. Lining the walls and filling endless wooden shelves were thousands upon thousands of them, not crumbled or half buried in the sand, but new and clean and vividly legible. It was clear that Lugalzaggesi and his men cared little about the contents of the room, for here and there they had callously pushed shelving down to make room for their stores, but the vast majority of the tablets were still intact. David knelt forward and gingerly picked up one of the cuneiform-encrusted tablets, and his heart started to race. Before him was the entire temple library of Lagash. He knew that scarcely a fragment of these tablets would survive into his era, that time and history would eventually destroy what Lugalzaggesi's thoughtlessness had already started. But for the moment they were intact, and he marveled at the wealth of knowledge, at the fantastic secrets and lost mysteries they most assuredly contained.

He turned to Grenville abruptly, and in an instant he understood what the old magician was up to. Nothing Grenville had said or done up until now had tempted David. He was intrigued by Grenville's powers, but nothing the old sorcerer had shown him had given him any real cause to take the bait.

He looked again around the torchlit chamber. But what a boon to an archaeologist such dark forces afforded. He felt dizzied at the prospects. What theories he could advance, what gross ignorances and gaping holes in history he could fill, if he had the opportunity even to translate a fraction of these tablets. And what other libraries might he have access to, what other battles might he witness, what other figures out of history might he talk to, actually meet face to face, and even interview?

Suddenly Grenville waved his hand, and the tablet David was holding flew out of his grasp and placed itself back in a niche in one of the shelves.

"You see," Grenville said quietly, "I told you not to be so certain that the path I have chosen is not worth the price."

He turned to leave.

"But can't I look a little longer?" David pleaded.

"Another time perhaps. Right now we must be getting back." Grenville motioned for David to walk in front of him, and together they made their way back out. Outside, they bid Lugalzaggesi and his priests good-bye, and David looked one last time at the mighty city of Lagash. He then glanced at the proud prince from Umma and realized with bitter irony that in a few years he would be defeated by an even more ferocious warrior king, the infamous Sargon of Agade. Then it would be Lugalzaggesi's fate to be brought in neck stock to the gate of Ekur and be ridiculed and spat upon by all who passed by.

They reached their chairs and sat back down, and as the entourage of Sumerians bowed their heads in obeisance, they lifted slowly into the air.

It was just before they were about to enter the wall of clouds that something strange happened. As they were soaring along, far in the distance there appeared a small but intense pinprick of light. It took several moments before David realized that it was zooming toward them. He squinted at it, trying to make out other features, but as it drew closer he realized it was little more than a bead, brilliantly luminous, and slightly golden in hue. Grenville also noticed it and seemed to be looking at it fearfully, and before David knew what was happening, it streaked toward them with lightning speed and struck the old magician in the side of the head, crackling furiously as it did so, and then soared off again, vanishing as quickly as it had appeared.

Grenville cried out with pain from the impact, and the moment he did David felt the powerful and steady force that gripped his chair shudder and loosen, and the next thing he knew they were tumbling over and over, plummeting downward. He screamed and struggled to hold onto his chair, and then out of the corner of his eye he saw a large ruby suspended on a chain come tumbling out of Grenville's robe and slip neatly off his head. Desperately the old magician reached out and grasped it with but two of his fingers, and they tumbled for a few seconds longer before he finally regained control of their chairs. They leveled off just seconds before crashing into a rocky escarpment that had appeared in the desert beneath them, and they once again glided upward into the clouds.

Grenville slipped the ruby back into his robe.

Back through the mists they traveled, back through the thunder and the darkness, until once again they were both resting peacefully on the floor in Grenville's study.

David looked around him just to make sure that they were indeed ensconced in the comforting solidity of the room before he turned to Grenville.

"What happened?" he asked.

"Just a phenomenon," Grenville returned.

"What kind of phenomenon?"

He looked at David crossly. "A phenomenon," he repeated. "It is just one of the rare but occasional hazards of time travel."

It was clear from the disagreeable tone of his voice that he was not going to tell David any more about the thing, but it was also obvious that whatever it was, not only had it very nearly caused them to tumble to their deaths, but it had scared the wits out of Grenville. He had all but lost his normally implacable composure, and his eyes darted about nervously as he apparently contemplated the meaning of the encounter.

David too was deeply shaken over the event, but he was

also excited, for it suggested at least that there were limits to Grenville's power, and forces that were perhaps greater than his magic.

Grenville continued in his agitation until finally, cursorily, he called the butler and instructed him to show David out. David looked at him one last time as he was leaving the study, and observed that he was still sitting in his chair, fidgeting and thinking, while behind him the fire dwindled, and the maharaja in its gold palanquin glistened as it continued its interminable crossings.

* * *

As he drove home David's thoughts were in a flurry of confusion. One moment he was overcome with excitement, hypnotized by the implications of his journey into the past, and the next he was in the throes of depression, and then perplexity, as he recalled the various points in their conversation where Grenville had become curiously evasive, or seemed to be hedging some point. It was when he was almost to the cottage that he thought of the most baffling thing of all. With the evening now behind him it struck him as extraordinary that Grenville should care so much about what he felt at all. In retrospect, Grenville had spent the entire evening trying to win him over, to seduce David into crossing over to his side. Why? Everything that he knew about the old magician suggested that his ruthlessness knew no bounds. If he really only wanted the genetic contribution of their children, why didn't he just kill David and Melanie? He had certainly not displayed any qualm about eradicating his adversaries in the past. What was so special about them that he had chosen instead to keep them alive?

When he arrived home he found Katy waiting up for him in the living room. The look on her face told him something was wrong.

"What is it, Katy?"

"It's Mom," she said, motioning for him to follow her upstairs.

"What about Mom?"

"She's really sick."

David followed his daughter upstairs. In the bedroom he found Mrs. Comfrey standing attentively at Melanie's side and there was the smell of vomit in the room. Mrs. Comfrey looked up with a concerned expression. "It's the Missus. She's terribly ill."

David rushed over to the bed and looked down at his wife. She was beaded with perspiration and her eyes were closed. Tuck stood worriedly at her side, gently stroking his mother's limp hand.

"Do you know what's wrong with her?" David asked the housekeeper.

For the first time since he had known her Mrs. Comfrey seemed definitely in a dither. "We brought her a cheese sandwich and some soup after you left, but she couldn't keep them down. It came on quite suddenly. She complained of feeling ill and the next thing I knew she was delirious. She finally fell asleep and I thought it best to let her rest."

David sat down next to his wife and felt her forehead. "She does have a fever," he said. All of the commotion caused Melanie to stir, and she opened her eyes and looked up at her husband weakly.

"Oh, David, I'm so glad that you're home."

"What is it, Melanie? What's wrong?"

"I don't know. Suddenly I just felt awful."

"Well you haven't been taking care of yourself. I told you to pull yourself together."

"It's not that," she said in a hush. "It's something else."

"What else, Melanie?"

"I don't know," she said in a voice so low that it was almost inaudible.

"Melanie, I can't hear you. What else, what is it?" he prompted.

"I just feel so strange," she whispered. "I feel as if . . . as if I've been drugged or something." She tried desperately to lift her head, but then she fell back to her pillow.

"Mom!" Tuck cried, as David pulled him close and hugged him. In his other hand he took Melanie's and was about to ask her something further when he saw that she had again lapsed into unconsciousness. He sat there for several minutes wondering what to do, and then finally, as he was about to place her hand back down beside her, he saw. In the middle of the white expanse of her arm was a large red welt.

His interest piqued, David leaned forward and examined it

more closely. The red swelling was about as big around as the end of his thumb and in the very center of it was a small red dot, not unlike the sting of a wasp or other insect. He turned around quickly and noticed that the window was open and the curtains were fluttering in.

"What is this?" he asked, and Mrs. Comfrey examined the mark perplexedly.

"Looks like a spider bite or something," she said. "Yes, that's it. Perhaps she's having an allergic reaction to a spider bite."

"Or some other insect," David countered as he walked quickly over to the window and shut it. And then he paused, gazing out into the darkness as he pieced together a possible picture of what had happened.

When Julia had leaped out of the window of Grenville's study he had not heard her hit the ground. Grenville had said that she had the ability to turn herself into an insect, and as he gazed back at the welt on his wife's arm he now thought it likely that she had done just that. For some reason she had transformed herself into a bee or something and had come in the window and stung Melanie. But why? Out of jealousy? Or out of the sheer malice of the act?

He did not know. He only knew that now, as he saw the health and well-being of his family slowly being whittled away before his eyes, whatever temptation he had felt for Grenville's offer quickly faded from his mind.

10

THE NEXT DAY Melanie was somewhat better, but still complained of nausea, and confined her appetite to toast and clear broth. No longer able to just sit around and wait for whatever was going to happen next, David resolved to make the only move open to him. His only hope lay in finding Grenville's Achilles' heel, so it was imperative he find out everything there was to know about sorcery and demonology. If there was one human being on the face of the earth who had sifted through the mountain of literature on the subject and might offer him some insight on the matter, it was Burton-Russell.

He called Grenville and with as untremulous a voice as possible asked for permission to make a routine trip to Oxford. After being assured that Melanie and the children would be staying behind, Grenville assented. Next, after giving Mrs. Comfrey strict orders to keep the children inside and to keep the windows closed, he went outside to the Volvo. In spite of the fact that he had been told that Julia did not come out during the daytime, he was taking no chances. After he got into the car he searched it from top to bottom for uninvited passengers. When he found none, he rolled all of the windows up and drove off, and it wasn't until he was miles beyond the valley that he rolled them down again.

He arrived at Oxford shortly after noon and made his way to All Souls College, where Burton-Russell had his office. David had not telephoned to say that he was coming. He had not wanted to take the chance of Grenville knowing his destination in advance. In spite of this, he had no serious worry that Burton-Russell would not be in. David knew enough about the old antiquities scholar to know that he would spend the better part of the morning and afternoon in his office in quiet study.

David gazed up fondly at the distinguished old facade of All Souls College before he went inside and made his way to Burton-Russell's office. He knocked on the door, and a croaky voice bade him to enter. Burton-Russell sat at his desk, surrounded by his usual avalanche of books, periodicals, photographic plates, and old manuscripts. In feature Dr. Aubrey Burton-Russell was a small man, with a narrow fringe of short white hair and pink-veined eyes. He had a reputation among his colleagues for being a bit dotty, and although he had a tendency to ramble and sometimes make points that only he himself understood, David knew that somewhere behind his foggy eyes there worked a formidable intellect.

He looked up at David with pleasant surprise. "Mr. Macauley, how nice to see you. Come in, come in. How thoughtful of you to drop in."

After they had exchanged amenities David surreptitiously scanned the room for insects. On seeing no suspicious intruders he sat down.

"To what do I owe the honor of this visit?" inquired the old don.

David swallowed nervously and was about to answer when he noticed that Burton-Russell's window was open a crack. "Do you mind if I shut that?" he said without explanation.

Burton-Russell looked at him quizzically, but nodded.

David crossed the room and shut the window. He paused briefly to look outside, and across the quad he saw the Roman dome of the Radcliffe Camera and its eighteenth-century Tower of the Winds. He found himself growing quite homesick for the safe spires and quiet greens of the ancient university.

He turned and faced Burton-Russell uneasily. He knew he had to phrase his questions carefully, for given that he did not know the extent and range of Grenville's powers, he could not take the chance of telling the old professor anything that might anger his captor.

"Well, I do hope you don't think me quite strange, but I

was wondering if you might tell me everything that you know about sorcery."

Burton-Russell blinked once or twice, but quickly took the question in stride. "I don't suppose you'd like to tell me why you are interested in this subject?"

David shifted his weight nervously. "It has something to do with a theory I'm working on, but for the moment, since my thoughts on the matter aren't as structured as I would like them to be, I wonder if I could beg your indulgence and refrain from telling you until I'm more certain of my hypothesis?"

Old Burton-Russell regarded him quietly, and for a moment the fogginess of his gaze seemed to lift as he assessed what David had just said.

"Very well," he said. "But you know you've aroused my curiosity enormously. No doubt this has something to do with the things you've been digging up out at that bog, and, of course, I'd like to know every detail. But for the moment I'll respect your wishes. What would you like to know?"

"Whatever you know," David returned. "Most specifically I'd like to know about demonology, about the tradition of a sorcerer being able to tap great power by forming an allegiance with a demon."

"Hmmm," Burton-Russell said as his eyes glazed over with a look that David knew meant he was going back through his voluminous mental archives. "That's a very sketchy subject. The most complete information we have on it dates from the Middle Ages and the Renaissance. During that time a number of historical figures acquired reputations of being magicians who had accomplished the conjuring up of demons, among them Albertus Magnus, Paracelsus, and Simon Magus."

"Do we know anything about their methods?" David asked.

Burton-Russell stroked his chin. "Well, we don't know much about the particular methods that these men employed, but in the British Museum and most particularly in the Bibliothèque de l'Arsenal in Paris, there are a number of manuscripts dating from this time that purport to tell one how it is done."

"Have you seen any of these manuscripts?"

"Yes, I've read quite a few of them. I even have photographic facsimiles of several of them." Burton-Russell stood, and despite the apparent chaos of the many books and papers in his office, he went directly to an incredibly cluttered wall of books and pulled two volumes out. He handed them to David, who accepted them greedily.

"They're called *grimoires*," he said, "which I believe is from the French word for grammar books." He pointed at one of the volumes in David's hands. "That one is called the *Grimoire of Honorius* because tradition alleges that it was written by a thirteenth-century pontiff, one Pope Honorius the Third."

"And how do they say to conjure up a demon?"

"Oh, the usual twiddle-twaddle. You draw a magic circle on the floor. You say a lot of funny words."

"Do the methods work?"

Burton-Russell looked suddenly startled. "Why, my dear boy, you're taking all of this rather seriously, aren't you?"

David blushed. "I'm sorry for asking such a silly question. I just thought . . . well, there are so many legends about the matter, one wonders if there can't be some small amount of truth to them."

Burton-Russell looked as if he were going to make some further quip when, on seeing the gravity of David's expression, seemed to decide against it. "Well who can say? Perhaps there is at that."

David opened up one of the books, glancing briefly at the cryptic symbols it contained. "I don't suppose you've tried any of these incantations?"

Burton-Russell smiled. "I confess that in my madder moments I've been tempted, but it is not as easy as it looks." He pointed at the second book David was holding. "That one is called *The Sacred Magic of Abra-Melin the Mage*, and alleges to have been written by a fifteenth-century adventurer who refers to himself only as Abraham the Jew. The ritual it describes for conjuring up a demon takes a full six months to execute and during that time requires that the participant abstain completely from all human company and, among other things, consecrates an entire building to be used solely for the purpose of the magical operation."

David's face fell.

"So you see, contrary to popular belief, the darker art is not something that one can dabble in on a random Saturday afternoon, but requires a prodigious amount of time, preparation, and dedication."

David considered the matter for a moment. "You said that

the most complete information we have about sorcery and demonology dates from the Middle Ages and the Renaissance.
How far back does the tradition of magicians conjuring up
demons go?"

Burton-Russell's eyes grew misty. "Oh, very far, to the very
birth of civilization itself. In the sand-buried cuneiform tablets
of Sumeria and Babylonia are mentioned the first dark summon-
ings of evil power, the first worries of ferocious spirits of the
night, of demons that wandered the marshlands in search of
hapless victims."

"The marshlands?" David said, perking up. "Why the
marshlands?"

"Well, as you know, civilization in the Mesopotamian basin
centered around the Tigris and the Euphrates, and although
these areas are surrounded on all sides by great deserts, during
the time that we are speaking of the land immediately bordering
these two great rivers was a network of vast marshlands and
tropical lagoons. I suppose the cultures of the Mesopotamian
basin chose these areas as the point of origin for such creatures
because the swamplands were often so treacherous and inacces-
sible, and it has always seemed to be a part of human nature
to populate the unknown with devils."

Burton-Russell stood up, his eyes scanning the bookshelves
for another book, but continued speaking as he did so. "In
the ancient tongues of the Near East the worm *worm* referred
to any creature that inhabited a wet or muddy area, and hence
they often referred to these creatures as 'Great Worms.'" He
found the volume he was looking for and plucked it from the
shelf, and David noticed that it was a copy of Sir E. A. Wallis
Budge's *Babylonian Life and History*. He thumbed through it
quickly. "Ah, here's a passage that mentions them, for example."
He read: "'After Anu had created the Heavens, the Heavens
created the Earth, the Earth created the Rivers, the Rivers created the Marshes, and the Marshes created the Worm. . . .
Came the Worm and wept before Shamash, before Ea came
her tears, and she said: "What wilt thou give me for my food?
What wilt thou give me for my drink? . . ." And Ea said: "I
will give thee dry bones and scented wood." And the Worm
said: "What are these dried bones to me? Let me drink of thy
children's blood, and eat of thy children's flesh, or I will set
thy teeth to tingle, and thy gums to ache."'"

Burton-Russell looked up from the book. "In the Bible the authors of the Old Testament corrupted the term and took to calling the Worm the Great Serpent, or Leviathan."

The words hit David like a bolt of lightning. He recalled Grenville saying that the bog came closest to what he might call Julia's natural habitat, and he realized now just how ancient a creature she actually was.

"And in the presence of these creatures one felt one's teeth tingle and one's jaw ache?"

Burton-Russell blinked several times as he looked back down at the book. "I suppose that could be one interpretation."

"And is there any mention in the old Babylonian texts of magicians bringing such creatures under control and harnessing their power?"

"There are vague allusions to it, but the first real mention of this sort of thing comes a little later in history. According to legend, it is said that in addition to being a wise and just leader, Solomon was also a powerful magician, and was learned in the ways of sorcery. According to Talmudic legend his mastery over demons was so great, in particular over a demon known as Ashmedai, that it was these dark creatures, at Solomon's command, who actually built the Temple of Solomon."

"Is it recorded how Solomon was able to effect such control?"

"Only that it was through an incantation, a pact of sorts, that Solomon had inscribed on a gem."

"Is there anything to suggest that these were the same creatures that were first written about in Babylonian texts?"

Again Burton-Russell looked startled. "My dear boy, you speak as if you think these things are real, as if demons are really only some hitherto-undiscovered life form that has been mentioned here and there in different legends."

"Oh, no," David stammered quickly, "I don't mean to suggest that. What I meant to ask is, are there any similarities of tradition, any motifs in the legends that seem cross-cultural?"

"Well, there is one, I suppose," Burton-Russell replied.

"What is that?"

"In the Psalms it is mentioned that the Canaanites, like the Babylonians before them, were forced to sacrifice the blood of their sons and daughters to these 'devils' in order to appease them."

David considered the information carefully. "I have one other question," he said.

The elder don looked at him expectantly.

From his pocket he withdrew a slip of paper on which he had written the unknown language with which Grenville had addressed Julia. He handed the paper to the older man. "Do you have any idea what language this is?"

Burton-Russell scrutinized the snippet carefully. "*Ip bur ib du ni,*" he read quietly. "Isn't that interesting? It definitely has a very ancient ring to it, but I just can't place it. It's reminiscent of Ugaritic, and even smacks a little of a very ancient form of Hebrew, but it's neither one, really." He stroked his chin contemplatively as he continued to gaze at the paper. "You know, I've seen this tongue before, I just can't place where."

He looked at his watch. "Oh, dear me. I'm late for my lecture."

David felt a pang. "Are you sure you can't place where you've seen it?"

"Well, if you'd be willing to wait for me, I'll only be gone an hour. And I'm sure if I think about it for just a little bit, I'll be able to recall where I've seen it."

Reluctantly, David agreed to wait.

After Burton-Russell left, he occupied himself by poring over the books on demonology that the elder don had given him, but to his chagrin they were awash in such mystic jargon that he could glean very little useful information from them.

As it turned out, Burton-Russell was gone longer than an hour. Indeed, he was gone longer than two, and when the third hour started to creep by, David realized to his dismay that if he did not leave soon, it would be dark before he got back home. He was just about to leave when Burton-Russell burst excitedly into the room carrying a large stack of periodicals.

"I think I've narrowed it down," he said. "I'm certain we'll find the answer to what language it is in one of these magazines."

"What makes you so sure?" David asked.

"Because I remembered that wherever it was that I saw it, it was in an article that I read sometime last spring, and so these are the only possibilities. Here, help me look," he said, handing half of the stack to David.

David sighed as he began the search.

It was some time later that Burton-Russell became suddenly excited. "I've got it!" he said. "It's from Ebla!" He looked at David. "Do you know about Ebla?"

David frowned. He knew only that it was an excavation site in the Middle East. "A little," he said. "Tell me more."

"Well, Ebla was once a mighty empire, as mighty certainly as Babylonia or Sumeria, but for some reason, after it was sacked in the third millennium B.C. it was totally lost and forgotten. It wasn't until 1964 that a team of Italian archaeologists excavating in northwestern Syria came upon its ruins as well as one of its temple archives with over twenty thousand clay tablets still intact."

Burton-Russell lifted up the paper and perused it with interest. "What is so amazing is that it could be so utterly forgotten, but in the temple archives they found the records of a vast commercial and cultural empire written in a hitherto-unknown Semitic dialect." Burton-Russell pointed at the scrap of paper on his desk. "Those sentences, my dear boy, are written in that dialect. They are phonetic renditions of phrases in ancient Eblaite."

David was electrified. "Can you tell me what they say?"

"Unfortunately, I cannot. You see, Eblaite seems to have both Semitic and Assyrian roots. It appears to be a protolanguage to both. The problem is that both Jewish and Arab scholars have tried to claim Ebla as evidence that the land is properly part of their heritage, and as a consequence the Syrian government has become so angry that it has put a halt to further work on the deciphering of the tablets."

"How old did you say the Eblaite civilization was?"

"It's been lost and buried for over forty-five hundred years."

David stood gazing off into space as he recalled Grenville saying that the language he was speaking with Julia would be totally unknown to David. The question that now dominated David's mind was, How was it that Grenville happened to be speaking ancient Eblaite? Was it possible that he was actually far older than he claimed to be? Was he really not from Avebury, but somehow a survivor of the long-lost civilization? As David considered the matter he realized that the evidence indicated that this was the case—Grenville's unusually dark complexion, his hesitancy in telling David his birthplace, his fluency in ancient Near Eastern languages, all suggested that he was really over twice as old as he confessed to being. But why had he lied? Why was he so afraid of David learning about his true origins?

"Are you all right?" Burton-Russell asked.

"Yes, quite all right." David looked at the older man. "Has any of the Eblaite language been translated?"

Burton-Russell nodded. "Yes, a few words." He handed David the periodical he was holding. "You'll find most of them in this article."

"May I borrow this?"

"Yes, of course."

David looked out the window and saw that it was getting dark. Melanie would be in a panic if he did not get back soon.

"You know, it's strange," Burton-Russell said with a trace of amusement.

"What's strange?"

"The civilization of Ebla and its entire written language have been lost and buried for over forty-five hundred years, and yet somehow one of its words managed to survive and find its way into our own language. We've used it for centuries, embraced it as if it were one of our own words, without ever realizing that it was really an artifact, the solitary survivor of a long-dead civilization."

"You're kidding," David said. "What word is that?"

"*Hallelujah,*" Burton-Russell returned. "It's one of the few phrases that's been translated from the tablets. It means 'praise ye the Lord' in ancient Eblaite."

David was thunderstruck. If there had been any doubt in his mind about whether Grenville and Julia were from ancient Ebla, it was now banished as he recalled the effect the word had had upon his monstrous adversary. He shook with excitement as he pondered the implications of what Burton-Russell had just said, and was just about to turn and thank the little man when suddenly a large bluebottle blowfly buzzed loudly past his ear and zoomed up toward the transom above the door of Burton-Russell's office. He looked at it, paralyzed momentarily with fear.

"That's funny," the elder don said, also noticing the fly. "They don't usually come out much after dark."

David continued to watch the fly as it buzzed along the door casing and, quickly locating a space between the transom and the door, exited into the hall. David turned to the little man beside him and swiftly bid him good-bye, and as Burton-Russell regarded him with surprise, David placed the periodical under his arm and ran out the door.

Out in the hall he looked around madly and finally spotted the fly about twenty feet down the corridor. He broke into a run to catch up with it. At the end of the hall there was a window and he hoped to see the fly bump repeatedly against the glass, to give some indication that it was just a normal insect that had gotten trapped in the building. But when it reached the end of the corridor it avoided the window altogether and with eerie determination neatly turned the corner and sped on. David also rounded the corner, nearly knocking down two aged dons as he struggled to keep pace with his diminutive quarry.

By now the blowfly had picked up speed and was about forty feet ahead of him. As he continued to run after it, a short distance in front of him two large doors opened and a class of undergrads suddenly started to empty into the hall. Within moments he was engulfed by an ocean of students, and he watched anxiously as far ahead an incoming don opened the front door of the building and the fly vanished into the air beyond.

Had it been Julia? Something told him that it had. He recalled that according to legend, Beelzebub, Satan's chief emissary on the earth, often took the form of a fly, but there was more to his conclusion than memory of that old myth. What frightened him was not only the fly's steely determination to get out of the building, but its deft ability to do so, to avoid simple obstacles that normally stymied other flies. He quickly made his way through the flood of students and down the ancient steps of All Souls College.

If the fly had been Julia his worry was now that she would make it back to the valley before he did, that she would warn Grenville of his talk with Burton-Russell, and, angered by David's indiscretion, Grenville would take some act of revenge against Melanie and the kids before he had a chance to get back to them.

He got into his car and sped off. While he was still within the confines of Oxford he tried desperately to keep the Volvo under the speed limit, but once he was outside on open road he tossed caution to the wind and pressed the accelerator nearly to the floor. When he finally arrived home and pulled into the driveway, to his horror he saw that the front door of the cottage was standing wide open.

He leaped out of the car and ran up to the house. Inside, the living room light was burning brightly, but there was no sign of activity.

"Melanie!" he called. "Tuck, Katy, Mrs. Comfrey?"

There was no response.

In a panic he started to search the house. It did not take him long to see that there were signs of a struggle. In the living room a chair was overturned and in the kitchen, the drawer that contained the knives had been completely pulled out and its contents emptied onto the floor.

"Oh, God!" he cried as he raced back to the front of the house. He was about to ascend the stairs when he felt something wet drip down onto his arm and he quickly wiped it off and noticed it was blood. He looked up.

"Oh, my God!" he cried again when he saw the body of a child, a young girl, garroted and hanging from the banister overhead.

"Katy!" he screamed as he bounded up the stairs, tears filling his eyes.

But it was not Katy. It was Amanda, her lifeless eyes bulging piteously as she dangled like a bag of laundry from a rope tied under her arms and suspended from the stair railing overhead. It appeared that she had been strangled by the rawhide cord on which he had placed the cross he had given her, and, indeed, that crudely hewn but sacred relic still dangled uselessly over her slumped face. The blood, he noticed, came from a small wound in her shoulder, a single bite mark that was distinctly Julia's signature.

Still terrified over what had happened to his family, he stepped around the body and continued upstairs.

Madly, he searched the children's bedrooms and found nothing. It was while he was searching the master bedroom that he heard a clunk and realized that it had come from the closet. Cautious, but desperate to find his family, he crept closer and quickly flung open the door.

Inside, Melanie and the children were huddled together, and

231

in her hand Melanie clutched one of the kitchen knives. She screamed and nearly lunged for him.

"Melanie, it's me!"

Still overcome by fear, she blinked several times before she would allow herself to believe it, and then she rushed forward into his arms. The children followed her, crying uncontrollably.

And then suddenly Melanie drew back, her face once again filled with terror. "How do I know it's you?"

Realizing that she feared he might be the demon, he tried to think of some proof he could offer her. "Ask me something, something only I would know."

"When is Tuck's birthday?"

"August twenty-sixth."

She seemed only slightly calmed. "Where did we go on our honeymoon?"

"We didn't go on a honeymoon—at least, not until a couple of years after we were married. And then we went to Ibiza."

"Oh, David!" she cried, collapsing once again into his arms.

He hugged his family for several moments before he finally drew back. "Where's Mrs. Comfrey?" he asked.

"She went into Leeming to visit an ailing friend."

He sat his wife down on the bed and Tuck and Katy clambered onto it beside him. "Tell me what happened," he said.

"It was her," Melanie said, still struggling to keep from sobbing. "The kids were in the living room and I was in the kitchen getting a drink of water. There was a knock on the back door and when I opened it Julia was just standing there, smiling fiendishly. I slammed the door in her face and locked it, but I could tell it wasn't going to hold her back. So I got a knife out of the kitchen drawer and ran and got the kids and we came up here and hid. I heard her come in and she stomped around the house, but I never heard her leave. So we just stayed in the closet until you got home."

"So you don't know what's out there?" David asked.

Melanie's eyes widened. "No, what?"

He shook his head. "Just keep the kids in here for a while." He stood up to leave, but Melanie grabbed at him and held him back. "David, my God, you're not just walking away without telling us. *What's* out there?"

He looked at her firmly. "Melanie, it's okay now. Everything is—"

But before he could stop her she had jumped up and run down the hall. He caught up with her just as she happened upon the body.

"Oh, my God!" she gasped as she turned and buried her head in his shoulder. David turned and saw that Tuck and Katy were coming out of the bedroom.

"Stay back there, kids!" he snapped angrily. He took Melanie gruffly by the shoulders. "Now will you please go back into the bedroom and see that the kids don't come out here?"

Melanie reluctantly went back in and shut the door behind her.

It was as he cut Amanda's body down that he saw the note. Written on a piece of embossed stationery and pinned to her dress was a message from the Marquis de L'Isle. It read:

> My good Professor Macauley:
>
> This is only a warning. I do not like what you did today. I will spare Professor Burton-Russell's life since this is your first offense, but I will not be so tolerant should such an event occur a second time. Next time, this could be one of your children.
>
> Yours most sincerely,
>
> Grenville

He cursed and crumpled the note in his hand. He looked down at the body. The first thing that struck him was that Amanda had been strangled by the cross that he had given her, and he wondered why Eblaite symbols affected Julia, but not Christian ones.

Secure in the knowledge that his own children were safe, he was swept anew with grief and outrage. It wasn't that he ever doubted that Grenville was evil, but somehow, as he looked at Amanda's dead body, it was as if he truly saw for the first time the extent of the wickedness he was up against.

Tormentedly, he carried the body outside, and saying a final prayer he placed it in the trunk of the car. It made him heartsick to subject it to this final indignity, but he did not want Tuck or Katy or Mrs. Comfrey to see it before he had a chance to drive it to Fenchurch St. Jude and turn it over to the constable.

Still summoning his every ounce of will power to fight back

the nausea, he cleaned up the blood and disposed of the rope, and then he went back upstairs. When he entered the bedroom he found Melanie madly involved in packing. Tuck and Katy were standing to one side and watching with alarm.

"What are you doing?" he asked.

"What does it look like I'm doing?"

"Melanie, you know you can't do that."

She turned on him with fury in her eyes. "Don't tell me what I can or cannot do! I'm taking the kids and we're getting the hell out of here!"

He pulled her harshly to one side of the room and lowered his voice so that the kids could not hear. "Melanie, I tried something today that I thought would help get us out of here, and that's why that child out there was killed. It was a warning, Melanie. If you try to just drive out of here Grenville will never let you get out of the valley alive."

She looked up at him torturedly, still half crazed with fear, and then she started to cry. Disheartened and defeated, he helped her back to the bed.

Tuck and Katy also began to cry. Katy looked up at him desperately. "Dad, what's happening to us? What's going on?"

He looked at his children, at the panic in their faces, and then he looked at Melanie. She had stopped momentarily in her sobbing and her eyes were wide with fear as she shook her head, trying to signal to him not to tell the children anything.

David looked back at Tuck and Katy, at the confusion and terror in their faces. He sighed. He had to tell them something.

He called them over and put his arms around them. "Kids, we're in a little bit of trouble," he said.

"David, *no!*" Melanie interrupted, trying to stop him.

He glanced at her disapprovingly and continued. "You know that man that Mommy and Daddy went to visit, the Marquis de L'Isle?"

They both nodded.

"Well he's a very bad man, and he's told us that we can't leave this valley."

"But how can he stop us?" Katy questioned.

"We don't know and that's what's frightening us," David returned. "We know that he has done some very bad things in the past and so we don't want to attempt to leave until we're certain that he can't hurt us."

"Can't we just call the police?" Katy continued.

David looked at her sympathetically. "Katy, trust me for the moment. If we could have called the police, we would have, but the Marquis seems to be a very powerful and very clever man, and we don't want to make a move until we're absolutely positive that it's the right one."

Both Tuck and Katy gravely absorbed what they were being told.

"Is he a gangster?" Katy asked.

"Something like that," David replied.

"Is he the one who shot the woman from Leeming?" she pressed.

David glanced briefly at his wife before he answered the question. "It doesn't really seem to be his style of doing things, but with the Marquis, anything is possible."

Tuck began to cry again. "Daddy, why can't we just shoot him?"

David hugged his son even tighter. "Because Mommy and Daddy don't just go around shooting people. That would make us just as bad as the Marquis is." He pulled Katy closer to him also. "Don't worry, we'll get out of this somehow. You've both just got to be very brave until we can figure out how."

He smiled and tried to wipe away his children's tears. "Oh, and one more thing. Mrs. Comfrey doesn't know about any of this. If she did it would put her in danger also, so this has to be strictly our secret. Understood?"

They both gazed at him dumbly.

"Understood?" he said even more firmly.

Falteringly, they both nodded.

* * *

Later that evening, after Mrs. Comfrey had gotten back, David drove into Fenchurch St. Jude and turned Amanda's body over to the constable. The constable accepted it solemnly, and although he glared at David as if he harbored the conviction that David was somehow to blame for this most recent act of ruthless savagery from the Marquis de L'Isle, he said nothing. It was an occurrence that the inhabitants of Fenchurch St. Jude had clearly long ago learned to accept without comment.

As David drove away he began to more fully understand the lifelessness, the look of bleak despair that he had seen in the faces of the people when he had first arrived in the valley.

He had been under Grenville's despotic rule for only a comparatively short time, but already it was taking its toll on him. His mind boggled at what it would have been like to grow up knowing nothing but Grenville's tyranny, to live and die as one's parents and grandparents had, fearful that one's every action was watched, that the slightest insurrection might result in sudden and unspeakable death.

He sat up all that night in the living room with a shotgun. He knew that it would provide him with at best only a temporary reprieve if Julia came stalking them again, but somehow it made him feel less helpless. As he sat there, drinking cup after cup of coffee to keep awake, he pondered all of the little mysteries hoping to find some clue that would help them escape the nightmare that they were now trapped in. He wondered again why Grenville did not just kill them and take Tuck and Katy into his own care. He wondered also why Grenville had so pointedly sought to conceal his true age, and why it was so important to him that David not know that he was from Ebla. David did not know why, but time and time again in searching for answers to these questions, his thoughts returned to the Roman couple. He had no substantial reason for why he felt that way, but he could not help thinking that the Roman woman's suicide, the fact that she had taken her own life instead of being killed by Grenville, was somehow the key to these mysteries.

The next morning when he looked in on Melanie, to his great distress he found that she had taken a turn for the worse. She was vomiting again and her breathing was faint and raspy. It was as if the events of the night before had taken whatever last small scrap of pluck and stamina she possessed. She also drifted in and out of unconsciousness, and her face was growing increasingly thin. As David sat with her, holding her enfeebled hand, slowly, painfully, he realized with growing disquiet that she was dying. It might take a week, or a month, but he realized that she would not be able to survive for long in the condition that she was in.

He sat with her all morning and most of the afternoon, and

finally, not knowing what else to do, he decided to pay one more visit to the campsite. He hoped that if he examined the bodies of the Roman couple once again he might find something that he had overlooked, some tiny fragment of information that could help him save the lives of his wife and children.

It was just as he was about to leave that Tuck came running up to him fearfully.

"Daddy, where are you going?" he asked, his face filled with dread.

"I'm going to the campsite. I'll be back in a little bit," David returned.

"Can I go with you?" he begged.

David looked down sadly at his son's forlorn expression. "I don't think so, Tuck."

Tuck looked devastated. "Oh, please, Daddy. Why not?"

"Because you've got to stay here and take care of your mother."

Tuck started to cry. "But Mom has Mrs. Comfrey to take care of her, and I'm scared to be left here alone. I want to come with you."

David was about to say something else when Katy also appeared, looking anxious.

"You're leaving again? Can I come too?"

David sighed. He did not think it was wise to take his children to the site of the excavations, but he could not turn down their desperate and pleading faces.

"Oh, very well," he said. "Come along."

"No!" a voice suddenly shouted from behind, and he looked up to see that Melanie had dragged herself out of bed and had come down the top several flights of stairs.

Seeing what had happened, Mrs. Comfrey rushed up behind her and tried to assist her back to bed, but Melanie fought her. She seemed almost delirious.

"Melanie," David said softly, "it will be all right."

"But it's almost dark!" she exclaimed.

"No it isn't. The sun won't set for another hour or so. I'll get them back before then."

She remained adamant. "No! You mustn't take them, it's too near the bog!"

Irritated that she was coming dangerously close to saying

things in front of Mrs. Comfrey that she shouldn't, and realizing that at least part of her anxiety was rooted in her debilitated mental state, David sent the children on out to the car.

"Melanie, they're upset and frightened. They just don't want to be left alone. They'll be all right."

He turned around to leave.

"But they'll be even more frightened if you take them to the campsite!" she called behind him. "You expect too much of them. They're not little adults. They're just children!" Her voice trailed off as he shut the door behind him.

He resented her apparent assumption that he was going to subject the children to anything at the excavations that would frighten them. Given their already fragile state of mind, he had no intention of letting them anywhere near the bog bodies.

At the camp he herded the children out of the car and led them toward the main tent. About fifteen feet outside it he stopped them.

"Now listen to me," he said, looking at them sternly. "I want you both to play right here where I can keep an eye on you."

Katy looked appalled. "You're not letting us come in?"

"No," he said in a tone of voice that stifled further argument.

"Well what are we supposed to do to pass the time?" she asked.

"You might try telling your little brother a story. But whatever you do, I don't want you to come into the tent, and I don't want you to wander off. We're very near the bog here and it would be very dangerous for you to just go strolling around."

Tuck looked off into the thicket nervously.

"Do you understand?"

"Yes," Katy said begrudgingly.

"Now, remember, stay where I can keep an eye on both of you."

David walked off toward the tent. Inside he found everything as they had left it. The first two bodies they had unearthed were now completely preserved and laid out on dry tables with sheets draped over them, but the bodies of the Roman couple were in separate tubs and were still soaking in the first of their chemical baths. David walked over to the woman. For some reason the pressure of the peat above her had been irregular and left her corpse both slightly elongated and slightly concave.

It was almost as if a wax model of a human being had been sat upon by a giant while it was still in the formative stages of hardening. Nonetheless, he started to drain off the chemical bath so that he could proceed with his examination.

Outside, the wind began to blow and caused the grass on the hills to rustle and move.

"Dad, the grass is moving!" Tuck called, suddenly panicky.

David looked up from his work. "Tuck, it's only the wind." Tuck seemed slightly reassured.

David finished draining the liquid off, and with a towel he began to pat the body dry. For the moment they had left all of the woman's clothing on, and even the fateful knife clutched firmly in her hands. From the activity of the chemicals in the peat she had also been left absolutely rigid, and she had been preserved lo these nineteen-odd centuries almost exactly as she had fallen just seconds after she had plunged the knife into her abdomen.

David looked at her face and felt a pang as he saw the sadness and desolation there. What had driven her to this act? he wondered. Was it really the witnessing of her husband's ghoulish murder, or was there some other secret that her ancient brain concealed?

Outside, the wind rustled once again, and Tuck became agitated. "Dad, I'm scared."

David looked up and saw that his son was looking around, anxiously. "Katy, aren't you telling him a story?"

"I'm trying to, but he won't listen," she whined back.

"Well, try harder."

He returned his attention to the body. Her flesh, once soft and supple, was now dry and leathery as an old shoe. He scrutinized her posture, the way she held her hands, but still he discerned nothing that piqued his attention. He tried carefully to shift her, to get a better view of the knife she held, when suddenly there was a snap and her hand broke neatly off at the wrist.

For some reason the mishap affected him almost as adversely as if the woman were still living flesh and blood instead of some strange permutation of something once alive, and he was filled with horror and anger over what he had done. He cursed as he looked at the cross section of her severed wrist, as brittle and ragged as an old tree limb. Perhaps it was the pressure he was under, or his exhaustion because of lack of sleep. Perhaps it was his concern and irritation with his wife, his loss of patience with his whiny children, or the total and agonizing frustration he felt over suspecting that he was close to something, but not able to pin down exactly what it was. But as he looked down at the shriveled body, as he pondered what secret the ancient skull contained that still eluded him, he wondered suddenly why he was doing it all. Grenville was right. He did grovel around in the mud and try desperately to wrest secrets out of fragments. Why was he struggling so hard? Why was he pushing his mettle to the very limit when still, no matter what he did, the world just continued to slowly collapse around him? Why didn't he just give up and go over to Grenville's side?

For several moments he remained lost in this thought, thinking of the worlds that would be opened up to him if he just accepted Grenville's offer, when, only half consciously, he noticed something peculiar about the concavity of the woman's body.

He barely had time to register the thought when outside the wind suddenly surged up powerfully and captured a piece of black vinyl plastic that had gotten wrapped around one of the tent's supporting ropes, sending it whipping through the air like some strange winged creature.

As fate would have it, it sailed right toward where Tuck and Katy were standing, and when Tuck saw it coming he screamed and suddenly broke into a run.

Horrified, David took off after him. "Tuck!" he cried, but Tuck just continued to run, heading straight toward the thicket that marked the edge of the bog.

Gripped by panic, David pounded after him. "Tuck, no! It's just the wind!"

But Tuck was apparently so overcome with terror that he was no longer cognizant of his father's cries. A wave of icy fear engulfed David as he saw Tuck vanish into the thicket.

"Tuck, please stop, Daddy will protect you!" David screamed, but when he reached the edge of the thicket he saw no sign of his son. He stopped, listening carefully, until he once again heard the crash of the underbrush, and then he took off in the direction of the sounds.

He caught a glimpse of Tuck only once more, just a flash

of the color of his jacket in the far distance, before he heard the splash.

"Tuck!" he screamed with such agony that it felt as if his vocal cords would rip from his throat. "Tuck, please!" He crashed frenziedly through the brambles, caring not at all that the thorns were ripping his skin, his clothes.

At last he reached the spot where he had last seen his son, but Tuck was nowhere to be found. As David looked frantically around only silence met his ears, silence and the ominous rocking of a tangle of lilies in one of the bog pools where only moments before something had apparently crashed through the floating mat of peat.

Without regard to his own safety, David dove madly in. Once submerged he struggled to open his eyes, but the icy water had become so clouded with peat from his thrashing around that he could see nothing. He quickly discerned that the bog pool appeared to be quite large, for as he swam farther downward he found no sign of bottom. He also, in his mad flailings, found no trace of Tuck.

Finally, his lungs on the verge of bursting, he started back up for air. When he reached the surface he came up under a matted tangle of vines and rotted debris and with superhuman strength he tore through them, gasping frantically when he once again saw daylight. In the distance he also heard Katy calling for him.

"Dad! Dad, where are you?"

"Katy!" he bellowed. "Don't come in! Run home and call for an ambulance!"

"Why?"

"Just do it!" he shrieked, angered that he was wasting precious time. He looked at his watch and realized that Tuck had now been under for almost a minute.

Taking several large gulps of air, he dove back down into the pitchy water. This time, more prepared for the descent, he reached bottom, or as he had expected, false bottom, and his hands plunged deep into the thick black ooze. He prayed that Tuck had not managed to submerge himself in this for if he had, David knew that he would never find him. Feeling his way carefully along the slimy bottom he penetrated another fifteen feet or so into the darkness. It was difficult going, for the bottom of the bog pool was littered with debris, old tree stumps and fallen branches, and David was forced to meticulously grope around them to make sure that Tuck had not gotten wedged underneath any of them. The water at the bottom of the pond was also icy cold and his fingers grew numb as he continued. Time and again he surfaced, ripping his way through the floating tangle of the lilies and gasping for air, only to dive down again to continue in his search. Finally, numbed from cold and exhaustion and in danger of drowning himself, he was forced to temporarily latch onto a floating log. He looked at his watch. To his great despair he saw that if Tuck was in the pond he had now been underwater for almost twenty minutes. David realized torturedly that already his hope of ever recovering his son alive was slim, but he realized that it was nonexistent if he did not continue. Filling his lungs he once again dove down into the murk.

It was a little while later, as he was fumbling wildly through the ooze of the false bottom, that his hand collided with the rubber sole of a child's shoe. Reaching out eagerly, he felt the solidity of a leg and he realized that he had found him. Calling upon his last flicker of strength, he carried the body to the surface. This time, with only one hand free, it was even more difficult for him to tear through to the open air, but finally he broke through and managed to reach the shore. Tears flooding his eyes, he laid Tuck's limp little form on a bed of ferns. Feeling for a pulse, he found none.

David's first urge was to wail, to let out all his grief and pain in one terrible cry of misery, but something inside him would not allow him to give up, to accept that Tuck was dead. Frenziedly, he collapsed beside his son and started to give him mouth-to-mouth resuscitation. After a minute or two of this, a slight stream of water came pouring out of Tuck's mouth, but it was not accompanied by any sound or movement to indicate that it was more than a phenomenon of physics, just an emptying of water from a dead body. David felt once again for a pulse, but still found none. Placing one hand on Tuck's diminutive chest, he pounded firmly on it with the other, and then again. He continued with his attempts at revival, alternately breathing into Tuck's mouth and then pounding on his chest, until suddenly a great flood of water poured forth out of him. David tilted Tuck slightly to one side, slapping him on the back to assist in the purge. And then he watched.

For several seconds Tuck remained motionless, the water continuing to stream from his mouth, and then suddenly he seemed to move. David ripped open his little shirt and placed his ear against his chest. To his uncontrolled elation he heard a faint beat. On Tuck's left hand a finger twitched, as weakly his body forced a cough and another flood of water came issuing out of his lungs. His heartbeat remained feeble and erratic and his eyes closed, as he desperately struggled to hold on to life.

David looked at his watch and realized to his horror that as near as he could determine Tuck had been underwater for almost thirty-five minutes. Now that his frenzied state of mind had diminished slightly, he wondered how it was that Tuck had survived at all, but his puzzlement quickly faded as he clung only to the hope that the ambulance would arrive in time. As he continued to rock his son gently in his arms he remembered also Winnifred Blundell's warning that sooner or later the bog always took, and he prayed that this time at least she had been wrong.

It was nearly dark before the ambulance finally arrived, accompanied by the police from Leeming as well as Grenville's Rolls. It did not surprise him that Grenville was here. He knew that after Melanie had called for the ambulance she would have worried about what Grenville would do when he found out, and she would have called him to apprise him of what was going on. The cars pulled to a stop and the ambulance attendants jumped out and rushed over. Within moments they had placed Tuck's still-unconscious form on a stretcher and had clamped an oxygen mask over his face.

Melanie also ran over, beginning to scream when she saw Tuck, and one of the policemen quickly took her by the shoulders and held her back.

Grenville got out of his Rolls and watched the proceedings sternly.

As the ambulance attendants loaded Tuck's stretcher into the back of the ambulance, David tried to comfort Melanie and Katy also ran over crying. It was only after both the police and the ambulance attendants were out of hearing range that Grenville strode angrily over.

"What in the bloody hell do you think you're doing having these people come here?" he demanded.

David looked at him wrathfully. He knew that Grenville

243

was going to be livid over his actions, but he no longer cared. "It's my son in there," he said. "He's nearly drowned. I had to call them."

Grenville was still fuming. "And what do you intend to do now?" he asked.

"We intend to go to the hospital and see that he's okay," David shot back.

"I won't allow it!" Grenville snapped.

"And what are you going to do to stop us?"

Grenville glared in the direction of the police, apparently weighing his options.

"If you kill them, not only will Tuck probably die and you won't have him, but you'll bring in an investigation that even you might have some trouble handling."

"Very well," he growled. "You've got me on this one. You and your wife may accompany your son to the hospital, but your daughter stays here."

Before David or Melanie could do a thing he pulled Katy away from them. Katy's eyes widened with terror and she was about to cry out when Grenville quickly passed his hand over her face and she fell into a bewitched sleep.

"She'll be at Wythen Hall until you return," he said. "And may I suggest for her sake that you keep me fully informed of what is going on, and you return forthwith." He gestured for his chauffeur to come over to take Katy's limp body and place it in the Rolls.

David stepped forward to stop him, but Grenville intervened, venom flooding his expression. "I warn you, Professor Macauley, do not push me any further, or I will kill all of these people, including your son, right here and now."

Convinced that Grenville was now telling the truth, David stepped back.

"No!" Melanie exclaimed as she watched Katy being taken away, but one of the policemen was approaching them and David motioned for her to be silent.

The ambulance started its motor.

"We're ready to leave," the policeman informed them. "Would you and your wife like a ride to the hospital?"

"Thank you," David returned, "but I have my car here. We'll drive ourselves."

"Very well," the policeman said, nodding. "If you don't mind we'll follow along also. We have a few questions we're going to have to ask you. Just formalities, you understand."

David nodded.

Before they left David ran up to the ambulance one last time and looked in at his son. "Any prognosis?" he asked the attendant who was still involved in administering oxygen to Tuck.

The attendant looked up. "How long did you say he was underwater?"

"Thirty-five minutes," David returned.

A shadow seemed to fall over the attendant's face. "Of course, we'll have to run some tests, but it's a miracle that you were able to revive him at all." He looked with concern at his partner. "I hate to be the one to tell you this, but I wouldn't get my hopes up about him ever regaining consciousness. Brain death generally occurs after five to ten minutes without oxygen. Even if we do manage to keep your son alive, it's doubtful that he'll ever come out of his coma."

The words cut through David like a sword. Numbed with shock, he assisted Melanie into the Volvo.

"What did he say?" she asked. But for the moment David could not reply. Both the ambulance and the police started their engines and David followed suit. As he turned the key in the ignition he looked at Grenville one last time.

"*What* did he say?" Melanie repeated, but still to no avail.

David's thoughts were a thousand miles away, and as he pulled up onto the lane he registered only the bottomless pain inside him and the glower on Grenville's face, illumed by the flashing red light of the ambulance as it receded into the distance.

11

AT THE HOSPITAL they waited for almost three hours before the physician attending Tuck, a Dr. Grosley, finally came out to talk to them.

Dr. Grosley was a tall man with a bald head. David searched his face for some hint of the news he was bearing. "How is he?" David asked. "Is there any hope?"

The doctor's expression remained grim. "Please sit down," he said, as he took a seat beside them. Before continuing he took off his glasses and wiped their lenses clean with a handkerchief. Then he replaced them and looked at David and Melanie somberly.

He cleared his throat. "As you know, something of a minor miracle has occurred in your being able to revive your son at all after he was submerged for so long underwater." He looked at David. "I must commend you for your efforts. As I understand it, they were quite extraordinary."

David nodded perfunctorily.

Dr. Grosley paused again, as if he didn't quite know what to say next. "I also understand that the lake your son drowned in was a bog lake and that the water was quite cold. Is that correct?"

Again David nodded. "Yes, that's correct. But why are you asking this? Is it important?"

Dr. Grosley pursed his brow. "In this case I'm beginning

to believe that it was quite important. In fact, for your son, the difference between life and death. I don't know if you have noticed, but in the news in the past several years there have been a number of accounts of this sort of thing. Last year a young boy fell through the ice in a river in Scotland and was under for forty minutes and then was successfully revived. And just this past winter a young woman was pulled from her automobile twenty-five minutes after plunging into an ice-encrusted pond and was successfully resuscitated."

"And were they all right?" David asked.

"In these two particular cases, after sufficient medical treatment both were able to resume normal lives."

"But how?" Melanie asked, grasping her husband's hand hopefully.

"Certainly part of their startling recoveries is due to advances medical science has made in such procedures as cardiopulmonary resuscitation and body-core rewarming. But a good deal of it is also due to a recently recognized phenomenon called the Mammalian Diving Reflex."

Both Melanie and David looked confused.

"Let me explain," Dr. Grosley went on. "You see, the reflex is triggered by the immersion of the face in cold water. This in turn stimulates the ophthalmic branch of the fifth cranial nerve, which results in apnea, bradycardia, and a redistribution of blood from the extremities to the central core of the body."

Melanie looked as if she were going to start crying again, and David looked at the doctor irritatedly. "Dr. Grosley, neither of us has any idea what you are talking about. Couldn't you please just tell us in plain English?"

Dr. Grosley blinked several times, looking sincerely apologetic. "I'm sorry. Do forgive me. All I meant is that when the face is immersed in cold water for any length of time, the body shuts down. It mobilizes all of its forces to supply the more vital organs such as the heart, lungs, and brain, with all of the available and oxygen-rich blood at its disposal. It seems to be a very ancient mechanism originally created by nature to allow seagoing mammals such as dolphins and whales to survive underwater. No one knows why human beings also possess the Mammalian Diving Reflex, but in cases such as this it can sometimes buy a little more time for drowning victims such as your son."

"But if I heard you correctly," David interrupted, "the two cases that you mentioned occurred in ice water. The water in the bog lake was cold, but it certainly wasn't near freezing."

"It doesn't matter," Dr. Grosley responded. "Even on the warmest day of the summer, when the surface temperature of a lake is seventy to seventy-five degrees Fahrenheit, the water at the bottom still only hovers around fifty degrees, and that's low enough."

"Are you trying to tell us that Tuck may be okay?" David asked.

"Not exactly," Dr. Grosley returned quickly. "What I mean to say is that we do not know yet. The fact that the water in the lake was cold and you were able to resuscitate your son after so long a time indicates the Mammalian Diving Reflex at least came into play, but the two cases I mentioned were two of the more remarkable ones. There have been other instances of MDR where the patients were resuscitated but still suffered considerable brain damage, and still others where the patients never came out of their comas at all. Now, we've run an EEG on your son, and we've discovered that there is still upper-brain activity, but all that tells us is that at least Tuck is not brain dead. But we have no idea if he'll ever come out of his coma, or—if and when he does—whether he will have suffered brain damage, and to what extent. Only time can answer these questions."

"So all that you are really telling us," David said, crestfallen, "is that there is hope."

"Yes," Dr. Grosley returned. "I'm not making you any promises, but there is at least hope."

Melanie started to cry and David put his arm around her as the doctor stood up. He waited to see if they had any other questions, and after several moments David looked back up at him.

"If Tuck does come out of his coma, do you have any idea when that might be?"

The doctor shook his head sadly. "No, I'm sorry, but we have no way of determining that. It could be in a few days. It could be months."

He was about to turn and walk away when suddenly he paused and gazed down at Melanie with a quizzical look on his face.

"Forgive me for saying it, Mrs. Macauley. I know you've been through rather a lot, but you do not look very well. Are you all right?"

Melanie looked up at the doctor as if she were not going to say anything, but then, sniffling, apparently changed her mind.

"Well, the truth is I haven't been feeling very well lately."

Dr. Grosley looked at his watch. "I have a few moments, would you like me to take a look at you?"

Melanie looked at David hesitantly and David nodded, urging her on. Finally, faltering, she turned to the doctor once again. "Very well."

＊　＊　＊

Melanie came away from the examination with a prescription for tranquilizers and the revelation that she was suffering from severe symptoms of stress. For the next twenty-four hours David and Melanie kept a close vigil over Tuck. All that night, as David sat up next to his son, his mind was racked intermittently by feelings of guilt over Tuck's accident, and then fear for his daughter's safety. He blamed himself for what happened to Tuck. He hated himself for ever taking Tuck to the bog in the first place, and he rebuked himself even more for not keeping a closer eye on him. Mixed in with this guilt was the worry that perhaps Melanie had been right, perhaps he had expected too much of his son, and if he had not this terrible thing might not have happened. As for Katy, David had no substantive reasons to suspect that Grenville was going to harm his hostage, but by now, at the very least, he had come to realize that the old sorcerer was as cruel as he was unpredictable, and even if he treated Katy with all of the decorum of his title, David knew that, should Grenville bring Katy out of her bewitched sleep, finding herself alone with the Marquis would be torture enough and would send her into a blind panic. And so, late that night, they drove back to the valley, and after picking up Katy, whom Grenville had mercifully left in her enchanted sleep for the duration of her incarceration, David reluctantly dropped his wife and daughter back at the cottage and returned to the hospital alone.

As the first day of Tuck's coma slowly grew into two, and then three, David's guilt intensified. He recalled clearly that shortly before the accident he had entertained the notion of accepting Grenville's offer of power, and he began to feel that, because of this, in some way beyond his reckoning the universe was punishing him, trying to teach him a lesson for having such cavalier thoughts. His excruciating bouts of self-reproach were punctuated only by moments of incredulity that he could be in this situation at all. As he passed the increasingly endless hours in the hospital waiting room watching the doctors and the nurses walking to and fro, he found himself wanting to shout out to them, to take them by the shoulders and tell them about the bizarre and terrifying plight that now held his family in a death grip, but even if he had harbored the hope that anyone would have believed him, he had come to believe in Grenville's powers too fully to have any confidence that this would help him out of the nightmare he was living.

It was on the fourth day following the accident, while David was getting some coffee out of a machine at the end of the corridor, that one of the nurses came running up behind him.

"Mr. Macauley, Mr. Macauley! It's your son. We believe he may be coming out of his coma!"

Tossing his still full cup into the trash, David hurriedly followed the nurse back to Tuck's room. There he found several other nurses standing around Tuck's bed with Dr. Grosley hovering over his son excitedly.

"His hands," Dr. Grosley instructed. "Look at his hands."

David looked down and saw that Tuck's tiny hands were twitching as if coursing with an unseen current. Although it was a minor act, the various onlookers in the room were responding to it with almost uncontrollable excitement. For the first time since the accident David also felt a surge of hope, but then he looked down and saw a large red welt on Tuck's arm. "What's that?" he asked.

"We took some blood to test for hepatitis from the bog water," Dr. Grosley was saying, when one of the nurses suddenly interrupted.

"His eyes!" she said excitedly.

David directed his attention to Tuck's eyes and saw that his lids had also started to quiver. Like a robot exploring long-dead circuits, the unseen energy shot through Tuck's still limp body, here causing a facial spasm, and there a twitch in his leg, until finally a rapturous cry rose from everyone in the room as Tuck's eyes slowly opened and he apparently struggled to focus on the faces around him.

David rushed forward and grasped his son's hand. "Tuck!" he exclaimed. "It's Daddy. Daddy's here." He looked hopefully down into his son's face, but Tuck just continued to squint confusedly, his gaze examining David, and then moving away and looking at Dr. Grosley, and then each of the nurses in turn.

"Tuck!" David repeated, but still Tuck paid him no special mind. He looked at David with neither fear nor recognition, as if he saw no more that was familiar to him in David's countenance than he saw in any of the other faces present.

David looked fearfully at Dr. Grosley.

"He may still be confused," the older man returned. "Keep trying. See if you can get him to say something."

David turned again to his son. "Tuck," he murmured softly. "Can you remember me? Do you know your name? Your name is Tuck. Can you say that? Can you say *Tuck*?"

Still Tuck only blinked perplexedly.

"Please," David begged. "Please can you say something? Anything?"

For the first time Tuck seemed to register that he was being asked to do something, and he looked at David slightly more penetratingly than before.

"*Tuck*," David said, mouthing the words more slowly. "Can you say *Tuck*?"

He paused and everyone watched Tuck with silent anticipation, and then finally the child opened his mouth. For a moment nothing came out, as he apparently experienced anew the feeling of having vocal cords, and then at last a slow and faltering cascade of syllables crept forth. But everyone in the room remained tensely silent, for the sounds that came out had been unintelligible and more like the slurred and impenetrable stammerings of a stroke victim than coherent human speech.

David's face fell and Dr. Grosley quickly grasped his arm comfortingly.

"Sometimes, if the speech centers of the brain have been damaged, many other functions still remain intact. Has your son learned to read yet?"

David nodded.

"Are there any written words, perhaps his name or something, that he would display a more than normal recognition of?"

David thought about it for a moment. "Yes, I believe so," he replied.

Dr. Grosley withdrew a felt-tip pen from his pocket and took a piece of paper from a tablet near the bed. "Write the word here in large, bold letters."

David did as requested. With slow and measured strokes he spelled out the word MOXIE. Dr. Grosley took the paper back from him and looked at the word, blinking several times and then smiling faintly.

"Now let's see," he said. He held the paper up a foot or two in front of Tuck's face and Tuck focused on the marking on the paper.

"Watch his lips to see if he tries to mouth the word silently," he instructed.

Again everyone in the room went silent, and for several seconds Tuck continued to scrutinize the word on the paper, the black against the white. But his lips did not move, nor did he register even the faintest hint of recognition. He looked up blankly at the people around him, still paying no more mind to David's face than he did to any of the others present. A pall fell over the room.

"I'm so sorry, Mr. Macauley," one of the nurses said, and David turned to Dr. Grosley anxiously.

"What does it mean?" he asked, whatever hope he had so recently fostered now rapidly slipping away.

Dr. Grosley's gaze became evasive and downcast. "I'm sorry," he said. "It appears that your son's brain damage is more extensive than we had expected.

"What does that mean?" David repeated.

Dr. Grosley looked at him grimly. "It's difficult to say. At the very least it means that your son as you knew him is no longer there. There may be remnants of his memories of who he once was somewhere deep in his mind, but the fact that he displays absolutely no recognition of you, or his name, or the word that we have just shown him indicates that this information is pretty much absent from his mind."

"And at the very worst?" David asked, detecting in the way that Dr. Grosley had couched his remark that there were darker tidings to come.

"Well certainly we now know that at least some brain damage

has occurred. However, given that we still don't know the extent of the damage, or what learning disabilities it has brought with it, it will still be quite some time before we can predict how much, if at all, Tuck might recover from his current condition. In the worst scenario he may remain like this forever, a perpetual infant. However, if the damage is not too severe, through therapy and a great deal of love and patience, in a few years we may be able to instill in him a few new memories, we may even, in time, be able to teach him to speak and read once again."

* * *

In the next several days it was discovered that Tuck's motor functions had remained unimpaired, and although he was wobbly he could still manipulate objects and walk by himself. However, he still continued to display no more than what had become a familiar and trusting acceptance of David's presence, and, in fact, displayed more excitement at the presence of a nurse that he had taken a liking to than he did toward his own father. Occasionally, he also persevered in his attempts at human speech, but these remained garbled and indecipherable, and Tuck seemed almost puzzled by this fact, as if something deep inside him recalled communicating with people in this manner, and was now baffled and frustrated at the process no longer working.

Learning the truth about Tuck's condition had also pretty much brought David to his knees. When he was with his son, or what was left of his son, he forced himself to be cheerful and encouraging, but when he was alone he was desolate. The loss of Tuck as he had known and loved him, combined with the unrelenting awareness of Grenville's stranglehold on his family, had left David a broken man. He didn't sleep much and he seldom ate, and by the time Dr. Grosley said it would be all right to take Tuck home and continue nursing him back to health there, David was like a man deranged, his hair tousled, his gaze blank and frightening, and his clothing unkempt. It was as he was out in the parking lot ready to bring the car around to pick up Tuck that he saw a figure approaching him in the darkness.

He looked up agitatedly, primed to run at a moment's notice, and then he realized it was Brad.

"Dr. Macauley . . . *David*," the younger man called out.

"Brad, what are you doing here?"

Brad stepped into the circle of one of the parking-lot lights and stood about four feet from David.

"I was so worried about you," he returned. "And Mrs. Macauley. I hadn't heard from you and then a friend of mine who's an intern here called me and told me what happened to Tuck. I'm so sorry."

David looked at his graduate assistant nervously. He was happy to see him, indeed, thrilled at the sight of a familiar and comforting face. But he was also afraid, for he knew that he was still bound by Grenville's command of silence.

"How is Mrs. Macauley . . . ah, *Melanie* doing?"

"Not well, I'm afraid," David stammered in return.

Brad's forehead furrowed as he shook his head sympathetically. "God, I'm sorry to hear about all of this. Listen, I don't want to pressure you about the digs because I know that's got to be the last thing on your mind, but is there anything I can do to help you out? Anything at all?"

David felt a wave of affection for the younger man flow through him and he yearned desperately to be able to open up to him, to let everything that was happening to him just come flooding forth, but he knew that he could not. "No," he said as the evening wind blew up gustily around them.

"Do you think I could maybe visit, come around some day this week to see how things are going?"

"No," David repeated quickly, fearing the consequences. He looked at the younger man and saw that his feelings appeared to be hurt by the brusqueness of his refusal. "I'm sorry, Brad," he said in a more amicable tone. "It's just that . . . well, you've got to understand Melanie's in pretty bad shape, and I appreciate your offer. I appreciate it more than you may even imagine, but I just don't want to chance setting Melanie off. I hope you'll be patient with me on this."

"Sure, whatever you say," Brad said softly.

David looked at his watch and then back at the younger man, his eyes filled with conflicting emotion. "I'm sorry, Brad. I really have to be going."

Brad looked bewilderedly at him as David fidgeted and prepared to leave.

"Dr. Macauley . . . ah, I mean, David?"

"Yes?"

"Are you sure everything's all right? I mean, I know you must be going through hell, but I get a strange feeling there's more to it than that, there's something else going on that you're not telling me." Brad reached out and took David by the arm and David looked down, realizing that such a bold gesture of affection probably took every ounce of nerve that the younger man possessed.

He looked up into the younger man's eyes and was swept again with the urge to confide in him. After all, what more could happen to him? What terrible blow could fate or Grenville deliver him that would make him any more miserable? The wind blew again, and he looked around nervously as he realized that even if Julia had taken the form of an insect, if they strode together full face into the wind she might never be able to flutter close enough to them to hear, to know that he was betraying any secrets.

His heart began to pound. "There is something I'm not telling you, Brad, but we've got to walk." He looked around again. "I don't want to be overheard."

"But there's no one else in the parking lot," Brad countered, looking even more concerned.

"It doesn't matter!" David snapped. "Follow me." He turned around and started walking into the wind.

They strode out into an open space in the parking lot and David continued to look fearfully about.

"Well, what is it?" Brad prodded.

David looked at the younger man once more and was about to tell him when suddenly he was swept with a constricting fear. Was he doing the right thing? Or was Grenville listening somehow, through some artifice that he didn't even know about?

He struggled to force the words out. "It's more fantastic than anything you've ever encountered before in your life. Brad, I don't expect for you to believe me, but certainly you know I'm not the sort of man to make something like this up. It's the most frightening thing I've ever been up against. It's—"

And then he froze in midword as the shadow moved about them. And he screamed.

"Dr. Macauley!" Brad called after him, but it was of no use. David just kept running until he reached the Volvo and got in, leaving the younger man standing in the halo of a parking-lot light and watching the lazy flutterings of an errant moth.

* * *

Melanie took her first sight of her son as well as anyone might have expected her to, and it broke her heart when he looked at her with the same vacant stare that he had first offered David. Tuck was still quite weak from his accident and slept a great deal, but over the course of the next several days his motor skills improved with such remarkable rapidity that he was feeding himself and walking around as if nothing had happened. His mental condition, however, did not improve, and he would occasionally scrutinize his favorite toys as if they were the most cryptic objects he had ever seen. He also continued to attempt to speak, and when he did so, would stammer incoherently with such a desperate longing to be understood that it never failed to unnerve them and send them from the room to conceal their tears. Try as they might to maintain an optimistic facade in front of Tuck, their own grief and disappointment soon seemed to become apparent to him, and he himself sunk into despair as if he too were tortured by the disabled brain that now entrapped him.

To assist them in their fight against the unrelenting gloom that now encompassed them, nature saw fit to batter the valley with a torrential rain, and it was after two days of this, when David could not fathom what else could possibly befall them, that they received a telephone call. Katy answered it, and after the caller had apparently identified himself, she laid the phone down and started up the stairs.

"Katy," David called after her. "Who is it?"

"It's Dr. Grosley," she returned.

"Well, let your mother sleep. I'll take the call," David said, starting toward the telephone.

"No," Katy returned. "Dr. Grosley asked especially to speak to her. He said it was important."

David hesitated, still wondering if it would be best if he took the call, but then gave in. "All right," he said, motioning his daughter on.

Katy roused her mother and a minute later Melanie came groggily down the steps in her nightgown. "Hello? Oh, hello, Dr. Grosley. . . . Yes. Well, I suppose so."

David stood in the doorway listening in to the call and

watching Melanie's expression with interest.

Suddenly Melanie went deathly white. "No!" she gasped. And then she fainted, the phone tumbling out of her hand and rattling against the floor.

"Hello? Hello?" came Dr. Grosley's muted voice from the receiver as David quickly knelt down by his wife to check her. He picked up the dangling telephone.

"Dr. Grosley, this is Mr. Macauley. It appears that my wife has passed out."

"Oh, dear," Dr. Grosley returned. "I do hope she wasn't hurt?"

David continued to examine his wife as he spoke. "No, I don't think so. I think she just fainted."

"I see. Perhaps she was just overcome by the news I gave her."

"Why?" David said worriedly. "What did you tell her?"

There was a pause before Dr. Grosley's voice once again sounded at the other end of the line. "Well, good news, I hope. Some of the results of the tests I ran on her just came back. It appears that she's pregnant. The two of you are going to have another baby."

David allowed the information to sink in and repeated it several times before he finally hung up. He might have been happy, were it not for the situation they were in and the fact that Melanie had taken the news even more disconsolately than he. Behind him Mrs. Comfrey had apparently been listening in, and she ran up excitedly.

"A baby!" she rejoiced. "The missus is going to have a baby! What a godsend. Praise be, that's what this house needs." She wrung her hands together excitedly and then stooped and assisted David in lifting Melanie into a chair. "I'll get Mrs. Macauley a cup of clear tea," she said then, scurrying off.

Katy looked at her father with concern. "I think there's some smelling salts in the upstairs cabinet."

"Thanks, Katy," David returned, ascending the stairs in leaps and bounds to get them. It took him only a moment to find them, but when he returned he found that not only had Mrs. Comfrey already brewed the tea, but had apparently poured the hot mixture down Melanie's throat.

"What did you do?" he demanded as Melanie coughed and sputtered several drops of it on herself.

"It's to revive her," Mrs. Comfrey returned, deadpan.

"But you might have choked her," David said. He uncapped the smelling salts and passed them beneath Melanie's nose. She stirred, her eyelids fluttering, but still she did not come to.

"That's funny," David said, passing the smelling salts beneath his own nose to see if they were still good, and the sharp scent nearly caused him to topple backward. The vial was definitely still potent. He wafted it once again beneath Melanie's nose, and again she stirred, pulling away from the pungent smell, but she remained unconscious. Growing increasingly worried, he lifted her up into his arms. "Help me get her upstairs," he said.

"Yes, good idea," Mrs. Comfrey returned, going up ahead of him. "I'll see that the bed's turned down."

He arrived upstairs and placed Melanie between the sheets.

Mrs. Comfrey retrieved a cold, wet washcloth and placed it on Melanie's brow. She looked up at David. "I don't think you need to worry. Having a baby does funny things to a woman, you know. She was probably just overcome by the news because of all the things that have happened lately. She'll come to."

Then, on seeing the tension in David's face, Mrs. Comfrey's expression became more concerned. "Mr. Macauley, if you'll forgive me for saying so, I'd say you could use a good stiff drink."

Surprised by Mrs. Comfrey's sudden display of considerateness, David pushed his hair back off his forehead. "I suppose I could at that."

"Well, why don't you go on downstairs and have one. I'll see to Mrs. Macauley and I'll call you as soon as she comes to," Mrs. Comfrey returned.

David smiled, touched by the thought, and nodded. As he passed Tuck's room he looked in and saw that he was fast asleep. He went downstairs and poured himself a double shot of Dewars' and downed it in three gulps. Still disturbed by Melanie's apparent horror over her pregnancy and his inability to revive her with the smelling salts, he started to pace. Outside the thunder cracked. The lightning flashed, and a moment later the thunder sounded again, and suddenly he got the most peculiar idea. It had been drifting around in the back of his mind for some time, something he had noticed before and had not paid enough attention to, and now, for the first time, he thought he was beginning to understand.

He grabbed his raincoat and put on his rubbers, and then shouted up from the bottom of the stairs, "Mrs. Comfrey, I'm going out for a drive. I'll be back in about half an hour."

"Okay, Mr. Macauley," Mrs. Comfrey called back.

He went outside and got into the Volvo. It was raining so hard that even with the headlights on and the windshield wipers turned up to their top speed he could barely see a thing, and no sooner had he started to back out of the driveway than he pulled the car neatly into a rut. Gingerly he pressed down the accelerator and heard the irksome whine of one of the wheels spinning uselessly in the mud. He rocked the car, regulating his action on the accelerator to its best advantage, but still the Volvo remained thoroughly stuck. Cursing, he got out and examined the damage, and saw that the car had sunk into the mud almost up to its bumper. Pulling his raincoat more tightly around him, he slammed the door and started off on foot.

Because of the rain, it took him longer than usual to reach the camp, and once there he was pleased to find that at least the portable lighting system still worked. After flicking them on he looked around the tent at the shrouded bodies on their various tables. Then he looked at the body of the Roman woman, still resting in her empty tub just as he had left her. He walked across the room and looked down at the strange concavity left on her abdomen by the weight of the peat. He wondered again at this peculiarity, which he had first noticed just moments before Tuck's accident.

She was such a perfect specimen, and such an important find historically that he had hoped he could perform the most modern procedures upon her, X rays and ultrasound scans, before resorting to the more crude methods at his disposal. But given the specialness of the circumstances he had no choice. Taking a scalpel in his hands, he carefully cut through her blouse, trying to injure its structure and pattern as little as possible, and then lifted it away. He gazed down at her naked body, the shriveled breasts and the puffy belly, elongated and tobacco brown. And then, taking a deep breath, he began to cut.

Outside, the rain continued to hit the fabric of the tent with such force that it sounded like a thousand little fingers snapping against the canvas, and the lightning flashed again. David continued with his ghoulish task and noticed that, as he had expected, the woman's flesh was still so tough that he was going to have to cut a perfect oval to be able to open her up enough to see inside. As if he were coring an apple, he moved the scalpel slowly around until he had completed a full circle. Then, taking hold of the neat skullcap of skin, he lifted it out as the thunder pealed once again.

Although he had been half expecting it, the sight that now met his eyes still caused his blood to run cold and a tingling darkness to move up his spine. Perhaps it was because it was the final proof of the antiquity of Grenville's power. Or perhaps it was because the evil that he was up against was now recorded so tangibly before him, and in a form that was easy for him to understand, to touch, and actually examine with his own hands. Whatever the case, what he saw frightened David, made him realize that he was in a fight for more than just his mortal soul, more than anything that he had yet experienced, for he now knew the Roman woman's secret, why Grenville had not allowed Julia to kill her, and why she had ultimately been driven to take her own life. She had been pregnant, and the child that she had carried was not a human child.

He looked down at the grotesque and leathery thing still slumbering in her womb, at its tiny but elongated fore and middle fingers, at its large and pointed ears, like dried bat wings plastered and curled on either side of its head, at its small, round mouth already lined with razor-sharp teeth, and its closed but massive eyes. Like everything that had been interred in the bog, the fetus had undergone a dark metamorphosis, had been preserved and mummified by its many centuries of burial in the peat, until it now looked unreal, more like a movie prop than something that had once been alive. But David knew that it had been alive. And he knew what manner of creature it would have grown into had it been allowed to mature.

As it continued to rain outside, a storm of thoughts passed through his mind. He realized that somewhere along the line, Julia, in some guise, had managed to either seduce or rape Melanie and that she had been too frightened or ashamed to tell him. Although he hoped it wasn't true, he suspected that the child she now carried was the same as the hideous thing before him. Melanie was aware of this fact, or at least thought it possible, and perhaps that was why she had fainted upon hearing she was pregnant. A wave of revulsion passed through David at this realization, but he suppressed it, knowing that he had to persevere until he had further pieced together all the facts that now confronted him.

If he was correct in his assumptions, perhaps that was why Grenville had not simply killed them and taken their children. It was probably never their children that he really wanted. As David thought back he recalled that one of the first questions Grenville had asked him was whether they had children and intended to have more. Certainly from this, Grenville could have determined that Melanie was a young and fertile woman, still capable of childbearing. This had perhaps been his plan all along.

As David continued in his mad race of thoughts he realized that this was probably why Grenville had sought so hard to court his favor, to win David over to his side. No doubt Grenville had been quite displeased when the Roman woman had, instead of giving birth to another minion for him, taken her own life. If and when the time came that Melanie discovered the true nature of her pregnancy, it would have been most useful to Grenville to have David as an ally, to help him prevent an incident like the Roman woman's suicide from occurring again.

With this thought came one final realization. David recalled the red welt on Melanie's arm and how similar it had seemed to the needle mark on Tuck's arm where the doctors had taken blood to test for hepatitis. What if the mark had not been a bee sting left by Julia? What if Grenville was secretly closely monitoring all of Melanie's bodily functions and already knew that she was pregnant? Given that he had not won David's favor, and that both David and apparently Melanie knew the true parentage of the child she was carrying, to prevent Melanie from doing something similar to what the Roman woman had done, Grenville had only one recourse. He would have to control Melanie completely, and to do that he would have to take her into his safekeeping.

The lightning flashed again and David looked out into the darkness. He knew Grenville well enough by now to know that he would not waste a second in accomplishing his task, and with David out of the house and a good distance away it was a perfect time for him to make his move. Suddenly overcome by terror, David looked one last time at the unspeakable thing on the table before him, and then ran out into the storm.

* * *

Lying in her bed, Melanie knew something was wrong. She was completely conscious, and yet it took every ounce of strength she had to move. She remembered the telephone call from Dr. Grosley, and she remembered realizing that it meant that now she was going to have to tell David about her encounter with that . . . that *thing*. She recalled also that she had fainted, and she had a dim perception of a hot liquid being poured down her throat. No, forced, and that she had almost choked. But beyond that, until this moment, everything had been darkness. Even opening her eyes was a Herculean task, and when she finally succeeded she looked around the room. First, she noticed that it was empty. And then she noticed that the rain was still beating briskly against the pane. And then she noticed that the hall light was on and she could hear singing.

It was a familiar voice and she recognized it immediately. As soon as she did, Mrs. Comfrey came padding softly into the room. In her hand she carried a cup of tea.

"Oh, you're awake," she said with surprise. "Well, I've brought you another cup of clear tea. Here," she said, lifting Melanie's head up to face the cup. "Drink it down. You'll feel better."

Instantly she started to pour the hot liquid into Melanie's mouth, and Melanie struggled to push it away. "Mrs. Comfrey, please. Can't you just set it by the bed and I'll drink it myself?" And then, as soon as she had said it, she realized that this was what had happened to her before, and suddenly it occurred to her, from Mrs. Comfrey's forcefulness, from the strange lethargy that now gripped her body, that she was being drugged.

Mrs. Comfrey looked at her disbelievingly. "Are you sure if I just leave it that you'll drink it?"

Trying to be as convincing as possible, Melanie returned, "Yes, of course I will."

Mrs. Comfrey remained dubious. "You promise?"

Melanie found her eyes trying to close again and she struggled to hold them open. "Yes, I promise."

"Well, I guess that's all right then. I'll just go get ready."

"Ready?" Melanie repeated. "Ready for what?"

"To go out," Mrs. Comfrey returned and looked slightly shocked as if she felt that it should be completely obvious to Melanie what she was talking about.

Melanie tilted her head and looked once again out the window. "But it's raining," she managed to say. But when she returned her head to its original position she saw only Mrs. Comfrey's back as she ambled out into the hall. For several minutes Melanie just lay motionless, wondering if she was imagining things, and staring at the window and then at the cup of tea.

Out in the hall she could hear Mrs. Comfrey walking up and down, cupboard doors opening and closing, and then she heard the unmistakable sound of water running, lots of it. Finally, mustering all of her strength, she used her arms as a pivot and swung herself out of bed. Sluggishly, she put on her slippers, and then, almost as an afterthought, she took the cup of tea and dumped it out the window. Slipping on her robe, she inched her way out into the hall. As she reached the door she heard the water stop and then a clunk and a plunk.

Was she dreaming? No, she wasn't dreaming. She could feel the wood of the doorframe too distinctly beneath her hand. And besides, everything—the chill atmosphere of the house because of the rain, the agonizing lassitude of her muscles—it was all too real. She heard a sudden plash of water, as of one liquid being poured into another. Her curiosity aroused, she crept down the hall. It wasn't until she was halfway down the corridor that she realized the light was on in the bathroom, and the door was ajar. And the sound was coming from in there.

For some reason it struck her as all very odd, and although she wasn't quite sure why, it seemed prudent to her to muster as much stealth as possible. Slowly, she approached the bathroom door, and when she was finally just an inch away, she leaned forward and looked inside.

To her slight embarrassment she discovered that the sounds were only Mrs. Comfrey taking a bath, and she was just about to politely withdraw when the smell hit her full in the face. It was a mind-bogglingly ghastly smell, the same horrible stench of decay that had drifted through the house for weeks, only a thousand times more potent, and madly Melanie looked about the bathroom for its source. Mrs. Comfrey seemed not aware of it at all, and continued to sit in the bathtub facing away from Melanie as she languidly lifted tumbler after tumbler of water and poured them over her back. Mystified, Melanie was about to pull away when she noticed something else. She blinked several times for she found it difficult to believe, but here and there it looked as if tiny chunks of Mrs. Comfrey's abdomen were actually starting to break away and were dangling in the flow of water, as if, were it not for forces unknown, she were in danger of simply falling into pieces. Baffled, Melanie continued to scrutinize Mrs. Comfrey's naked torso, and then she saw. In the base of Mrs. Comfrey's spine, as neatly as if they had been shot into a cadaver, were two bullet holes surrounded by a corpselike aurcole of gray.

Melanie gasped and Mrs. Comfrey turned around. Undismayed, she said: "Are you ready, dear? We'll be going soon." She stood, pulling a towel around her, and stepped out of the tub.

Terror-stricken, Melanie stumbled backward as she realized now why Mrs. Comfrey wore such heavy perfume. She clambered to right herself after her fall, and Mrs. Comfrey observed her animation with slight surprise. "Oh, now, didn't you drink your tea?" she asked with the amiability of an old nanny.

She started for Melanie and Melanie took a step backward.

"Why are you doing this?" she gasped. "What are you and why are you here?"

Mrs. Comfrey looked puzzled. "Why, I'm your nurse. I've been watching over you all along. I'm to be the midwife at your baby's birth."

Before she even finished the sentence Melanie had panicked and broken into a run.

"David!" she cried. "David!" But when there was no answer she dashed into Tuck's room and lifted him up into her arms. When she rushed back out into the hall she noticed that Mrs. Comfrey was in her room with the door open and was leisurely dressing.

Still running, Melanie went quickly down the stairs.

"David! Katy! Where are you?"

"What is it, Mom?" Katy said, coming over to the stairs.

"Where's your dad?"

"He went out."

"Oh, no!" Melanie gasped. "Did he take the car?" Not waiting for an answer she ran to the window and looked out. To her relief she saw that it was still in the driveway.

"Katy, run out and get in the car, now!"

Seeing the panic in her mother's face, Katy did as she was bid. Tuck stirred in Melanie's arms, his eyes rolling around in confusion. Melanie grabbed her purse with her set of keys to the Volvo in it and ran out into the rain.

"Mom, what is it?" Katy asked, crying, when they were all in the car.

"Lock all the doors!" Melanie barked back as she started the car. At the front door of the house Mrs. Comfrey appeared in her raincoat and hat.

Melanie hit the accelerator and the wheels of the Volvo spun uselessly.

"Oh, no!" she cried, the drug that had been in the tea still tugging at her will.

Mrs. Comfrey started down the steps.

Melanie hit the gas pedal again, rocking the car back and forth. "Oh, no! Oh, no! Oh, no!"

Katy looked out the car window at Mrs. Comfrey's approach, and discerning that the older woman was the cause of Melanie's unholy dread, became even more agitated. "Mom!" she screamed. "What is it? What's going on?"

"Don't let her in!" Melanie gasped. She continued to madly rock the car as Mrs. Comfrey trudged slowly toward them.

"Mrs. Macauley," Melanie heard her say above the whine of the tires. "It's quite stuck. I saw it happen out the window. Mr. Macauley couldn't even get it out."

"Oh, where is he?" Melanie exclaimed as she burst into tears. She continued to rock the car, pounding the accelerator again and again as Mrs. Comfrey's deathly white hand tapped incessantly against the window.

"It's no use," Mrs. Comfrey shouted. "There's no place for you to run to."

Her sobbing had now become convulsive, and Katy was also screaming and crying, but Melanie would not give up. Desperately she kept trying to rock the Volvo out of the ditch as she watched Mrs. Comfrey walk away and retrieve a large stone. Mrs. Comfrey carried the stone back to the car, and with the same ruthless affability, smiled in the window at Melanie.

"No!" Melanie screamed as she stomped the pedal even more frantically. With supernatural strength Mrs. Comfrey's thin, scarecrow arms lifted the stone high above her head, and she was just about to bring it crashing down through the windshield when suddenly the Volvo found traction on something and lurched up out of the ditch. Once in the lane Melanie floored it, and they went speeding down the road. It was a short-lived victory. They had traveled only a few hundred yards when suddenly the road, a virtual bog itself from the rain, simply gave way beneath them, and like a piece of butter sliding off a hot skillet, the car slid back down the muddy cascade and buried itself up to its headlights in the mire.

Realizing there was no hope of getting it out, Melanie grabbed Tuck and ordered Katy out of the car. Their feet sank up to their ankles in the mud as they struggled to get out the car door, and to Melanie's continued horror she saw that Mrs. Comfrey was running toward them and was only about a hundred yards away. Not knowing what else to do, she wiped the rain out of her eyes, and then reached back into the car and pulled the trunk release. Then, pushing Tuck back into the car, she went and got the tire iron out of the trunk.

By this time Mrs. Comfrey was closing fast upon them, and she seemed not at all concerned by the weapon in Melanie's hand. In a mindless panic, Melanie braced herself, and just as Mrs. Comfrey was lunging for her, she swung the tire iron around and brought it crashing into Mrs. Comfrey's side. There was a sort of squelching sound and Mrs. Comfrey pitched to the left, but she did not fall. The thunder cracked and the rain continued to pour down as Mrs. Comfrey sedately surveyed the damage. The tire iron had hit her full in the rib cage and had even left an apparent dent, but no blood trickled out, only a sort of white ooze. Mrs. Comfrey looked irritatedly at Melanie, for the first time displaying a hint of anger.

She lunged again, her white hand becoming clawlike as she grabbed for Melanie's throat, and Melanie swung the tire iron again, this time catching Mrs. Comfrey full in the neck. Again Mrs. Comfrey careened to one side, but still she did not fall, and again Melanie brought the tire iron crashing down and hammering into her attacker. This time the flesh of Mrs. Comfrey's neck split open like a ripe melon and a white substance came out. Before Mrs. Comfrey could recover, Melanie got in another blow and then another, until, to Melanie's unabated horror, chunks of Mrs. Comfrey's shoulder started to fall away, revealing her decaying insides, which possessed the consistency of a sort of crumbly cheese. Her vision now blurred by crying, Melanie just continued her assault until Mrs. Comfrey's head came clean off, and indeed much of her upper torso had been whacked away, but the headless body battled on. It was clear it was about to die, but still it stumbled forward, groping furiously.

No longer thinking clearly, Melanie screamed and stumbled blindly in the opposite direction, not stopping to hear if the thing was still pursuing her, and then suddenly she ran into a pair of comforting arms. Her crying was uncontrollable as she realized that it was David back from the digs, and she looked up, longing for even so much as a glimpse of his reassuring face. But it was not David. It was Grenville. "I've been waiting for you," he said as he closed his hand tightly about her wrist. Melanie looked past him and saw that his Rolls was parked just a little distance up the lane and the chauffeur was already carrying Katy, kicking and screaming, to the car.

"What about the boy?" the chauffeur asked.

Pulling Melanie sharply to his side, Grenville directed his attention to Tuck who was still sitting in the Volvo.

"Leave him," Grenville returned. "I think that Professor Macauley's wife and daughter will be hostages enough."

* * *

When David neared the cottage the first thing he saw was the Volvo half buried in the ditch, its headlights still shooting up into the pouring rain. And then he saw the tiny figure running toward him. At first he was frightened, not knowing who or what the approaching figure was, but then he saw it was Tuck. He looked worriedly into the Volvo and saw Melanie's purse and the keys in the ignition, but no sign of either his wife or his daughter. And when the lightning flashed he saw the remains of Mrs. Comfrey.

"My God, what has happened here?" he murmured as Tuck reached him. He looked around one last time before he swept Tuck up into his arms and ran toward the house. He was halfway there before he realized with amazement that at least Tuck had seemed to recognize him, or recognize that he represented some sort of port in the storm.

When he got to the house he wrapped a blanket around Tuck and placed him in one of the living room chairs. Then he searched the cottage from top to bottom. His heart sank when he still found no sign of his wife or daughter. He did not know what had happened to Mrs. Comfrey, but given that there was no trace of either Katy or Melanie he could only imagine that Grenville now had them. He was about to collapse when in the living room he discovered that Tuck had slipped out of his blanket and was now pacing in front of the fire, his tiny hands clasped behind his back.

"Tuck?" David said, curious at his strangely adult behavior.

For the first time Tuck seemed almost to know the name, and he looked at David with concern.

"Tuck, do you understand me?" David asked excitedly.

In reply, Tuck babbled a stream of the nonsense syllables that had now supplanted his once intelligible vocabulary, and then looked at David beseechingly.

David rushed forward and, kneeling down, took hold of both of Tuck's arms.

"Tuck, you know what happened, don't you? You're trying to tell me, aren't you?"

Again Tuck slurred out a stream of nonsense, and again David was struck by not only the apparent and desperate intentionality behind it, but by the increasing aura of power that seemed to be emanating from Tuck, the rapidity of his mastery over motor function, and the growing sharpness of his eyes. Now more than ever David got the unnerving feeling that somewhere deep in Tuck there was a working mind, a conscious and thinking being that was as frustrated by the wall of babble dividing the two of them as David was.

"God, I wish I understood you," David muttered, and Tuck also rattled out something with a sigh. Only this time David caught something in Tuck's speech that caused him to freeze with astonishment.

"What did you say?" he asked, and Tuck looked up at him, searching David's eyes for some hint of meaning, and then, apparently finding it, he repeated the syllables.

David would have been moved enough at the fact that Tuck had repeated the same sequence of phonetic sounds twice in a row. But what really staggered him, caused his very heart to stop, was that he had recognized one of the syllables. It sounded to him disturbingly like ancient Eblaite. Thunderstruck, he repeated one of the few phrases he knew in the language, the sentence that he had first heard Grenville say to Julia.

No sooner had he said the phrase when Tuck's own eyes widened with amazement and he reached up and gripped David's arms excitedly. He shot something else back at David, and not knowing what else to say, David repeated a word that he knew was one of the terms by which the Eblaite people knew themselves.

"*Ibri,*" he proffered.

At this Tuck's rapture knew no bounds. "*Ibri,*" he repeated, nodding. And then, wringing his hands together excitedly and hopping around, he cast his gaze up toward the ceiling. "*Hallelujah, hallelujah, hallelujah!*"

12

FOR THE REST of the evening they went around the house pointing at objects and feverishly telling each other the words in their respective languages for those things. With the aid of the article that Burton-Russell had given him and a notebook and pen, David started to construct a lexicon of the ancient tongue that Tuck was now speaking. Lacking the proper stylus and the wet clay for which Tuck, or whoever was now inhabiting his body, could use to record his own tongue, David carved a small wedge in the end of a raw potato. Then, giving the makeshift writing instrument to Tuck along with an ink pad and a notebook, he watched with astonishment as Tuck proceeded to deftly stamp out an explosive stream of cuneiform into his tablet. Had David experienced the phenomenon under other circumstances he might have taken the time to meticulously write down phonetic renditions of each of Tuck's ideographs. But for the moment he was less concerned with the procedures of his science, and far more concerned with simply breaking through the language barrier of whoever, or whatever, was now in possession of Tuck's soul.

They worked at their respective notes right through until dawn, and the morning was punctuated only by a telephone call from Grenville, informing David that his wife and daughter would be safe as long as he remained quiescent and tried nothing. The telephone call was brief and in it David discerned nothing to indicate that Grenville was in the slightest way cognizant of the miraculous transformation David was witnessing in his son.

Exhausted, they took a brief nap, and to David's surprise, Tuck was up only a scant hour later, walking around the house and animatedly thumbing through magazines. David fixed them a small lunch and then they continued with their work, toiling once again through the night. By the morning of the next day it was obvious that Tuck had assimilated far more English than David had Eblaite. He still had a good deal of trouble with syntax and was completely baffled by certain words, but all in all it was apparent that the intellect now inhabiting Tuck's body was a formidable and extraordinary one, and voracious for everything that David could teach him.

By the third day David no longer even tried to keep up with his compilation of a lexicon in Eblaite, and instead assumed only the role of tutor, answering Tuck's relentless barrage of pantomimed and crudely phrased questions, and rattling off such a mountain of information that he found it difficult to conceive anyone could absorb it all. But absorb Tuck did, until finally he was able to open up written books and actually glean certain fragments of meaning from them.

Curiously, even as Tuck's grasp of English grew, he remained reluctant to attempt actual discussion with David, and limited their exchanges to a battery of one-sided interrogations. When David tried to question why this was Tuck returned succinctly: "Not yet proficient." By the end of the week Tuck no longer even needed David, and spent long hours sitting in a window seat in the living room and turning pages of books with a speed that left David agog. As quickly as David retrieved a stack of volumes from his library's shelves, Tuck finished them and put them back, until slowly David's awe became mingled with fear as he wondered not only what was transpiring in his midst, but whether it was a benevolent force, as he had blindly assumed, or perhaps something far more sinister and even dangerous.

Over the course of the weekend Tuck devoured virtually every volume in David's library, and when Monday morning came rolling around, his eyes brimming with all of his new knowledge, he fell into a deep sleep. David sat up next to him all the while he slumbered, wondering if perhaps some watershed had been reached, but it wasn't until late that night that Tuck awoke once again.

He glanced at David briefly, and with a look of serious determination slipped out of bed. David followed him downstairs and into the kitchen, and then he looked at David once again.

"I'd like a beer," he said.

David was taken completely off guard and stared down at him aghast. His first reaction was to absolutely refuse the request, but then, on seeing a glimpse of something exhausted, but strangely ancient and powerful, in Tuck's now unfamiliar gaze, he reconsidered.

"Very well," he said. "Just go easy on it. It's not going to take much to get you drunk."

"I am well aware of the limitations of this body," Tuck returned cryptically.

His conscience still staunchly rebelling at the idea, David went to the refrigerator and, taking one of Tuck's tiny cartoon-adorned cups, filled it half full of beer. He handed it to his son and waited nervously for him to drink it.

"Please, just a little more," Tuck said, handing the cup back.

Still jarred by the notion, David poured another small gurgle into the cup.

"Shall we sit?" Tuck returned, motioning at the kitchen table. They both sat down as David continued to keep his eyes trained on the cup in Tuck's hand. He felt himself stiffen as Tuck lifted it and took a sip of the amber liquid.

A sour expression came over his face. "This is beer?" he asked. David nodded and Tuck shook his head sadly. "Then the tavern keeper should be flogged for watering." He set the glass down and looked at David. "I know you must be wondering what is going on. I am now ready to answer all of your questions."

A rush of excitement passed through David. "What has happened to you?" he shot back quickly.

Tuck's expression grew somber. "I assume that what you are really asking is what has happened to your son?"

David nodded as a wave of disquiet swept through him.

"I do not know," Tuck returned. "Let me just say that when I came upon this body, your son had already departed it."

David's face went pale. "And who are you?"

Tuck took another sip of beer. "My name, phonetically translated into your manner of speaking, is Ur-Zababa. If I am not mistaken you are currently locked in combat with an entity I know as Malakil. I am also sure you have discovered by now that he is an individual of not unformidable power. Long ago I was his teacher. I am responsible for everything he knows."

A tide of darkness came over David, both at the news that his son was indeed dead, and at the realization that if the personality before him was Grenville's teacher, was in possession of all of the knowledge that Grenville possessed and more, there was no telling what mortal peril David was now in.

His apprehension must have been written all over his face for Tuck, or Ur-Zababa, as he now called himself, quickly spoke again. "There is no need for you to be alarmed. You will find that I am cut from quite a different cloth than Malakil." He took another sip of beer as he gazed off soberly into the distance. "It is true that I taught Malakil everything he knows, that I gave him the keys to his power. But the infamies he has committed are of his own creation, and no one has been made more remorseful by his wickedness than I." Tuck, or the entity that now inhabited his body, once again returned his attention to David. "That is why I have entered into this time," he said. "I mean to see that Malakil and the evil that he has wrought are brought to an end."

David blinked several times, excited by what he had just been told, but unable to divorce himself from the perception that the figure before him was still Tuck, was still only a child, and certainly no match for Grenville.

"But how?" he asked.

Ur-Zababa frowned. "It is true that it will not be easy. The body of your son is still recovering from his accident, and I am still weakened by my transition into this world, but I am not completely without my resources. To begin, I would like you to tell me all that you know about the man I know as Malakil, how you met him, and everything that has happened since. Please try to recall even the most insignificant details. I need to know everything to be able to amass a plan of attack, and sometimes it is the most trivial occurrences that provide the most valuable insights."

"What?" David said, standing. "You're going too fast. You

tell me that my son is dead and that you've taken over his body, and you expect me to just take this all in stride as you go on asking your questions?"

For the first time a hint of compassion came into the small face before him. "I'm sorry. I know you have been through a great deal. It's just that we do not have much time. You see, I already know some of the things that are going on. I know that your wife is pregnant and that the birth will be no normal birth. I know also that the only reason Malakil has allowed you to remain alive until now is that he needed you, needed to maintain the status quo so that your wife would not suspect what was going on. But now that your wife has become pregnant and he has taken her into his safekeeping, his purpose in needing you alive is over. It is only a matter of time before he kills us both."

David thought about this for a moment. "And what do you propose to do to stop him?"

Ur-Zababa regarded him pointedly. "I'm not sure yet. But I know one thing. If I am to have any hope of succeeding, you must tell me everything that you know."

David stared at the little boy sitting across from him at the table, grief and disbelief still tugging at his soul, and then, taking a deep breath, he conceded. He told Ur-Zababa everything, from Brad's first discovery of the bog bodies to Melanie's fainting when she received the phone call from Dr. Grosley, and when he had finished, Ur-Zababa pondered everything that he had said for several minutes before he spoke.

He shifted his weight and laced his tiny fingers together thoughtfully. "First, let me begin by saying that you should not judge your wife too harshly for allowing herself to be seduced by the demon, whatever form it took. The bog-myrtle wine that Malakil gave you the first time you visited his home was most assuredly a powerful aphrodisiac. Even when I knew him Malakil was especially skilled at the manufacture of potions, and given what you have told me about the demon eluding you when you chased it around the lake, I would suspect that that is the evening that the seduction took place."

David thought about this for a moment and recalled his own strange feeling that he had been drugged after drinking the bog-myrtle wine. "But why Melanie?" he asked. "Why did Grenville or Malakil, or whatever his name is, wait over two thousand years before attempting to bring about such a birth again?"

Ur-Zababa knitted his brow. "Because such a birth can occur only once every two thousand years. You see, magic is a thing of cycles, of rhythms and cosmic pulsations, and the birth of a demon through a human mother is one of the most difficult magical operations of all. It can occur only when the planets are in a very special alignment with the stars, for then and only then are the two worlds close enough together to allow a transition between the world of the demon and the world of the human to take place. This alignment occurs but once every Great Month, or roughly every two thousand years— the time it takes for the precession of the equinoxes to cause Earth to pass from one astrological age and into the next. The last time this occurred was when the Roman woman stumbled so haplessly into Malakil's clutches. And when the advent of the Great Month before that occurred, over two thousand years previous, Malakil still lived in Ebla. It was then, while he was still my student, that he took a young girl of Ebla and through a powerful and forbidden conjuration engendered in her the seed of what was to become the demon you know as Julia."

"What were you in ancient Ebla?" David asked.

"A sorcerer, of course."

"And did you obtain your power from a demon?"

Ur-Zababa looked at him sharply. "No. I have never taken the forces of darkness as my ally and I never will. I derived my power by following a different path." The boyish gaze once again became distant. "But I could not stop Malakil from embarking upon a path of evil. I never even suspected that such a desire lay hidden in his heart." He looked at David with a tortured expression. "You see, I taught him the ways of darkness. I taught it to him as part of his education, so that he could fight it if he ever came up against it. I never suspected that he was embracing each terrible secret as I revealed it to him. That is why I must stop him now, because I am, in a way, responsible for all of the atrocities that he has committed, and to put my own soul at peace I must bring his life to an end."

"But how?" David asked. "Do you have power?"

"Not yet," Ur-Zababa replied, looking at his small hands as he held them out before him. "I am still too newly incarcerated in this body. It will take a little while before I can adjust its frequency, the vibration of its molecules, to more completely accommodate the flow of my power. And even then, I'm afraid, my energy level will be no match for Malakil's. I have simply been away from this plane of existence for too long to manifest the full of my abilities in so short a time."

David grew worried. "Then how do you propose to best Malakil?"

"Through cunning," Ur-Zababa returned. "Cunning and surprise."

David's interest increased.

"You see, Malakil is not without his—what is your expression?—Achilles' heel. And he will not be expecting anyone to know what that Achilles' heel is, because at present he has no idea that I am here. Thus, he will not be as cautious as he should be about protecting his one vulnerability. However, as soon as my powers start to manifest themselves he will sense their presence. He will at first not know what they mean, and may assume that it is just a disturbance in the fabric of space and time. But he will soon figure out that I am here, and that means that we will have to move quickly if we are to preserve our element of surprise."

David trembled with excitement. "But what *is* his Achilles' heel?"

"The jewel," Ur-Zababa replied. "The ruby that he wears around his neck. It contains the pact he made four thousand years ago with the powers of darkness, his covenant with Julia. It is the jewel that enables him to maintain his dominion over her, and to tap her power. Without it Malakil would be as subject to her wrath as the rest of us."

"You mean that Julia would turn on him?"

"If she was hungry. Or if Malakil was lucky she might simply return to her own world. Whatever the case, one fact remains. Demons are at heart ferocious and solitary creatures, and the only reason that he has her allegiance is that he possesses the jewel."

"Does that mean that without it Malakil would be powerless?"

"Without it the brunt of Malakil's power would instantly vanish, but he would still possess a small amount of power. However, without the jewel, at least we would have a chance of overcoming him."

David thought about what Ur-Zababa had just said. He directed his attention once again to the little magician. "A while back Malakil took me on a voyage into the past and a strange incident occurred, an incident in which he nearly lost his ruby pendant."

Ur-Zababa smiled faintly and nodded.

"Do you know anything about that?"

"I was the bead of golden light that attacked Malakil," Ur-Zababa confessed. "It was Malakil's fatal mistake to return to the era in which he knew me. That was how I was able to locate him and follow him back here."

"But how? Do you exist only in the past, or have you lived in some other form these past four thousand years as Malakil has, or what?"

Ur-Zababa smiled consolingly. "To begin you must understand that the past is not dead. In fact, strictly speaking, there is no past. At a certain level of perception one begins to realize that all time exists at once. It is only the current limitations of your consciousness that make it appear that you are moving along a linear and frozen track of time. The reason that I was able to once again locate Malakil is that he returned to a time when I, in the form of Ur-Zababa, was not yet dead. But in truth, the entity that sits before you now has lived in many times, and has gone far beyond Ur-Zababa, and now exists properly in a plane of existence that you do not yet have a vocabulary to describe."

"Is it heaven?"

"Not as you think of it, for to call it heaven would be to limit it, and in truth it is far more splendid than any heaven of which you can yet conceive."

"And what about Tuck? Is Tuck in this place?"

Ur-Zababa smiled again. "If you can call infinity a place. The truth is that reality is vast, far vaster than you have yet dared to imagine, and all that I can tell you is that Tuck is somewhere in that infinity, doing what it is necessary for his soul to do."

David felt both painfully empty and comforted.

"Now I have a question for you," Ur-Zababa went on.

David regarded him curiously.

"In all of your experiences with the demon Julia did she ever give you any reason to suspect that she was uncomfortable with her body temperature, that, like a person coming down with something, she was unable to decide whether she was too warm or too cold?"

"Well, now that you mention it, she did seem to alternate between sitting before unusually large fires and then suddenly preferring the damp chill of the bog."

"Fires that were too uncomfortably warm for you to sit very close to?"

"Yes," David returned, startled.

"And when she assumed her secondary forms, forms in which she no longer looked like normal matter, but glowed, did her flesh have a pitted look as if it were in an advanced state of decay?"

David nodded again. "Yes, but how did you know?"

"Because it only stands to reason. Properly speaking, Julia should have perished at the end of the first Great Month of her sojourn upon this earth. It is a credit to Malakil's power that he was somehow able to extend her survival for a second. But she will not live beyond this one. From what you have told me it appears that even now she is in the process of dying. That means it is even more imperative that Malakil usher her successor into this world. For him it is very literally a matter of life and death."

Ur-Zababa's expression became more troubled. "I now have a most difficult question to ask you, one that you are perhaps not going to take kindly to my asking. Will you please try to understand that it is the seriousness of the situation facing us that forces me to even ponder such a possibility?"

Falteringly, David nodded.

"We will do everything that we can do to stop Malakil, but if by some chance we should fail, and if it comes within the realm of opportunity for you to end your wife's life by your own hand, would you be willing to consider that as a final option, to save future generations from untold centuries of Malakil's madness?"

A cold and existential hush fell over David's soul. "No! Please, you cannot ask that of me."

Ur-Zababa raised his hand. "Before you decide, there is something else that I have not told you."

David looked at him with increasing dread.

"A young demon is far more powerful than an old one. The

power that Julia now provides to Malakil may seem prodigious, but it is only a shadow of what it once was. In her youth, during the first several centuries of Malakil's covenant with her, untold thousands went down before his might. You must believe me when I tell you that the only reason he has confined his reign of terror, lo these many centuries, to just this tiny valley, is he has not had the resources to extend them beyond. But power is a game to Malakil, and he is a destroyer of worlds. You would be astonished if I told you how many of the wars of the ancient world were fought at his inspiration, how many civilizations fell as a result of his machination and wrath. It was he who ordered the sacking of Lagash. It was even his treachery that brought about the fall of Ebla."

David allowed these words to settle in for several moments before he spoke. "And you think that if Malakil's power were restored to its fullest he would no longer confine himself to just this valley?"

"I don't *think* where Malakil is involved. I *know*. If he were to have such power again, it would be tantamount to unleashing such a floodgate of darkness upon this world that even all of the wisdom and artifice of your current civilization could not stop it. The earth would become a playground of evil."

David was about to say something else when Ur-Zababa stopped him. "It is not a decision that you have to make now. Hopefully, if all goes well, it is not a decision that you will ever be faced with making. But if all else fails I want you at least to know the full extent of what is at stake."

David nodded slowly and after several minutes of quiet rumination he spoke again. "I have another question. The first time I saw Julia in her true form the word *hallelujah* seemed to have an adverse affect upon her. However, another religious symbol, the sign of the cross, doesn't seem to do anything to her. In fact, she even strangled the little girl Amanda with a cord on which I had suspended such a cross. Why does one religious symbol affect her and the other not?"

"Because *hallelujah* comes from the language in which Malakil's pact with Julia was written, and the belief system in which the demon was originally conjured up always holds dominion over it. That is why if and when we come into possession of the ruby pendant, any commands we then give to Julia must still be in Eblaite, otherwise they will have no effect over her."

"Does that mean that I can protect myself from Julia simply by saying 'hallelujah'?"

Ur-Zababa shook his head. "No. The first time you frightened her off probably only because you surprised her. She wasn't expecting anyone to say anything to her in Eblaite, and when you did you must have given her quite a start. She might have even jumped to the conclusion that you were a rival magician such as myself. But now that Malakil has most assuredly enlightened her on the matter, saying hallelujah will only have a slightly jarring effect upon her, like a brisk slap. Unless, of course, you are in possession of the ruby pendant. Then the word would cause her searing pain, and at least keep her at bay if I were not yet present to tell you what else to say. That is something it may be useful for you to remember."

David accepted the words thoughtfully.

"I have one more question."

Ur-Zababa looked at him.

"When I have visited Malakil's home on several occasions I have sensed a strange presence in the house, an almost whispering energy. Do you know what it might be?"

Ur-Zababa smiled. "You are very sensitive. It is evil that you have sensed. The demonic world is always very close to Malakil, and it is its presence that you have sensed. It is that same ability to sense things beyond the borders of the physical senses that will ultimately alert Malakil to my presence here. For the moment my power is too weak to have aroused any suspicion in him. He may have sensed my coming when I first entered Tuck's body, but only as a small pinprick in the fabric of space and time, a faint disturbance that the excitement of the moment most assuredly made him forget. But we must work quickly because as I grow stronger he will begin to sense that something is amiss."

Ur-Zababa's eyelids fluttered as if he were about to fall asleep. "And now," he ended, "I must rest if I am to have the strength necessary to begin awakening my own power. Otherwise we will have no hope of ever overcoming Malakil."

* * *

For the next several days Ur-Zababa did little that appeared very remarkable to David except sleep in incredibly brief stints, eat only raw vegetables, and spend endless hours on folded knees in the middle of Tuck's room, meditating. David looked

281

in on him often, hoping to see something that would rekindle his faith that they had any chance against Grenville, but by the end of a week he was once again in the throes of depression over their plight.

As Ur-Zababa seemed to eat less and less, David started to eat and drink more, and when the following Monday rolled around, in a fit of soothing gluttony he got a pot roast out of the freezer and cooked the entire thing for himself. It was while he was gorging down a healthy portion of it that he heard a low sort of rumbling tremor pass through the house. He paused, listening carefully, and at first dismissed it as nerves. But then he heard the sound again. This time it lasted longer than before, and as he sat there wondering if he was actually perceiving it, he noticed that some salt he had spilled beside his plate had begun to vibrate, each tiny crystal moving about like an individual in a milling crowd.

Wiping his hands, David stood up from the table. By the time he had reached the kitchen doorway the tremor had passed, but it was only a few seconds before it came again, like a glacier moving in its slumber, or a train passing somewhere in the night. He ran up the stairs.

As he moved down the hall he realized, as he had suspected, that the mysterious vibration was coming from Tuck's room, and nervously he crept forward and pushed the door open. Instantly, the hall was filled with a soft but strangely brilliant light. In amazement, David looked in and saw that Ur-Zababa was still sitting in a trance on the floor, and that the same strange light was now moving in patches over his body as it swirled off and filled the room with a turbulent, but eerily silent, cyclone of luminescence. At first it was the noiselessness of the glowing whirlwind that attracted his attention, for it moved with such force and turbidity that it seemed it should be roaring, only it was not. However, as he continued to stare into the storm of light that was like a phosphorescent liquid in a blender, in some distant part of his mind he slowly became aware of a sensation of voices, not one, but thousands, lifted in a chorus of celestial singing. He also perceived that the maelstrom now surrounding Ur-Zababa was slowly pulsating, and that its rhythm coincided exactly with the low rumble that filled the house.

As he stood transfixed by the spectacle before him, he got

an inexplicable but distinct feeling that the light was aware of his presence. No sooner had he gotten this impression when the light suddenly spoke to him, not in words, or even sounds, but in feelings. It told him that everything was all right, and to be patient for a while longer. And then, out of the swirling vortex of energy, a vapory tendril reached out and gently pushed him back into the hall. As soon as it had done this the door abruptly swung shut with a hush and a puff of glistening mist.

For another two hours David sat out in the hall, mesmerized, as the walls and the floors of the house rattled and the room beyond continued to seethe with unknown energies. Occasionally the forces rumbling within became so intense that brilliant shafts of light would stream out from the cracks around the door, and once or twice David even thought that the door itself was going to blow out of its frame. Then finally, as suddenly as the activity had manifested itself, it ceased, and everything was quiet. After several minutes David heard someone walking around in the room, and a moment later the door opened and Ur-Zababa looked up at him calmly.

The energy disturbance that had enshrouded his body was now gone, and he seemed changed not at all, save that he appeared a little more rested.

But his gaze was frighteningly determined. "The time has come," he said.

"Tonight?" David questioned.

"Tonight."

He looked at his watch. "But it's already past seven."

"It doesn't matter," Ur-Zababa went on. "My power has now returned, or at least a portion of it has, and Malakil will have most assuredly sensed its coming. It is only a matter of time before he or Julia pays you a visit to see if you have had anything to do with it."

"What do you mean a *portion* of your power?" David asked worriedly.

Ur-Zababa looked at him somberly. "I told you that I was too newly incarcerated in this body to tap the full of my power."

David's consternation increased. "Do you have a plan?"

"Of sorts, but it is not going to be easy. Let's go downstairs and I will tell it to you."

David turned and went down the stairs, Ur-Zababa following.

In the living room he sat down on the sofa while his diminutive companion remained standing. Ur-Zababa flexed his fingers in front of him and started to pace.

"Exactly how much power do you have?" David asked, his agitation increasing.

"Please," Ur-Zababa said, "that will become obvious as I explain to you the plan I have in mind. Now, will you please trust me and allow me to continue?"

Begrudgingly David listened.

Ur-Zababa once again lapsed into thoughtful pacing. "To begin, do you recall about what time it was when you first saw Julia assume her true form and visit the feeding grounds in the bog?"

"Just about midnight, I guess."

"And what time was it when she left the manor house the evening that you had your conversation with Malakil?"

"Much earlier. Maybe nine or nine thirty."

Ur-Zababa grimaced. "That is unfortunate. I was hoping there would be more regularity in the times that she went on her nightly prowl." He considered this for a moment. "We are just going to have to proceed on the assumption that midnight is closer to her usual feeding time, and the fact that she left the house earlier the night of your visit was due to the unusualness of the circumstances."

"Why? Is there some reason that your plan requires that Julia be in the bog?"

"Not in the bog. Just out of the house." Ur-Zababa looked at David almost apologetically. "You see, when I told you that a portion of my power had returned, what I meant is that I have enough power to perhaps catch Malakil off guard. But the modicum of power that I now possess would certainly be no match for Julia, unless of course we gain possession of the jewel."

"How do you propose to catch Malakil off guard?"

Ur-Zababa smiled faintly. "I intend to put him to sleep."

"You have enough power to do that?"

Ur-Zababa nodded. "Unless Malakil has figured out that I am here, and has had the foresight to cast a spell specifically designed to counter it, I have the power to put him and his entire household into a deep sleep for at least ten minutes, perhaps a little longer."

David looked only slightly encouraged. "What happens during those ten minutes?"

"You go in and get the jewel."

"What about Katy and Melanie?"

Ur-Zababa sighed. "I suppose you are going to insist on bringing them out as well?"

"Of course I'm going to bring them out. It's my wife and daughter that we're talking about here."

"But they will be safe once we have the jewel. And besides, your wife is the last person Malakil is going to want to harm."

"And Katy? Didn't you say that Malakil would retain some of his powers even after we take the jewel? Isn't there a chance he will be so outraged that he will seek revenge against Katy?"

Ur-Zababa looked suddenly sheepish, as if he had anticipated this but considered getting the jewel so important that he had not wanted to mention it. "Yes," he conceded. "That would certainly be a logical move for him to make."

"Then I at least have to get Katy out. And if I've gone to all the trouble to get Katy out I might as well bring Melanie out along with her."

Again Ur-Zababa sighed. "Yes, if you insist. But you must understand, the spell I cast will put them into a deep sleep as well. That means that once you are in Malakil's house they will not be able to answer you if you call out their names in your attempts to locate them. It also means that even if you do happen to discover which room or rooms they're in out of the dozens Malakil has there, because they will be asleep, you will have to carry them out bodily. And you must do all of this within the space of ten minutes, and still make sure that you have left time to retrieve the jewel, for without the jewel it will all be for naught. Do you think that you will be able to manage?"

David nodded, realizing that the task he was setting for himself would be difficult if not impossible. But he knew also that he could not go into the house, be so near to Katy and Melanie, and not do something to get them away from Grenville's clutches.

"Where will you be during all of this?" he asked.

"Not far from the house," Ur-Zababa returned. "I must use part of my power to keep Malakil from sensing my presence, and that demands that I not approach too closely. It also demands that I remain motionless during the whole time that Malakil and his household are asleep, so I may sustain the concentration necessary to keep them in their slumber. That is why I will not be able to assist you in your endeavors. It is also why I must go to the house alone, and why you must time your arrival at the house to coincide exactly with my casting of the spell. It would be taxing my powers too much to try to shield Malakil from sensing both of our presences should we arrive together."

"You mean Malakil could sense our presence even if he or Julia were not watching?"

"Oh, yes, Malakil is a very special organism, and in a sense even the air around him is an extension of his being. He can detect a person of my energy emanation several miles away, and a normal human being, or even a small animal, if it approaches within several thousand feet. In a sense, Malakil exists in a web of being that surrounds him like a bubble."

David suddenly recalled the strange behavior of the bittern that he had seen flying over Wythen Hall the first time that he had visited Brad at the excavations, and realized that it must have collided with what Ur-Zababa was now calling the bubble of Grenville's being. His mind also continued to reel with other thoughts. He was horrified that Ur-Zababa was not going to be able to accompany him into the house, for he knew that their greatest risk of failure was most assuredly in the fact that he was going to have to tackle such an enormous task alone. He also realized that he himself was going to be in considerable peril at least until Ur-Zababa cast the spell that put Grenville into his temporary slumber.

"So what you are telling me is that Malakil will most likely be aware of my approach?"

Ur-Zababa nodded.

"What makes you think that once he's aware of my approach he's just going to sit by and do nothing until you cast your spell?"

"Curiosity," Ur-Zababa replied. "Since he will have sensed the energy disturbance that the coming of my powers has caused, and since it is possible that you, as his greatest adversary, have had something to do with that disturbance, he will at least want to talk to you before he kills you."

"Great," David returned. "So how do we make sure that I

time my arrival to coincide precisely with your casting of the spell?"

Ur-Zababa looked at the watch on David's wrist. "Do you have another one of those?"

David thought for a moment. "I think Melanie has a spare one in her jewelry box."

"Then you must get it for me, and we will set them so they beat as one."

"You mean synchronize them."

"What? Oh, yes, synchronize them."

Another worry crossed David's mind. "What if Malakil *has* had the foresight to cast a counter spell? How will I know not to enter the house?"

"I will try to get word to you somehow," Ur-Zababa offered. "But if for some reason I am unable to, you must also rely on your own wits to tell you that."

"And if by some miracle I do get the jewel, what do I do with it?"

"You get in your car and you drive away, and I will meet you a little farther down the road. Since the commands must be given to Julia in Eblaite, I am obviously the one who will have to take over from there."

"What if Julia happens to show up during all of this?"

"I'm afraid that is,—how do you say it?—the one wild card working against us."

"You mean that the sleeping spell would not work on her?"

"Nothing that I can do will have any power over her until I am in possession of the ruby. It is for that reason we must pray that she indulges in her usual habit of passing the night in the bog, for if she does show up, all will be lost."

David looked fearfully at the darkened window. "How do we know that she has not already shown up, that she is not out there watching us even now?"

"Because I would have sensed her presence," Ur-Zababa returned. "I am far more sensitive to the pain in the jaw than you are."

* * *

Ur-Zababa's last revelation, that all would be lost if Julia intruded on their plans, did nothing to quell the growing knot of fear in David's stomach, and for the next several hours he tried every trick he could think of to try to calm himself. First, he got Melanie's watch and scrutinized it like a hawk for over an hour to make absolutely certain that it was indeed in sync with his own. Then, he paced up and down the stairs and through the rooms. And finally, as midnight approached, he got Ur-Zababa a pair of Tuck's tennis shoes and a small navy-blue jogging outfit that he had purchased for Tuck shortly before coming to Fenchurch St. Jude. On such a clandestine undertaking he reasoned that Ur-Zababa should at least wear something that wasn't visible in the moonlight.

It was as the clock struck quarter to twelve that Ur-Zababa appeared behind him in the living room.

"I should be leaving soon," he said.

David looked down at him and as he did so, over his fear, he felt another amorphous veneer of emotion, a darker and deeper panic.

"What is it?" Ur-Zababa asked, seeing the change in his expression.

"I don't know. Just worried, I guess."

"Well, you must calm yourself. We both must be as concerted and determined in this effort as our will allows."

"I know," David said. He handed Ur-Zababa the outfit.

"What is this?"

"I thought you should wear something that would be less visible in the night."

Ur-Zababa smiled grimly. "Being sighted visually was the last thing that I was worried about, but I suppose it is a good idea." He went into the back part of the house and put the outfit on, and when he returned he handed David a small object wrapped in a cloth.

David opened it, and his heart sank when he saw that it was a knife in a leather sheath, one of the hunting knives from the gun room, and that Ur-Zababa had carved into its handle a row of mystic symbols.

"What is this for?" he asked, already knowing the answer.

Ur-Zababa became even more somber. "As you know, it pains me more than I can express to tell you this, but if all else fails, perhaps you can use it . . ." His voice trailed off.

David went pale. "On Melanie? No! Please!" He handed the knife back to his little companion.

Ur-Zababa refused to accept it. "Take it," he begged. "If, in the end, you do not have the courage to use it, I will understand. To perform such a deed would be asking more of you than one has the right to ask any man. But please, remember that there is far more at stake this evening than just our own lives. And please, take the knife so if that terrible moment comes you will at least have the choice."

Every fiber of David's being still rebelled against the notion. "But why must it be a knife?" he asked, his voice cracking. "Why not a gun?"

"Because that is the way it must be," Ur-Zababa returned quietly. "The symbols I have written on it give the knife a special power. It is the only way that we can be assured of success."

His head spinning, David fought back the lump in his throat and reluctantly accepted the knife.

Ur-Zababa picked up the watch, ludicrously feminine, and strapped it on his wrist. "I want you to leave precisely twenty minutes after I have left. It should take you another ten minutes to drive to Wythen Hall, and when you do, at twelve thirty-five exactly, I will have cast the spell. I can guarantee you ten minutes undisturbed in the house, no more. Malakil will most likely be in the study with the ruby around his neck. The servants, of course, will all be asleep, so they will not bother you. Once you have gotten the ruby and your wife and daughter are out of the house, drive away and I will join you down the road."

Ur-Zababa looked up at David and motioned for him to stoop down. When he did so the little magician placed both of his hands on the sides of David's arms and patted him firmly.

"May Nabu watch over us," he said.

"Nabu?" David asked.

"The god of wisdom," Ur-Zababa explained, "and the patron saint of all those seekers of knowledge who work for the good."

"May Nabu watch over us," David repeated.

With that Ur-Zababa smiled and then turned and strolled out into the night. It was as David watched him vanish into the darkness that he realized what had caused him to experience the second veneer of panic. As the last feature of his little companion, the band of white rubber on the backs of tennis shoes, was swallowed up by the blackness, he realized that he could not divorce himself from the feeling that somehow it was Tuck who was now walking off into the night. It was Tuck who was now going up against Grenville, and it was Tuck who would be in danger if he encountered Julia, who risked being torn limb from limb so that not even his countenance, the last vestige of what had once been David's son, would remain.

Fighting back his remorse, he looked down at his watch.

It was ten minutes after Ur-Zababa had left that David heard a sound. At first he could not determine what it was, but then it was clear to him that it was the sound of a car pulling up.

Stunned, he ran to the front window and looked out. He felt a rush of adrenaline when he saw the headlights click off and heard the car door open and shut. There was a crunch of gravel, and the sound of footsteps. And then a firm knock on the door.

Trembling, David slowly opened the door and was amazed to see Brad standing on the step beyond. "What are you doing here?" he demanded.

Brad looked slightly surprised. "Aren't you going to ask me in?"

"But you don't understand," David said, glancing nervously at his watch. "Now is not a good time. I have—"

"—Professor Macauley," Brad interrupted. "I think I know what is going on."

Shocked, David hesitated and then reluctantly let him in. "What do you mean?"

Brad became his normally diffident self. "Well, I don't know exactly what is going on," he stammered. "But I know that something has happened to you. I know that you are up against something . . . well, something very strange, something that's got you by a stranglehold, and I want to help."

"But what makes you think that?" David asked, still being evasive.

"Well, among other things, the fear you displayed when you saw the moth the other night. It was just like the incident in the pub." Brad glanced sheepishly down at his feet before looking up again. "I know you, Professor Macauley. For the villagers of Fenchurch St. Jude to be so frightened at a moth is one thing. But you, your feet are firmly on the ground. If a moth has you that upset it has to be because something quite extraordinary is going on. Please. You can confide in me. You can tell me what is going on."

Again David felt a wave of reluctance, but at the same time

another part of him was crying out to tell the younger man what was going on. He looked at his watch and realized that he had only another five minutes before he had to leave. In a flash of hope and excitement, it occurred to him that if Brad were to help him once they were in the house, if he were to assist David in finding Katy and Melanie and getting them out as well as the jewel, it might be the only way they could achieve such an impossible task before Grenville woke up. And besides, if they were going for broke anyway, what did breaking just one more of Grenville's rules matter? He turned to the younger man and, like a dam bursting, something broke within him and he decided to take Brad into his confidence.

"You're right," he said. "I am up against something unbelievable. Something very evil and very dangerous and I do need your help. But I don't have time to tell you about it now." He looked at his watch. "We have to leave immediately and I will tell you about it on the way."

Looking baffled, Brad nodded.

"This way," David directed. He recalled that he had left the car keys in the kitchen and he figured that they might as well exit through the back door.

They walked down the hall and through the kitchen, and it was just as they were leaving that it happened. The pot roast that David had fixed for himself earlier was still sitting on the counter, and as he opened the back door he turned and saw the younger man grab a quick bite and pop it in his mouth.

Brad smiled when he saw that David was watching him, and wiped his hand on his trousers before following.

At first his action did not register in David as abnormal. David was so excited at the idea of having someone help him once he was in Grenville's house that he didn't even pay attention to the danger alarm going off inside him. But then, as they exited into the darkness, he recalled that Brad was a vegetarian, that unless his life-style had changed radically, he would never have deigned to take a bite of meat.

David stopped and looked at the younger man standing just inches away from him in the moonlight, and with a chill he realized.

It was *her*.

Ur-Zababa had said that it was only a matter of time before Grenville sent her to find out what was going on. With her shape-shifting abilities Julia had molded herself to look like Brad so that she could gain David's confidence and determine what he was up to.

"So you have a plan?" the younger man asked innocently.

David froze, reading new meaning into the inquiry, and then he remembered that he had also heard a car. He looked out into the driveway and saw what appeared to be Brad's rusted Volkswagen sitting beside his own car in the moonlight. Had he been wrong? Was it really Brad's car, or was it only an apparition, an artifact of magic conjured up by Grenville to further convince him of his graduate student's authenticity? He looked again at the younger man. His every feature, even his mannerisms were all perfect.

David's heart was pounding, and he realized that if it was Julia, the last thing that he wanted to do was alert her to the fact that he was on to her. "Yes, I have a plan," he said. "But we have to get into the car, and I will tell you about it on the way."

"Where are we going?" his companion asked.

"I will tell you that on the way also," David returned, trying to buy more time as he figured out what he was going to do.

As they approached the car their feet crunched softly in the gravel and David was struck by the surreal nature of the dilemma facing him. If he was wrong, if the person walking beside him really was Brad, then enlisting his assistance might be his only hope of surviving the evening alive. But if he was right, if the figure beside him was something far more sinister and untoward, then his slightest slip or miscalculation might bring the full of his adversary's true ferocity down upon him.

David's flesh tingled as they both got into the car.

He started the engine and pulled out of the driveway before he spoke again. "I've got to warn you, you're not going to believe what I'm about to tell you."

"Try me," his companion countered.

As rapidly and succinctly as possible, David told the figure next to him the bare bones of everything that had happened up to and including the coming of Ur-Zababa's power. He reasoned that if the person sitting next to him really was Julia he had to make it sound good, had to fill in the gaps between everything that she and Grenville had already suspected, to gain her trust. On occasion as he spoke, Brad in turn appeared to express rather convincing signs of doubt and disbelief, but he also, David thought, seemed to stiffen at the mention of Ur-Zababa's name.

"Okay," Brad offered when David paused. "This is all very hard to believe, but I trust you, Professor Macauley. If you say it's so I'll believe you, but what is the plan?"

David froze, his throat tightening when he realized the final reckoning was at hand.

"Do you remember that time when we were in Germany together, in Wiesbaden?"

"Yes, why?" Brad returned.

"Because we made a pact there. We promised that if one of us was in trouble the other would always help him out. I just wanted to make sure, before I told you the plan, that you still were willing to uphold your end of the promise."

"Yes, of course I am," Brad replied. "Now, what is the plan?"

David drew in his breath before he continued. At least now he knew. He and Brad had never been in Wiesbaden together. They had never made such a promise to one another. The creature beside him was, indeed, Julia.

His companion shifted impatiently.

"The plan is this," David said, hoping that he had not aroused his adversary's suspicion with his pause. "Ur-Zababa is waiting for me at Nobby Fork. He has challenged Grenville to meet him there and Grenville has accepted. What Grenville does not know is that Ur-Zababa has a secret weapon, something that will drain Grenville of all his power so that Ur-Zababa can then take possession of the jewel." David looked at his watch. "I was supposed to go there in case he needed my assistance, but perhaps you could go instead, and I will be able to go to Wythen Hall and see if I can obtain the release of Katy and Melanie."

"I had better go to Wythen Hall too," the figure beside him said.

"Why?"

"Because if Grenville is still there you might need my help."

"He won't be there," David argued. "He's already on his way to meet Ur-Zababa."

"And you say Ur-Zababa has a secret weapon, something that Grenville does not know about?"

"Yes."

"Then I had better go to Nobby Fork." His companion looked out the car window. "Stop here."

"Why?" David said, stopping the car.

"Because I know a shortcut through the bog. I can be at Nobby Fork on foot in five or ten minutes."

David watched as the younger man got out of the car. He knew that Julia really wanted to intercept Grenville and warn him about his impending doom. "What is the secret weapon?" he asked.

"A magic circle," David replied, hoping that his response would sound credible to the demon. "If Grenville steps inside it he will be drained of all his power."

His adversary seemed to accept the information. "You go on to Wythen Hall," he said. "I'll meet you later."

David nodded and anxiously pulled off into the night.

He could scarcely believe that it had worked. Had Julia actually believed it? She seemed to have. He looked again at his watch. He had five minutes to make it to Wythen Hall if he was going to keep on schedule, and hopefully Julia would be occupied for at least fifteen minutes or so before she realized that she had been duped. He hit the gas.

As the old manor house came into sight David's apprehension increased, and he remembered what had happened to Luther Blundell when he had attempted a similarly uninvited approach. He looked out over the grounds and hoped that somewhere out there Ur-Zababa was this very moment casting the spell that would put Grenville and his household into a deep sleep. He hoped also that Julia had not gotten wise to his ruse, for he knew that if she returned unexpectedly he would not fare nearly so well when forced to tangle with her a second time. At length, he reached the end of the drive and stopped the car. He took the keys out of the ignition and got out.

As he approached the house he was gripped once again with the fear that something had gone wrong, that even now Grenville was watching his approach. He recalled that Ur-Zababa had said if that were the case he would have to rely on his wits, and he looked up anxiously at the windows, searching for some hint of movement, but still he saw none. He reached the door.

For a moment he half considered knocking, reasoning that

if someone answered he could argue at least that he was merely paying a visit to beg for the release of his wife and child. But then he remembered that it always took the butler several minutes to respond, and he did not want to risk wasting precious time. Summoning all of his courage, he pushed against the ancient wood and the door opened.

He stepped in and then stopped. Inside, the house was dimly lit and deathly silent, but he knew that this meant nothing. It had always been a house with the quietness of a tomb about it. It occurred to him that if Grenville had become wise to their plans, and had cast a spell to counteract Ur-Zababa's own, it would be just like him to remain in hiding anyway, and to allow David to labor under false hope for as long as possible before pouncing and revealing that it had all been a trap. With this fear in mind David listened for a moment longer, searching for the slightest creak or rustle of clothing, but the only sensation that greeted him were all the smells that he had noticed 'n previous visits, the mustiness and faded richness of the woods, and the faint, cool redolence of the stone.

Still detecting no hint of movement, he started up the stairs. He deduced that the most likely place for Grenville to keep Katy and Melanie would be the upstairs bedrooms, and that was where he decided to begin his search. Cautiously, he turned the handle of the first door he came to, and discovered that it was not a bedroom at all, but a linen closet. He moved on to the next.

The next three rooms he looked into were, indeed, bedrooms, but all were empty and looked as if they had been empty for quite some time, with everything neatly in place, and dusty, and even faint traceries of cobwebs hanging in their corners.

It was as he was about to round the corner at the end of the hall that he froze and flattened himself against the wall. Just around the corner he could see a person sitting. From his outfit it appeared to be one of the liveried footmen, but he could see only his shoes and trousers, and he could not tell if he was unconscious or not. Slowly, he inched forward, spying more and more of the person, until at last his slumped head came into sight. He appeared to be in a deep slumber. More than that, in a wall sconce beyond was a torch, and to his astonishment he saw that the flame itself no longer even flickered, but was motionless, as if it had been frozen in a frame of film. It appeared that Ur-Zababa's spell was very much in effect.

Realizing that he no longer had to be quiet David took off running, madly flinging doors open, and no longer even bothering to close them. Most of the rooms he came to were bedrooms, but one was an upstairs parlor and actually had a servant in it lying slumped on the carpet, where only moments before he had been engaged in polishing a candelabrum. David looked at his watch and was horrified to see that four minutes had gone by and he still had not found any trace of Katy or Melanie. He ran up to the third floor.

To his great relief he found Melanie in the next room he came to and was surprised to see that the room itself was quite grand, with inlaid floor, a fantastically painted ceiling, gilt cornices, and a huge Elizabethan bed canopied in Chinese silk. Melanie, as he had half expected, was lying on the bed, deep in her enchanted sleep, her hands and feet firmly bound to the bedposts to keep her from harming herself. Wasting no further time, he ran over to her and cut her tethers with the knife that Ur-Zababa had given him. Then he lifted her limp body up into his arms and quickly carried her downstairs.

Running as fast as he could with his load without risking a fall, he placed her in the car and looked at his watch. Seven minutes had now passed; he had only three left. He ran back inside and up to the third floor.

In the room next to Melanie's he found Katy lying curled up on a sofa where she had apparently been crying, and he quickly carried her downstairs. Because she was lighter he was able to run faster with her in his arms than he had been able to with Melanie, but still, as he slid her onto the car seat he noticed that he had only a little over a minute left.

Giving it every ounce of strength he had, he tore back into the house. He prayed that Ur-Zababa had been right about Grenville being in his study as he scaled the steps two and three at a time. By the time he reached the doorway to the tower room his heart was beating so rapidly that he feared he had pushed himself too hard, but he knew he could not pause. He opened the door and went in. As he did so, for a fraction of a second he was swept with the fear that if Grenville had cast a counter spell, he might have arranged only to protect

296

himself. But to David's great relief he saw the old sorcerer sitting in a chair before the fireplace, his head draped limply backward and apparently in a deep stupor. As further evidence that Ur-Zababa's magic had permeated even their adversary's inner sanctum, the fire in the fireplace, like the torch near the footman, was eerily motionless, frozen in midflicker, and an unearthly pall of silence hung over the room as if time itself had been temporarily suspended in Wythen Hall.

David knew that he had only a few seconds left and he did not even pause to glance at his watch, but strode quickly across the room and stopped directly in front of the old magician. Once again Grenville wore the dressing robe of gold and black brocade fringed in Russian sable that he had worn during David's last visit, and clearly visible around his neck was the glint of a gold chain. Tingling with anticipation David reached down and lifted the chain up until the large ruby that he had first seen in his near-plummet to his death, came falling out. For the first time he noticed that magically embedded in its depths was a thin sheet of gold leaf on which was delicately inscribed a small but dense passage in cuneiform. Carefully he lifted the chain up over Grenville's head and for the briefest of moments dangled the ruby before him, when suddenly he was terror-stricken to see a soft play of light dancing over his arm. He did not have to ponder the matter for long to know what it meant. The fire behind him had once again begun to burn normally. And then suddenly, before he had time to even consider what to do next, Grenville's hand bolted out like a serpent striking and latched around his wrist with an almost crushing grip. In a panic David tried to pull away, but could not, as Grenville's head tilted forward, his eyes began to glow like blast furnaces, and he let out a guttural scream of rage.

Not knowing what else to do, with his free hand David flung the ruby away, and it rattled across the floor. Seeing where it landed, Grenville returned his incendiary gaze to David and in a burst of outrage flexed his fingers and sent David crashing across the room and into a set of bookcases. As David struggled to right himself he saw that Grenville was quickly rushing over to retrieve the ruby, and he leaped up. No longer thinking of himself or the consequences, he lunged forward and hit the old sorcerer full in the back, bringing him crashing down into one of the study tables. Again Grenville turned, his eyes still glowing like hot embers, as he shot a fist-size fireball at David, and then another. David dodged the first one, but the second grazed his hip, sizzling like a match head gone awry as it passed, and he screamed out with pain. As the fireball continued on, it zoomed across the room and sailed into one of the wall tapestries, setting it on fire.

"No!" Grenville cried, reaching out once again to grab the ruby, and again David lunged forth bringing his entire body smashing down on the old sorcerer's arm and stopping it in midreach. Grenville screamed again, but before he could do anything David picked up the ruby and threw it with all of his might out the window. It crashed through the glass and fell down into the darkness beyond.

Instantly Grenville yanked his arm out from under David and stood up, and David also stood. He glared at David with such rage and venom that a veritable wave of energy seemed to roll off of him like a hot wind, and at the same time the glowing embers of his eyes collapsed even farther into their sockets until the inside of his skull appeared to be nothing more than a swirling inferno, and mirrored eerily the growing fire on the tapestry behind him.

"You are a fool!" he rasped. "You could have had it all!"

"You would never have shared your knowledge with me," David shot back.

"You are wrong," the old sorcerer returned. "I liked you. Had you played the game differently I would have considered making you my apprentice. But not now. Now you die."

Reaching up into the air he suddenly plucked a sword from the nothingness and brought it crashing down. Somehow David managed to jump out of its way and narrowly missed being cleaved in the shoulder. As soon as he had made his move Grenville brought the sword slicing through the air once again, and this time as David rushed to get out of its way he tripped over one of the chairs and went crashing onto the floor. No sooner had he fallen than Grenville was upon him, pinning him down with the point of the sword leveled against his chest. He pulled the sword up, readying for the plunge, and as he did so David looked up into his eyes, the eyes of the person about to become his executioner, and was stunned to perceive the same strange emptiness, the same soulless ferocity that he had first seen in Lugalzaggesi's eyes. In that moment of crystal-line awareness that comes perhaps only when a man is facing death, he realized that that was the source of Grenville's ruth-lessness. His cruelty was not a product of his complexity or intelligence, but an ancient remnant, a look into the barbarity of the distant past.

He brought the sword plunging downward, and David screamed, certain that his death was imminent. But at the very moment that the sword was about to penetrate his flesh, it exploded and vanished in a cloud of glittery sparkles. For a few seconds Grenville looked down, dumbfounded, at his empty hands, and David too looked around, wondering what had happened. At first he discerned nothing, but then out of the corner of his eye a shadow moved and he turned his head in the direction of the movement and saw.

Standing in the doorway was Ur-Zababa.

Grenville too looked in the direction of the intruder, and at first he blinked perplexedly, not understanding. But then a look of terrible recognition came over his face. "You!" he shrilled.

But before he could react further, Ur-Zababa had rolled his hands out one after the other and sent what looked like several large soap bubbles of electrical energy zooming across the room. They hit Grenville with explosive force, knocking him off his feet, and David quickly crawled out of the way.

"The ruby?" Ur-Zababa cried. "Where is it?"

"I threw it out the window."

Seeing that Grenville would not be down for long, Ur-Zababa motioned for David to follow. "Then we must make haste to find it!"

He ran out of the room with David right behind. On the way down the stairs they collided with the butler, and the old servant made a feeble attempt to stop them, but they pushed him out of the way.

"We must hurry," Ur-Zababa warned. "We have only a few seconds before Grenville will be after us again." Saying this, he opened the front door and they ran outside. They headed toward the left of the house, and were just about to round the corner where he had thrown the ruby when another figure appeared suddenly out of the mist.

It was Julia.

She had once again assumed her feminine form, and as David looked at her whatever hope he had possessed of getting away alive quickly vanished. He recalled that Ur-Zababa had warned there was only a slim chance that his powers would be a match for Grenville's, but Ur-Zababa had stated clearly that they would definitely be no match for Julia's.

No sooner had they collided with her than Grenville appeared at the door behind them. He seemed only a shadow of his former self. His face appeared even more gaunt than normal, and his eyes no longer glowed. He was breathing heavily and his legs were trembling as if it were taking every ounce of his energy for him to even stand up. It appeared that his powers were just about gone.

David looked back at Julia and noticed that she was staring at her former master, her eyes wide with alarm. He wondered how she would react. Ur-Zababa had said that without the ruby Grenville would be as subject to Julia's wrath as they were, but what did that mean she would do next? Did it mean that they still had hope?

She continued to eye Grenville up and down, her consternation growing as she apparently discerned what had happened to him. He kept his stare riveted on her, his gaze beseeching and still smoldering with rage.

"Get them," he said finally. "Especially the boy. It is Ur-Zababa."

David returned his attention to Julia and saw that she was now staring at his little companion malevolently. And then, without warning, she opened her mouth and emitted a searing scream of rage as she lunged for them. He managed to jump out of the way, but she caught Ur-Zababa by the feet, her teeth gnashing as her mouth transformed into something inhuman. Flailing frantically, Ur-Zababa managed to pull away and ran a short distance farther into the moonlit clearing. For a second or two David watched in horror as Julia went after him, after the empty shell of what had once been his son, but then he realized he was wasting precious seconds. He looked at Grenville and saw that his attention was glued to the confrontation taking shape before them, his gaze transfixed and dripping with venom.

Taking advantage of the distraction, David turned and ran to where the ruby should have fallen. He dropped to his knees, moving his hands in wide arcs through the wet grass. In the clearing among the twisted trees he saw Ur-Zababa unleash a fireball, feeble and sputtering, but Julia, now totally metamorphosed into the demon, grabbed it and squelched it with a sizzle and a puff of steam. Exerting what appeared to be one of the last flickers of his power, Ur-Zababa caused a javelin to materialize in midflight, and it sliced through the air and penetrated Julia's chest with a hideous susuration. Undaunted, Julia emitted her laugh of clicks and throaty rattles as she pulled the spear out, and the wound bubbled and frothed and quickly healed itself. She broke the javelin in half and tossed it to the ground.

His best efforts foiled, Ur-Zababa started to slowly pace backward as Julia moved in for the kill. She lunged again, grabbing for him with one of her massive hands, and he managed to avoid her by only a fraction of an inch. His small size seemed to provide him with a slight advantage, but David knew that it was a losing proposition. Julia was merely basking in the final moments.

David's search became even more frenzied as Julia grabbed for Ur-Zababa again, giggling froggily. Madly, he moved his hands through the wet grass as Ur-Zababa tried desperately to circle around to Julia's side, but she skillfully reined him in, like a cat toying with a mouse. She began to drool as the clicking in her throat became even deeper, and David realized that she was salivating, readying for the final strike. He knew that he had only seconds to go.

Suddenly, as Julia was just about to make her move, his hand hit something solid in the grass. He had found the jewel.

Without thinking he stood up instantly and screamed, "I've got it!"

Distracted by his outburst, Ur-Zababa looked in David's direction, and the moment he had turned his gaze away from Julia she swung out and hit him in the side of the head, knocking him unconscious.

David looked aghast at his fallen companion, and then at the jewel in his hand as all eyes were upon him. He felt a sinking feeling. Without Ur-Zababa and his knowledge of Eblaite, possession of the ruby meant nothing.

"Why don't you give it to me," Grenville murmured weakly from beside him. "It will do you no good."

David looked down at the ruby and then back at his opponent. "Never," he returned.

In spite of the fact that he was on the verge of collapsing, Grenville snorted with amusement.

"Very well," he said. And then, looking truculently at David, he reached out his hand, and drawing on some last glimmer of power caused the ruby to fly out of David's grasp and across the lawn and into his own hands. As soon as it touched his fingers a shudder passed through him, and his power slowly started to return.

At the same moment, Melanie and Katy, who had been watching the entire spectacle from the car, ran over to David's side.

"Why didn't you drive away?" he snapped.

"You didn't leave us the keys. And besides, I couldn't leave you."

He looked at his wife, sadly searching her gaze as he realized how much he loved her. He looked at Ur-Zababa lying unconscious on the ground, and then at Grenville, the ruby securely in his hand and Julia once again doting at his side.

"Forgive me," he said, as he grabbed Melanie by the shoulders and pushed her down to the ground in front of him. Then, pulling the dagger Ur-Zababa had prepared for him, he held it up against her throat.

"David, what—"

"Shut up!" he demanded, his eyes filling with tears. Katy looked on, petrified.

For the first time Grenville also looked concerned. "What do you hope to accomplish by doing that?" he asked.

"You know what it will accomplish," David returned.

Melanie made a move to get away, but he held her tightly. She looked at him with disbelief.

"And what makes you think that I will not get the dagger away from you as simply as I just gained possession of the jewel?"

David looked down at the row of mystic symbols on the dagger. "Because Ur-Zababa anticipated that move. He consecrated the knife so that you would be powerless to stop what I have to do."

Grenville's eyes opened even wider as he tried to affect an air of unconcern. "Come now, Professor Macauley, I'm sure we can work something out. If you refrain from doing anything rash I will spare your life and the life of your children."

"What about my wife?"

"I'm afraid that even if you allowed her to live she would not ultimately survive the process that has taken over her body."

David shook his head. "Then I might as well end her life now."

"Daddy, no!" Katy screamed and David pushed her away.

Becoming even more agitated, Grenville took a step forward. "Very well," he said, his gaze darkening. "If you spare your wife's life, if you turn her over to me, I will share my power with you. I will teach you *all* that I know."

David's first response was to say no, to shout out that he could never be party to the unleashing of another Julia, an even more unfathomably powerful Julia, but to his great surprise something deep within him was once again ineluctably drawn to Grenville's offer. It was as if every drive, every intellectual curiosity that he had ever experienced suddenly came to the fore, clamoring for its due. He thought of the library of Lagash and all of the other lost libraries of the world that would be available to him if he had Grenville's power. He thought of all of the puzzles of the past that he would be able to solve—how the pyramids had been built, how Joan of Arc really died, and what had caused the Mayan civilization to vanish. And he thought of the multitude of other unknown vistas that would be opened up to him, the limitless worlds that he would become privy to, the laws of physics that he would rewrite. And for a moment he almost gave in. But then he looked into Grenville's eyes, and although he did not know precisely what the word meant, he knew that if he went along with Grenville's plans, he would be damned.

"I cannot do it," he said, trembling, as he raised the knife into the air. "I cannot allow the child that she carries to come into this world."

By this time Melanie was in a state of shock and no longer resisted. Summoning every ounce of courage that he possessed David readied for the plunge. He looked at the knife one last time and was just about to bring it down when Julia suddenly turned to Grenville.

"What child?" she asked, bewildered.

303

David froze as he looked at the expression on Julia's face. Was it possible that she did not know? And then, in a flash, the pieces came together and he understood. Julia was unaware that Melanie was carrying her progeny. Given that such a birth could occur only once every two thousand years, she was perhaps even unaware that she had the ability to impregnate. That was why Grenville had not allowed her to maul the Roman woman. He had not wanted her to discover that the Roman woman was pregnant, that he was planning on replacing her. It was even why in their current conversation he had so meticulously avoided any specific reference to Melanie's pregnancy, referring to her condition as simply *the process that has taken over her body.*

David suddenly wondered why Grenville had kept such information from Julia, but judging from the look of fear spreading across Grenville's face, he thought he understood that also. His heart pounded as he tried one last desperate ploy.

"Julia," he called out. "Do you realize that you are dying?"

And then, from the look of hurt and betrayal she gave Grenville, he knew that he had been right. How had Grenville put it? *We are all obsessed.* At some point in the distant past she might have been only a ferocious spirit kept at bay, and the ruby might have been the only thing binding her allegiance to Grenville. But she had been with him for over four thousand years. She had grown used to him, and in her own curious way perhaps even loved him. That was why she had not turned on him even when he had not had the ruby. It was also why Grenville had taken such pains not to tell her that Melanie was pregnant. He knew that she would not take kindly to her being replaced.

"It's true," David said, driving the last nail into the coffin. "The night of the dinner, the night that you seduced my wife, Grenville performed a magical operation that enabled you to get her pregnant. He did it because he no longer wants you around. You are weak and you are dying, and even now he has planned it so that my wife is carrying your successor."

As Julia continued to stare at Grenville, the look of guilty terror that filled his face told her that what David was telling her was the truth. Without warning she reached out and knocked the ruby from Grenville's hand.

"Replacing me!" she shrieked, and before Grenville could react she gripped him by the arm and pulled him violently toward her.

"Please, Julia," he stammered. "Let me explain!"

"Replacing me!" she keened mindlessly as her nostrils flared. And then, letting out an insensate roar of anger, she was upon him like a panther, biting deep into his neck and shoulder.

Grenville screamed as blood spurted down over his brocade robe, and for a moment David was frozen by the sight. But then, seeing the ruby lying in the grass only a few feet away, he retrieved it and ran over to Ur-Zababa's side.

As David lifted the little head into his arms, Grenville screamed again and there was a terrible crunch as Julia crushed one of his arms.

Furiously David patted Ur-Zababa in the face and felt a wave of joy when his eyelids fluttered and he began to come to. By this time Grenville's screaming had begun to wane and he emitted one last nerve-shattering cry as Julia crushed his rib cage with her massive hands and then tossed his lifeless body to the ground.

She turned toward David, clearly intent on continuing her revenge, when she saw the ruby in Ur-Zababa's hand.

"The time has come," Ur-Zababa said. *"Ib ba ikbal ma."*

Julia looked suddenly horrified.

"Ib shal malaku," he continued. *"Nig mala eem shibura. Nig mala eem shi."* He held the ruby aloft in his fist. "Now you return to your own world."

He made a gesture with his free hand in the air in front of him and suddenly a dark cloud formed behind Julia. It expanded quickly, dense and churning like a thundercloud, as a brilliant lavender light began to flash within its depths. For a moment Julia looked as if she were about to run, but suddenly a fissure formed from top to bottom in the cloud and a tremendous roar of wind enveloped her. As the fissure continued to open, David could see that beyond was a landscape more fantastic, more unspeakably foreign than any he had ever previously beheld. For as far as the eye could see, against a deep indigo sky, was a vast expanse of dark and jagged mountains, twisted escarpments and grotesque rock formations, all barren and wracked by a cacophony of strange sounds, great groanings

305

and howlings, and a shimmering sound, as of the buzzing of a thousand flies, only more metallic, like the clashing of cymbals, or the shaking of many thin sheets of aluminum.

With a final gesture of his hand, Ur-Zababa caused the wind to reach hurricane proportions, and it whipped up around Julia in a swirl of dirt and debris, sucking her back through the fissure. And then, with a clap of thunder, the hole between the worlds vanished, and the lawn became silent save for the crackle of the fire now engulfing the house behind them, and the cries of the servants as they fled into the night.

13

THAT NIGHT, WHEN they arrived back at the cottage, David was filled with foreboding to find that Brad's rusted Volkswagen, apparently not a product of Grenville's magic, was still in the driveway, and the next day he found Brad's body where Julia had left it, only a hundred feet from the house. It seemed that in the end he really had come to offer his assistance, only Julia had intercepted him and had adopted his plan with the same facility with which she had temporarily adopted his appearance.

About a week later Dr. Grosley performed an abortion on Melanie, and although they told him they had wanted the pregnancy terminated out of purely personal reasons, after the operation David discerned in Dr. Grosley's deeply unsettled expression that the fetus must have already possessed at least some of the disconcerting features of its father. In spite of this they deemed it prudent to tell Dr. Grosley nothing.

As for telling their story to anyone, even if David had possessed the inclination to brave the scorn and ridicule that would follow such a disclosure, any enthusiasm that he might have possessed for such a venture was further diminished by two important discoveries.

The first was that although the malevolent aura that hung over Fenchurch St. Jude had clearly dissipated, its inhabitants, out of deeply ingrained fear and lifelong habit, still obstinately refused to betray Grenville's secret in any way.

The second was even more dismaying to David. In the unlikely event that he did decide to tell his tale to anyone, he knew that his ace in the hole, the one piece of physical evidence that he possessed, would be the demon fetus preserved in the Roman woman's body. However, when he visited the excavation site on the day following Melanie's abortion, to his great distress he discovered that because he had cut into the body of the Roman woman before he had sufficiently preserved her, the fetus had begun to decompose, and was now little more than an amorphous mass.

It was ten days after their final encounter with Grenville, as he stood surveying the valley for the last time with Katy and Melanie sitting in the car a short distance away, that he received what he at first thought was the final blow. He had submitted his discovery of the bog bodies for publication, but had turned over what work was left to one of his colleagues, and Ur-Zababa stood at his side as he looked somberly at the excavations for the last time.

"David," Ur-Zababa said, interrupting his reverie.

He looked at the little figure beside him.

"You shouldn't feel badly," Ur-Zababa continued. "What you did was necessary and good, and you have every right to be very pleased with yourself."

"But what about you?" David asked.

"What about me?"

David swallowed. "Well, I'm afraid I've become quite fond of you. Are you going to keep my son's body, or are you going to leave it, and if so, what happens then?"

Ur-Zababa smiled softly. "I'm afraid I'm going to leave it. I must return to the place where I belong."

David's gaze dropped.

"But you mustn't be sad," Ur-Zababa cautioned. "Everything has a beginning and an end. That's why flowers die and leaves fall off the trees."

David looked up at him again as he recalled that they were the words that he had said to Tuck, but still he did not understand the real meaning of what he had just been told.

Ur-Zababa became silent for a moment as if he were listening to a voice somewhere deep inside his head. "Yes," he said quietly and almost to himself. "I think your father knows that you have moxie."

David's eyes widened. "Tuck?" he asked.

Ur-Zababa smiled. "He is here."

"Is he alive?"

"I told you that he was. I told you when you asked that he was right where he was supposed to be."

"But is he here, in your body . . . *his* body?"

Ur-Zababa nodded.

David would have been angry were he not so happy at what he had just been told. "But why didn't you tell me? Why did you allow me to believe that he was dead?"

"Because I knew that you never would have allowed me to use his body."

"Of course I wouldn't. You had no right."

"But I did have a right. You see, when I came upon him in the cold waters of the bog, I asked him. He gave me his permission to be the dominant soul in his body for a while. He wanted to help." Ur-Zababa paused. "You have a very special son, David." He smiled. "And Tuck has a very special father."

He took both of David's hands into his own. "I leave you now. I wish you and your family great peace and happiness. And I hope that perhaps in some distant space and time we may meet again.

With that, his eyes closed and remained shut for only a fraction of a second before they opened again, this time sparkling with a familiar light.

"Hi, Dad," the familiar voice chimed.

Tears filled David's eyes as he swooped his son up into his arms. "Oh, Tuck, I missed you so much."

"I missed you too, Dad," Tuck returned, and they both hugged each other so tightly that Tuck grunted.

It was on their way back to the car that he saw something different, something eerily wise in his son's eyes.

"What is it, Tuck?" he asked.

Tuck smiled, but his gaze remained dreamy. "It was just so amazing," he said in a voice that now seemed curiously older than its years.

"What was?"

"Everything," he said shaking his head, his eyes still glazed with wonder. "I know so much, Dad. I just know so much."

David smiled, but he was almost a little frightened. What

did Tuck know? Where had he been in the past several weeks, and what had he seen? As they got into the car and Tuck scrambled over to greet his mother, David realized that in sharing a body with Ur-Zababa, Tuck had no doubt also absorbed some of his information. This basically pleased David, for he had always expected a lot from his son. But as he turned the key in the ignition he realized that in some ways it meant that Tuck was now perhaps far wiser than he, and in the years ahead he wondered what Tuck would become. And what unfathomable wisdoms Tuck would eventually expect from him.